THE
OMEGA
FACTOR

PREVIOUS WORKS BY STEVE BERRY

COTTON MALONE NOVELS

The Kaiser's Web
The Warsaw Protocol
The Malta Exchange
The Bishop's Pawn
The Lost Order
The 14th Colony
The Patriot Threat
The Lincoln Myth
The King's Deception
The Jefferson Key
The Emperor's Tomb
The Paris Vendetta
The Charlemagne Pursuit
The Venetian Betrayal
The Alexandria Link
The Templar Legacy

STAND-ALONE NOVELS

The Columbus Affair
The Third Secret
The Romanov Prophecy
The Amber Room

CASSIOPEIA VITT NOVELLAS (WITH M. J. ROSE)

The End of Forever
The House of Long Ago
The Lake of Learning
The Museum of Mysteries

THE
OMEGA
FACTOR

STEVE
BERRY

HODDER &
STOUGHTON

First published in Great Britain in 2022 by Hodder & Stoughton Ltd
An Hachette UK company

1

Copyright © Steve Berry 2022

A CIP catalogue record for this title is available from the British Library

Hardback ISBN 978 1 399 70631 5
Trade Paperback ISBN 978 1 399 70632 2
eBook ISBN 978 1 399 70633 9

Printed and bound in Great Britain by Clays Ltd, Elcograf S.p.A.

Hodder & Stoughton policy is to use papers that are natural, renewable and recyclable
products and made from wood grown in sustainable forests. The logging and manufacturing
processes are expected to conform to the environmental regulations of the country of origin.

Hodder & Stoughton Ltd
Carmelite House
50 Victoria Embankment
London EC4Y 0DZ

www.hodder.co.uk

could learn a great deal. Previously, I've dedicated two books to Frank, but it seemed only right to thank him one last time. He will be greatly missed.

The dedication for this book is a bit unusual. Novelists deal in the world of imagination. A novel is, by definition, not real. Sure, there are facts and people and things that might be real, but the plot, the conflicts, crucibles, and conclusions are only a story, designed simply to entertain the reader.

Walt and Roy Disney also dealt in the world of imagination. Walt was the dreamer, a visionary. Roy was more grounded, practical, the financier. Neither could have flourished, though, without the other. Dreams languish unless somebody can find a way to transfer them into reality.

That was what Roy did for Walt.

Together they were an amazing creative team who produced some of the most enduring characters, places, and stories in human history.

Their relationship was a close one, but not perfect. They disagreed and fought, as brothers do, but, in the end, they always came back together. Both seemed to realize that neither was complete without the other. Proof of that came after Walt died in 1966. The dream of a second theme park on the East Coast was just that, a dream. Its creator gone. But Roy made it his mission to see to it that the "Florida project" came to fruition. On October 1, 1971, that happened when Roy formally dedicated, not Disney World, but what he renamed as *Walt* Disney World.

Seventy-nine days later Roy died.

So this book is for the two Disneys, Walter Elias and Roy Oliver, imagineers extraordinaire, creators of the incredible, two men who continue to spark wonder, produce joy, and touch the world.

Every day.

ACKNOWLEDGMENTS

This is my first book with the Hachette Book Group. My sincere thanks to Ben Sevier, senior vice president and publisher of Grand Central, for taking a chance on an old guy like me. To Wes Miller, my editor, whom I've greatly enjoyed getting to know and working with. He's a man of remarkable insight. This book became much better thanks to him. Then to Tiffany Porcelli for her marketing expertise; Staci Burt, who handled publicity; and all those who created the cover and made the interior of the book shine. A grateful nod also goes to Sales and Production who made sure there was a book and that it was widely available. Thank you, one and all.

A deep bow goes to Simon Lipskar, my agent and friend, who made this book possible.

A few extra mentions: Jessica Johns and Esther Garver, who continue to keep Steve Berry Enterprises running smoothly. Nathalie Dumon, who showed Elizabeth and me around Ghent and provided some early research materials. Noah Charney, the expert on all things relative to the Ghent Altarpiece. And Christophe Masiero for helping out with my French.

As always, to my wife, Elizabeth, who remains the most special—and most intuitive—of all.

One other sad point. During the writing of this book, the man who pushed me to learn the craft of writing passed away. Frank Green lived a long and productive life. Many writers, myself included, owe him a great deal. He was a tough taskmaster, generous with his time, and if you kept your mouth shut and ears open you

For Walt and Roy Disney, who left an extraordinary legacy of inspiration and imagination

Like a dog that returns to its vomit,
is a fool who reverts to his folly.

Proverbs 26:11

PROLOGUE

His pursuers were gaining, so Jan van Eyck prodded the horse with a jab from his boots. The animal seemed to sense their quandary and increased his speed, blasting out each breath of the cool mountain air in a torrid wheeze.

Jan was alone, being chased in terrain that was both unfamiliar and hostile. When he'd first spotted the Moors, before midday, he'd counted nine on horseback. Two more had joined the chase since. The task he'd been sent to achieve was vital to his benefactor, capture was not an option, so he urged the steed forward with a snap of the reins.

He knew his ride well. A good horse, with quickness and intelligence, could, and had, succored him many times. When ill, a horse was cared for with more wisdom than was vouchsafed to most Christian denizens. Horses were the means whereby kingdoms flourished, and the coursers, the palfreys, and especially the destriers responded to affection with an unmatched loyalty. He knew of one knight who returned home from war and was not recognized by his betrothed but was instantly embraced by his faithful stallion.

He stared ahead.

Jagged, snow-topped mountains rose all around him. To the west, like a sphinx on the desert plain, a svelte peak stood detached, its upper folds sheathed in silvery white, another spur of the pointed Pyrénées shadowed far behind it. He did not need to stop and listen to know that hooves were beating across the meadow behind him. He'd wanted to make his way north unnoticed. It was a mere two-day ride from Tormé, on the Spanish side of the mountains, to Las Illas on the French side. The refurbishing of the ancient town into a new fortress had only recently been completed, and he knew its presence, so close to the border, was a source of friction to the Moors.

Though Navarre and Aragon both were in Christian hands, Moors still freely roamed northern Spain. Slowly, the *reconquista* was driving the Arabs southward. Castles and towns were being regained every year. Eventually, surely, the Moors would be forced to board ships and return to Africa, ending six hundred years of occupation. But, in the meantime, they continued to spoil churches, sack convents, and waylay travelers, especially those who ventured too far south and dared to cross the Pyrénées.

His mind flashed to the warriors behind him.

Moor meant simply "dark," and the deep olive of their skin stood in stark contrast with the loose-fitting white tunics, the colorful turbans, and the scarfs that draped their necks in a kaleidoscope of silken thread. They were a brutal lot, a clear menace, and he did not want to face their crescent-shaped scimitars or their mounted archers. He'd been expecting follies of arrows, but the pursuit so far had been through thick stands of fir and pine, so clear shots had been unobtainable. He hated archers. A true warrior should only come to battle with an ax and sword in hand. What had the poet said? *Coward was he who was the first archer.*

He allowed his attention to switch from the ground to the route ahead, relying on his horse to make sure the footing was true. A blast of crisp wind swept through a nearby cleft and slowed his progress. The trees around him began to change, the firs diminishing, towering pines now dominating. Each trunk reached audaciously toward heaven, many twisted as if in pain, most bereft of limbs.

He winced.

There would now be more opportunities for the archers.

The horse slowed and twisted a path through the pines, avoiding granite boulders and leaving a clear trail across dainty edelweiss. A stillness wrapped the dusky forest. The musty scent of twigs and boughs filled his nostrils. Above, the sun was warm, the clouds low, which meant rain might eventually become his ally. But, for now, any storm was too far away to be of assistance.

He stopped the horse and risked a look behind him.

No one was in sight.

He tried to listen for some sound that might betray the Moors' presence, but the clicking of grasshoppers interfered. He emerged from the trees and found a path leading eastward.

A signed paper in his saddlebag certified that he was the duly authorized representative of Philip the Good, the reigning Duke of Burgundy. By trade, he was an artist. Philip's court painter. But by service he was a spy, in the employ of the duke. His current mission had taken him into Spain on a reconnoiter of local roads and territories. His attention to depth and detail, his skill and accuracy with pen and brush, was what distinguished his art. The duke liked to say that his visual cunning was unmatched. But unlike his paintings, where the real world only inspired what he represented, when on a covert mission what he produced had to be an exact match. On this trip he'd sketched valuable maps that led to important mountain passes, all vital to any army in the future.

Jan was broad-shouldered and solid in limb. His brown hair had grown out, stubby like a brush—his beard long and ragged, which made his pallid face look even paler. Normally, he'd be clean-shaven, but he'd intentionally not shaved the past few weeks, the facial hair adding a measure of welcome disguise. His head was lean, large, and some said square, with a high brow and a fine straight nose. It helped that he spoke Spanish and understood the local customs. All of which made him the perfect spy.

Another breeze brushed past and he savored a quiet moment. His skin was wet and hot, his legs achy. Beneath the mantle he was clad in heavy mail. A weighty aventail bit into his neck and chin. He'd dressed for battle, ready for whatever might come his way, and eleven Moor horsemen had accepted his challenge. He wondered if someone in the last village had given him away. It was a Christian community but, as he'd been warned, the Moors had eyes and ears everywhere.

He reached down and stroked the horse. The animal flattened his ears and accepted the affection. The twitter of a finch came from an adjacent tree. He half expected the clash of an ax or the buzz of a saw, but there was no sign that anyone else loomed nearby. Before him, another pass opened and beyond spread the brilliance of an emerald-breasted valley. A clearly defined trail wound a path ahead through a thick stand of beech. He urged the horse forward and sat up in the high saddle, thinking perhaps he'd lost his pursuers. He'd be glad when he could remove his ponderous metal clothing and enjoy the comfort of night. He should make Las Illas before sundown.

Ahead, on one of the trees, something caught his attention.

He approached and stopped.

Carved into the trunk of an enormous beech was the image of a bird. Great care had been taken with its representation. The plumage and beak distinct, its mighty wings held close and tight, ready for flight.

He recognized the vulture.

The Spanish called it *quebrantahuesos*. Bone smasher.

And he knew why.

He'd watched in awe many times while the great raptor had dropped its prey from the air onto rocks, breaking the bones and making it easier to get at the rich marrow. Strange that someone had taken the time to so beautifully depict such a predator here. Below the bird were letters. Not of a language he knew, though he recognized the Arabic symbols. Around him the rock crannies groaned from the wind. He was deciding on what next to do when the stillness was disturbed by a low swoosh that quickly grew in intensity.

He knew the sound well.

Arrows piercing the air.

In the next instant three tips sucked into the earth just ahead of him.

His head whirled around.

The Moors had rounded a bend in the trail and were fast approaching. He urged his horse forward. Their first shot had been off, but they would be more accurate with the next folly. He allowed his right hand to drift from the reins to make sure that his battle-ax was still held by its leather strap to the saddle. He might soon need the weapon.

He entered the mountain pass.

To his left rose glaring white cliffs. Box brush clung to every crevice. An inky-black forest loomed to his right. He almost diverted the horse into the trees, but his lead on the Moors was good and he thought he might be able to outrun them. He had to be either over or near the border, and he doubted the Moors would follow him into French territory.

He rounded a bend in the trail and ducked beneath an out-stretched limb. His horse was in full gallop, the hooves skimming across the hard ground. He saw another of the carved vultures in a trunk ahead, along with more Arabic symbols. Just as he passed the tree the horse's front legs found a soft patch of shale and together they plummeted toward the ground. He knew what was coming, so he leaped as the animal pounded the earth and hoped his suit of mail would protect him from the worst of the fall.

He slammed into the hardpan next to the horse. While he rolled left, the horse tumbled on, a sickening whelp signaling that the animal was in pain. He somersaulted several times. Chain mail dug into his sheepskin shirt. He brought his arms to his head and shielded his face from rocks as he careened off the trail. He continued to tumble until finally coming to rest against the gnarly roots of one of the beeches.

He sat still for a moment and assessed the damage. There was pain, a multitude of cuts and scrapes, but nothing excruciating. He tested his arms and legs. Nothing seemed broken. He moved his head from side to side. His neck was unaffected. Jesus, almighty God. He'd been lucky. The smell of mold and moss filled his nostrils. He immediately listened for sounds of the Moors.

But there was nothing.

The thought of his pursuers roused him to his feet.

He pushed back the coif and allowed the hood to droop onto the nape of his sweaty neck. He swiped blood from his brow, then staggered back to the trail. The horse was on its feet, ready.

What a tough stallion.

He looked to the right.

The Moors were farther down the trail, still atop their mounts, simply watching him. Thankfully, they were far enough away that their bows would be useless. He waited for them to charge. He would be easy prey since both his sword and ax were with the horse. Good thing. He might not have survived the fall with those strapped to his waist. He stared at his enemy and decided that if they advanced, he would flee into the woods and take his chances. Perhaps he could disarm one of them and gain a weapon.

"They will not come forward," a voice said from behind him.

The language was Occitan.

He turned and spied a black-garbed nun who stood alone in the center of the trail. No feature on her face betrayed a shred of fear or anxiety. Odd. He could not decide which was the greater threat— the known antagonists or this out-of-place character.

"What do you mean?" he said, staying with Occitan, then turned his attention back to the Moors.

"They will not come forward," she said again.

He did not take his eyes off the riotous band.

"There is no danger," the nun declared, the words calm, like the echo of a voice from heaven.

"They are a mighty danger," he made clear.

"Not here."

But he was unconvinced.

So he decided to test the declaration.

He took a few steps forward and raised his arms above his head. He crisscrossed them back and forth and screamed at the horsemen in the language of Aragon, which they would surely understand. "Come forward, you cowards, and do battle."

They did not accept his offer.

"Are you afraid of a single man, unarmed? Of a nun?"

No response came from their dark, scathed faces.

He lowered his arms.

"By God, you are afraid," he yelled.

Ordinarily, to challenge a Moor was to invite a fight to the death. Arabs had not held power in the Iberian Peninsula by being weak. Yet these heathens merely turned and trotted their horses away. He wondered if his eyes were deceiving him. So he continued to watch until they disappeared around a bend, and all that remained was dust twisting in the air. He turned back to the nun and wanted to know, "The birds carved to the trees. What are the words in Arabic beneath?"

Somehow he knew this woman could answer the inquiry.

"The devil will have his own."

"Those are *their* words?"

The nun nodded. "We adopted it from them. A warning from long ago."

He stepped close and noticed the chain around her neck and the symbol, in silver, it supported.

A *fleur-de-lys*.

He'd seen knights, kings, and dukes display them. But a nun? He pointed. "Why do you wear that?"

She beckoned with an outstretched arm.

"Come, and I will show you."

PRESENT DAY

CHAPTER 1

GHENT, BELGIUM
TUESDAY, MAY 8
8:40 P.M.

Nick Lee rushed toward the flames and smoke, growing more concerned by the moment. He'd flown to Ghent to see a memory that had haunted him for a long time, the images of her as crisp and vivid as if from yesterday, not nine years ago. They'd come within a week of marriage, but a life together had not been meant to be. Instead, she chose another path, one that had not, and would never, include him. His words at the time had stalled in his throat. Hers were definitive.

I have no choice.

Which seemed the story of *his* life.

A volatile mixture of good and bad, pleasure and pain. Right place, wrong time? Definitely. Wrong place, right time?

Damn right.

More than he liked to admit, in fact.

He'd started in the army as an MP, then tried for the Magellan Billet at the Justice Department but was not offered a position. Instead the FBI hired him, where he stayed five years. Now he worked for the United Nations Educational, Scientific and Cultural Organization, more commonly known as UNESCO. Part of the UN since the beginning, its mission was to advance peace through education, science, culture, and communication. How? Mostly through initiatives like World Heritage Sites, a global digital library, international literacy days, and a thousand other programs designed to promote, preserve, and sustain human culture.

He was employed by a small appendage within that giant beast. The Cultural Liaison and Investigative Office. CLIO. A play off the Greek goddess Clio, the muse of history. Officially, he was a credentials-carrying UN representative, which definitely opened doors. In reality he was boots on the ground. Trained eyes and ears. A field operative. Sent where needed to deal with artistic and cultural issues that could not be resolved through conference calls, ceremony, or diplomacy.

Sometimes you just have to kick a little ass, one of his bosses had said.

He'd been there right after ISIL plundered Iraqi churches, museums, and libraries. On-site in the Maldives when radicals dynamited Buddhist artifacts. In Timbuktu, after the Battle of Gao, when parts of that ancient city were ravaged by war. His job, first and foremost, was to stop any cultural destruction. But if that wasn't possible, then he'd deal with the aftermath. He'd come to learn that many so-called cultural purges were simply smoke screens for the hasty acquisition and subsequent sale of precious artifacts. Fanatics weren't entirely stupid. Their causes needed money. Rare objects could easily be converted to a stream of wealth that was virtually untraceable. No worries about bank accounts being seized or frozen by foreign governments. Just make a deal with reclusive buyers more than willing to supply gold, cryptocurrency, or cash in return for the seemingly unobtainable.

Thankfully, this trip to Belgium did not concern anything threatened, except perhaps his heart. He'd been looking forward to seeing Kelsey again. She was here in Ghent doing what she did best. Art restoration. It had been a mutual love of art that had first drawn them together. Then something wholly

12

unexpected, at least from his point of view, pried them apart. He'd never seen it coming. Should he have?

Hard to say.

Nine years had passed since they last saw each other face-to-face. Their parting had not included any tearful farewells, hugs, handshakes, words of comfort, or encouragement. Not even an argument or anger.

Just an end.

One that had left him stunned.

Their communications since had been through social media. Not much. Electronic comments here and there. Just enough to stay in touch. She had her life and he had his, and never should the two mix. He'd many times wondered if maintaining any contact was a good idea, but he'd done nothing to curtail it. Was he a glutton for punishment? Or maybe he just wanted her in his life, however that might be?

Two weeks ago she'd suggested in a Facebook direct message that he come to Ghent. A first. An invitation to visit. Which made him wonder. Good idea? Bad? But once she'd told him what she was working on, he'd decided, what the hell, why not. Now he was here and the building he'd been sent to, per her texted directions, was on fire.

Was she inside?

He ran faster.

He was a few blocks over from the ancient Cathedral of Saint Bavo on a darkened street amid Ghent's old town. All of the buildings around him seemed a tribute to Flemish architecture, a gauntlet of brick brownstones with stoops and chimneys. He was not far from the famed Graslei. A stunning ensemble of riverside guild houses spanning centuries and styles. Once part of a medieval port, one of the oldest sections in a town dating to the fifth century, it had been a focal point back when Ghent acted as the center of Flanders' wheat trade. The district now was a touristic hot spot with a high concentration of café patios. He was hoping to have a late supper with Kelsey at one of them after seeing what she'd promised to show him.

The building ahead, ablaze in smoke and fire, rose three stories to a stepped-gable roof, but all of the destruction seemed localized on the ground floor. People had gathered in the narrow street, watching, but no one was moving to help. He ran up and asked if the fire department had been notified. An older woman said in English that a call had been made. He heard sirens in the distance and decided not to wait for their arrival. Instead, he bolted toward the front door in six quick steps and pushed the heavy wooden slab inward.

Intense heat and smoke poured out.

He grabbed a breath and plunged inside a large studio, metal racks of art equipment and supplies lining the walls. Tables filled the center. All consistent with a workshop, where Kelsey had told him she wanted to meet.

But no fire raged here.

"Kelsey," he called out.

He heard a noise from the next room and headed toward the open door. There, he saw Kelsey engaged in a struggle with another person. The figure was black-clad, in tight-fitting clothes, the head and face hooded. It was hard to see much through the smoke, the only light coming from a raging conflagration on the other side of the room that was rapidly burning, the flames crackling and curdling like the sound dried wood made in a hearth.

He moved to help, just as the black figure pushed away and landed a kick to Kelsey's gut that staggered her back. The attacker used the moment to bend down, grab something from the floor, then disappear into the smoke. He blinked away the burn from his pupils and found Kelsey.

14

He helped her from the floor, gentle with his touch, and they fled the room. "You okay?"

Her eyes were red, watery, and wild. Her gaze changed from rage, to fright, to recognition. "Nick." She coughed out the smoke from her lungs and nodded fast. "I'm fine. Really. I'm okay."

The curtain of time parted in his mind. It was like nine years ago again, and that familiar connection clicked. But he forced his thoughts to the present. "We have to get out of here."

She shook her head. "I have to stop the fire."

"Help is on the way. They'll do it. Let's go."

She would not budge. "Nick, go after her—"

Her?

Two policemen burst into the room.

"I'm okay," Kelsey said. "Get my—laptop back."

One of the uniforms came close to help, and the other wielded a fire extinguisher that he began to use on the flames.

"Please," she said. "Go."

Part of him said to stay and make sure she was okay.

But another part knew what Kelsey wanted.

And it wasn't comfort or protection.

So he hustled off into the smoke.

CHAPTER 2

Bernat de Foix dropped his napkin on the plate and turned his attention to the young man sitting across from him. They'd just broken a three-day fast. A last tribulation, all part of what they'd both been working toward for over a year. Fitting that it would finally occur here, within this ancient fortified city.

Humans had lived on this mount adjacent to the slow-moving river Aude since the Neolithic Age. It had been the Visigoths who founded the grand walled Cité de Carcassonne as an oppidum on the historic trade routes that once linked the Atlantic Ocean to the Mediterranean Sea. All that former glory, though, was gone. Now it all existed as a mere paraphrase of what had once been. Its hotels, souvenir shops, and cafés were busy year-round accommodating tourists wanting to experience the past. The Hôtel de la Cité was the only five-star establishment within the olden walls. A mix of the neo-Gothic and art deco styles, it stood in a quiet corner beside Saint-Nazaire Basilica. Tonight, he'd specifically avoided all of the popular restaurants scattered across the cité and dined in his suite, requesting that Andre Labelle join him.

"I must tell the hotel chef how much I enjoyed the meal," he said to the younger man.

And he meant every word.

The stuffed courgette blossom in tomato velouté had been the perfect starter. The local trout, baked with mushrooms and sweetbread, the ideal second course, augmented with some roasted cauliflower in brown butter. Dessert had been particularly exquisite. Crème brûlée with hazelnuts, topped with chocolate sauce and a scoop of caramel ice cream.

A feast fitting for this grand occasion.

"Are you ready?" he asked.

Andre nodded. "I have been for a long time."

"And you wish to fully accept?"

"I do."

"You know what that entails?"

"In every way."

"Your past sins? Have you atoned for them? Are you remorseful? Prepared to lead an exemplary life from this day forward?"

"I am."

He was pleased. "Then proceed."

Andre rose from the chair and dutifully knelt on the carpet. "Thou just God of all good souls, thou who art never deceived, who dost never lie or doubt, grant me to know what thou knowest, to love what thou dost love, for I am not of this world, and this world is not of me, and I fear lest I meet death in this realm of an alien evil god."

The declaration had been delivered in perfect Occitan, the language in which the prayer had first been uttered more than eight hundred years ago. Precious words that drew a stark contrast between the *just God of all good souls* and the *alien evil god* of the physical world.

"If God wills it," Bernat said, "good souls, like yourself, can have knowledge of the world of the Father. Whether we can have knowledge of the other world, in this life, or only in the next, remains to be seen."

Andre's head remained bowed, eyes to the floor. Reverent. Respectful.

"Do you wish the *consolamentum*?" he asked.

"With all that I am," Andre said.

"Have you properly prepared?"

The head nodded. "I am ready."

"For every duty that might be required?"

"Every one."

Andre had begun his journey three years ago as a *credente*, a mere believer. He had shown both promise and desire, so when he'd requested further training—to test his sense of faith with rigorous examinations—the Elders had been pleased. He'd been allowed to participate in seminary, the *maison des hérétiques*, where his devotion had been honed and tested. Now, after lengthy fasts, vigils, and prayer, he was ready for the final step.

Only a Perfectus could administer the *consolamentum*, the laying on of hands, which meant that every new Perfectus stood at the end of a chain linking them all the way back to the apostles and Christ himself. The ceremony marked the transition from *credente* to one of the elect. Not a cleric or a priest or anything special, merely believers who'd chosen to become teachers, their task to aid other believers in becoming part of the Perfecti, too. Each one lived a solitary life, at the last phase of their worldly existence, practicing self-denial, finally assured that they would never again return to the physical world. Long ago their name had been born as an insult, reflecting how the Holy Roman Church saw them as "perfect heretics." But they'd kept the label as a badge of honor, out of defiance, signifying an element of completeness in their spiritual lives.

"Shall we keep going?" he asked.

Andre nodded.

It was during the *consolamentum* that the Holy Spirit inhabited the Perfectus' corporal body as a symbolic death from the material world and a rebirth in the Spirit. The ceremony was striking in its simplicity. Unlike other religious baptisms no water or anointing oil were required. No towering churches laden with idols, or priests clad in gold-embroidered robes. Only belief and devotion cemented the bond, most times administered in the forest, beside a lake, in the mountains, or before a hearth in the homes of those wanting salvation. Once done, any deviation from the righteous path and you were no longer a Perfectus. The journey to salvation had to be restarted. The *consolamentum* had to be immaculate, without blemish, that element necessary as a counter to the corrupt priests and bishops that had existed in the thirteenth century and whose profane acts were still allowed to go unpunished. The cursed Catholics had long considered the rite a distorted imitation of their own baptismal ritual. But that was not the case. Instead, the *consolamentum* dated back to the earliest Christian church, handed down from generation to generation without the interference of priests or popes.

"Pray God to make a good Christian of me, and bring me to a good end," Andre repeated three times.

He'd been fully apprised on Andre Labelle by those who'd worked with him over the past three years. Thirty-one years old. Possessed of an arrest record. Petty theft. Assault. Disorderly conduct. Once a wild, impulsive man who never admitted a mistake living what some would say was a wanton, reckless life. Thankfully, he'd come to the attention of another Perfectus who'd started him along the right path. Andre had been born not far away to the south, in the Roussillon, where nature loomed larger than life and mystery reigned. An extraordinary place with a rich heritage full of all sorts of legends and tales involving Moors, Charlemagne, and Roland. Andre was reflective of the hearty stock bred there. A slim, muscular youth with dull black, curly hair and a flat nose that projected a tough-guy look. Only the dark eyes betrayed the clouds of pain that still haunted a troubled mind. But every report Bernat had received had noted an exemplary record and a deep dedication to the faith. The road to salvation stretched long and narrow, reserved only for those in full possession of their faculties and enjoying the support of the Elders, which Andre had earned.

Bernat stood from the chair. "Proceed with the *melhoramentum*."

An Occitan word meaning "improving," which began with an acknowledgment that the Holy Spirit dwelled within the Perfectus standing before you. An initiate had to believe that to be the case or none of what was about to happen would matter. Andre stayed kneeling on the carpet and folded his hands, bowing three times. "Bless me, Lord. Pray for me. Lead us to our rightful end."

He provided the correct response. "In our prayers, I ask from God to make a good Christian out of you and lead you to your rightful end."

"I will devote myself to God and the Gospel," Andre said. "I will no longer eat meat, eggs, cheese, or fat apart from oil and fish. I will not swear any oaths and will never forsake the sect out of fear of fire, water, or death."

"Do you have anything to confess?"

Part of the ceremony was a cleansing of the soul.

"Only that my pride and arrogance can, at times, still get the better of me."

"We could all say the same thing."

"But mine must be controlled."

"Then do that. Without fail. Please recite the Pater Noster."

Andre murmured the Lord's Prayer. Bernat took the moment to step over to the desk and retrieve his Bible. He opened to the Gospel of John, then held it above Andre's head as had been done for centuries by other Perfecti. "*In the beginning was the Word, and the Word was with God, and the Word was God.*"

Andre began to tremble.

"The light shines in the darkness and the darkness has not overcome it. There was a man sent from God whose name was John. He came as a witness to testify concerning that light, so that through him all might believe. He himself was not the light, he came only as a witness to the light. The true light that gives light to everyone was coming into the world. He was in the world, and though the world was made through him, the world did not recognize him. He came to that which was his own, but his own did not receive him. Yet to all who did receive him, to those who believed in his name, he gave the right to become children of God, children born not of natural descent, nor of human decision or a husband's will, but born of God."

Andre's head stayed low, to the floor, accepting the Holy Spirit into his heart, cementing his choice to become a Perfectus.

Now the most important part.

"The Word became flesh and made his dwelling among us. We have seen his glory, the glory of the one and only Son, who came from the Father, full of grace and truth. He cried out, saying, 'This is the one I spoke about when I said, "He who comes after me has surpassed me because he was before me."' Out of his fullness we have all received grace in place of grace already given. For the law was given through Moses and grace and truth came through Jesus Christ." He paused and allowed the moment to take hold. Finally, he asked, "Are you at peace?"

Andre rose up but stayed on his knees. "Totally."

"Stand."

Andre came to his feet and Bernat stepped close, reverently laying the Bible atop Andre's head and gently kissing him once on each cheek.

The kiss of peace.

"Welcome, my brother. You are now one of us in every way."

Tears had formed in the brown eyes. This arrogant petty criminal was now a part of the one true faith. All new Perfecti were assigned a *socius*, a comrade who shared, for a time, in their labor and hardships. He'd specifically asked to be Andre's.

"You will serve me," he said. "Until you strike out on your own to serve all believers."

Andre nodded.

Bernat laid the Bible down and walked across to the glass-paneled doors that led out to a spacious terrace. He opened the doors and gestured for Andre to follow him outside. Cool crisp air tingled his nostrils. A perfect mid-spring evening. The more modern section of Carcassonne, known as the Bourg with its crisscrossing mesh of paved streets, could be seen below in the distance, the rooftops lit to the night. He was an ardent student of history and knew about all that had happened here eight hundred years ago. Every detail. The good and the bad. He drew strength from that legacy.

Which he would need in the coming days.

"It is time," he said.

Andre nodded in agreement.

They were both here, in Carcassonne, for the same reason.

He smiled. "Let it begin."

CHAPTER 3

Nick quickly worked his way through the heat and smoke, aided by an open door and windows that were being smashed by firemen, allowing the soot more ways out.

One of the policemen followed him.

What was happening here? Hard to say. But whatever it was seemed intentional. He flushed those disturbing thoughts from his brain and plunged out into the Belgian night, filling his lungs with clean air. Ahead, fifty yards away, he caught sight of the black figure racing away down the quiet street.

Carrying a laptop.

"I'm going after whoever that is," he told the cop in English.

"This is a police matter," the man said in English, too. Thank goodness. Foreign languages were tough for him.

He found his UN credentials and flashed them. "I can handle this."

The cop studied them, nodded, then displayed a radio. "I will alert others and have help come your way."

Good idea.

Nick raced off.

Ghent was familiar to him, as he'd visited twice before. It sat at the confluence of the Scheldt and Leie Rivers. Still a university city, once the largest town outside of Paris, it had been one of the richest places in northern Europe. It remained a city of merchants. Markets lay scattered everywhere, places where you could find anything from a quart of fresh strawberries to the collected works of Dickens. All that among pedestrian-only cobbled streets, a thousand-year-old fortress, churches, a cathedral, several medieval towers, and a constant string of spacious squares and tall spires. Once a year in July it celebrated itself with a huge nine-day festival of music, art, and fun, which he'd attended a couple of years back.

He stepped up his pace and began to close the gap on his target. Thankfully, he stayed in excellent shape. Exercise had always been a release for him. He liked to push himself with a little pain and a lot of sweat.

The black-clad figure turned a corner ahead.

He followed, now surrounded by two lines of multistory, polychrome façades. No billboards, neon, or high-rises in sight. Just an Old World charm from an unpretentious simplicity, the aging hand of time dominating. Most of the rows of stepped-gable houses were full of hotels, banks, souvenir shops, retailers, bars, and cafés, everything put to good use as though it were not a priceless relic from another epoch. These were residences. The ground-floor doors dim, lights burning only here and there in the upper windows. A few cars sat parked, which he sidestepped, keeping pace with the woman ahead. He only knew she was a woman because of Kelsey.

Go after her.

A part of him wanted to do whatever she wanted. Some things never changed. But what was so important about that laptop? He had no idea but added that inquiry to his growing list of unanswered questions.

For the past five years he'd traveled the globe trying to preserve, or sometimes save, history. You'd think that the locals would appreciate their heritage far more than he did. But sadly, that was not the case in most places. In fact, the greatest threats to historical preservation came from those most familiar with the place or thing. Why was that? Familiarity bred contempt? Maybe. But most likely it was just indifference. Here, though, arson, criminal damage to property, and theft had occurred. Not to mention the assault on Kelsey. All intentional. He hoped the fire had been contained but, from what he'd seen, it appeared that another work of art had been lost. One precious thing after another gone. His job was to prevent that from happening. And he was good at it, the only field officer on CLIO's payroll.

A loner.

Which he liked.

His personal life had evolved into much of the same.

Since Kelsey there'd been relationships here and there, but none lasting more than a few months. Everyone had been measured against her, and none had met the grade. Frustratingly, Kelsey stayed etched into his mind. Her pale, almost translucent complexion. High cheekbones, green eyes, and hair that once hung long and perfectly straight, the color of cinnamon. A beautiful woman in every way. He knew it was stupid. Time to move on and all that bullshit. But he'd found that hard to do. So he'd done nothing. Just worked hard. Traveled the world.

And hoped the next best thing would come along.

His quarry turned another corner and he kept racing ahead, the gap between them closing. They passed through a piazza with an eager, active night crowd. The woman stayed to its edges and disappeared down a side street. He could not lose her. With some polite phrases he eased his way through and followed. Another corner turned and they were now riverside, paralleling a waist-high stone wall. He had the impression she wasn't just running away. She was headed to a specific place. Luckily, few people were around here to either get in the way or be placed in danger. Was she aware he was following? Hard to know.

Sirens suddenly pierced the air.

Three cars, blue and red lights flashing, emerged from one of the side streets. They turned and headed for a small cobbled square that spread out from the quay wall, their headlights cutting huge swaths of light in the darkness. It was like they'd sensed her, the black-clad figure now being boxed in with nowhere to go.

The locals worked fast.

He stopped about a hundred feet away, shifting his weight forward, ready to sprint or weave, depending on what was about to happen. His breath expelled in sharp whooshes, drying his mouth. The woman backed to the stone wall and glanced over the side, as if assessing the situation. The headlights angled toward her and, in the instant before she was fully illuminated, she tossed the laptop over the side. Into the river?

The cars screeched to a stop.

Doors opened.

Men with guns emerged, shouting. In Flemish. The woman whirled around and faced the police, one hand down, behind her back.

More shouts.

The concealed arm appeared from behind her.

A shot rang out.

From the police.

More rounds were fired.

Which seared the woman's chest and sent her lean body spinning like a dancer. The sight sickened him. Sure, he'd seen his share of violence, but was this necessary?

Neither hand held a weapon.

She slid along in a marionette's dance, then fell forward unable to protect her face, which smacked hard into the pavement near a stone fountain.

He did not move.

Luckily, he was not near enough to draw attention and the police were focused on the body, advancing ahead with guns pointed. He glanced over the wall. Long fingers of shadow clutched the water in a tight grip. He caught a blur of movement in the darkness and the outline of a boat drifting away from a concrete walk that edged the river.

Nothing would be learned here.

So he hopped over the wall, hung by his fingertips, then dropped to the concrete below.

CHAPTER 4

Bernat left Carcassonne with Andre, driving nearly an hour east to Béziers. The town occupied a bluff above the river Orb a mere ten kilometers west from the Mediterranean coast. One of the oldest settlements in France. Neoliths, Celts, Gauls, Romans, and Visigoths all had occupied it at some point or another. Bullfighting was its current claim to fame. A million people came every August to witness the spectacle. But on July 29, 1209, the feast day of St. Mary Magdalene, something happened here that changed the world forever.

The army was camped outside the city, a vast expanse of tents and bivouacs, a solid mass of men, horses, and carts encircling the fortified walls. It had arrived yesterday after a march from Lyon intent on capturing 222 heretics, about 10 percent of Béziers' population, that the residents were known to be harboring. The warriors had come in response to a call to arms made by Pope Innocent III. The West was accustomed to papal crusades, as it had been waging those since 1095. But all of that venom had been directed at Muslims and the bloodshed occurred far away in the Holy Land. This was to be the first crusade directed against fellow Christians conducted entirely in the heart of Europe. More precisely in a region known as the Languedoc, a proud and independent arc of mountainous terrain stretching from the Pyrénées in the south to Provence in the north. The land of wind, olives, grapes, and sea. Troubadours and traders. Sharing a culture and language with Aragon and Barcelona. A bastion of independent thinkers and capitalistic burghers. Where Christians, Jews, and Muslims lived and worked together in harmony.

Here also flourished a new religion. A pacifist brand of Christianity stressing that salvation could be obtained through a detachment from natural goods. One whose origins were wholly unknown, but one that proclaimed itself the true faith, more ancient than Catholicism, tolerance and poverty its keystones.

It had migrated from the East, after gaining footholds in Italy and the Rhineland. Its central doctrine proclaimed that the world was the creation of a dark evil force. Rex Mundi. King of the World. Encompassing all that was corporeal, chaotic, and powerful. Matter was corrupt. Anything that existed in the world was corrupt. Civil authority was a fraud. And if that authority was based somehow on a divine sanction? Like the Holy Roman Church?

That was even worse.

Followers believed the soul was trapped in the body, an imperfect creation within the domain of evil. The object of life was to escape this hell on earth and seek the God of Light who ruled the eternal spiritual domain, unsullied by the taint of matter. Each believer had to choose to renounce the material world. If not, after death, they kept returning, over and over, occupying new bodies, experiencing new lives, until they were finally ready to reject all that was physical. Once done, they were elevated from a mere believer to a Perfectus, capable then, at their next death, of ascending to a blissful, forever state ruled by the God of Light.

The cosmology was one of dual principles.

Evil was seen. Good was not.

An absolute separation of spirit and matter.

They had no need for sacraments, churches, bishops, popes, tithes, or taxes. Those were all part of the physical world that did not matter. Women were equal to men in all respects. No swearing of oaths, no saintly relics, no worship of the cross, which had been nothing more than an instrument of torture. No violence or military service. No eating of food that came from any procreative act. Marriage was meaningless. Having children cruel, as it brought another heavenly soul into evil. Christ had once come, but only as an apparition to spread the dualist truth of Good and Evil and start the chain of believers, which had continued for centuries unbroken. The whole concept was attractive, seductive, and popular. In Italy they called themselves Cazzara, after the Greek katharos. *In Germany they were the Ketzer. In France they acquired the label* Cathari. *Latin for "pure." From that evolved the name that stuck.*

Cathar.

The Holy Roman Church tried and failed to ban them in 1179. It claimed Cathars practiced unnatural vegetarianism and advocated the extinction of mankind, and that Perfecti were clearly homosexual since they always traveled in pairs. An attempt to overpower them with priests and monks trying to convert the wayward failed in 1203. By July 1209 the Cathar religion had taken firm hold in the Languedoc. Not only with the peasants, but also with the nobility, bourgeoisie, and wealthy burghers. Local Catholics, who were no fan of Rome and all its rules and dogma, supported friends and neighbors in their religious choice. It helped that most of the Catholic clergy were corrupt and that Cathars lived virtuously. To the people of the Languedoc the enemy was anyone who challenged the authority and autonomy of the powerful viscounts of Toulouse, Foix, and Carcassonne. Which the Holy Roman Church did routinely. Catharism cast a simplicity that many found appealing. Love thy neighbor and the peace that goodness and honesty brought. Cathar homes were open and welcoming. Rome tried to label it heretical, but the fact remained that the Cathars were far more than a differing philosophy. They were a full-fledged, open competitor.

Gaining ground.

Which required extermination.

And that explained why an army of twenty thousand men waited outside the walls at Béziers.

They'd come from all over. The Papal States in Italy. The Militia of the Faith of Jesus Christ. Hospitallers of the Holy Spirit. The Knights of Saint George. The duchies of Burgundy and Brittany. The counties of Nevers, Auxerre, Aurenja, and Saint-Pol. English volunteers. The duchies of Austria and Berg. The Electorate of Cologne.

They would ultimately stand against the counties of Toulouse, Valentinois, Astarac, Comminges, and Foix. The viscounties of Béziers, Carcassonne, and Albi. The lordships of Séverac, Menèrba, Tèrmes, Cabaret, and Montségur. The marquisate of Provence. The crown of Aragon. And a host of exiled knights.

Not a single Cathar participated, as violence was repugnant to them.

To eliminate the need for a bloody fight, an ultimatum was issued. Hand over the 222 heretics and Béziers would be spared. The offer was considered and rejected, one of the local burghers remarking that they would rather drown in the salt sea's brine than betray their friends. The message was clear. The local Catholics planned not to cooperate.

So another way would be utilized.

Warfare then was a matter of siege rather than pitched battles on open fields. But the crusaders could not afford a lengthy stay, one that would deplete resources and allow the enemy time to organize. Many more battles would be required and their knights were bound to only forty days of service, the nobles who commanded them distrustful of one another, the mercenaries that had been employed wholly unpredictable.

But a siege seemed the only way.

Until fate intervened.

A small group of men from Béziers ventured outside the city walls *in an exhibit of force designed to annoy the enemy. They hurled insults and killed one of the crusaders, tossing the body into the river Orb. The mercenaries—godless, lawless, and fearless, men who never showed a drop of mercy—were stirred to action. They charged, barefoot, dressed only in shirts and breeches, brandishing hand weapons. A brawl ensued. The mercenaries advanced and managed to breach the city gates, which had been opened to allow the retreating burghers to reenter.*

A fatal mistake.

Within minutes bands of crusaders were inside the city.

The Dominican monk Arnold Amaury, there as the pope's legate, in supreme command, was queried. How do we know if someone is Catholic or Cathar? To be spared or executed? *Amaury considered the inquiry, then declared that* the Lord knoweth them that are his. Kill them all. He will recognize his own.

Which was exactly what happened.

Panic and frenzy reigned. Private homes were breached. Throats cut. Women raped. Plunder taken. Many of the residents sought sanctuary within the churches. But the doors were forced open and all inside slaughtered. Men, women, children, babies, invalids, priests. No matter. All were put to the sword and the town burned.

Ten thousand died.

Within a few hours the grand city of Béziers was laid to waste with corpses and blood, the streets filled with brigands fighting among themselves over the spoils.

The Albigensian Crusade had begun.

Through the windshield Bernat spied the lights of Béziers.

Truly, a monument to resilience.

The town had survived the centuries, today a center of French wine production. It still sat on a hilltop with its cathedral, great squares, vast esplanade, and picturesque streets. He was particularly fond of its rugby team, which had twelve championships to its credit. About seventy-eight thousand people lived there. But only one of those residents concerned him at the moment.

During Andre's probationary period it was learned that, like so many other Cathars, the younger man had been born and raised Catholic, attending a regional parochial school in southern France. As a boy he'd been active in the Catholic Scouts, which was where he first met Father Louis Tallard who, over a twenty-year period, had managed to sexually abuse nearly thirty scouts, one of whom had been Andre Labelle. Complaints were filed and Tallard had long ago been relieved of his parish, but he had been allowed to return to active duty—working administratively—after he supposedly confessed his sins and repented. Incredibly, no criminal prosecutions were initially pressed. All of which illustrated the hypocrisy and arrogance of the modern Holy Roman Church. No other institution had systematically protected sexual predators to such an extent. Finally, three years ago, after much uproar, Tallard had been formally charged with multiple counts of sexual abuse and the rape of minors. Those cases remained pending, dragging through the courts with no resolution, all while Tallard continued to wear the white collar of a priest.

Bernat bypassed central Béziers and drove along a perimeter highway a few kilometers north, beyond the town, on a deeper foray into the ever-thickening forest. Finally, he turned off the highway onto a dirt path, rutted and dusty, lined with grassy ditches and tumbled-down wooden fences. The farmhouse he sought sat back, among the trees. Tallard had retreated there after being charged, trying to fade away, hoping to be forgotten.

He drove close to the small, shabby cube of a house and parked. Another vehicle was already there. He and Andre stepped out into the night. The moon peeked through racing clouds overhead. He led the way as they marched toward the front door across a layer of thin grass. A man waited. Short, stout, fair-skinned, bearded.

"Is he ready?" Bernat asked.

"Like a Christmas turkey."

He nodded his appreciation and opened the door. Inside was a hodgepodge of décor, the place messy, made even more so by some overturned furniture and two broken lamps, all signs of a struggle. Louis Tallard lay on his back, sprawled across an oak table, his hands and arms tied to each of the table's four legs, his head angled downward over the side. Tallard was fifty-nine years old, short, lean, wiry-limbed with lined features, sporting a beard and mustache. Tape blocked the mouth from speaking or breathing. A wild look filled the priest's blue eyes. Good. He had every reason to be afraid.

"Wait outside," he told the man, who left, closing the front door behind him.

That was the thing about paid help.

They did exactly as they were told.

He faced Louis Tallard, who cocked his head upward. The man wore a dirty sweatshirt and faded jeans. At least he was not dressed in a clerical suit or sporting a white collar.

"I am Bernat de Foix. I was born and raised in the *Comté de Foix*, as you would say in French, or the *Comtat de Fois*, as I would say in Occitan. My mother's ancestors flourished there from the eleventh to the fifteenth centuries. The title of count was first assumed in 1064 by Roger of Foix, who inherited the town of Foix and the adjoining lands, passing them on to his heirs for generations. The town still stands, as does the castle, but the lands no longer belong to the de Foix family. They were lost long ago. Are you familiar with them?"

Tallard shook his head quickly back and forth indicating no.

"No matter. I thought it only fitting that you know your inquisitor. That was a courtesy your fellow priests once showed others." He pointed. "Do you recognize this young man?"

34

Another violent shake of the head for no.

"This is Andre Labelle. Seventeen years ago you sexually molested him."

More shakes of the head.

"You deny the allegation?" he asked, incredulous.

Tallard nodded yes.

"As is your right. So we must now determine the truth."

The Albigensian Crusade lasted twenty years. Though billed as a religious war to root out heretics, it was nothing more than a land and power grab under the guise of religion.

And a slaughter.

Burnings, blindings, hangings, the rack, even corpses exhumed and defiled. No atrocity was too much. Hundreds of thousands were affected. In the end the Languedoc was politically realigned, bringing it solidly within the sphere of the French crown, diluting any influence from Spain. From 1209 to 1215 the crusaders experienced great success, capturing Cathar lands and perpetrating unspeakable acts of violence against civilians. From 1215 to 1225, a series of revolts allowed many of those lands to be regained by the local nobility. A renewed crusade resulted in the recapturing of the territory, driving Catharism underground by 1244. After the papal armies left something else arrived. Something equally as bad. An Inquisition. Sent to eliminate all remaining vestiges of Cathar belief left in the wake of the crusade. Most of the inquisitors, like Arnaud Amaury who'd led the crusaders, were Dominicans. In 1233 Pope Gregory IX charged the Inquisition with the absolute extirpation of the Cathars. Soon the Franciscans joined in the effort, but it was the Dominicans who left a legacy of bitterness that had endured right up until today.

"When your fellow priests came to town as part of the Inquisition," he said to Tallard, "they would announce their arrival days in advance, and everyone was invited to confess their sins. If you owned up to relatively minor misdeeds, were prepared to swear fidelity to the church, and were willing to provide useful information about others, you were given a small penance and the matter was closed. But a failure to confess, or to provide useful information on your family or friends, was taken as a lack of commitment to the one true church. And dealt with accordingly. Most were burned at the stake. Horrible, wouldn't you say?"

He did not wait for a headshake in reply.

"They were after the Perfecti," he said. "The few remaining devoted Cathars. Men and women who were not willing, under any circumstance, to swear an oath, let alone one of fidelity to the Catholic Church. So those who refused to provide information on the Perfecti were dealt with harshly."

He motioned and Andre ripped the tape from Tallard's mouth. The man worked his jaw, swallowed a few times, and sucked in repeated deep breaths. Then the priest yelled, "What do you want?"

"Justice," he said.

"For what?"

He allowed his gaze to bore in. "For the evil you have done."

"Are you going to kill me?"

"We do not kill."

A puzzled look came to the priest's face. "You're Cathar?"

"We are," he said with pride.

"That religion died centuries ago."

"Unfortunately for you, that attempt to exterminate us failed."

Relief flashed through the bound man's eyes. "Cathars deplored violence. In every form."

"True," he said. "But that does not mean we are merciful."

CHAPTER 5

Nick landed softly, the rubber soles on his shoes aiding with the impact. No one had seen him roll over the side of the stone wall, the dark sky above him constantly strobed by blue and red lights. Thankfully, the commotion was farther down the quay and the darkness had provided ample cover. But the whole river could be lit to the night in a matter of minutes. The boat with the laptop was still drifting away on the current. He had to follow, so he crept over to a small wooden dinghy tied to the concrete walk that edged the water. He released its mooring lines and pushed off, glad to see two paddles lying inside.

There'd been no need to kill that woman. None at all. Yes, one hand had been concealed and, once revealed, a moment of indecision had occurred. But even if she'd been armed none of those policemen had been in any danger, considering the number of loaded weapons aimed her way. She'd been shot on impulse. And from stupidity. She was far more valuable alive. Now whatever she knew had died with her. He was licensed and sanctioned to carry a weapon among member states, fully trained in its use, but he rarely toted one. If the truth be told, he hated guns.

And for a good reason.

Which only a few people knew.

He'd carried a weapon in the army and the FBI, never firing it in the line of duty. Thankfully he'd discovered that in his current job guns were more a nuisance than a source of protection. They raised more questions than were ever answered. So far he'd managed just fine without one.

He hoped Kelsey was okay. This was not the reunion he'd envisioned. Not even close. But what had he expected? Kelsey was a full-fledged, vow-taking daughter of Christ. A sister in the Congregation of Saint-Luke. After their breakup he'd learned what he could about the religious order, trying to understand what happened. Kelsey had always been a devout Catholic, but she'd kept her beliefs close, sharing them only when appropriate, cautious when expressing herself. He'd always chalked that hesitation up to just being a private person when it came to religion. So he'd never fully realized the depth of her devotion.

Until the end.

"I have a calling," she said to him. *"One that has been talking to me for some time. One I've ignored. But I can't any longer."*

"What are you saying?"

"I can't marry you. I plan to take my vows and become a nun."

Another man? Another woman? Okay. He could deal with that. But God? What could he have said that would not have sounded selfish? Though he'd been stunned beyond belief, he'd accepted her decision and, together, they'd canceled the wedding. Two weeks later she began her postulancy. Now she was Sister Kelsey MacKenzie Deal.

Instead of Mrs. Kelsey Lee.

More sirens wailed in the distance. This was turning into a busy night for Ghent police and fire.

Since moving to Paris he'd often fantasized about exploring the corners of Montmartre or having lunch atop the Eiffel Tower with someone special. Perhaps even visiting the haute-couture *maisons* on Avenue Montaigne, the elegant boulevard that bound together the houses of Dior, Chanel, Valentino, and Louis Vuitton along with an exorbitant collection of high-end jewelers. Paris was all about fashion and romance. No one could visit without some feeling of having come home, its dingy grandeur one of the few sights left in the world that truly stirred emotion. So far he'd found no one to share those sights and sounds with.

But he wasn't giving up hope.

Maybe one day.

Ahead, the motor to the boat he was pursuing cranked.

Not good.

No way he could keep pace by rowing.

Luckily, the boat barely puttered along. Surely trying not to attract attention. There were speed limits within the city. The banks on both sides of the river were lined with houses, shops, and restaurants. Portions were lit. Others not so much. He'd passed three boats out for the night, both low to the water, designed to fit beneath the many bridges that provided only minimal clearance.

He grabbed the oars and decided to add a little speed to his drift. The current was helping, but only enough to keep him barely moving. He kept his gaze locked on the boat about fifty yards away. Its occupant seemed unaware of being followed. Otherwise they would have used their horsepower advantage and sped away. Thankfully, the ever-increasing darkness blotted him from sight.

Ahead he spotted the Gravensteen, a fearsome twelfth-century fortress, lit to the night. Once the seat for the Counts of Flanders, it had been first modeled after a Syrian crusader castle, he knew, then remodeled in the nineteenth century to reflect what Victorians thought a medieval castle should look like. It came complete with a moat, turrets, and arrow slits built originally to thwart Viking invasions. He'd toured it once.

The boat ahead passed the fortress.

Now about a hundred yards separated them.

Ghent's downtown was chopped up like a puzzle, its pieces outlined by rivers, tributaries, and canals. Hard to go in any direction and not find water. Luckily, here the river was straight, devoid of bends, more empty boats at anchor against the stone walks and walls at the edges. He grabbed his bearings and realized they were heading toward the northern reaches of town, the buildings on either bank becoming progressively darker. He kept paddling, trying not to lose the other craft.

He'd come a long way from the FBI's Art Crime Team. Cultural trafficking was a looming criminal enterprise. Billions of dollars were stolen annually. The FBI had long operated a team of twenty agents, trained and supported by another special team of Justice Department prosecutors. The twenty were divided into five units of four, each responsible for cases in an assigned geographic region. His team had been headed by a no-nonsense special agent named Bill Muntan and oversaw the southwest United States. During his five years with the FBI hundreds of millions of dollars in looted art and cultural treasures had been recovered. Then, on a rainy Thursday afternoon, his life changed.

"*UNESCO is looking for a field asset,*" *Muntan said to him.* "*This is something new for them.*"

He'd worked with UNESCO several times on cases. It possessed a wealth of information and access to even more. But he'd been unaware that it employed active assets.

"*They want someone young, eager, and hungry,*" *Muntan said.* "*I thought of you.*"

"*I like my job now.*"

"And I'm not particularly fond of losing you. But if the UN is going to get into the same hands-on business that we do, I want a friend over there. Someone I can call on and who will call on me. I like to have friends in places."

Point made. So he'd taken the job.

And never regretted it.

The past six years had been the most exciting and productive of his life. His professional success seemed due to an alchemy of intelligence, courage, and a capacity for hard work. He was now thirty-seven years old, fit physically and mentally, with a solid career and the prospects of even more.

So what else mattered?

At the moment retrieving Kelsey's laptop had vaulted to the top of his must-do list.

A part of him wanted to be there for her.

No matter what.

Ahead, he saw his target ease toward the east bank of the river. He stopped paddling and watched as a black figure hopped from the boat and headed up a set of stairs to street level. It was hard to tell if the form was male or female. A lit building stood at the top, across the street from the river, a few parked cars hugging the curbs in front. He watched as the figure topped the stairs, laptop tucked under one arm, crossed the street, and stepped through a gate in what appeared to be an iron fence. The figure then vanished through the building's front door.

He resumed paddling.

A light came on in a second-floor window, near the center of the rectangle. He made his way to the same quay, secured the dinghy, and climbed the stone risers. At the top, he crossed the quiet street and approached the iron gate. The building beyond was a four-story, brick rectangle with two projecting wings that stretched from either side toward the back. It was flanked on one side by more multistory brick buildings that all faced the river. Its roof was steeply pitched slate dotted with dormers. The spiny tentacles of tall blooming trees rose close to the walls. Windows sheathed by opaque curtains allowed only a halo of light to seep outward in the upper stories, the pedimented front door shielded by a porch and lit by two iron fixtures. He saw no cameras or other overt security, and the gate itself was unlocked. But what really puzzled him was the sign near the main entrance.

CONVENT FOR THE MAIDENS OF SAINT-MICHAEL

CHAPTER 6

Sister Claire Haffner slipped the black hood from her head. Sweat soaked her short brown hair and dark brow. Her eyes were filled with tears for Sister Rachel. She'd heard the gunshots. Had her friend sacrificed herself to ensure that the operation was successful? Was she hurt? Dead? Captured? Impossible to say. But why had she chosen to toss the laptop down and remain on the street exposed, vulnerable?

"The panel's destroyed. Take this and go."

That's what Rachel had said. She'd caught the laptop, then watched as her friend vanished from sight. The next thing she'd seen were the strobing lights. Then heard the gunfire. An unsettling sound. One that had broken her heart. With no choice she'd made her escape on the river following Rule #1. The objective took priority.

Always.

She stood in the convent foyer and allowed the familiar silence to calm her shattered nerves. This convent, here in Ghent, was for the aged, where the maidens lived out their later years after a lifetime of faithful service. The building had existed for three centuries, built specifically in Ghent for a reason. And yes, the women here were aware of the mission and had helped with preparations, but they'd intentionally not been briefed on all its particulars. Those details were only for the order's abbess, who was hundreds of miles away awaiting a report.

She closed her eyes, steadied herself, then climbed the stairs to the second floor. Her room was one of several kept ready for visitors and faced the street. She, Sister Rachel, and Sisters Ellen and Isabel had arrived three days ago from the south, reconnoitering the workshop and determining when and how best to act. The operation had been planned for some time with care and diligence. The order had not survived for fifteen centuries by being impetuous or foolish.

She entered her room and switched on the light.

The small cubicle contained only a desk, wardrobe, lamp, white-cane chair, and iron-framed twin bed with a crucifix hung above. Bathrooms were shared down the hall, similar to a dormitory at university. She and her fellow maidens owned little to nothing in the form of material possessions. Whatever they needed was provided by the order. She'd long ago adjusted to a life of simplicity, devotion, and duty. What she was not accustomed to was failure.

She peeled off the black spandex from her hot sweaty skin. A report would have to be made to the abbess, but she could not bring herself to make the call. At the moment she needed solace.

Which had always served her well in the past.

One of her earliest childhood memories had been a realization that she wanted to be on God's side. Religion had been important to her as far back as she could remember. She'd earned a degree from Tulane University and wanted to teach music in elementary school, thinking that by doing so her life would be given to God.

Then she met Sister Anne.

An older woman who'd visited the Catholic church in Shreveport, Louisiana, on a search, one that Claire herself would later repeat many times. On that day she was employed by the Caddo Parish Public Schools, devoted to her music students. She'd listened to Sister Anne talk about the signs of a religious vocation—dedication, determination, and a little voice in your head that leads the way—thinking the whole time she was talking only to her. More conversations followed and Sister Anne invited her to attend a retreat at a nearby convent. There in that quiet reverent space she'd begun, for the first time, to truly listen to God's voice, pondering what he might be asking of her.

Why not be of service to me? the voice kept saying.

Why not?

She'd always been possessed of a mind of her own, not one to crave the strength or attention of others, and always respectful of authority. All traits, she came to learn later, that Sister Anne searched for in recruits. That woman had possessed terrific instincts. Which were needed in her line of work. Anne had been the gatekeeper. The first person that every recruit dealt with. The one that had to be convinced. The selection process was tough and arduous. Only one to two women were found every few years.

And for good reason.

She recalled thinking about her own decision for several months. Finally, she quit her job and joined the Maidens of Saint-Michael.

She lived a year as a postulant, then devoted another year to canonical study, residing in the convent as a novitiate. Temporary vows came next, which bound her to three more years. If after all that time she still was sure then, and only then, were final vows taken. Most orders bestowed a ring on that day that signaled a marriage with Christ. The maidens were different. Each received a silver necklace with a *fleur-de-lys*.

Hers had hung around her neck for sixteen years.

She slipped on a robe, walked to the bathroom down the hall, and showered, hoping the water could rinse away some of her anxiety.

But it had no effect.

She returned to her room and dressed in her habit. The order had long ago abandoned the white-sleeved tunic, scapular, and stiff coif of a headdress. No floor-length black dresses or rosary belts either. Instead, inside the convent they wore plain gray smocks, simple low-heeled shoes, with a matching gray veil that showed their hair and face. Outside the convent, though, they dressed as needed for the particular situation.

Like tonight.

She sat on the edge of her bed and stared at the laptop. Her mind and body felt dull and heavy. For so long she'd basked in the halo of confidence that success generated in the young. But her luck ran out tonight. She'd warned the abbess. Told her, and the other maidens, that this was not worth the risk. Now there was Sister Rachel's sacrifice to weigh.

But how much of a sacrifice had it been?

She stood and left her room, navigating the halls to the convent's inner chapel. The building was deserted. It was time for nightly prayers in the outside main church. Inside the dimly lit chapel, an older woman knelt in one of the pews, hands folded underneath her chin. Claire crossed herself and knelt too, praying for forgiveness, but all her effort brought was the unaccustomed dampness of renewed grief to her eyes. The older woman stopped praying and turned to face her.

"What happened?" the older woman asked in French.

"Sister Rachel has been taken. She might even have been killed or injured."

And she told her what happened.

"The abbess must be informed."

"This is her fault," she said.

46

"Keep your opinions to yourself."

She glared at the older woman. "I don't need any lessons on my duty."

"I would hope not."

"This entire thing was unnecessary. And you know it."

"I know nothing, other than what a majority of the maidens wants. As should you too. What of the main objectives?"

"Accomplished. It's Sister Rachel who needs our help."

"That's a decision for the abbess."

She knew this woman was nearing eighty, a maiden for nearly sixty years and a former abbess, now retired. Once a capable guardian, like so many other women who'd come before her, now she lived here in seclusion and safety, enjoying a hard-earned rest, far away from the realities to the south.

She was curious. "Did you ever have to deal with death?"

"Once."

She knew that in the time leading up to and including World War II, there'd been several fatalities within the order. Ever since, though, she'd always believed that things had remained relatively calm. But this woman was speaking of a time long after the war.

"I was unaware," she told her elder.

"There is much you do not know." The older woman laid a hand on her shoulder, the small appendage shaking with a slight palsy, worry lines heavy on her face. "We all believe that you will one day be abbess. You are a devoted guardian. But please don't forget your vows."

None of that mattered at the moment.

Only Sister Rachel.

So she bowed her head.

And prayed.

CHAPTER 7

Bernat considered himself an experienced, worldly man with an infinite capacity for patience. But the sight of the bound priest swept waves of revulsion through him. And not for the older man's predicament. No. His thoughts were with the victims of this sexual predator. He'd spoken the truth when he'd told Tallard why they'd come.

For justice.

"Waterboarding was one of the most common tortures employed by the Spanish Inquisition during the fifteenth century," he said. "This has never been a secret. It is attested to by reams of letters, debates, manuals of instruction, and copious records of trials that include verbatim accounts of the torture sessions. I personally have read some of those in the historical archives of Spain. But it was not invented there. Since the thirteenth century it had been widely used by European civil and ecclesiastical courts. Unlike the Americans in the twenty-first century who wanted to label it 'enhanced interrogation,' it is clearly torture—and was meant to be that from the start."

Tallard's eyes were wild with fear.

"The Holy Roman Church used it extensively here, in the

Languedoc, when the Inquisition came after the Albigensian Cru-sade. And they were quite methodical with its application. When ready, the inquisitors and a recording secretary adept at speed writing would gather in a chamber. Everything that happened was written down. Sort of the electronic recording of its day. But unlike today, back then an attending doctor could rule the accused unfit to be tortured and order the procedure stopped." He paused. "Of course, that rarely occurred."

Then he smiled, enjoying this man's anxiety.

Andre returned with a pitcher filled with water.

"Once the accused was brought into the chamber, he or she was offered six opportunities to make a full and voluntary confession. Fear, in the presence of imminent pain, was generally enough to loosen an accused's tongue. It was only when fear did not work that torture was applied, with each step of the procedure, each jar of water, each turn of the winch, each question and choked-out answer, duly noted by the recording secretary."

The priest angled his head up and screamed for help.

Bernat slapped the back of his hand across the fool's face, sending the head back down over the table edge. "There's no one to come to your aid."

"You're insane."

He tossed a practiced show of casualness Tallard's way. "I prefer that label to what you are." He faced Andre. "Tell him."

The young man stared down at the priest. "Do you remember me?"

"No."

One.

"I remember you," Andre said in a low, dry voice. "The smell of your sweat. The touch of your clothes. Your wandering hands. The way you held me tightly against you."

"Lies. Lies. Lies," Tallard yelled.

Two.

"The way you tried to put your tongue in my mouth. I was eleven years old and could not avoid you."

"You are mistaking me for someone else. I feel for you. I truly do. But it was not me."

Three.

"You would always say I was *your little boy*. That you loved me and that what was happening was our secret and I must not tell anyone."

Tallard shook his head in denial.

Four.

"And I told no one," Andre said. "Not my parents. Friends. Other priests. The nuns. No one. I kept it all to myself for twenty years."

For the first time Andre's voice cracked. Horrible memories surely flooding back. Bernat had been warned that this could occur. No matter. Evil had to be faced. Tonight.

"You both must believe me," Tallard spit out. "I have never done such things. Never."

"This young man," Bernat said, "and others say otherwise. The charges you currently face say otherwise. Are they all lying?"

"No. Of course not. I would never want to minimize their pain. But it was not me."

Five.

"You have been shielded for a long time," he said, keeping his voice in a hushed, reverent tone. "By bishops who thought they could sweep it all away with no accountability. By Rome who turned a blind eye. By prosecutors who did not want to be bothered. By the public-at-large who seemed not to care. But your crimes are clear. There is no doubt as to your guilt. So I will give you one last chance to confess."

A strained silence descended as Tallard surely weighed his options. The truth? Or another lie? This demon had surely for so long denied who and what he was that reality no longer mattered. His psyche was convinced either that he never did anything wrong, or that whatever he'd done had been wholly consensual. Never mind his victims were innocent children who worshiped him as the embodiment of all that was sacred and good, something predators like this bastard used to maximum advantage.

"It. Was. Not. Me," Tallard said.

Six.

He shrugged, a gesture that signaled disdain and dismissal. "Then we shall proceed and, hopefully, extract the truth."

Andre reached down into the vinyl bag he'd brought from the car and removed a set of iron prongs. Bernat moved toward Tallard's head and wrenched the neck upward, forcing the man's mouth open. Inquisitors who'd worked their madness in Spain christened the tool a *bostezo*. Ironic, since the word meant "yawn." Tallard struggled as Andre forced the prongs into the mouth and pried the jaw open with a solid grip on the iron handles. From his pocket Bernat removed three long strips of linen, which he shoved to the back of the mouth, causing the priest to gag. Andre maintained his hold on the iron handles, keeping the mouth from closing, making swallowing impossible. Modern applications used a towel over the face soaked with water to cause the victim to feel like they were drowning.

Inquisitors were far crueler.

He lifted the pitcher and poured a small amount of water onto the linen strips. Eight hundred years ago a jar would have been suspended above the victim, the water allowed to slowly trickle onto the cloth, which maintained a nearly constant sense of drowning.

Tallard choked on the water that found his throat, struggling to breathe.

He kept easing the liquid into the open mouth and onto the cloth.

More gasps.

He stopped. "Have you anything to say? Indicate with your head yes or no."

The stubborn fool never moved. He resumed pouring. The sensation had to be excruciating, but he felt nothing for this monster. Breathing was becoming increasingly difficult. Tallard tried to cough and choke out the water but the prongs made that impossible.

Finally, the man broke.

And nodded his head over and over.

That had not taken long.

He stopped the pour, slid the linens out, and motioned for Andre to withdraw the prongs.

"All right," Tallard said, swallowing and breathing hard. "All right. I will tell you... everything."

"If you don't, then the next application will be far worse, with no letting up."

Tallard nodded in understanding.

He set the water pitcher down and motioned. Andre produced his phone and activated its video recorder. They listened for fifteen minutes as this man, ordained by Holy Orders, supposedly part of an unbroken line back to the twelve apostles, described how he sexually abused boy after boy, Andre included.

Bernat raised his hand. Andre switched off the recorder. "I can't listen to any more."

"I did what you asked. I confessed."

Now for the most important question. "Have you told anyone this before?"

Tallard hesitated, and Bernat sensed that he had. To make the point clear, he reached for the pitcher.

"No. No. Please. No more. Yes. I told the archbishop."

There it was. Exactly what he'd come for.

The Most Reverend Gerard Vilamur.

"Archbishop Vilamur knows all of this?" he asked.

Tallard nodded. "Everything."

"For how long?"

"Several years."

Just as he'd suspected.

"I want you to say that again, slowly." He motioned and Andre tapped the recorder back on. Tallard repeated what he'd said about the archbishop.

Andre tapped the screen, stopping the video.

Bernat's phone vibrated in his pocket. He stepped back and checked the display, which revealed a text marked with a red exclamation point.

Not good.

He opened and read the message from the curator of the cathedral in Ghent. The Just Judges panel has been destroyed in a fire. Total loss. It was a deliberate act of vandalism. Perpetrator escaped, police are in pursuit.

He was shocked and a multitude of questions were raised by the startling information. Thankfully, his job here was finished, so he stepped back and motioned for Andre to gather their things, including the water pitcher. No evidence could be left behind.

He headed for the door.

"Where are you going?" Tallard said. "You can't leave me here like this."

"Not to worry."

He stepped outside with Andre and closed the door. The man from earlier, and one other, waited near their car.

Both walked over and he nodded.

They disappeared inside the house.

He and Andre stood in silence.

"It's good that we don't kill," he said in a low voice. "That we do not fall to their level. Not then. Not now. Not ever. But it is also good that those two men don't believe as we do."

Andre nodded. Ever so slightly. Then a wisp of a smile formed at the corner of the younger man's lips. Smug. Self-contained. As if nothing was more important than their success.

And nothing was.

CHAPTER 8

Nick pushed through the iron gate in front of the convent and quickly worked his way around to the rear of the building. Knocking on the front door had not seemed like a smart play. The convent sat at the end of the block on a corner lot dotted with tall trees. Lights illuminated the red-brick walls and he was mindful of the many windows, but all of their shades were drawn, and what lights did burn were heavily filtered. The structure itself was elegant, the pinnacles and fleurons on the window gables definitely Old World. He wasn't sure what he planned to do. This was a convent, after all. But some serious felonies had occurred, a woman was surely dead, and one of the participants in all those crimes had fled here.

So this place was fair game.

Not to mention that the laptop was here too.

He rounded a corner and studied the rear of the building. A group of rectangles topped by low gables surrounded a large open court. They were timbered, the roofs in varying tones and tints, their façades deeply furrowed with the washings of countless rains. At the far end of the courtyard, opposite the main building, standing alone was what appeared to be a steepled church. Lights burned inside and he heard the soft chant of collective singing. Within the courtyard were walkways, trees, and benches, all lit by lamps on iron posts. Then he spotted what he was looking for.

A back door into the main building.

Movement caught his eye as the door opened and a woman exited. She wore an ankle-length gray dress with a veil on her head. He sought cover back around the corner and watched as the nun hustled toward the church, which she entered.

No sense wasting time.

He trotted across the open space, passing through a long trestle with a vine-hung gallery, to the rear door. He lifted the latch for the Gothic door and entered. He stood in a kitchen, the space crowded but orderly, one side dominated by a large fireplace. A sharp scent of rosemary laced the warm air. Stout beams hung overhead that displayed a variety of Delft plates. The wood floor had attained that satiny finish that came from long usage and tireless cleaning. No one was around and he heard no sounds. Hopefully, the residents were all in church.

He headed down a short hall and found a wooden staircase that wound upward. Nothing elaborate, most likely a back route that allowed quick access up and down. He slowly climbed to the second floor, the risers announcing his presence with a melody of squeaks, and stepped off into another corridor, this one wider than below, with a stone floor and rugs that acted as runners. True to a convent nothing adorned the walls, all painted a soft pastel color. Light came from sconces, the shadows trembling with their flicker. Doors lined both sides of the corridor, each open and spaced symmetrically apart.

The nuns' private rooms?

He stepped cautiously to the first open doorway and spied inside, seeing a small cubicle, sparsely filled with a mix-match of furniture. He listened and heard no sounds on the floor.

The next room was similar.

As was the next.

The light that had come on after the woman entered the building? That had been in a room facing the street, toward the middle. He grabbed his bearings and realized he was at the rear, so he hustled ahead down the corridor, past more open doors, turned a corner, and made his way to the other side. More open entrances lined the way. Still no one in sight. He was taking a huge chance. Expectation ached in the pit of his stomach. But the nerve of an alley cat was sometimes required to get the job done. And no one had ever accused him of being bashful.

He made another turn.

This one leading to a corridor with more open doors to rooms that fronted the street. As he passed each he stared inside, seeing nothing until he came to one toward the middle of the floor. Lying on the bed was a bundle of black clothing.

And a laptop.

He stepped inside and saw that the bodysuit and hood were similar to what the arsonist had worn. He stared around, looking for anything that might shed light on who he was dealing with. There were a few toiletries, a brush, rosary, and a Catholic missal. He opened it and read what was written on the inner flap.

To Claire, May God always walk with you.

Okay. At least he had a first name.
Along with the laptop.
Time to get out of here.

CHAPTER 9

Nick grabbed the laptop and headed for the outer hall. He hesitated a moment at the door and checked for anyone around. Hearing nothing, he scampered out and began to retrace his route. It seemed like it was time to involve the local police. Kelsey had wanted her laptop returned. Okay. Mission accomplished. But that woman back in town and the one who'd escaped to here were involved in God knows what. Nuns or not, they'd broken the law and had to be dealt with. That meant by the locals. Of course, before any of that could happen, he needed to leave without being seen.

He turned a corner, passing more of the open doors.

Not far to go.

Suddenly, someone appeared ahead, from around the next corner. A young woman in a long gray dress, her auburn hair bound by a veil. Maybe late twenties, petite, with a pale face dotted with freckles that glowed with good health.

Until she realized that a stranger was inside the convent.

Then her countenance changed from calm, to surprise, to something else altogether. She advanced toward him, yanking the length of her habit up above her knees, pivoting off her right foot, and planting her left heel into his chest. He'd hesitated, never thinking that a nun would use a roundhouse kick on him, so she'd gotten the best of him. He was thrown back against the wall, his breath exploding outward. Pain shot through his head, short-circuiting his brain in a starburst of sparks that exploded before his eyes.

That hurt.

He slumped, feet skidding on the carpet, but managed to keep a grip on the laptop. He got hold of his senses and regained his balance, but the nun was not backing off. Two quick steps and she was back on him, angling her knee and shifting her weight, raising her right leg upward and throwing another kick, sweeping one side to the other, aiming for his left lower shin, just above the ankle.

A move designed to break bones.

He dropped back and barely avoided contact with her.

It was a calculated move on her part and well executed. The woman advanced again, her actions swift and natural with no hesitation. There seemed no quarrels of conscience within her. But this was not his first rodeo. And after those kicks, chivalry be damned. He feigned confusion and drew her closer, staggering upright, weaving his head in supposed disorientation. She took the bait and he pounced, gripping the laptop with both hands, swiping it hard across the side of her face.

Metal smacked skin.

She teetered, then dropped toward the floor with an unconscious grunt. He quickly reached out and braced her, lessening the impact.

She lay still.

"Sorry about that," he whispered.

And he got moving.

$$\Omega$$

Claire opened her eyes, stopping the prayer at the sound of a commotion from beyond the chapel. The older nun heard it too. Anything loud within the convent drew immediate attention since this was a place of silence. She crossed herself, rose from the pew, and fled the chapel.

Out in the corridor she stopped and listened but heard nothing unusual. She turned a corner and headed back toward her room. Another turn and she saw someone lying on the floor. She rushed over to find Sister Ellen, one of the women who'd come north with her, unconscious with a nasty bruise on the left side of her face.

She managed to stir her to consciousness. "What happened?"

"Man...here. Had the...laptop."

Alarm swept through her.

She sprang to her feet and ran to her room, seeing immediately that the computer was gone. *No. This can't be.* Not after all that had happened. She reached into her habit, removed a phone, and dialed a number.

"We have an intruder. I need everyone back inside. Now."

She knew that nearly all of the sisters were in the church conducting nightly prayers, including Sister Isabel, the fourth member of her contingent, whom she'd just alerted. The security of the convent came above all else, including prayer. Most of the women were beyond their prime, but she'd brought three able acolytes with her. One of them was Sister Rachel. The other was lying woozy on the floor.

The final one?

On her way.

In the meantime she needed to find the intruder.

Ω

Nick heard an alarm sound.

In a convent?

Nothing about this place made sense. But he couldn't dwell on that abnormality. He needed to leave and he was rapidly making his way toward the wooden staircase he'd used to climb to the second floor. From there he'd descend to the kitchen, then out the rear door. But when he arrived at the top of the stairs he heard voices below, along with steps clonking up the wooden risers.

That wasn't good.

He turned and rushed back down the corridor he'd just traversed, feeling like a rat inside a maze with little room to maneuver.

The pulsating alarm stopped.

Apparently the troops had been mobilized. There'd be people behind him shortly. Ahead? Unknown. So he stopped at a corner and cautiously peered around the edge.

A woman, older than the one who'd attacked him, appeared at the far end of the hall wearing a gray skirt and veil. She stopped for a moment at the T-junction, then kept going, not coming his way. He heard voices behind him and realized he couldn't stay exposed any longer. So he hustled forward and darted into an open door, entering one of the sparsely furnished cubicles. He knew it would do nothing but attract attention if he closed the door, so instead he assumed a position behind it, watching through the crack created by the hinges as three more women dressed in gray skirts passed the doorway and kept going.

"What's happening?" a female voice said in English.

"Sister Ellen was attacked. There's a man inside the convent and he has the laptop I retrieved. Find him. Fast."

That had to be Claire giving orders.

A heavy tramp of feet headed off down the hall in both directions. He hoped with the doors to every room wide open they might overlook searching them, concentrating on the corridors and exits.

So how was he going to get out?

Ω

Claire dispatched her sisters to search the corridors. Some of the older nuns also joined in. She'd already ordered the exit doors locked and guarded. No way anyone was going to leave.

The bigger question, though, the one that really bothered her, was how she had been located in the first place.

Ω

Nick stared around at the tiny bedroom, focusing on the window that faced the front of the building. He stepped over and checked the sash, which was held shut by a brass latch. Hinges allowed it to swing out at a ninety-degree angle. When he'd first arrived he'd noticed the exterior architectural adornments, particularly a ledge that encircled the second floor. Now, much closer, he saw it was about ten inches wide, made of stone. Trees grew close to the walls, but not here, more to the side where the building wrapped around to another wing. If he could get to the corner he could use the thick limbs to make his way down to firm ground.

Foolish? Maybe. But he had no choice.

So he stuffed the laptop into his pants at his waist where it could remain, hopefully, out of the way. He hopped up and climbed out, flattening his body to the wall, arms extended upward, palms pressed hard to the brick. The sheer drop down to dark shrubs was at least twenty feet, probably more.

Which could break a bone.

He pushed the sash back, nearly closed, so it would not be

readily noticed, then wedged along, one step at a time. Thankfully, the wall was rough, offering plenty of ridges and crevices for his fingertips, and heights were not an issue for him. He passed more windows that opened into other cubicles, all of which were sheathed from the inside by shades. Hopefully, the nuns were focused inside, never thinking about a high-wire escape.

He found the corner.

But the stone ledge did not round it smoothly. Instead it stopped with a gap that stretched around the corner to where the adornment began again.

Just great.

The tree he was seeking was on the other side of the corner. A stout limb within easy reach from there. His balance was being affected by the bulky laptop tucked at his waist. After a quick assessment he leaned out from the wall as far as he dared, swinging his right leg around the corner, searching for the ledge. Once found, he planted his foot and thrust his weight around the corner, reaching with a hand that found more rough brick. His left foot came down perilously close to the end of the ledge, his heel not secure. He strained his weight forward on the ball of one foot, clutching for any handhold as he could feel his body wanting to fall. His fingernails tore against the brick, then caught a small chink, digging in. He kept moving, now on a much darker side of the building, pressing his body flat against the wall.

He was fairly invisible here, as there were no outside floodlights on this side of the building. Anyone below would have to stare directly at him to make anything out in the darkness. He kept edging ever closer to the tree that nestled next to the outer wall. He made it there and grabbed the thick branch with both hands. Then worked his way toward the trunk and climbed down to the ground, the sweet smell of the grass and leaves thick in the air. He was still within the convent grounds, so he stole a few glances around and jogged toward the iron gate. He made it out and was turning to leave when a window on the third floor opened. He quickly sought cover behind a parked car and watched as a woman appeared in the lit rectangle.

He recognized the face.

The same woman from the corridor.

Claire?

She poked her head out and looked down, seeing the barely open sash one floor below. She banged a protesting fist on the sill, lingered for a moment, then withdrew from the window, closing the sash and drawing the sheers together.

He mentally sorted through all of the elements in the situation, searching for options. He'd learned long ago that his job demanded a more moderate personality. No hotheads allowed. Patience over impertinence. Skill over force. Diplomacy instead of confrontation. He was an official United Nations envoy without any law enforcement authority whatsoever. To get the job done he had to inspire trust, not generate controversy. But what he'd just done violated all of those principles. He chalked it up to Kelsey. She had that effect on him.

The excitement began to pass.

And the possibility of failure faded.

He ran quickly down the street, disappearing into the night.

CHAPTER 10

11:05 P.M.

Bernat strolled up the cobbled incline toward the open gate that led back inside Carcassonne. The city's towering ramparts stood defiant, brightly lit in all their awesome glory. Across their summit stretched a widow's walk protected by merlons and battlements, flanked by towers that had acquired a host of fanciful names. The Tréseau with its Gothic windows and vaulted rooms. The circular Tower of Justice. The ever-present Bishop's Tower. The Valde, a cylinder five stories high that had long ago accommodated both a toilet and a well. Each had once served a specific purpose, faithfully protecting the city and its residents, a need that existed no more.

He realized that most of what could be seen was part of a fanciful nineteenth-century makeover that had saved Carcassonne from demolition. So he should be grateful. The whole place could not exist. But the fact remained that little of what had once been had survived. Which had not stopped the city's tourist board from conjuring up fanciful romantic images. Its motto—A *dream you can live with*—was not subtle in any way.

After the massacre at Béziers, the next major target for the Albigensian Crusaders had been Carcassonne. Well fortified at the time, but conveniently vulnerable thanks to an overflow of refugees. The invaders marched the eighty kilometers between Béziers and Carcassonne in six days. The siege lasted a mere week thanks to a cut in the city's water supply. When it surrendered its inhabitants were spared, forced to leave, as one contemporary chronicler described, *in only their shifts and breeches*. Everything else, including all of their personal possessions, remained.

What an insult.

He passed through the arched tunnel that opened into the city. The path was twisty and inclined so that any attacker would have to turn corners and run uphill. Closed souvenir shops lined both sides. He had to admit that the restorers had done a good job preserving the narrow winding paths, half-timbered façades, and cobbled squares. At this late hour few people were around, the tourists all gone for the day. He entered one of the squares that fronted the Castle of the Counts, a twelfth-century edifice reinforced by a moat and barbican that transformed it into a citadel within a citadel. Now it was just one more stop for visitors to make.

Tonight he'd felt like those papal crusaders from long ago here on a mission. Only in reverse. Where they'd killed out of politics and greed, he'd avenged a horrible wrong and sent a message to his enemy. In that last regard he and the crusaders were similar. He could only hope that the Most Reverend Archbishop Gerard Vilamur would understand the gesture.

He turned and walked away from the castle, heading toward his hotel, his footsteps echoing off the uneven cobbles to the arcades of the steeped roofs. Everything around him stood sheathed in shadows. That feeling of anxiety, one he'd grown accustomed to while growing up but had fought to eliminate as an adult, had seeped back into his bloodstream. Any broken thread in the complicated fabric of his plan could ruin everything. Where before the path had seemed clear, and destiny had filled him with confidence, now he wasn't so sure.

Uncertainty.

A state he did not care for.

It could be fatal. No question. But it could also be an asset, forcing him to be ready to deal with what fate might throw his way—adjusting, adapting, or reversing course altogether. The human brain didn't mind risk, so long as the odds were known. But when the outcome became ambiguous? Totally unpredictable? That was another matter. Unfortunately, he now found himself squarely within that state.

The ball had started rolling.

But where would it end up?

He entered the Hôtel de la Cité, obtained his room key from the desk clerk, and climbed the stairs to his suite. Andre was staying with a friend who lived below the mount in the modern section of the city. The new Perfectus had said nothing on the drive back from Béziers, but it was clear that a measure of satisfaction had been drawn from what happened.

His phone purred just as he stepped inside the room and closed the door. The curator in Ghent. He answered the FaceTime call and the screen filled with a chaotic scene of smoke, firefighters, and police.

"That looks bad. What's happening?" he said to the phone's microphone in English.

"The arsonist was a woman, whom the police killed while she was trying to escape."

"Have they learned her identity?"

"Not yet. But they're working on that."

"Could you scan around? I'd like to see more."

The image on the phone moved and he recognized the restorer's workshop, where he'd visited several times, its windows shattered, smoke still seeping out, firefighters surveying the damage. The pan continued until he saw an ambulance parked at the end of a narrow street, Sister Kelsey Deal sitting on the back being treated by paramedics.

"Could you go to her?" he said to the curator.

The image went jittery as his man walked closer to the ambulance and spoke to the paramedic. The nun sat with a blanket draped around her. She spoke a moment with the curator, then faced the camera.

"Monsieur de Foix," she said. "I am so sorry, but the panel is gone."

"It's not your fault," he said.

And he meant that.

"I was the restorer. It was entrusted to me. Whatever happens to it is my responsibility."

"He's right, sister, it is not your fault," he heard the curator say from behind the camera. "Nothing that happened is your fault."

"I tried to stop her," she said. "But was not able."

He could see that she was terribly upset. As was he. They were only a few days away from the world learning the panel's long-held secret.

"I am so sorry this has happened," he said to her again.

"The curator tells me," Sister Deal said, "that the remaining panels of the altarpiece are untouched, safe in the cathedral. Just mine was attacked."

Which made no sense.

Why burn it?

CHAPTER 11

Kelsey stared at the phone screen and the face of Bernat de Foix. Everything seemed unreal, distant, too dreadful even to contemplate.

The *Adoration of the Mystic Lamb* or, as it was more commonly known, the Ghent Altarpiece, was one of the world's great works of art, created in the early part of the fifteenth century, at the threshold of the Renaissance, by two brothers, Hubert and Jan van Eyck. It comprised twelve oak panels measuring, when fully opened, twelve feet high by seventeen feet long.

A triptych, it consisted of a large central panel and two wings, one to each side, which could be folded shut. The upper register of seven panels represented heavenly redemption and included images of God, the Virgin Mary, and John the Baptist. They were flanked by panels of angels playing music and, on the far outermost, the naked figures of Adam and Eve. The central panel of the lower register showed a gathering of saints, clergy, and soldiers attendant at an adoration of the Lamb of God. Four other panels showed groupings of people from across the world, making their way to the celebration, all overseen by the dove of the Holy Spirit.

Closed, the rear images were grisaille, grayscale, the images meant to appear like stone sculptures, with no ornaments or jewelry. Opening the altarpiece revealed the vivid earthly reality in which Christ assumed a human form, giving way to the awe-inspiring beauty of the kingdom of heaven, where the Savior was worshiped for all eternity. Hundreds of figures populated the twelve panels. They ranged from elders to bishops, confessors, martyrs, hermits, saints, knights, and judges. The level of detail was amazing and unprecedented, the liberal use of tint and hue nearly overwhelming. Egg-based tempera had been the paint base of choice for the time, but the van Eycks had been revolutionary. They'd used linseed and nut oil. Which permitted more detail and subtlety, as the oil made the paint translucent, capable of layering, adding depth to what had once been flat. Not the first artists to be so bold, but definitely the first to maximize its potential.

The merchant and mayor of Ghent, Jodocus Vijd, and his wife Lysbette commissioned the altarpiece as part of a larger project for a chapel in Saint Bavo's Cathedral. Most likely Hubert van Eyck conceptualized it, but died in 1426. His brother Jan, the court painter for the Duke of Burgundy, Philip the Good, then finished the commission. Its completion and installation was officially celebrated on May 6, 1432, just in time for the baptism of Philip the Good's son.

Which began an anything-but-peaceful existence.

During religious troubles in 1566 and 1578 the panels had to be hidden away from Protestants attacking Ghent. In 1794, after the French invaded Flanders, the four central panels were plundered and taken to Paris. They were returned in 1816, after Waterloo, but then the panel's two outer wings were pawned by a renegade vicar. When the church failed to redeem them, the wings were sold to an English collector who sold them for an even more outrageous sum to the king of Prussia. Until 1918 they were exhibited in Berlin. A few of the panels remaining in Ghent were damaged by fire in 1822. Others were sent to a museum in Brussels for safe-keeping. In 1894, several were sawed and separated so their fronts and backs could both be displayed facing forward. During World War I, the Germans wanted more of the panels. But the cathedral's canon smuggled them out of the country and hid them away until after the war. The Treaty of Versailles required the return of the panels sold to Prussia and, for the first time in centuries, all twelve were reunited in Belgium.

In 1940, before Germany invaded a second time, a decision was made to send the altarpiece to the Vatican. But it only made it to the French Alps. In 1942 Hitler ordered the panels seized and brought to Germany. They eventually ended up in the Altaussee salt mine where, in 1945, the US unit known as the Monuments Men saved them from being blown up before the Allies arrived, returning them to Saint Bavo's in Ghent, where they had remained ever since.

By any measure it was one of the greatest works of art ever created. But it had been repeatedly stolen, given away, sold, sawed, hidden, falsified, censured, and nearly blown up. All totaled the altarpiece had fallen victim to thirteen separate acts of violence and seven outright thefts, bestowing upon it the distinction of being the most violated art object in the world.

Not surprisingly, considerable damage had accrued from the centuries. Many cleanings and restorations had occurred. The first were in the late sixteenth century to remove a thick layer of candle soot from the forty thousand masses that had been said around it since 1432. More cleanings happened in 1617 and 1731. Each one seemed to do more harm than good.

Unfortunately, nothing that old ever survived intact.

Over time, layers of varnish had engulfed the original paint and excessive overpainting had obliterated much of what the van Eycks had initially created. The whole thing became caked in dust and blistered, raised flakes of paint had broken off, wax had built up, warping had occurred, cracks had lengthened, and even mildew had set in. A minor effort was made in 1950 to repair the effects of war neglect but accomplished little. Finally, eight years ago, over two million euros were raised by the Royal Institute for Cultural Heritage for a major scientific restoration, utilizing all of the latest modern techniques. One at a time the panels were removed from the cathedral, taken to a workshop, and meticulously restored. The rest remained on display. Eleven had completed the process and were back in Saint Bavo's awaiting the last.

The twelfth panel.

Bernat de Foix had provided the hundred thousand euros needed to fund its restoration. The other eleven panels had undergone filming, X-radiographs, sketchings, models, and intricate tests. Their restoration had even been broadcast online through Flemish public television, cameras recording all of the key moments. But none of that fanfare happened with the twelfth panel. No cameras. No press. Nothing. Costs were kept down by employing a Catholic nun, trained as an art restorer, rather than a more expensive professional. Over the past nine years Kelsey had worked on a cadre of important art projects. Plautilla Nelli's *Crucifixion*, restored for the San Salvi Museum. The self-portrait of the Spanish artist Velázquez, damaged from flooding at the Uffizi Gallery in Florence. Violante Siriès' *Madonna*. All of which had led her here, to Ghent, and the twelfth panel. She'd gained a reputation from her perception, bearing, and organizational talents. The local archbishop had specifically requested her services. But she harbored no illusions. She'd been chosen because of the panel's peculiar provenance.

It was a copy.

The original had been stolen on April 10, 1934.

Sometime during that night the twelfth panel was removed from its oak frame. A note was left in its place, written in French.

Taken from Germany by the Treaty of Versailles. A clear reference to its plunder by German forces during World War I. It was only returned to Belgium in accordance with the Treaty of Versailles. The subsequent police investigations were inept, the only serious search for its whereabouts occurring years later. Twenty days after the theft, the bishop of Ghent received a ransom demand for one million Belgian francs, which authorities refused to pay. A second note arrived in May. Negotiations ensued from then until October over the course of eleven more letters. At one point, the twelfth panel's back side, a grisaille painting of St. John the Baptist, was returned in a supposed act of good faith. But the main panel, known as *Justi Ivdices, Just Judges*, was never seen again.

On November 25, 1934, a man named Arsène Goedertier—a discount broker, artist, inventor, and politician—suffered a heart attack. On his deathbed he confessed to knowing where the master-piece had been hidden. He told his lawyer, "I alone know where the *Mystic Lamb* is. The information is in the drawer on the right of my writing table, in an envelope marked 'mutualité.'" The envelope was found, along with carbon copies of the ransom notes and an unsent note that said the panel "rests in a place where neither I, nor anybody else, can take it away without arousing the attention of the public." Goedertier died without revealing anything further.

But had he worked alone?

Speculation ran rampant, many believing that Goedertier had to have had inside help. Eventually, the whole cathedral was searched and even x-rayed to a height of ten feet. The war memorial at Melle, erected in 1934, was broken into on the theory that it might have been the hiding place. But nothing was ever found and the theft remained an unsolved mystery.

The missing twelfth panel was replaced in 1945 by a copy painted by a Belgian named Jef Van der Veken. The copy was based on another copy that had been painted in the mid-sixteenth century for Philip II of Spain, kept at the Royal Museums of Fine Arts of Belgium. To blend his copy, painted on a two-hundred-year-old cupboard shelf, Van der Veken applied a layer of wax that generated a similar aged patina. Kelsey had been working to remove that layer of wax when she made a remarkable discovery. Beneath the reproduction was another painting.

The original *Just Judges*.

All of the panels had been created the same. A hard, ivory-colored layer, an emulsion of chalk powder and glue, had been first applied to the wood. Next came an underdrawing, outlines made of figures. Then thin layers of paint were applied one atop the other. Each layer allowed for different hues of light to pass through, reflecting off one another, creating a luminosity of color. Most experts thought Hubert van Eyck completed the underdrawing, with Jan painting atop what his brother created. Van der Veken had simply painted over the van Eycks' original, and his "copy" had stood inside Saint Bavo's since 1945, taking its place with the original eleven other panels resting, as the thief had proclaimed, "in a place where neither I, nor anybody else, can take it away without arousing the attention of the public."

But how had that happened?

Impossible to say. Especially considering everyone associated with the theft and its aftermath was dead.

And why destroy it now?

An even better question.

She'd first reported the find to the cathedral's curator, then to her prioress, and finally to Monsieur de Foix. All of them had urged that nothing be said until her removal of the overpaint had been completed. Thankfully, the panel was small and she was working alone in a workshop blocks away from the cathedral, an easy measure to ensure total privacy. The fact that the panel was a reproduction, of little to no artistic value, there simply for completeness

74

of the work, made secrecy that much easier. No one cared about the twelfth panel. Except some woman who set it on fire.

Prior to tonight Kelsey had removed nearly all of the wax and overpaint, revealing the original fifteenth-century *Just Judges* in all its glory, her eyes the first to see it in a long time.

"Do not fret over this," de Foix said to her through the phone, bringing her thoughts back to reality. "As I said before, no one holds you responsible. But Sister Deal, I must ask. Your records, were they destroyed in the fire?"

She knew what he meant. She'd carefully recorded high-resolution digital images of the panel from every angle after the overpaint removal. Similar to what had been done with the other eleven in years past. Those images were publicly available on the internet on a site known as Closer to Van Eyck for anyone to study. She'd hoped hers would join that cache. She noticed how Monsieur de Foix had phrased his question cleverly, careful not to reveal anything about the original's resurrection, a fact that only four people in the world should know. So she chose her words carefully too.

"The arsonist stole my laptop with the images," she said.

"They were not backed up?"

"I was told to adhere to strict security, with no copies. But someone is pursuing the laptop, as we speak."

Someone who was once, and still is to some degree, most special.

"Let's hope that effort is successful."

She agreed.

CHAPTER 12

Nick kept moving.

No one had followed him. He was north of central downtown, among dense clusters of residences and commercial establishments. Of course, if the maidens did decide to take to the streets in pursuit he'd be a bit of a standout toting a laptop. So he decided to get as far away as he could.

Fast.

His mind tumbled around a mixture of anger, relief, disbelief, and exhilaration. The young woman who'd confronted him inside the convent had handled herself with skill. Two more members of the same convent had engaged in arson and theft, one probably dying in the process. None of them were anything like the nuns he remembered from childhood. Most of those had been older women who spread terror through classrooms. He hadn't been born Catholic. His parents were a religious mix. One Methodist, the other Presbyterian. Neither was devout. Sundays in their house were off days. Fun times. Church not on the schedule. He'd attended parochial school, as his parents had insisted that the education there was superior to the local public system. Nuns had been scarce, only accounting for a few of the teaching positions.

But they'd been tough. No nonsense. All business. Caring, though. He still recalled Sister Regina. Soft-spoken. Patient. He'd struggled with math in the sixth grade, but she'd helped him through.

Parochial schools in the 1990s were different from a generation before. They'd needed students and revenue, so rules were adjusted and more non-Catholics were granted entry. Being an outsider he hadn't been required to take catechism, attend mass, or be part of the altar boy service. Which was good since, for him, as a Protestant, it was a church service not mass. No one showered him with money after a first Holy Communion. No confession of sins every Saturday afternoon. Then there was the ash on the forehead every spring, near Easter. He and a few others in his class were the only ones not marked. Maybe all that pomp and ceremony had shoved him away from religion. Hard to say. But meeting Kelsey certainly caused a reassessment. Never, though, had she forced him to make choices that he might have found uncomfortable. She had faith. But she always recognized that it was her personal choice and everyone had to decide for themselves what to believe. Religion had never been a divisive element between them.

Until the end.

"I can't ignore what's inside me anymore," she said to him. *"I'm so sorry, Nick. I love you dearly. But I love God more."*

He'd told her he understood. And part of him had. But another part had found it all inexplicable.

He kept moving and entered one of the many cobbled squares, this one surrounded by cafés. Guests huddled around the outside tables, pawing and nibbling, talking in a variety of languages. Twenty euros to a maître d' bought him a call to a taxi service, which arrived a few minutes later and drove him back to where it had all begun.

Emergency vehicles were parked at the end of the street that led to the workshop, the path too narrow for their girth. People were being kept back by the local police. He approached one of the uniforms and flashed his UN credentials, which gained him access beyond the barriers. He walked down the dimly lit route between the olden buildings, the scent of charred wood heavy in the night air. Smoky wisps continued to seep from the workshop's shattered windows. He approached closer and could see that the interior was a black mess. Beyond the building, at the other end of the street an ambulance was parked and he spotted Kelsey, a blanket wrapped around her. He headed that way, relieved she was okay, and she saw him. He held up the laptop, signaling that he'd been successful.

She stood, shed the blanket, and rushed to him. "I can't thank you enough, Nick. I was afraid it had been lost."

He handed over the computer. "Mind if I ask what was so important about this?"

"It has the images I made on it." Her voice was low, in a whisper. "Of what I found."

Now he was curious. "What did you find?"

She shook her head, a piece of her red hair falling across her cheek. "We can't discuss it here."

He got the message and nodded. "I assume the panel was destroyed?"

"It's ash. That's why this"—she motioned with the laptop—"is so important."

But he wondered why images of a 1945 copy of the *Just Judges* carried any value. He started thinking like a CLIO field asset, his inquisitive mind churning away. But he agreed with her that this was not the time or place to have an in-depth discussion. Still, he wanted to know, "Do you know anything about the Maidens of Saint-Michael?"

"That's an odd question."

"And a full explanation also falls into the category of not now, later."

She smiled. "I get it. And, yes, the convent is located on the north part of town. It's a retirement home for the members of that order. They do some volunteer work throughout Ghent. I met one of them."

"Older women?"

She nodded.

"Anyone named Claire?"

He could see her mind was working, assimilating the bits and pieces he was tossing out, trying to make sense of them.

She shook her head. "No one by that name."

He'd probed about as far as he wanted to go for the moment. "I'll be back in half an hour or so."

"What are you going to do?" she asked him.

"Throw what little weight I have around."

CHAPTER 13

Claire realized that the intruder had escaped. She'd found an open sash on the second floor and assumed he'd used the outer ledge to make his way to the trees, then down to the ground. That suggested a level of training and nerve, especially given the fact that the man had brazenly invaded a convent. A professional? The police? Or something else? What had been a partial success had now turned into a total failure with one person missing in action.

This was perhaps the most difficult thing she'd ever faced. But adversity was not something she ever shied away from. Growing up Black in Louisiana had come with a whole host of challenges. She'd never been a political activist, but she had been mindful of her rights, facing down her share of ignorance, hate, and racism. The world was full of good and bad. In the convent race meant little to nothing. The maidens came from all walks of life and every corner of the globe. Each was special. Chosen. Then trained. Sure, there'd been challenges here and there. Nuisances that had required some correction. But nothing on this magnitude. Of course, the altar-piece had always represented the greatest threat. That was why the maidens' retirement community had been based in Ghent for over three hundred years, providing ready eyes and ears nearby.

Just in case.

She'd learned that being a maiden meant making a conscious choice to live outside normality, in a private world that totally influenced your entire life. Some religious orders were cloistered away, apart from the world. Hers cast the appearance of such, but in reality they surreptitiously engaged humanity on a daily basis. Being a Maiden of Saint-Michael came with challenges not faced by any other religious order. There were thousands of abbeys and convents. Some quite famous, like the Carmelites. Others not so much. Each had their own mission and purpose, usually reflected in their creation and history. All of them involved an oath to celibacy, poverty, and a total commitment to God. The maidens swore a fourth pledge. *Veritas Vita*.

The truth, the life.

The cursed Jan van Eyck, who created the Ghent Altarpiece with his skillful brush and cunning mind, even added those words to the lappets on the main altar of the center panel. Thankfully, in nearly six hundred years, only a precious few had ever grasped their significance. And now, with the twelfth panel's destruction, any chance of that ever happening again had been made that much harder. The original was gone. No images of it existed anywhere else in the world except, if their intel was to be believed, on Sister Deal's laptop.

Which was now back in play.

Time had taught her how to live and work among a collective with little privacy, pooled resources, no intimacy, and a total setting aside of all personal needs for the good of others. Most initiates, like herself years ago, had led meaningful but uneventful lives. Suddenly finding yourself confined inside a closed space, with strangers of varying nationalities and ages, could definitely be overwhelming. Most adapted. Some never did and left before taking their final vows. A lack of personal choice was not for everyone. But she'd found a certain degree of freedom in submission. Decisions and concerns that had once been part of her everyday life no longer mattered. You had to give up something to get something. And, for her, what she'd gained was a great inner peace.

Daily life for most of the maidens was a combination of prayer and routine. Everyone had a role. Some cleaned rooms. Others worked the gardens, or cooked meals, or washed clothes. A few rose to administrative duties, keeping the books, paying bills, answering correspondence. All participated in the convent's social calling of working with the poor, the disadvantaged, the sick, and the mentally ill. All also served as guardians. Some in the field, the rest at the motherhouse. Individual desires were cast aside for a singular higher principle.

Veritas Vita.

The truth, the life.

Which, for them, carried a great meaning.

The responsibility for making all of that happen lay squarely within each individual maiden, as Sister Rachel had unselfishly proven. To be sure that no one ever faltered, once a year each maiden drafted a statement, expressing a clear desire to continue with the order. If that wasn't possible, any of the women could freely move to another convent or return to secular life.

Their choice. Always.

Which she liked.

Sister Rachel had only recently composed her statement and elegantly explained an unwavering devotion and a deep desire to continue serving. Rachel was young, not even forty years old, with twenty to twenty-five more years ahead of her before retirement. The Maidens of Saint-Michael had always stamped an end point on service. Sixty was the preferred age, though some had continued to sixty-five. The current abbess was sixty-four and there was already talk of who would succeed her. That person would be chosen by the maidens, in a vote, which had to be unanimous. Many had already approached Claire privately and said she would have their support. But she wondered if that loyalty would survive what had happened here on this horrible night.

She entered the convent's main church, where the fourteen older maidens and the two remaining from her contingent had gathered. Sister Ellen sported a purple bruise to the right side of her face. Claire walked down the center aisle and stood before the main altar. She was not the senior woman present but based on the situation, she was the on-site leader for the designated operation. That gave her command. She explained all of what had happened, leaving nothing out. Everyone assumed the risk, so everyone was entitled to complete information.

"We are surely being tested," she said when finished. "The panel has been destroyed, but those high-definition images are just as threatening. We will have to retrieve that laptop computer." She paused. "I'm not sure how I was tracked here. But I was. So I accept full responsibility for the failures that have occurred."

"We cannot abandon Sister Rachel," one of the older women said. "It is not our way."

"We will deal with that," she said. "But not now. There is something more pressing. We must prepare."

"For what?" one of the women asked.

"More visitors."

CHAPTER 14

Nick retraced his route from the earlier chase, ending back at the quay overlooking the river. The police cars were still there, as was the woman's body, sheathed by a plastic tarp. People had gathered and were kept back by uniformed officers. He approached one, flashed his credentials again, and asked for access.

Which was denied.

Instead, the uniform radioed to someone and a few moments later a man—stockily built, with a heavily jowled face, high brow line, and wide mouth—approached. He introduced himself as Inspector Zeekers of the Federal Police. More specifically from the General Directorate of Judicial Police, the main investigative arm. The fact that it was the Federal Police here, not the locals, spoke volumes.

"I am curious," Zeekers said, "what is the United Nations' involvement?"

"An art treasure was just destroyed. That always interests us."

"It was a copy. Of little value."

"That it was. But the fact that someone went to a lot of trouble to destroy a copy raises questions."

"And you just happened to be nearby?"

"I was here, in town, visiting the restorer who was working on the panel."

"How utterly...fortuitous."

"That's the way I look at it. Can I see the body?"

The man shook his head. "This is a local matter. Not an international incident."

He'd encountered this type of resistance before. Law enforcement all across the globe possessed one thing in common. Like bears and their dens, they guarded their territory. But part of UN membership came with jurisdictional concessions. One of those, laid out with specificity in Section 9, Part C, Paragraph (f), was the unconditional acceptance of UN assistance with the "loss, theft, or destruction of a cultural work risen to the level of world recognition." He'd invoked those words so much that he knew them by heart, along with the correct citation from the member-state agreement.

He repeated them, then produced his cell phone. "We can either get this over with now, or Brussels will be giving you a call." He motioned with the phone. "Your choice, Inspector."

Zeekers thought only a moment, then caved, as most did. Something about their government knowing they existed bothered them. Unlike in America where the locals could give a rat's ass whether you called Washington.

He followed the man across the cobbles to the body, where Zeekers peeled back the yellow plastic. A cocoon of illumination from tripod lights lit the scene. The black hood had been removed to reveal a woman in her mid- to late thirties, blond hair cut short, her face like a waxen mask, pale white with no makeup, bruised badly from the impact to the ground. A dark pool of blood welled across the stones from several bullet wounds, the entries neat, the exits not so much.

"Any idea who she is?" he asked Zeekers.

"No identification was found. We've taken her fingerprints, so that may provide the answer."

"Why was she killed?"

"The officers reported that they thought she was carrying a weapon. When she made a threatening move, they fired."

Not exactly what happened, but he wasn't going to admit he was anywhere near the scene. "I assume your division was called in on the chance the rest of the altarpiece might be in jeopardy?"

"That thought had occurred to us. We've dispatched additional security to Saint Bavo's. All is safe."

"And that's why the police carried loaded weapons tonight?"

Normally, Belgian authorities, like many across Europe, rarely toted live ammunition in their guns.

"We were alerted to a possible terrorist situation," Zeekers said. "We responded accordingly. Which is procedure. I see your point. This woman was clearly unarmed and the police fired too quickly, but bad things happen in situations like this."

Nothing here was certain besides a woman's needless death. Nothing could be proven until more details were unearthed. Names. Dates. Times. The minutiae were what always mattered. Then it would all have to be verified. His mind ran through a familiar debate. The one he had with himself every time when he had to involve local officials. The second rule of working the field was knowing your opponent. The first was to identify your friends. Here? Both calls were easy. That convent had to be searched and he had zero authority to make it happen. But this guy? Inspector Zeekers of the General Directorate of Judicial Police? He could ring that bell.

Nick stood from the body.

Zeekers bent down to replace the tarp.

But something caught his eye in the light. Just beneath the

black outer garment, on the right shoulder, where the thin material had been shredded by an entry wound into the pale skin.

"Wait," he said.

He crouched back down, carefully parted the shards of Lycra and spandex, and revealed a small tattoo.

"A vulture?" Zeekers asked.

"It appears so."

And strange for a nun to be sporting one. Perhaps it had been applied before this woman took her vows. Something meaningful only to her. That was possible. Then he noticed a chain around her neck.

"You see that?" he asked Zeekers.

The inspector crouched down and carefully tugged the links out from the gash in the bodysuit, revealing a silver medallion dangling at its end.

A *fleur-de-lys*.

Personal to her again? Or something more?

"Mind if I take a few pictures?" he asked.

Zeekers nodded.

He found his phone and snapped an image of the tattoo, the medal, and the woman's face.

Then he faced Zeekers.

Time for truth.

"There's somewhere we have to go, and there's someone who has to come with us."

CHAPTER 15

Kelsey stepped from the police car in front of the convent for the Maidens of Saint-Michael. Nick had returned and explained the situation—which, at first, had sounded fantastical. But once she realized he was serious her skepticism had changed to intense curiosity.

Thank goodness he was here.

For so long she'd lived a solitary life, mostly away from her family and friends. Fulfilled? Absolutely. Complete? Working on it. Satisfied? That one was still on the table. She'd definitely made the right choice devoting herself to God. Every day she felt an intense inner satisfaction. But hurting Nick? That she regretted with all her heart.

She'd hoped time had helped him to better understand. That was one reason she'd finally suggested a face-to-face meeting after so many years. She wanted to say again how sorry she was for the pain and judge for herself the degree of his healing. It was important that he was okay. They'd once trusted each other, and, to some degree, she'd violated that trust, however justified her actions might have been. He hadn't been her first love, but he had been the last and most important.

Her person.

She'd specifically chosen the Congregation of Saint-Luke for its dedication to culture, and its desire to draw people toward faith through the beauty of art. The order was started by a Carmelite nun who'd lived in Florence during the 1930s. She'd noticed among the city's many museums and fresco-covered churches that there were few to no works by women, and what did exist lay unseen in storage rooms. So she embarked on a quest to find and restore the lost artworks of Florence's forgotten female artists, digging into museums' archives and dusty deposits. By the 1960s she'd formed a new religious order dedicated to the evangelist Luke, the patron saint of artists. Her recruits shared that passion, many becoming skilled restorers. Hundreds of works, most from female artists, had been brought back to life by the sisters of Saint-Luke. Eventually, the convent targeted its recruitment to women either trained in or passionate about art, and Kelsey's early restoration work had definitely come to their attention.

She'd realized her artistic calling in college and, by age twenty-eight, when she joined the sisterhood, she'd already assisted on several notable American restoration projects. Her superiors spoke highly of her skills, and she hadn't wanted to lose her passion for art. She entered the convent to do more, not be shut away. Many convents kept to themselves, maintaining the old ways. But many more did not. The Vatican II Council in the 1960s changed everything. Latin was abandoned for English. Religious names were dropped in favor of your birth name. Choices were provided for what work you could do and where you would do it. Family connections were encouraged, not prohibited. The Congregation of Saint-Luke had long embraced those reforms, which had allowed her to satisfy both of her inner desires.

Three police cars had accompanied the one she and Nick had ridden inside. No sirens or flashing lights. Just a quick drive north through light traffic. Two cars parked out front while the others turned, rounded the corner, and their uniformed occupants headed for the rear courtyard that Nick had told them about.

Nick led the way through an iron gate to the lit main entrance where he banged on the heavy slab of oak. An Inspector Zeekers directed more uniformed police to stand ready. A few moments later the door opened, revealing an older woman dressed in a plain gray dress and light veil. She had neatly clipped silver-gray hair and a face as smooth and rosy as a child's. She introduced herself as the resident mother superior.

Zeekers stepped forward. "Forgive this intrusion, but we have reason to believe that a criminal has sought refuge here."

The older woman's face tossed a puzzled look. "It is the middle of the night, Inspector, and this is a convent. A house of God. We provide no sanctuary for criminals."

"This man says otherwise."

And Zeekers pointed at Nick.

"Forgive us, sister," Nick said. "But there's a woman dead not far from here who might be part of this convent. And I followed another woman straight here. I entered the building and retrieved a laptop that had been stolen. All that occurred after her accomplice set fire to a part of the Ghent Altarpiece."

"You were here?" she asked, incredulous.

He nodded.

"Those are incredible accusations you made," the mother superior said. "I certainly hope you have proof."

"My own eyes and ears are not enough?"

"Not in this instance."

One of the uniforms approached and whispered into Zeekers' ear. A concerned look spread across the inspector's face. "There is no motorboat or dinghy in the river across the street."

Kelsey watched as Nick considered the information.

91

Nick found his phone and displayed the screen to the mother superior. "This is the dead woman. Do you recognize her?"

The nun gave the image a quick glance, winced at the sight, then shook her head. "She is not of this convent."

"Is Sister Claire?" Nick asked.

"There is no nun here by that name."

Kelsey watched carefully. She had no reason to believe that Nick was lying or exaggerating. Not his style. And he had retrieved the laptop.

"Mother Superior," she said. "I noticed that you answered the inquiries with *not of this convent* and *no nun by that name here*. Have you ever seen the woman pictured on the phone and do you know, or know of, a Sister Claire?"

The older woman stared her down. "And you are?"

"Sister Kelsey Deal of the Congregation of Saint-Luke."

The mother superior's face remained set in stone. If she was cornered, nothing revealed her predicament. "Let me be clear, there are no criminals here, nor any Sister Claire."

Still not an answer, which only raised more questions in Kelsey's inquisitive mind. And she could see that Nick and even Inspector Zeekers were not convinced either.

"Mother Superior," Zeekers said, "we have no choice. I must search the premises."

"Inspector, we are but a group of aged sisters who serve the poor and live out our remaining days in peace. We have nothing to hide. Please, search away. I will wake the sisters who are asleep."

Zeekers gestured toward the officers, but Nick stopped him and said, "We just need to see one room. On the second floor."

The older nun led them upstairs and he walked to where he'd found the laptop. The door was wide open. He stepped inside and saw only the furniture from earlier. Nothing else.

"There's no need to look any further," Nick said to Zeekers. "Whatever was here is gone."

Kelsey studied the mother superior, trying to gauge the situation. Her own prioress was a well-disciplined, bookish woman with a no-nonsense approach too. But there was one thing she could say about her superior. Never had she lied.

Unlike this woman.

They left the room and descended back to the entrance foyer. All of the uniforms waited outside. Zeekers apologized for the intrusion and left out the front door, along with Nick.

Kelsey lingered a moment and faced the older nun. "I hope you go and pray."

"For what?"

"Forgiveness for your deceit."

And she left out the door.

CHAPTER 16

Nick entered the small apartment where Kelsey had been staying for the past few weeks. They'd left Zeekers, who'd agreed with them that the mother superior was lying. But, without more, there was little they could do. The maidens had certainly covered their tracks. But that didn't mean they did not bear a thorough investigation. He'd given Zeekers his recommendations but the inspector had been noncommittal on what would happen next. The arsonist was dead. The laptop retrieved. Only a copy of the *Just Judges* was destroyed. And nothing led from the convent to anywhere else.

"*Seems like finding Sister Claire would be easy,*" he said to Zeekers. "*There has to be a list somewhere of all the women connected with that order.*"

"*I'm sure there is, and that will be the first place we start. But ask yourself, if they were that careful to sweep things clean, don't you think they were equally careful with their membership rosters?*"

Good point.

But it was still worth the effort, along with identifying the dead woman, who almost certainly had been a nun too.

None of that was his problem, though.

His was standing across the room as Kelsey switched on some lamps.

"The diocese supplied this apartment," she said to him. "Part of the compensation for my services."

"They pay you?"

"Not me. But they do pay the convent. It isn't much. But it helps us survive."

Zeekers had told her not to leave Ghent for a few days. Nick didn't like the implications, the suggestion that Kelsey might have somehow been complicit. Time, though, for some answers.

"Tell me why the laptop was so important?"

And he listened as she explained what she'd found beneath the copy of the *Just Judges*, along with the high-resolution images she'd made.

"That's an incredible find," he said to her. "Congratulations, you solved a nearly ninety-year-old cold case."

"It was an amazing feeling, stripping away the overpaint and seeing that masterpiece again."

Interestingly, no one had informed the police about the treasure that had lain beneath the copy. Kelsey had not said a word and the curator of the altarpiece, who'd been waiting for them when they returned from the convent, had not reported that fact either. Zeekers was operating on the assumption that a copy had been destroyed. It now being the original would definitely change everything.

"Why not tell the police the truth?" he asked her.

"That's not a decision for me. I was told to tell no one."

"You were going to tell me."

She sat on the settee. Her red hair hung loose, which made her look much more like the woman he remembered. "You're different, Nick. I didn't see the harm. Besides, you were always good at keeping a secret. And a public announcement was coming shortly anyway. The curator was already making plans for a press conference to announce it to the world."

He liked that he was being placed in a category by himself. "You look tired."

"I am."

The laptop sat on the cushion beside her.

"Thank goodness I recorded those images," she said. "I have the entire panel mapped in high res. Which I only finished two days ago."

"Who knew that?"

"I kept my prioress informed, the curator, and, of course, Monsieur de Foix, who funded the restoration. He was coming to Ghent in a few days. I planned to show him everything."

"Tell me exactly what happened earlier."

"I finished working and closed the workshop around 5:30. I wanted to come back here, rest a little, clean up, and change clothes. I did that and returned a few minutes before you arrived. When I came in through the front door I heard someone in the other room. I entered just as the fire started. I saw the woman in black and tried to stop her. That's when you appeared."

"That was a foolish risk you took."

She rubbed her stomach. "My gut is sore from that kick. But I had to protect the panel and"—she pointed at the laptop lying next to her—"those images."

Something else occurred to him. "Did anyone know you would be returning to meet me?"

She shook her head. "Not a soul. I considered it no one's business."

Interesting. Had the intruders known she was gone, but not known she would be returning? Clearly yes, since the last thing they would have wanted was an interruption.

"Do you usually leave your laptop there?" he asked.

"Always. It's safer than carrying it around. Of course, I didn't realize someone was targeting my work. How would I?"

But the two women who'd orchestrated the burglary clearly knew everything.

"Tell me more about what you found. Secrecy doesn't really matter much anymore."

"No, I guess it doesn't."

He heard the defeat in her voice.

"When it was created in the early 1940s, the copy of the *Just Judges* was intentionally coated in a wax layer to artificially age it, so it would appear like the others. Over time that wax had thickened and darkened. It looked terrible. Part of my restoration involved a complete removal of that layer. During the removal I knew some of the underlying paint would come off. It's unavoidable, and I just repair it as I go. When some did come off, that's when I saw the underpaint. Which in and of itself is not suspicious. Artists paint over things all the time. But when I noticed that the underpaint was exactly like what had been painted over it, that changed things."

"So you started taking more off?"

She nodded. "The copy was worthless and could be replaced. So I removed it and discovered the original *Just Judges* beneath. Right there. Totally intact."

Amazing. He was definitely intrigued. "Who created the copy?"

"A Belgian by the name of Jef Van der Veken. He was a conservator, copyist, and infamous art forger of old masters. Really good at it, too. He was hired in 1939 but did not deliver the panel until 1945. Of course, World War Two came in between so there was nowhere to deliver it to. He was quite talented and did a wonderful job. But now we know he had the original below to help him. His copy was added when the altarpiece was returned to Belgium after the war as a place keeper. Nothing more. But there has always been some controversy associated with it."

He listened as she explained how Van der Veken signed the back of the reproduction, then inscribed it with a poem.

I did it for love.
And for duty.
And to avenge myself.
I borrowed from the dark side.

"His contemporaries, as well as the police at the time, were baffled by the verse. But he refused to explain himself in any way, and took whatever he knew to the grave in 1964."

"Looks like you solved that mystery too."

"It's still odd. I've been thinking about what he might have meant for the past few weeks. He did it *for love* and *for duty*? *To avenge myself*? What did he mean? And borrowing from the dark side? That's a strange choice of words."

He agreed. But those motivations really didn't matter anymore. "Tell me about de Foix."

"I don't know a lot about him. I was told he's the owner of an auction house in Toulouse. A man of means and a known art collector."

"Anything about him ever strike you as suspicious?"

She shook her head. "Not a thing. He was genuinely shocked when I told him what I found."

"And I imagine people weren't lining up to donate money for the restoration of a twentieth-century reproduction."

She grinned. "To say the least."

Which made the man even more suspect. "Have you met de Foix?"

She nodded. "Twice. He came to see my work. Both times he was complimentary and professional. He was supposed to return here in a few days. Why all the questions about him?"

"Because there's a leak. Somebody talked. Those women knew exactly where to go, what to get, and what to do. That means they had good intel."

"But why destroy the panel? That makes no sense. It was priceless."

Good question. But he decided not to press any further. The police and the cathedral authorities would be doing plenty of that over the next few days. And it was their job to investigate, not his.

"We never got to visit," she said to him with a smile. "I was so looking forward to that."

"Me too."

And he meant it. Seeing her, talking to her, it wasn't nearly as painful as he'd envisioned. "Maybe we could have lunch tomorrow, before I head back to Paris."

"So soon?"

He nodded. "I need to head back by tomorrow evening."

"How exciting it must be to work for UNESCO. Do you like it?"

"I think I found my niche. I've enjoyed my time there."

"Then, please, tomorrow, before you leave, let's have lunch and I want you to tell me all about it."

He'd missed talking to her. Though he was sociable and enjoyed people, he wasn't all that forthcoming with others. Kelsey had been the one exception. He'd never been afraid to tell her anything, and that intimacy had eluded him over the past nine years. No other woman had measured up. Maybe one day. He certainly hoped so. But not yet.

He turned for the door, then a thought occurred to him. "How about I hold on to that laptop tonight. No one knows I exist."

"I think that's a good idea. I was told to keep it safe."

"Why didn't the curator take it?"

"I didn't offer it to him. Nor did he ask."

And she handed it over.

He'd wondered what it would be like to be near her again. Long ago his love for her had evolved into something different, something respectful of the path she'd chosen in life. She was a woman he'd *once* loved, someone he still admired and missed. His hope was that this visit would allow them the opportunity to evolve from occasional social media posts to something more personal. What friends would do. And he desperately wanted to be her friend.

Something told him she wanted the same.

"Thank you for doing what you did," she said. "You may have saved things."

He smiled. "Glad it worked out."

"I'll see you tomorrow."

That she would.

CHAPTER 17

Claire settled into the seat of the private plane, rented hastily at the Ghent airport. No time existed for cars or trains and there were no commercial flights available at this late hour.

But she had to leave Belgium.

Now.

The flight south would take a couple of hours. She should be tired but she wasn't. The pilot had brought along some drinks and sandwiches, but her appetite seemed gone too. She was dressed in street clothes, ditching her habit since this journey needed to go unnoticed. But the chain with the pendant remained around her neck. With her thumb she gently felt the outline of the *fleur-de-lys*. Its presence always brought her comfort. However fleeting that might be at the moment.

Thankfully, only a precious few in the world knew the true significance of the *Just Judges* panel. Most of those were members of her order. Others lay within the Vatican. Two diametrically opposed sides. At war with each other for centuries. A conflict that had remained dormant for the better part of the nineteenth and twentieth centuries.

But that had not always been the case.

* * *

The four-month trial had ended.

An inquisitorial court, composed of dozens of judges and a hostile presiding officer, had convicted and sentenced Joan of Arc to death. They decreed that her supposed visions did not exist and her explanations for wearing men's clothing—that heaven had ordained it—were blasphemous. She was found to be bloodthirsty, idolatrous, rebellious, and working at the instigation of the devil. The verdict? Death. But since the church could not lawfully carry out an execution, the nineteen-year-old was handed over to secular authorities for execution.

On the morning of May 30, 1431, two priests appeared in her cell and pronounced that the time for reckoning had come. She was dressed in a rough gray tunic and led through the streets of Rouen to the old market square. A jeering mob lined the way, clamoring for her demise. Not unexpected given that Philip the Good, the Duke of Burgundy, enjoyed widespread local support, and it had been the duke himself who'd turned her over to the English for trial.

Nearly a thousand soldiers accompanied her on the walk from the prison, there to ensure not only that the crowd behaved but that no rescue attempts would be made. Four platforms had been erected. One for the ecclesiastical judges, another for the secular judges, a third from which a sermon would be delivered, then a fourth, the highest, which held the stake. Joan wore a paper miter upon which was written "Heretic, Relapse, Apostate, Idolater." A placard had been erected that proclaimed, "Joan who had herself named Pucelle, liar, pernicious person, abuser of people, soothsayer, superstitious woman, blasphemer of God, presumptuous, unbeliever in the faith of Jesus Christ, boaster, idolater, cruel, dissolute, invoker of devils, apostate, schismatic and heretic."

She was short and stocky, strong and resolute, with the spirit of a tomboy and the energy of a missionary. Her face was ruddy and weather-beaten, like that of a thousand other country girls, with deep watery eyes that seemed to seek out and feel others' pain. Much in the way of legend would later blur reality. But there were some truths. Her Christian name was Jeanne and she passed her childhood and adolescence in Domrémy with the d'Arcs. She claimed to have heard the voices of the Archangel Michael, Saint Margaret, and Saint Catherine, all telling her to support the dauphin Charles as king and free France from English domination. Eventually, she and the dauphin met and he approved of her visions. She was examined by the church, which also approved. Ultimately, she participated in ending the siege of Orléans and was instrumental in the consecration of the dauphin as Charles VII. But she fell captive to the Burgundians, outside Compiègne, who turned her over to the English.

Now she would die.

After all the requisite pomp and ceremony, along with a final sermon delivered to the penitent, Joan was led to the stake and bound to it by chains. The executioner had been instructed to not place her close to the flames so that she would not quickly asphyxiate from the smoke and death would come more slowly.

The kindling was lit and the hem of her robe caught afire.

Within moments she was engulfed.

A priest stood before the pyre, holding a crucifix, and prayed for her soul. She uttered loud groans and asked forgiveness, saying that Charles was not responsible for anything she'd done. Her final word has been clouded by myth, but the most often one repeated was Jesus.

The crowd watched and jeered as she died before their eyes.

Once the fire had subsided, her naked body was exposed for all to see. She was still recognizable, chained to the stake, most of her flesh charred away. This final indignity revealed, as one observer noted, "all that belonged to a woman." Important since many had believed she was a man. When they'd seen enough, the executioner poured oil, charcoal, and sulfur on the carcass and set it afire again. It burned for hours, past nightfall, reducing the flesh and bone to ash.

The executioner had been ordered to toss all of the remains into the river so as to discourage any relic hunters. But the man had been greatly affected by the death, proclaiming that "we have burned a saint." He was not diligent in returning and fulfilling his duties. So under the cover of darkness three women gathered the warm ashes from the pyre and stole them away. What was eventually thrown into the water were the ashes from three sheep that had been butchered and burned by those women a few days earlier.

Those three women had not been ordinary. Like Joan herself, they possessed a deep resolve and an unwavering commitment, each bound by oath. They were maidens. As was Joan. All of them part of a group that carried an ancient name. One bestowed on them out of respect and fear.

Les Vautours.

The Vultures.

Apt because, like their namesake, they never killed.

Joan herself had come to the maidens only a few months before the voices started in her head. She'd left the motherhouse and ventured north, throwing herself into the Hundred Years' War. Her impetuousness and stubbornness had generated success, but eventually they both led to her death.

At a mere nineteen years old.

But other maidens had risked their life to make sure that her remains were brought back to hallowed ground.

Claire had always drawn strength from thinking about those past maidens, especially Joan. Extraordinary women who pledged themselves to an extraordinary mission, one that had never been in favor with the Roman Catholic Church. Quite the contrary, in fact. So much so that, during the Albigensian Crusade, an effort had been made to locate and eradicate *les Vautours* along with the Cathars.

Which failed.

The one saving grace of tonight was that no public announcement had come revealing that the original *Just Judges* had been found. For whatever reason cathedral authorities had not, as yet, released that information. Perhaps they had been waiting to see if the laptop could be retrieved, as it was the only evidence to back up their claims. The idea had been to destroy the panel and retrieve the electronic images before any announcement ever happened. Half that goal had been accomplished. They needed to finish the job. Because once the world was told about what had actually been destroyed, the Vatican would know *les Vautours* had struck.

And it would act.

What a mess. Sister Rachel was exposed. The convent in Ghent had been violated. And far too many directional markers now existed. Which those in the know—

Could easily follow.

Ω

Bernat sat on the terrace and enjoyed the solitude. The time was approaching midnight. Carcassonne had settled down for the night, the lights in the distance fewer and farther between. The day had been both a success and failure. He'd been waiting for this moment his entire adult life, ever since he discovered the truth about himself. He'd long lived by a single mantra. One of long standing in the Languedoc. *Qui court deux lièvres à la fois, n'en prend aucun.* He who runs after two hares at the same time, catches neither.

So true.

Concentrate on one task at a time and devote your full attention to it. Trying to accomplish two things at once usually produced double mediocrity. Something well done was something done with dedication. Phase one was complete with the confession of Father Tallard. Andre had duly recorded everything, the e-file now waiting for him in his inbox, ready for phase two.

Qui n'avance pas, recule.

Another important mantra.

He who does not move forward, recedes.

Life does not stand still. There was only evolution or devolution. *Expect poison from the standing water*, the English poet William Blake once wrote. How true. To be stagnant was the same as to recede. He had to persevere. Move ahead. And he intended to do just that.

A text from the curator in Ghent an hour ago had told him that the electronic images had been recovered. Excellent. Things might be salvageable on that end. Finding the original *Just Judges* had been a sure thing. A way to finally establish himself within the art world and generate some worldwide notoriety. He was grateful for his inside information. True, Cathar beliefs about the evil of the physical world remained, and wealth was definitely part of that, but some modern accommodations had been made to ancient doctrine, all brought about by being nearly wiped out.

Survival.

That took precedence.

He'd invested a hundred thousand euros, which slid his foot in the door. Months back he'd agonized over how he would maneuver any restorer to look beneath the overpaint. But Sister Deal had come through on her own, making the discovery and allowing him to stay back out of the way.

Which had been perfect.

But why would someone destroy the panel? Why steal the electronic images? What was the point? It was all so strange, but he assumed Belgian investigators were working on determining answers.

He'd already answered the curator and asked for a copy of Sister

Deal's images. He'd been assured they would be forwarded along tomorrow. And the press conference they were planning for next week or the week after? That would go ahead too, only sooner, in the next day or so, with the narrative changing to now include the deliberate attack.

He stared out into the night.

A lot lay ahead.

A cruel spring had long wound tight inside him. He was too strong and too mature for a bout of nerves, but he could not deny the sudden fatigue that had overcome him. Like a marathoner who'd mistimed his final surge and burned himself out a hundred meters too soon, he wondered if he possessed the will to keep going and cross the finish line. Life had taught him that satisfaction was bought in fractions, tiny amounts here and there that eventually balanced the whole.

And led to the God of Light.

He reached over to the metal table and retrieved a copy of the day's *La Dépêche*. The regional newspaper was published throughout the Midi-Pyrénées region. A photograph of Archbishop Gerard Vilamur, the titular head of the archdiocese of Toulouse, appeared on the front page, along with a story of his possible elevation to cardinal in the coming months. In the ambient glow from the lights in his room, seeping out through the open terrace doors, he studied the prelate's features. The fleshy lips. Wide nose. An owlish face adorned by thin wire-rimmed glasses. The head topped with a perfectly coifed mop of wavy dark hair. The mouth split into a toothy, annoying smile.

"Time to end you," he whispered.

CHAPTER 18

Archbishop Gerard Vilamur loved everything about his chosen profession. He'd joined the priesthood fifty years ago as a young man of twenty-seven, rising through the ranks to monsignor, then bishop, and finally archbishop. He was presently one of only fifty-six hundred bishops that existed within the Eastern and Latin Catholic churches.

The next logical step upward was the red hat of a cardinal, and the Vatican had assured him that one would soon be coming his way. For several decades he'd faithfully served the archdiocese of Toulouse, a conservative enclave that dated to the fourth century, with competent and steadfast leadership. Which was no small feat. It spanned sixty-four hundred square kilometers. Nearly eight hundred thousand Catholics. Six hundred and two parishes. Two hundred seventeen priests. One of the few metropolitan archdioceses left in the world.

His own personal fiefdom.

As bishop he could perform the sacrament of Holy Orders, ordaining new priests. He was responsible for teaching doctrine and governing the religious lives of all of the Catholics who lived within his borders. He supposedly sanctified the world, representing the church in an official capacity. His office traced back to the apostles, who had been endowed as *special* by the Holy Spirit. Over a billion Catholics believed that such a transmittal of good-ness had continued through an unbroken succession of men from then to now. Bishops were required to be men of good reputation, possessed of outstanding faith, with high morals, piety, a zeal for souls, wisdom, and prudence. Each had to be older than thirty-five, ordained for at least five years, and in possession of a doctorate or at least a licentiate in sacred scripture, theology, or canon law from an institute of higher studies approved by the Apostolic See. Not many ever bothered to obtain such a higher degree, so there was a catchall in canon law that allowed a bishop to simply be a true expert in those same disciplines.

Whatever that meant.

No matter.

He'd earned his doctorate in theology through study and hard work. He carried the additional label of *arch*bishop because his diocese had existed for so long. It traced back to St. Saturnin, sent by Pope Fabian to Christianize Gaul in the third century, who became the first bishop of Toulouse. The current basilica bore both Saturnin's name and his bones. The church stretched over a hundred meters, shaped like a cross and built to last of stone and brick. Its tower was unusual, eight-sided, five-tiered like a cake, and topped with a spire. Its ceilings were vaulted, beneath which were Romanesque sculpture, intricate capitals, and a beau-tiful sequence of relief panels representing Christ, the saints, and angels. A number of radiating chapels displayed important relics. An ambulatory wrapped the nave and side aisles, allowing for an uninterrupted walk while viewing the chapels, even while mass was being said.

Which had been done for a reason.

During the time of Charlemagne the church became an important stop for pilgrims on their way to Spain and the famed Santiago de Compostela. Every accommodation had been made so their visit would be memorable and their donations generous. Today, the basilica was the most complete Romanesque structure in France, the largest in Europe, perched at the northern edge of the city's old quarter. It carried the stamp of a World Heritage Site, protected by myriad international laws and regulations.

He was here, inside the basilica, on this glorious morning to rededicate the tomb of St. Saturnin, which had just undergone an extensive renovation, paid for by visitors and patrons, like in the old days. The ceremony had been planned for some time, the renovations only completed a few days back. Many of the priests from the surrounding parishes had come, along with his six subordinate bishops. He too had once been subordinate to his predecessor, serving for nearly a decade before being elevated to archbishop, with the added designation of *metropolitan* to denote his dominance over the other six.

But he wanted a cardinal's hat.

The article in yesterday's newspaper had been flattering. He'd only cooperated with the reporter since the young lady was known to be generous to the church. The story had dealt with both himself and what was happening here today with the rededication. Hopefully, the clerks in Rome who monitored public relations from around the world had taken notice and passed the article on to their superiors. The pope had assured him privately, on more than one occasion, that he would eventually become a cardinal. His age was a factor, as he was nearing eighty, which would disqualify him from participating in any conclave. But it was not unusual for elders, like himself, to be rewarded late in life for their faithful service. In fact, it happened all the time. All he had to do was be patient and show the requisite humility expected from his position. That meant do nothing that might irritate Rome or the vicar of Christ himself. Word was the pope was considering naming a batch of new cardinals by Christmas. Equally promising was the fact that two of France's six cardinals had reached the age of ninety, both retired, which meant new blood was needed.

He'd worn his formal liturgical vestments. Miter, chasuble, gloves, ring, and white dalmatic, along with his pallium, with two crossbars instead of one, bestowed onto him by the last pope at the time of his elevation to a metropolitan archbishop. This occasion demanded formality. He was due back in his office across town by 11:00 for the start of his daily appointments. The priests who'd arranged for the ceremony were busy herding everyone closer to the tomb. He lingered near one of the side chapels and allowed the patrons to get settled before heading over. The air was warm with that hint of incense and melted wax that seemed to linger inside old churches. This was one of the world's great houses of worship, loaded with history and heritage, and filled with treasures that still drew people. He considered it a great honor to oversee it.

But it was time to move on to bigger things.

His phone vibrated.

He usually did not keep it with him when in church, but since this was merely a dedication ceremony, he'd switched it to vibrate and slipped it inside his pant pocket. Only a precious few possessed the number. Some family members. Half a dozen close friends. His staff. The majority of calls he received on any given day were from his private secretary. So it could be important. He had a moment, so he retreated into one of the side chapels and slipped the phone from his pocket.

A text.

He tapped the screen and read the message.

In all caps.

FOR YOUR EYES ONLY. YOU, OF COURSE, WILL NOT FIND IT ENLIGHTENING. BUT OTHERS WILL.

The text came with an attachment. He debated whether to open it, but his curiosity got the better of him.

He tapped the screen.

Then watched and listened in horror.

CHAPTER 19

Nick had taken a room in one of Ghent's finer hotels. He wasn't on CLIO's expense account, which had a rather meager per diem. Instead, this trip was all personal, the costs totally his. But he was paid a good salary. More than enough for him to comfortably live in Paris. So he could afford a couple of nights in a five-star establishment. He liked quality hotels. Something about the atmosphere, the attention to detail, the focus on service appealed to him. In another life he might have been an excellent general manager.

Instead, he'd pursued law enforcement.

A bit odd considering his roots. His parents were both Olympians, earning a gold medal in pair figure skating at the 1980 Lake Placid games. They'd been quite a team, defeating a heavily favored Soviet pair on American soil. Big news at the time, which had become more a footnote after the underdog Americans earned gold in hockey. They retired after that and married, but both remained active in the sport, still traveling the world as television commentators.

Madeline and Jack Lee.

Parents to five children.

His older brother followed in their footsteps, earning his own Olympic gold in speed skating. Which made him, and rightly so, a bit of the golden child, named for their father, Jack Jr. Now he was married, with two daughters, and owned a real estate firm. Two more brothers also came along before him. Aaron was a doctor who, along with his husband, Michael, worked as a humanitarian with several international outreach organizations. Gabe had the most mysterious of the sibling occupations. He worked with the CIA. But doing what? Nobody knew, and he refused to discuss it. Best guess? He was a senior analyst at Langley, probably high in the ranks, as he'd been with the agency for over a decade. Unmarried, he liked to play the field and had broken more than a few hearts. But, as he liked to say, he just wasn't the marrying type.

Nick and his twin sister, Natalie, rounded out the five. She'd been born first by a mere thirty seconds, which made him the runt of the litter, something none of the other four ever let him forget. Figure skating had been in her blood from an early age. She'd competed in the Olympics but fell short of a medal. No matter, she'd given it everything she had and that's all that mattered.

Nick and Nat. That's what the others called them.

Not surprising that he was closest with her. They even had the same middle name. Parker. In honor of their maternal grandmother, who'd also been a world-class athlete. Natalie remained single, working as a much-sought-after figure skating coach for future hopefuls. A true workaholic. She and Kelsey had once been close, but the breakup left some bitter feelings that Nat had yet to expunge. True, she understood Kelsey's calling, but breaking her brother's heart came with repercussions, whether God was involved or not.

Quite a group.

114

All ambitious.

Raised in an atmosphere saturated with education and challenge, all of it bred into them by genetics and a solid upbringing.

Sport had never been a passion for him, though he'd showed promise as a hockey player in college. There was talk of him playing professionally, but he nixed the idea, preferring instead to join the army. His parents had understood. It was his life and he had to lead it the way he wanted. Having a wife? Children? A family? Sure, he'd love that. But when Kelsey left those dreams went with her. Forever? Not likely. And surely one day someone would come along and rekindle that dream.

Thankfully he had his family.

At least once a quarter most, if not all of them, gathered somewhere for dinner. Of late, Paris had been the best locale to accommodate their various traveling schedules. They were due for another meal next month.

He needed to head back to Kelsey's apartment, but first he placed a call to his boss at CLIO. That position was something of a revolving door. He'd had three other supervisors over the past five years. Two good. One not so much. The current holder of the appointed position seemed intent on making a mark.

Reynaldo Pena.

A Spaniard with a degree in European art history from the University of Córdoba in Andalusia. He'd worked as a conservator at several mainstay museums, most notably the Belvedere in Vienna. He'd actively sought the CLIO position, which was an improvement from his last boss who'd seemed to hate every minute of her time there. Pena was also proactive and had not hesitated to involve the agency where needed.

Which he liked.

Nine a.m. in Ghent meant 3:00 a.m. in New York. But CLIO ran around the clock and Pena had made it clear that he was always available, night or day. So Nick placed the call, which was answered promptly.

"You don't sound like you were asleep," he said to Reynaldo.

"I was doing some reading."

He explained all that had happened, leaving no detail out and finishing with, "The bottom line is that part of one of the world's greatest works of art was intentionally destroyed. And the vandals knew what they were burning."

"I remember what one commentator said. *Napoleon robbed it, Calvinists nearly burned it, the Nazis were desperate to own it, and part of it has been missing for eighty years*. The Ghent Altarpiece has quite a history."

"This was planned out," he said. "They burned the panel and took the laptop, which means there's something on the images those nuns are prepared to die for. Did that woman last night realize the police would kill her? That's hard to say. But she willingly tossed the laptop over the wall and faced them down."

"You're curious?" Reynaldo asked him.

"Who wouldn't be?"

He hadn't explained to Pena about Kelsey, only saying that he'd come to town to visit an old friend. Anything more seemed a bit too personal for their all-business relationship.

"I need you back in Paris," Reynaldo said. "A couple of new scenarios are developing."

He didn't want to leave.

Not yet.

"Could I have a couple of days? Something's happening here that I think requires a look."

"My gut tells me no but, I have to say, you've piqued my curiosity. Okay. Take a look. If nothing materializes by Friday morning, let the locals handle it and head back to Paris. Understood?"

"I got it."

"Keep me posted."

"Like always."

He ended the call, delighted that he now could spend more time with Kelsey. And all under the guise of "work-related." Her laptop rested on the hotel room's work desk. His own sat beside it.

Time for a little research.

He grabbed his computer and opened the search engine, typing in *Maidens of Saint-Michael*. Which had a website. He chuckled. Didn't everybody? He found the site, then clicked the History tab and read.

The order went way back. A charter dated July 14, 1007, executed by Count Wilfred and his wife, Guisla, donated land to the church, located on the north side of the Canigou, a mountain in extreme southeastern France, right along the Spanish border. They also provided wheat, sheep, a mule, a silver chalice, fine linens, forty books, and the funds to erect an abbey in honor of Our Lord Jesus Christ, that it will have sisters under the Rule of Blessed Father Benedict and, in accordance with his will, that they serve the Almighty God in perpetuity. The abbey was eventually built and survived countless wars and the French Revolution, which had not been the fate of most in the region. According to the site, the maidens followed Christ according to the Gospel, seeking God in community through a life of prayer and service of others. They sought God together, having all things in common, living in simplicity, in relative silence and solitude. Hospitality was a key to their values. Those who arrived at the abbey to share in the prayer and peace were never turned away.

They made three traditional vows.

One of stability with a commitment to live where God called. A second to obedience, agreeing to listen to God and to live under the authority of an abbess, with mutual obedience to others in the community. Then a final one for a conversion, turning one's whole life to God, striving to become more Christ-like. As expected, included within all of that were pledges to chastity and poverty.

He scrolled down further and read how the Blessed Virgin Mary played an important role in the spirituality of the order. Then something caught his attention. The fleur-de-lys is special to the maidens as a symbol of their devotion to the Virgin Mary and all that she held dear. It resembles both the iris and the lily, two flowers long associated with the Mother of God. The lily is a symbol of virginity and purity. A species of white daylily only blooms during the time of the Assumption, in mid-August. The iris, or Sword Lily, is an emblem of Our Lady's Seven Sorrows.

Which explained why the dead woman was wearing one around her neck.

He read on and learned that the search for God through a life of prayer was the maidens' primary activity, but principles of education and gentility remained at the heart of the order. They operated a school in a nearby town, along with hosting retreats and catechesis. Other activities, according to the website, included raising animals, gardening, and making altar breads for sale to churches. He wondered where martial arts training and paramilitary operations figured into their overall mission.

Especially the willful destruction of cultural icons.

He had a ton of questions.

With no answers.

He kept scrolling around the site and learned that the Abbaye de Saint-Michael, the maidens' motherhouse, located in the high Pyrénées, was open to visitors and thousands came yearly for a guided tour. There were even guesthouses where people could stay, sharing in the peace and prayer, enjoying a break from the business of everyday life.

Really now?

Only the one sister he'd taken down, and the mother superior, had seen his face.

Should he test the odds with a visit?

Why not.

Seemed like the right play.

CHAPTER 20

Claire faced the abbess and explained everything that happened in Ghent. The older woman stood still, a slight crease in her spine, both hands behind her back, the dark eyes focused like lasers.

"The information we had," she said, "indicated that the workshop closed around 5:30. Which is what happened. We waited three hours before proceeding. Nothing indicated that Sister Deal would return. She had not the previous two nights. Somehow attention was drawn to Rachel and she was pursued. She threw the laptop down to me and stayed to face her pursuers. We have to return and help her."

"Rachel is dead," the abbess said.

Claire closed her eyes just as they began to tear. *No. This can't be.*

"The police shot her."

Anger grabbed her. "You were warned."

"That I was. By you. Of which I do not require a reminder."

She bit her tongue and stayed quiet.

"We have to look at the larger picture," the abbess said. "Determining Rachel's identity will be difficult, but not impossible for the police. Of course, their searching our convent in Ghent provides quite the arrow pointed straight to here. Do you have any idea how that man located you?"

She shook her head. "I slipped away in the boat and quietly made it back to the convent. I was unaware of being followed."

"But followed you were."

The words bit into her. On purpose.

"You blame me for Rachel's death," the older woman said. "But you have exposed us all. The man who followed you is an investigator from the United Nations named Nicholas Lee. Thankfully, your prompt action in sanitizing the convent and leaving helped when the police returned to search the premises. There was nothing to find. It was Lee's word against ours."

But she still felt the barb. Sharp. Deep.

The abbess was not noted for niceties. She was a small, sparrow-sized woman, brutally honest, a no-nonsense Italian who'd led the order for the past fifteen years. Practical and pragmatic, attuned to the slightest change in moods. Up until a few weeks ago they'd never had a cross word, which explained Claire's rise to Vestal, only one step removed from the abbess herself, essentially the second in overall command. But all that changed when the *Just Judges* reappeared. The abbess had one course. Claire another. But she'd pushed her objections aside and done her duty.

With unthinkable results.

"Your failures could be devastating," the older woman said. "For us all."

"There would have been no failures if we had simply left things alone." And she meant it. Then, she wanted to know, "Is there confirmation that the panel was destroyed?"

"The press reported that it was a total loss. But curiously they continue to speak only of it being a copy. Not a mention of the original that lay beneath. But that could change at any moment. I am told that the press conference that was coming in a week or so will most likely be moved up. Sister Deal's electronic images still exist for the world to see. Which could be worse than the original, in their detail. So the problem has not changed. Only now there is a spotlight shining right on us."

They stood in the abbess' office, located in the abbey's extreme northern wing, which afforded them privacy. A magnificent view of the adjoining peaks was provided through the open windows, a straight drop down outside about a hundred yards to a river gorge below.

She'd fled Ghent, correctly surmising that the police would come to the convent. If not during the night, surely by morning. Prior to leaving, all vestiges of their presence had been removed, including the boat she'd used and a dinghy that had been found tied to the dock. The two remaining sisters, Isabel and Ellen, had stayed on, finding rooms in a downtown hotel, ready to act once their course was set.

"The convent was searched?" Claire asked.

"Just the room you occupied. Signore Lee led them straight there. Sister Deal was also present and accused the mother superior of being a liar. Which, of course, she was."

The abbess was right. Her failures had placed everyone in a tough situation.

"All of this must be addressed with the collective," the abbess said.

Claire agreed.

She trusted the maidens as they trusted her. Each leaned on the other in good times and bad. Her own personal journey to here had started out of a sense of loss. Her mother and father had both died within an hour of each other, after fifty-four years of marriage. They'd been inseparable in life and so it would be in death. As their only child she'd buried them near the bayou and tried to understand why they'd been taken. By then she'd been a teacher for several years, and it wasn't six months later that Sister Anne appeared at Christ the King Catholic Church. She'd never really considered joining a convent. But the more she thought about the idea, the more a religious life had appealed to her. Of course, at that time she had no thoughts of what was to come.

She was not just a nun.

She was *les Vautours*.

The abbess' eyes began to soften. The scolding might be over. For all her rigidity this woman, flush with life, was also known for compassion. She presided over the maidens like a queen bee, but always with politeness and etiquette. Today's anger was unusual. The maidens had unanimously chosen her as their leader in one vote after another. All abbesses had to stand for selection every two years, and could be removed anytime from the position by a unanimous vote. Who led the order was just as important as the maidens themselves. That person made all tactical decisions, judging any threatening situation, assessing the risks, and dispatching eyes and ears to deal with problems. Good judgment was essential. Recklessness could be fatal. The collective depended on a responsible, mature, competent woman to lead them. There'd been bad choices in the past, but those were rectified by a swift removal. The current abbess was known for her competence. But her time was coming to an end.

She knew it. And the sisters did too.

"I am sorry," she said to her superior. "For my mistakes."

"As am I, in not listening more closely to you and the others."

She heard the pain in the voice.

The older woman pointed a finger. "But contrary to what you may think, the Vatican is attentive. They are out there. Watching. Waiting for us to make a mistake. And we just accommodated them."

She had to say again, as she had weeks ago, "We don't know they are watching."

"Don't be a fool, Claire. They are most definitely watching. Our only salvation has been they did not know where to look. We have remained hidden in plain sight for a long, long time. But you may have just solved that problem for them."

"May I have the opportunity to fix things?"

"How would you do that?"

"I would first retrieve Sister Rachel's body. She is entitled to a proper burial, here, among us. It could also help chill the trail."

"And that laptop?"

"I would also obtain it. Or, at a minimum, destroy its memory."

"Both would now be difficult feats, considering the situation."

The abbess' eyes maintained a steady, noncommittal gaze. Claire fought for control over her voice as she said, "But not impossible."

The older woman appraised her with a stern gaze. "I will address Sister Deal and the laptop through other, more manageable, means. Ones I was hesitant to use at first, but which now are imperative. As to Rachel, I will not make that decision. We will place it before the collective."

She bowed her head. "Yes, abbess."

"If the maidens so desire, your next efforts must be totally successful, without any error."

"I understand."

"For your sake, and ours, Claire, I hope you do."

CHAPTER 21

Nick sat in Kelsey's apartment as her fingers skipped across the keyboard and she called up the images she'd methodically scanned onto its hard drive. He'd walked over, with her computer, from his hotel immediately after talking with his boss.

The *Just Judges* appeared on the screen.

The oak panel was about sixty inches tall by twenty inches wide. A gradually withdrawing landscape showed a group of people on horseback making their way toward the New Jerusalem, depicted in all its glory on the main center panel, where they all would worship the Lamb of God. Expert consensus was that the ten people depicted in the *Just Judges* were administrators and politicians from Jan van Eyck's time. But with the original gone there'd been no way of confirming that until now.

"The Ghent Altarpiece is twenty-four pieces that fit together front and back, akin to a double-sided jigsaw puzzle," Kelsey said. "It's a fairly simple construction. What's difficult is piecing together the iconography in each panel. How they go together. What they mean in relation to the others. Nothing here was painted haphazardly. There's a purpose to every single thing depicted. Experts have wrestled with what those purposes and meanings are for six centuries."

125

"I've read a few articles," he noted. "There's a lot of speculation and debate about the whole thing."

"To say the least. The *Just Judges* is probably the most complex, message-wise, of the twelve. Each of the ten riders most likely expressed a particular story. We know van Eyck worked from a plan. What that was, though, has been impossible to determine. It's truly in-the-eye-of-the-beholder. What we do know is that the altarpiece is loaded with hidden detail and symbolism. In its entirety, when opened, it's a mystical poem of the Eucharist and the sacrifices of the Lamb, all occurring with Christians, the church, and the world adoring. Eleven of the panels have been totally mapped and minutely studied. Let me show you an example."

She tapped the screen and called up the image of a seated bearded man holding a scepter in one hand, his right fingers outstretched and pointed skyward. He occupied the top spot above the center panel in a clear place of prominence.

"Many think this is God the Father, overseeing the story of salvation," she said. "But he wears a papal tiara, there are no wounds in his hands, and he's wearing shoes, which usually doesn't connote Christ."

He saw the contradictions. "More of that mysticism?"

"Probably. It's a magnificent image. But let me show you the genius of van Eyck."

She tapped the keyboard and zeroed in on the cylindrical glass scepter that the figure held in his left hand. The detail on the enlarged image was amazing. Nick could see creases in the skin, cracks in the fingernails, the crisp folds in the cloth. Like a magnified photograph instead of paint with brushes.

"If all that is only revealed at high resolution," he said, "how did van Eyck paint it in the fifteenth century?"

"He was a trained miniaturist, skilled in the technique. Look at the scepter."

He focused on the translucent image.

With paint, van Eyck had created a reflective surface where light entered the transparent medium, then a portion bounced back through a long white line on the right side of the staff, creating a reflection in the pigment. Even the skin from the fingers was visible on its back side, looking through the staff. Incredible. He had to keep telling himself that this was not a photo.

"Jan van Eyck elevated the use of oil paint to a whole new level," she said. "The entire altarpiece is filled with this type of minute detail. Only now, after a thorough cleaning, and with the use of digital technology have we been able to reveal it all."

"And you're sure what you found was the original *Just Judges?*"

"There's no question. I had the original."

"So why would someone burn it?"

"I've been thinking about that all night. There's no definitive answer. But there are legends."

Now he was intrigued.

"The Ghent Altarpiece, like the *Mona Lisa* and some of the other great works of art, has always been surrounded by riddles. Outwardly, and in its simplest form, it's an ecclesiastical polyptych, a retable, an architectural feature set up at the back of an altar. Religious art. But, like I said, the notion of an abstract or a timeless painting was regarded as absurd in the fifteenth century. Art in that time period included messages, however subtle they might be. And many people have read a lot into this particular polyptych."

He listened as she explained how some found *unmistakable* references to the crusades, the Knights Templar, Teutonic Knights, even supposed incantations attributed to a variety of pagan origins.

"But it's all nonsense," she said. "Look at this."

And she clicked on the *Knights* panel depicted on the website, the one directly adjacent to the *Just Judges*. Nine horsemen in battle gear, three wearing crowns, were riding toward the center panel and the adoration. She zeroed in on the lead horseman, wearing silver armor and sporting a shield with a cross of blood. At the current resolution the cross on the shield appeared solid red. But as she magnified the image, letters began to form in the red paint.

ds fortis adonay sabaot v. emel el i.h.s. xr. agla.

"Some observers add *ominu* to the *ds* to form *dominus*, and *manu* to the *emel* to make *emmanuel*. But that's taking liberties with the inscription."

"What does it mean?"

She shrugged. "It's an odd mixture of Latin, Hebrew, Greek, and Coptic and is barely understandable. I read somewhere that it could be some sort of Middle Ages magical formula that was inscribed on weapons to make them stronger. Supposedly, it was written by the hand of God on a parchment found when Jesus was taken down from the cross." She smiled. "See what I mean? People have read many things into van Eyck's work."

She told him about more wild theories. References to the Holy Grail. The Golden Fleece. Alchemy. And the philosopher's stone.

"Supposedly, van Eyck was passing on these secrets to later aspirants through hidden messages in the work."

She looked lovely sitting at the kitchen table. Electric, alive, and beautiful, her voice soft but strong. She wore her order's dark-green smock with white trim and a high collar. No coif or veil shielded her red hair. She'd offered him coffee, but he'd eaten breakfast at his hotel. He was more interested in sizing up the playing field. He only had two days to work this and was determined to help in any way he could.

"There's something in the images you made that other people either want, or want kept secret," he said to her. "Something that woman died for."

"Were you there?"

He nodded. "I saw it all."

Her eyes warmed. "I know how bad that must have been."

"I would have preferred not to have seen that. But I did."

She gripped his wrist. He smiled and let her know that he appreciated the gesture.

She withdrew her hand. "All those other crazy theories aside, let me say that it would not be shocking if we discovered that a true secret did lurk somewhere in the altarpiece. A learned theologian advised Jan van Eyck. Most likely, Olivier de Langhe, the prior of the Ghent church at the time. Even more important, this was the only work of Jan van Eyck's intended for public display. All of his other paintings were private commissions. So van Eyck knew a lot of people would see the altarpiece. The only question seems to be, what's there that required the *Just Judges* to be destroyed?"

A phone chimed.

Not his. Kelsey's.

She reached for the unit and answered, listening for a few moments, then saying, "Yes, ma'am. I'll be there." She ended the call. "That was my prioress. She's here, in Ghent, and wants to see me."

He was intrigued. "When and where?"

"One p.m., at Saint Bavo's. She wants me to bring my laptop."

That pricked his interest. "Did she say why?"

Kelsey shook her head.

"Your convent is how far away?"

"Three hours by train."

"And your prioress came all that way?" His statement was rhetorical, but the answer was easy. "You said only three people knew what you found and that you'd recorded those images."

She nodded.

He'd originally thought his next move was to head to southern France. Not anymore. The next move might have just come to him.

"The curator wants me to email the images file to him," she said.

"I assume Monsieur de Foix will be privy to those images too?"

She nodded. "Of course."

That eliminated two of the three suspects.

"Any idea why your prioress is so interested in those images?"

She said nothing.

But he could see the questions forming in her mind.

"Don't email the images," he said. "Not yet. First, if you'll allow me, I have an idea that may give us the answer about your prioress."

CHAPTER 22

Archbishop Vilamur had to force himself through the rededication ceremony, saying the right words, smiling at the right time, careful with the cameras, which had been numerous.

But the video he'd been sent kept replaying through his mind.

Father Tallard was a problem, one that he'd tried several times to either ignore or suppress. He'd only been a monsignor when Tallard committed his crimes, another man then in charge. But that archbishop was dead and the problem of Father Tallard remained alive. Nobody would care that he'd inherited the issue. He was the current archbishop. His job was to safeguard the church and its members. He'd removed Tallard from any and all parishioner duties and ordered that he stay out of sight. But he'd not taken the man's collar. Even after formal charges had been brought, he'd opted instead to allow the criminal process to play out. That course, along with every other decision he'd made relative to Tallard, had been approved by the Vatican and all had remained relatively quiet the past three years. Sure, there'd been news accounts here and there. Victims raging about the lack of justice. But none of that lasted long. Thankfully, the public had become somewhat anesthetized to clerical sexual abuse claims.

One more seemed not to matter much. But now this. A recorded confession? While tied to a table?

That was an entirely different matter.

Sensationalism?

Sure. But that's what people loved.

Other than Tallard, his diocese had been relatively free of abuse allegations. Not a single substantiated case had arisen during his tenure, which he liked to remind Rome about. His public comments had always been focused on zero tolerance, along with a respect for secular authority to charge, try, and sentence abusers. So far, Tallard had vehemently denied all of the allegations. The church had quietly arranged for him to have competent counsel, but everything was now in doubt. To this point Tallard had smartly remained silent. Clearly, the video had been obtained by coercion. But by who? Victims? Zealots? And why send it to him with the rather cryptic *For your excellency's eyes only. You, of course, will not find it enlightening. But others will.*

Really?

Was the statement about enlightenment meant to convey that Tallard had already privately confessed his sins? Vilamur had heard Tallard's confession himself, every word protected under French law as confidential. Only two people knew that had happened. Had Tallard confessed that too? An admission not recorded? One that *others* would learn?

He had to know.

So he'd changed back into his black suit and collar and left the church right after the ceremony ended, driving away from Toulouse. He'd called his office and instructed that his appointments into midafternoon be canceled, manufacturing a story that one of the bishops needed to speak with him. The drive from Toulouse to Béziers was about two hundred kilometers, four-laned highway most of the way.

It took him only two hours to make the journey.

The house north of town had been obtained by Tallard's lawyer as the perfect out-of-the-way locale where nobody would pay the disgraced priest any attention. The farmhouse sat amid the dense local forest, with few neighbors. Tallard had been told to not venture out except to buy food, which should be done from different stores each time. No patterns. No routine. No consistency where the press or a victim might recognize him. He'd also been told to grow a beard and mustache to further complicate things. So far all of the deceptions had worked. Not a word had appeared about Tallard in the media or on the internet. Everything possible had been done behind the scenes with the authorities to delay the trial for as long as possible. It had not helped that the French government recently pledged to toughen laws on child rape. That move came after a massive online movement saw hundreds of victims share accounts about sexual abuse within their families. A draft bill had already started being debated in Parliament. Thankfully, that was months or years away from becoming law, if ever, and the local prosecutor was a friend, with a cooperative personality.

He found the farmhouse and parked out front.

He'd never thought a trip here necessary. He'd been kept informed of Tallard's case covertly, along with a report on all activities—which, to this day, had been minimal.

The day was warm and sunny. Before leaving the car he removed his white collar. Better not to announce his profession so openly. He stepped out and approached the front door and noticed it ajar.

He stopped.

This was foolish. He should not be here. But it had to be done. He was the only one who could make this inquiry. Especially considering that someone else apparently knew all about this problem.

He stepped to the door and knocked.

No reply.

"Louis," he called out. "Louis."

He pushed the door inward, which squeaked on its hinges. He stared into the small unlit den, everything all awry, as if from a struggle.

Then he saw Tallard.

Bound to the kitchen table, the body limp, head dangling down from one edge, the mouth and eyes wide open, the tongue protruding.

He stepped inside and approached the table.

Tallard was dead.

Which solved a whole host of problems.

And he would be thrilled by the fact except for what lay atop the body.

Two crosses. Made of wood. Both painted yellow.

The color brought context to the message.

When the Inquisition came to southern France to eradicate Catharism, repentant first offenders were ordered to forever wear a yellow cross on their clothes, called *las debanadora*, which meant in Occitan "reels" or "winding machines." The term came from the

Cathars comparing the cross to a reel and line, by which the wearer could be hauled in at any time for a second offense.

And that meant the death penalty.

Its presence here, eight hundred years after the fact, lying atop a Catholic corpse, was meant as a signal.

The other yellow cross, lying beside it, completed the message.

Many mistakenly called it the Cathar cross. The image was for sale in every tourist shop across the Languedoc as a supposed Cathar souvenir. But it had nothing to do with the Cathars. It was the Cross of Occitan. The heraldic design was first used in the coat of arms of the counts of Forcalquier, in the twelfth century, and by the counts of Toulouse on thirteenth-century coins and seals. It later spread to other provinces. Such a cross, upon a blood-red background, still made up the flag of modern-day Occitania. It was also found in the emblems of Midi-Pyrénées, Languedoc-Roussillon, and Hautes-Alpes, as well as in countless cemeteries and at country crossroads.

Old and new.

Atop the body of a sexual deviant. A priest of the Roman Catholic Church. He closed his eyes.

Dear God.

What was happening?

CHAPTER 23

Bernat's phone signaled an incoming call from Andre. He'd stationed the young man outside Father Tallard's farmhouse, among the trees, to wait and watch.

"He came," Andre told him when he answered. "Then left in a hurry, with the two crosses."

Perfect. Exactly what he wanted to happen.

"Were you able to record him?"

"I have a full video and pictures. His presence is well documented. He removed his collar before entering."

"Little good that will do him."

He prided himself on being quite knowledgeable about Cathar history and philosophy. But there was one other subject he'd become an expert on too. Gerard Vilamur. He'd studied that prelate for a long time and knew, without question, that once the archbishop saw that video he'd go straight to Tallard. He'd have no choice. That was why he'd so carefully phrased the text that accompanied it, and edited out the last part where Tallard admitted that Vilamur knew it all.

That, he would save for the next message.

The idea right now had been to draw the archbishop to the scene and create more incriminating evidence.

136

"Send me the video," he told Andre. "Then head back here."

He ended the call.

Things were on track with Vilamur.

And also in Ghent.

No one, other than Sister Deal, himself, and the curator, had laid eyes on the original *Just Judges* since 1934. Of the twelve panels for the Ghent Altarpiece only one had been stolen, then its back side returned, so only the *Just Judges* itself would be gone.

Why?

Investigators had pondered that mystery for a long time.

As had he.

What later generations would call the Hundred Years' War raged from 1337 to 1453. It pitted the English, along with some rebellious French allies, against the remaining French nobles in a struggle not only for territory but over who should be the rightful king of France. Over the course of 116 years, five generations of kings from two rival dynasties fought incessantly for the throne of the largest kingdom in western Europe. By 1429 it had devolved into a battle over whether Henry VI of England or the French dauphin, Charles, would assume that throne.

And the English were winning.

Then something wholly unexpected happened.

The appearance of seventeen-year-old Joan of Arc at the siege of Orléans sparked a revival of French spirit, and the tide began to turn against the English. They had laid siege to Orléans in 1428 but had been unable to take the city. In 1429 Joan persuaded Charles to send her to Orléans, saying she had received visions from God telling her to drive out the English. Her religious fervor raised the morale of the troops, and they attacked, lifting the siege. Inspired by Joan, the French claimed several more English strongholds along the river Loire. Those victories opened the way for the dauphin to march to Reims for his coronation as Charles VII, which happened on July 16, 1429.

Ultimately, the war affected alliances throughout France. Some nobles remained loyal to Charles, while others aligned with the English. The most powerful to take the English side was Philip, Duke of Burgundy and Count of Flanders, Artois, and Franche-Comté. Philip fervently believed that Charles had been involved with the murder of his father, John the Fearless. So he waged a civil war on Charles, which eventually entangled itself in the larger Hundred Years' conflict. In 1420 Philip formally allied himself with Henry V of England against Charles.

On May 23, 1430, Philip's Burgundian troops captured Joan of Arc and sold her to the English, who orchestrated a heresy trial against her conducted by pro-Burgundian clerics that ended in her execution. The Hundred Years' War continued for twenty-two years after her death. Eventually, Philip switched sides and joined with Charles VII, helping the French to finally banish the English from the continent. That move cemented his control over Burgundy and elevated him to the status of kingmaker.

Philip's reign as duke was a long and enlightened one. So much so that he acquired the label of the Good. He eventually presided over an extended period of peace, which encouraged a flourishing of thought dominated by knightly chivalry. Though poverty remained rife, burghers grew wealthy from increased commerce and developed a highly genteel lifestyle. Philip himself maintained no fixed capital and moved between his two richest territories, Burgundy and Flanders, and his various palaces, the main ones being in Brussels, Bruges, and Lille. His court was regarded as the most splendid in Europe, a leader in taste and fashion, which catapulted Flemish goods into the most sought-after commodities in Europe.

During his forty-eight-year reign Philip added six hundred illuminated manuscripts to the ducal collection. He commissioned tapestries, jewelry, paintings, and other works of art. The Burgundian school of composers and singers rose to prominence. He was a serious patron of artists and only the best of the best worked for him.

One artist in particular always had his favor.
Jan van Eyck.

Bernat had studied van Eyck.

Born in Belgium sometime between 1380 and 1390. No one knew which year for sure. By 1422 he worked at The Hague as a master painter, then in 1425 he became Philip the Good's court painter and confidant. So close were they that Philip became god-father to one of van Eyck's sons. He also undertook a number of confidential spy missions abroad on Philip's behalf for both diplomatic and intelligence purposes, and the Duke of Burgundy came to rely upon him.

Only about twenty works have ever been definitively attributed to van Eyck, all signed with his *Als ich kan*, As I can, which he added in Greek characters. He painted both secular and religious subjects as well as commissioned portraits. Philip paid him well and allowed him the artistic freedom to create whatever and whenever he pleased. All of his works emphasized naturalism and realism, creating a new level of virtuosity in the use of oil paint, the Ghent Altarpiece his crowning achievement. History labeled van Eyck a Renaissance man a hundred years before there was such a thing, and he lived a full life, dying in 1441. Now the resurrected *Just Judges*, existing only as images on a computer screen, was set to reappear before the world.

And he'd be a part of that.

But first he had to twist the knife he'd inserted into Gerard Vilamur—

One more time.

CHAPTER 24

Kelsey entered Saint Bavo's Cathedral, Ghent's largest and most monumental house of worship. A rugged, hulking structure. A blend of French and Gothic, its portrait gallery, bishop's seat, mausoleums, side chapels, and tombs all reflective of its special role as an episcopal church. Ten centuries of precious art was displayed inside.

She marveled at its interior with single aisles and short transepts, striking for its simple dignity and high arches. A vertical grandeur unfolded in massive columns that stood on high plinths, as if reaching for heaven. The many sandstone ribs in the complex vaults stretched in stark contrast with the unadorned brick walls. Across the nave she admired the elegant black-and-white high choir near an opulent rococo pulpit, curiously topped with a golden serpent. The church seemed welcoming without trying too hard. Touristy, but not overly so. It had been a cathedral since the sixteenth century and had borne witness to a multitude of historic events. Most notable it served as home to *The Adoration of the Mystic Lamb*. The altarpiece occupied a former baptismal chamber, displayed in all its glory by special lighting behind bullet-proof glass.

140

She entered the chamber.

The majesty of the restored panels immediately caught her eye. The colors so vibrant, so alive, as if just painted a few days ago. Her prioress waited, admiring the altarpiece. About half a dozen other people were inside too. An attendant stood off to the side and kept watch. Photography was strictly forbidden, and security cameras watched everything. The older woman greeted her with a smile. They both wore the green smocks and veil of Saint-Luke.

"Are you truly okay?" the prioress asked.

She nodded. "I took a kick to the chest. But I'll survive."

"I was so concerned when I received the call, for your safety. I'm relieved to know that you were not harmed."

Kelsey carried the laptop, which she'd been instructed to bring. "We were able to retrieve this, though. Thankfully, my images survived."

The others drifted out, the attendant following, and they were left before the altarpiece alone. Eleven panels stood open under the indirect light. The space for the twelfth marked by a placard that read "Being restored will return soon" in several different languages. But it wouldn't return.

Not ever.

"Kelsey," the prioress said, "I came here today first and foremost to make sure you were safe. I am grateful to God that is the case."

She appreciated the concern, which seemed genuine.

"You are a lovely woman and a most talented restorer. Our convent is honored to have you."

"Why do I hear a *but* in there?" She could see that the older woman was conflicted. "What is it?"

"Before I came to the Congregation of Saint-Luke, I served for many years with the Maidens of Saint-Michael."

She connected the dots. "They have a convent here, in Ghent."

The prioress nodded. "They do. It's a retirement home. The motherhouse is in southern France. I served there for nearly ten years. I then moved to our order, a promotion of sorts, for my many years of loyal service."

The chapel remained empty and they stood off to one side of the display. It was hard for her eyes not to focus on the magnificent painting, her mind drifting back to the conversation earlier with Nick. What she'd told him was true. Works of art like this were not produced solely for beauty. They were more like ancient billboards, serving God and church, educating and edifying. Designed to strengthen Christian ideals through majestic images, and to send subtle messages, the fabulous aesthetics more a means than an end.

What was this painting trying to say?

She desperately wanted to know.

Her prioress' concern for her safety seemed more a lead-in for what she really wanted. Nick had told her to be patient and not press. *Let it unfold at her pace.* Her relationship with this woman up to now had been minimal and businesslike. Most sisters rarely spoke of their past or their families. Those thoughts were kept private. Some had a need to open up to anyone about anything, but most spoke little of their life before the convent. So the prioress' admission about her own past was surprising.

"Why are you telling me this?" she asked.

"I want you to understand what I am about to ask of you."

She braced herself.

"I require you to give me your computer and all of the images you have regarding the twelfth panel. Are they there, on the machine?"

She nodded.

"No copies?"

"None."

"I understand that you participated last night in a police search of the maiden's house here in Ghent."

"How would you know that?"

"You did not inform me that such occurred."

Not an answer. "One of those sisters, or a woman whom they offered sanctuary to, stole this computer. Another set fire to the *Just Judges*. We had every right to investigate."

"There is never a good reason to violate the sanctity of a convent. Not ever. The Maidens of Saint-Michael deserve their privacy. Never would they harbor criminals."

She was not comforted by the observation. "One of those women is dead."

"I know. I am asking, as your prioress, for you to walk away from this matter and return to the convent."

"I can't do that."

Another knot of people drifted into the chapel and began admiring the altarpiece. The prioress motioned and they exited back into the church and found a quiet corner in the expansive nave.

"Then I'm ordering you to do as I stated," the prioress said. "I was hoping it would not come to that, but you leave me no choice."

When she took her final vows, she pledged to obey her lawful superiors according to the rules of the sisters of Saint-Luke. Though there were elements of a democracy within a convent, it was, by and large, a totalitarian state with one person in absolute charge. That oath meant something to her. But she wondered how much it meant to the prioress.

With no choice, she handed over the computer.

"Thank you," the older woman said. "Now please return to

the convent immediately. Your services here are no longer required."

She knew the correct reply. "Yes, ma'am."

"Is there a password required to access this machine?"

She nodded.

"I need it."

She provided the information.

The older woman turned to leave, then hesitated and looked back. "I'm sorry this happened to you. Please know that I'm doing what I can to make this difficult situation right. I hope you understand."

She nodded.

And the prioress left.

She watched as the woman headed for the cathedral's main doors and exited, the laptop tucked safely under one arm. A moment later Nick walked over. He'd been watching it all from another corner in the cathedral. She kept her eyes locked on the doors in the distance.

"You were right. She's connected to the Maidens of Saint-Michael." And she told him everything, then said, "She sold me out. She sold the *Just Judges* out. She told the maidens about the images and where to find them. The only thing she didn't know was about you."

"She ask about copies?"

She nodded. "I lied."

Which had been difficult, but necessary. Hopefully, God would understand. Nick had suspected that the leak was close to home. The curator and Monsieur de Foix had both requested copies of the images, so it made no sense that either would have harmed the panel. That narrowed the leak down to the only other person who knew of her discovery. So they'd uploaded a copy of the images to a CLIO server, safe behind a firewall and password-protected file, then erased them from the laptop. Nick had also activated the Find My Computer option, so they were now able to track the laptop's journey.

She turned and faced him. "What's going on here?"

"That's hard to say. But I think we're on the right path to finding out."

CHAPTER 25

TOULOUSE

Archbishop Vilamur was back in his residence. He'd fled the farmhouse, leaving Father Tallard's body for others to find. He'd been extremely careful inside, touching nothing other than the two crosses, which he'd brought back with him. No way he was going to leave those for the authorities to find. Bad enough that a pedophile priest had been strapped down and murdered, he could not afford the sensationalism that either one of those artifacts would generate in the media. Adding to his misery a new text message had come through his phone as he was driving back. From an Unknown Number. He'd pulled over to the side of the highway and tapped the screen.

Beware. Les Vautours still live. As do the Cathars.

Les Vautours?

The vultures. What in the world were they?

He'd never heard of them.

He decided that he had no intention of taking this heat by himself. Every single thing he'd done regarding Father Tallard had been approved by the Vatican, and he had the emails to prove it. Not once had he made a decision independent of them. He'd followed Rome's orders to the letter. So he reached for the rectory's landline and dialed Italy. After a staff member in the Vatican took his call, he explained the situation, in abbreviated form, expressed a desire to talk with the presiding official, and hung up.

Twenty minutes later the phone rang.

"This is Hector Cardinal Fuentes," the voice said in English, laced with Spanish inflection. "I understand you have a problem."

He was taken aback. He'd called the Congregation for the Doctrine of the Faith, the department within the Curia that dealt with clergy sex abuse complaints. Fuentes had nothing to do with that. Instead, he headed the Pontifical Commission for Sacred Archaeology. Pius IX created the commission in 1852 to care for the Roman catacombs and *conduct explorations, research and study so as to safeguard all of the oldest mementos from the early Christian church.* Talk about broad. That could pretty much include anything and everything. He only knew of Fuentes thanks to his own interest in church archaeology.

"I don't have a problem, Eminence. *We* have a problem. But what does that have to do with your area of expertise? And how are you even aware of the situation?"

"I received a call from the Congregation for the Doctrine of the Faith. They apprised me of your communication."

"That answers one of my inquiries. What of the other?"

"You mentioned *les Vautours.* Do you know what that is?"

"I have not the faintest idea. Could you enlighten me?"

"I can. But I choose not to at the moment, and I would ask your patience."

He realized he had no choice. "Of course, Eminence. I am at your disposal."

Another smart play. He knew that Fuentes was part of the pope's inner circle. One of half a dozen cardinals who acted as an unofficial papal cabinet. Angering or irritating him would not be smart. The man had involved himself in this quagmire for a reason.

Which had to be important.

"Has there been any indication, prior to this, of Cathar activity in your diocese?" Fuentes asked.

"Beyond rumor, gossip, and lore? Nothing. They are the things of legend, here for tourists. Occasionally, from time to time, we hear of their possible presence. But nothing definitive."

"And what do you know of them?"

"Forgive me, Eminence, but I do not concern myself with a religion that disappeared six hundred years ago."

"*Disappear* is such a generous word. More like the church extinguished them."

"The church did that to a lot of people. We were quite proficient in the art of killing."

No sense mincing words. History was clear. Cathars had been slaughtered by the tens of thousands. The Waldensians, and other religious groups across southern Europe and northern Italy, were murdered at the same time too. Maybe as many as a million overall. The Spanish Inquisition tortured and killed untold numbers. During the fifteenth century, Hussites were slain by the thousands. In 1572 Pius V ordered the death of twenty thousand Huguenots. Nearly 40 percent of the Protestant population of Germany was killed by Catholics during the Thirty Years' War. And the Jews. They'd been murdered indiscriminately by Christians for two millennia.

"I am aware of your master's thesis," Fuentes said. "'A Statistical Analysis on the Use of Deadly Force by the Holy Roman Church from AD 1000 to AD 1900.'"

He was impressed. But his personnel file within the Vatican would surely contain a copy. All part of his work history, which would soon come under sharp scrutiny with his consideration for elevation.

"You checked me out before calling?" he asked.

"Force of habit."

More red flags started to wave.

"*Les Vautours*," Fuentes said, "are a subject that interests me. When you mentioned them in your call earlier, my office was alerted. That is why you are speaking to me and not them."

"Are they some sort of radical, clandestine group? Would they have killed Father Tallard?"

"Vultures in nature do not kill," Fuentes said. "The group who took their name practices the same principle. So no, they would not have harmed anyone."

He wanted to know, "Why is this happening to me?"

"I am wondering the same thing. My first impression is that there are two separate, but not mutually exclusive, motivations here. The dead priest and the Cathar implications seem directed at you. The vulture reference seems directed somewhere else. Until today, there has not been any indication of their presence for nearly two hundred years."

Now he was intrigued. "Care to explain that last statement?"

"We have been actively searching for this group for a long time, particularly since the 1930s. Some here thought they existed in secret, apart from society, cloistered away. Others believe they are hiding in plain sight, under another name, as another entity, right before us."

"I had no idea."

"I'm sure you did not," Fuentes said. "But while the vultures may be a shadow, that priest's corpse is real. The video you received is real. Clearly you have an enemy."

"I would say *we* have an enemy. But that enemy just eliminated a big problem."

"And recorded a confession on video first. Hence why I think there are differing motivations here. You do realize, if this information goes public, that red hat you seek will prove elusive."

"You are well informed."

"That I am."

Fuentes was right. If that video was sent to the media the damage would be irreparable. No containment possible. True, everything he'd done had been with Rome's assent. But that would never be admitted, and, to save himself, he'd be forced to challenge them with the evidence he'd kept. Of course, that would end his clerical career. He'd lose his archdiocese and be forced off into oblivion.

No one won in that scenario.

But he did not want to be the fall guy either.

Thankfully, it could be a while before Tallard's body was found. The man had no family, no friends. The deal had been for Tallard to stay out of sight and allow time to work its magic. Perhaps the witnesses might recant, forget, or die. So far that had proven a sound course. The murder itself would surely be chalked up as some sort of revenge killing. But that assumed the recorded confession did not surface.

"I called to inform you that I am coming to Toulouse. I will be there tomorrow. In the meantime, I want you to keep me personally posted on any further developments. Here is my mobile number."

Vilamur jotted it down. He had a million questions, but realized their talk, for now, was over. He'd save them all for tomorrow. "I shall keep you informed, Eminence."

"And one more thing, Archbishop."

He waited.

"I will be anxious to hear why this blackmailer is focused on you."

And the call ended.

Dammit. His nerves were rattled. Anxiety surged through him. He was vulnerable. Exposed. Which had surely been the point of sending him the video in the first place. But what *did* this have to do with him?

Impossible to say.

Yet he also doubted Fuentes would believe him. He needed to calm down. There were engagements he had to attend later. Appointments that could not be delayed.

But before that happened he needed more information.

He left the rectory.

CHAPTER 26

ROME

Hector Cardinal Fuentes entered Le Sacre Grottes Vaticane, the Sacred Grottoes of the Vatican, a vast underground graveyard beneath St. Peter's Basilica. Once damp and dark, visited only by torch or candlelight, from 1935 to 1950 everything had been excavated, transformed, and equipped with electric lights.

It came in two parts.

The necropolis, seven meters down, was a city of the dead, mausoleums lined up alongside an ancient street, mostly pagan graves built of bricks. Four meters higher, three meters below the floor of the basilica, lay the grottoes themselves. Ninety-one popes and a litany of other priests, bishops, and secular monarchs back to the tenth century were buried there. The holiest tomb was that of St. Peter himself, the first bishop of Rome, who occupied a place of great prominence. But whether the bones resting there be Peter's or not was all a matter of faith.

As was most everything else to do with the Roman Catholic Church.

The Pontifical Commission for Sacred Archaeology was created and specifically charged with oversight of the grottoes, which ranked among the most visited sites within Vatican City. Millions of tourists came every year, generating many more millions of euros from entrance fees needed to maintain the site. It seemed a never-ending cycle of decay, restoration, more decay, and more restoration. Usually, people filled the various chapels, corridors, and chambers in a silent procession.

But not today.

The grottoes had been closed all week for some needed electrical repairs. They would reopen on Sunday, four days hence. Today, all was deserted and quiet. The perfect place for a private chat.

He made his way down the low, semicircular corridor that wound beneath the basilica and past St. Peter's tomb. An intentional shadowy, twilight illumination preserved the mystical subterranean atmosphere. Waiting for him was an old friend. Leonardo Dati. A slim, black-haired Portuguese cleric and current Master of the Order of Preachers. The Dominicans. Black friars, named for their black cloaks worn over white robes. They were founded in 1216 by a Spanish priest to preach the Gospel and oppose heresy. Currently, there were 5,747 Dominican friars, including 4,300 priests. The master was chosen from among them and served a set nine-year term. Dati turned as he approached and they walked deeper into the grotto, stopping below the third arch, toward the nave, at the tomb of John Paul I. He told Dati about the phone call from the metropolitan archbishop of Toulouse.

Every detail. Nothing omitted.

"It seems things are moving," Dati said in Italian, "but in varying directions. This is unexpected."

That it was.

He and Dati had been monitoring the developments out of Ghent. His office had been advised a month ago about the rediscovery of the original *Just Judges*, made by a nun from the Congregation of Saint-Luke, a group known for their dedication to art restoration. The painting had come back from the dead, unseen since 1934. It had been fortuitous that the find had been made by someone within the church and, so far, Sister Kelsey Deal had performed her job admirably and kept her discovery secret. Fuentes had been waiting to view the fully restored original panel and see for himself what, if anything, was there to find. Then the attack happened. By a woman lying dead in the Ghent morgue.

"Do you think the reference to the Vultures, made to this archbishop, relates to what is happening in Ghent?" Dati asked. "Or merely random. Coincidental."

"I have never been a fan of coincidence. The subject of *les Vautours* is not one you hear every day. Yet, here we have a mention, then an attack on the panel. I think they are related."

"Cathars knew of *les Vautours*," Dati said. "If the Cathars still exist, as the message noted, then that reference could have been passed down among them."

"My thought too. But it troubles me that this has even arisen."

"Thankfully, we have a team of friars in Ghent, awaiting orders."

They'd been dispatched right after word of the panel's destruction had come from the cathedral's curator.

"The high-resolution images of the panel should be forwarded to me shortly," he told Dati.

Thanks to the curator, with whom he'd established a working relationship. Which solved one problem. But the metropolitan archbishop of Toulouse had raised a new one.

"The dead woman is a *Vautour*," he said. "There's no question in my mind. She is the best tangible lead we've ever come across."

"Interesting that they remained women from the beginning," Dati said.

He nodded. "It appears so."

The friars in Ghent had viewed the dead woman's body and

sent an image of a vulture that had been tattooed on her left shoulder. Through officials at Saint Bavo's he'd also learned that a United Nations investigator was on the scene and had penetrated the local convent for the Maidens of Saint-Michael, retrieving a laptop that had been stolen from Sister Deal during the attack. That drew a straight line from the burned *Just Judges* panel to the maidens.

"We investigated the maidens," Dati said, "along with other convents in southern France, a long time ago. Nothing unusual was uncovered."

"Hiding in plain sight is always best. And they have not survived for so long by being stupid."

Two paths were available. They could go straight to the maidens' motherhouse in southern France. Or they could start with the retirement home in Ghent. He weighed the pros and cons, then said, "We will focus on the convent in Ghent and see if we can rattle some of those old nuns."

Dati nodded.

He pointed to the tomb of John Paul I. "He served a mere thirty-three days. A lifetime of preparation and dedication for a little over a month as pope. What a waste." He paused. "I want more."

"And I want you to have it. We Dominicans are ready to serve as a communion of brothers."

He liked that. No question where the friars stood.

"The time has come to stop dreaming, stop planning, and make it real," he said to Dati. "I need the confidence of the cardinals, and providence has dealt us a golden opportunity to gain it. I am not going to squander that."

"Neither will I."

That's what he liked about this man.

Definitive. Decisive. Determined.

The perfect ally.

"I will personally handle the situation in Toulouse," Fuentes said. "I want you to deal with those maidens in Ghent. We have to know for sure."

Dati bowed, ever so slightly, agreeing.

He acknowledged the show of respect with a nod. "Here's what I want you to do."

CHAPTER 27

Nick had developed a whole host of instincts. He'd started honing them with the FBI, but the past few years on an international stage had allowed him to really perfect them. He hadn't been sure the prioress was a problem, but he'd been curious enough to find out. The older woman probably thought that no one would consider her appearance here in Ghent suspicious. One of her sisters had been attacked. It would be only natural for her to be concerned. She also existed in a cloistered world where her word was the law and no one questioned her actions or motives. He lived in a world where every single thing came under sharp scrutiny.

"She sold me out," Kelsey said again.

He was tailing the prioress, who'd left the basilica with the laptop. He was in communication with Kelsey through his phone, her voice audible thanks to earbuds, and Kelsey safe back in her apartment. He was out on the streets of Ghent, the prioress thirty yards ahead and in no hurry. For the past fifteen minutes they'd meandered about. He could almost read the older woman's thoughts. *Who'd be following me?*

"She's a good woman," Kelsey said in his ear. "The other sisters, and I, have great respect for her. That's why this is so hard."

"You have to assume that she's doing what she believes is the right thing," he whispered back.

"That's what I keep telling myself. But she still sold me out and allowed a great masterpiece to be destroyed."

He knew that lying was tough for Kelsey. On their first date she'd made it clear that she preferred straight talk. If he didn't want to see her again, just say so. No need to make excuses or hedge. The truth would be just fine. He loved that about her and, when the time came to end things, she'd practiced what she'd preached and not minced words. Of course, earlier, she'd lied to her prioress about copies of the images but, as he'd explained to her, sometimes in his line of work, to get to the truth, it had to be done.

He passed through a cobbled square where a statue of Apollo stood watch. Water flowed from a fountain. Outdoor cafés were doing a respectable early-afternoon business. Lots of hustle and bustle all around with people moving in every direction. The prioress kept going, exiting onto a side street labeled Biezekapelstraat.

He followed.

Music leaked out overhead from open windows. They turned again onto another street and passed by Ghent police headquarters. He'd momentarily thought she might be headed there and that they'd misjudged her.

But she kept walking.

Saint James Church stood ahead adjacent to another large square. The river Leie flowed beyond, beneath a low-slung bridge. He saw the Gravensteen looming on the far bank. They were headed in the general direction of both the old castle and the convent, the way he'd taken last night on the river.

The prioress never made it to the bridge.

She stopped in the square and entered a fruit market that had been set up for the day. He lingered back and used the crowd for protection. Birds flitted across the cobbles in quest of tidbits.

The prioress loitered within the market, finally stopping at a booth selling fresh flowers.

"She's waiting for somebody," he whispered.

"I asked to be sent overseas," Kelsey said in his ear.

"Where'd that come from?"

"When I completed my novice training, I was asked where I'd like to serve. I chose France. I could have stayed in the United States, we have a convent there, but I wanted to go far away."

They'd never had a conversation about what happened afterward. It all happened so fast. She told him. The wedding was canceled. She entered the convent. Gone.

"I thought not dragging things out best," she said. "Not being around, or nearby. My course was clear, and I knew I'd hurt you. I would have given anything not to hurt you, Nick. I had to follow my conscience, over my heart. You said you understood, but you really didn't, did you?"

"I do now," he said. "But that took time."

He kept his eyes locked on the prioress, who busied herself with perusing the flowers offered for sale.

"I loved you, Nick. I still love you. I'll always love you."

"And I you." The words were bittersweet to hear and even harder to say. "But it's tough competing with God."

She chuckled. "He doesn't compete. He doesn't have to."

No, he doesn't.

"I was hoping we'd have this conversation," she said. "It's another reason why I wanted you to come here. The main one was I just wanted to see you again. Of course, I never dreamed all this would happen."

"The unexpected seems to follow you, Kelsey."

Two women approached the prioress. Both mid-thirties, one with short hair, the other longer. One was the woman who'd attacked him last night. The one he'd KO'd with the laptop. She bore a violet bruise with brown shadows on the side of her face. Both women wore gray dresses below their knees and veils that draped their necks. Perhaps they thought their religious garb would offer an added measure of protection since, after all, who'd ever suspect a nun of doing anything wrong? They certainly hadn't come from the convent. No. They'd vacated that refuge last night before the police arrived.

Smart play. So he wasn't dealing with dummies.

He was safely hidden behind one of the booths, out of their sight. The women chatted for a moment. Three nuns in a friendly conversation. Not a soul paid them any attention. Then the prioress handed over the laptop and left. The prioress had been easy to follow. These two, though, were another story. He noticed how they both seemed constantly aware of their surroundings. Checking the lay of the land. The one with the laptop headed off first, the other with the bruise lingered behind, off to the side, watching, ensuring that no one was following. He'd been with the police last night at the convent, and though they'd only encountered the mother superior, his face was definitely familiar to at least one of them.

Thankfully, he was a step ahead.

"She just gave the laptop to two Maidens of Saint-Michael," he told Kelsey.

"I have the blue dot blinking on the map," she said.

Kelsey had his computer with the tracking program that came with every Apple. No need for him to follow. Technology would do that for him. Finally, both nuns left the square, headed south, in the opposite direction of the bridge that led over the river toward the convent.

No surprise there.

"It's all good," he said to Kelsey, wanting to give them both some comfort. "Don't feel bad about following your convictions. You did what you had to do. Yeah, it hurt. But I'm a big boy. The main thing is that you're happy with the choice."

And he meant it.

Sure, he'd love to be the one who made her happy. But seeing her, and realizing that she actually *was* happy, loosened the grip on his chest that he'd lived with for nine years.

He liked to recall the good times. And there were many during the three years they were together. They met in a bookstore. The Poisoned Pen in Scottsdale. They both lived in Arizona. He working for the FBI. She for the local museum of contemporary art. They'd each had an interest in a travel log written by a woman who spent a month in Bali. With only one copy in the store he'd insisted she take it, but asked for a cup of coffee together in return. Three hours later they had dinner, then spent the next few days getting to know each other. The mutual attraction had been there from the start. No question. Was there such a thing as love at first sight? Before Kelsey he would have said no. Now? He wasn't so sure. They dated two years before he proposed, and their honeymoon would have been in Bali.

But that was not to be.

"Do you still have a lock on the laptop?" he asked, his mind returning to the problem at hand.

"They're moving south. And, so you'll know, I am happy."

Good to hear.

He headed after the laptop, but stayed back, down a narrow side street lined with rows of shops that sported residences above. Plenty of people moved all around. More than enough cover.

"I handled things all wrong," she said to him. "I had my doubts for several months before the wedding. I should have said no when you asked and explained my dilemma then. But I thought it all an illusion. Something I could ignore. I was wrong."

If she'd left him for someone else there were emotions at

the ready. Jealousy. Anger. Bitterness. Resentment. But to join a convent and devote your life to God? That one did not come with instructions. Her going radio-silent afterward had actually helped, since at the time he hadn't known what to say to her anyway. Instead, he dealt with the pain privately and, over time, learned to live with it. His family helped. Thank goodness he'd had them. Now, all these many years later, he knew that her rejection was not personal in any way. Far from it, in fact.

"Bali would have been great," she said.

He agreed.

"They've stopped," she told him in his ear.

He halted too.

"Still not moving," she said. "The dot is blinking over the Novotel Gent Centrum. A hotel."

Which made sense.

They had to flee to somewhere last night.

Okay. The bait had been taken.

Now set the hook.

CHAPTER 28

To the most revered Charles VII, by the grace of God most high King of the Franks, your faithful and humble bishop sends greetings and the courage of Charlemagne. Concerning those things you have charged me to do, I wish Your Nobility to hold as a certainty that I have neither allied myself with the enemies of your crown, nor have I shown friendship toward them. In accordance with my vow to prize you with sincere affection and to strive to place myself at your command, as time and place require, my only desire is to protect you in the affairs of Toulouse.

But if you would take up the arms of your right hand and the shield of your protection and raise yourself to deal a

STEVE BERRY

blow for the aid of Toulouse, more firmly
and freely would we follow the path of
your armed forces. It is not only I who
mourn, all the people are consumed with
unspeakable sadness as we see our land,
which the vigor of the kings of the Franks
adorned with liberty, be in danger of
falling to the English or the Moors to
whom it does not belong. Let not Your
Highness be affronted that I dare speak
thus to you, most dear lord. For the more
I am the special servant of both the Lord
and your crown, the greater is my sadness when I see that crown fall from the
height of its due state.

Not only in Toulouse, but from the
Garonne to the Rhône, I see adversaries
hurrying to accomplish their boast, that
by subjecting the members of your kingdom to servitude they will more easily
make its head totter. Good king, take on
your vigor. Bring your strong arm to our
region, that the audacity of your enemies
may be put down and your friends may be
comforted. Do what is necessary so that
the prelates and princes of our region,
along with les Vautours, guard Toulouse
both when you are there and when you are
absent. Strive to restore it to its due condition. I ask, and others plead, that you
give no heed to the cost of doing this, for

164

you will recover a hundred times whatever you spend, and your name, which is now but a shadow among us, will be exalted by all. Valete, valeant qui vos amant.

Vilamur laid the ancient document down.

It had sat safely within the diocese's archives for centuries. He'd come straight over after ending the call with Cardinal Fuentes. He was curious whether any reference to the words *les Vautours* was anywhere among the olden records. A few years back everything on file had been digitized and scanned electronically. So it had taken the archivist only a few moments to locate the sole reference. A letter from Pierre du Moulin, who served as archbishop of Toulouse from 1439 to 1451.

The archivist had also placed the letter in historical context.

The Hundred Years' War was then waning, but the English from the west and the Moors from the south continued to ravage the Languedoc. The French did little to stop the carnage, satisfied with the chaos those raids created among the southern nobility, who'd always harbored an independent streak toward the monarchy. So the local bishop, fearful for what was happening around him, penned a plea to a distant king. Apparently the letter never found its way from Toulouse north to Charles VII. Good thing. The king might have taken offense with the valediction, which struck the archivist as thick with irony. *Valete, valeant qui vos amant.* Goodbye from those who love you. But, as was explained, *valete* meant "be strong" as well as "farewell." So the king might not have appreciated the implication of weakness.

The singular reference to *les Vautours* came without explanation or elaboration, and the archivist, a trained historian, could not say who or what they were. He'd never noticed the reference until today. Some sort of fighting force? Mercenaries? Another of the countless medieval societies that sprang up everywhere? Impossible to know. Even more puzzling was why those words were of such importance to the Vatican.

The archivist also reminded him that the cache of documents the diocese maintained had been ravaged over the centuries. Particularly during the Albigensian Crusade, when the pope's forces had taken Toulouse. A lot had been lost, so there was no telling how many other references might have existed. The one surviving mention was a bit innocuous and meaningless. Regardless, he'd asked the archivist to see what he could learn about anything related to Vultures and report that information directly to him.

He left the archives and headed back to the rectory.

At the moment the video confession was more pressing. It had come to his private mobile number, not the one associated with the diocese. How that number had been obtained was just another of the many questions that remained unanswered. He'd already deleted it from his phone but realized that offered little to no protection. Whoever made it certainly controlled its distribution.

And he was at their mercy.

Bishops all over the world had been toppled on the mere allegation of a cover-up regarding claims of clergy sexual abuse. Like him, most had probably done exactly what Rome had wanted but, in the end, they became sacrificial lambs. Even several cardinals had fallen victim. Was he next?

It certainly looked that way.

He walked back to the rectory, greeting several people he knew. His office had already called twice looking for him, but he'd texted his assistant and told him that he would be unavailable for another hour or so. Thankfully, as archbishop, no one questioned him. The appropriate excuses would be made and appointments rescheduled. Inside, he sat in his den and tried to make sense out of what was happening. His housekeeper had returned and offered to prepare a late lunch but he declined.

No appetite.

He closed his eyes and allowed the silence to wash over him. Thirty years he'd worked to get to this point. Obtaining a red hat and cardinal's robes would be his crowning achievement. No way he would ever be pope, nor did he particularly want to be. Being a prince of the church would more than suffice. Doubtful he'd ever even get to vote in the Sistine Chapel for a pope before he turned eighty. Just three years away. The current Vicar of Christ showed no signs of failing health.

His phone vibrated.

He thought at first to ignore the call. Probably his office again. But he decided that he'd acted strange enough for one day. No sense piquing the interest of everyone around him by not answering.

He checked the display.

Unknown.

Ordinarily he'd never answer.

But today was anything but ordinary.

He pushed Accept.

"Are you listening carefully?" a male voice said.

"Who is this?"

"The person who sent the video."

He closed his eyes. "I'm listening."

"I want you at Montségur, at 4:00 p.m. today. Alone. If you do not come, or bring others with you, that video will be headed to the media. Are we clear?"

"What do you want?"

"You at Montségur at 4:00 p.m."

The call ended.

CHAPTER 29

Claire stood in the center of the chapter hall. Though she was physically back home, in France, her thoughts were hundreds of miles away in Ghent, wondering what was happening. The maidens had gathered, all twenty-three then in residence, the only ones missing the two still in Ghent on assignment and Sister Rachel, her body most likely in a morgue. Her colleagues sat upon plain wooden benches that fronted long pitted oak tables. This was where they took meals and gathered for important discussions. The abbess had opened the session with a prayer, explained all that had happened, then turned the floor over to her.

"I take full responsibility for everything that occurred last evening," she said in English. "I want that clear. I was the one in charge and things did not go as we expected."

"It was an ill-gotten plan that resulted in the death of a good woman," one of the maidens called out.

Anyone was allowed to speak without restriction or recognition, though civility was required.

"There was no need for such a rash act," another added. "It did nothing but draw attention to something that had no attention."

168

Several others chorused their agreement.

Another meeting less than a month ago had decided on the course to be taken. The vote had been a narrow one, with a significant minority, herself included, arguing that the *Just Judges* panel should be ignored. It had been gone since 1934 and there was no real danger emanating from its reappearance. That same minority was now re-expressing their objections, but with the added ammunition of Sister Rachel's untimely death.

"I need not be reminded of your concerns," the abbess interrupted and said. "A majority wanted the panel destroyed."

"No one wanted anyone to die," another said.

Claire faced the older woman. "Of course not. Sister Rachel sacrificed herself to ensure those images came into our possession. I doubt she thought the police would kill her. Merely arrest her. What happened was their fault, not hers, or ours."

Her voice stayed firm, the tone certain, and she meant every word.

"We are not here to re-debate our previous decision," the abbess made clear. "The Vestal and I have already had that discussion earlier. I am well aware how you, and she, feel. So please focus on the issue at hand."

To be abbess was to be absolute ruler. That person could appoint and depose any of those beneath her. She decided if novices were to take their final vows and if maidens would continue in the order's service. She made every decision within the convent and was their mother in a great many ways, treated with the greatest reverence, the person they all turned to in time of trouble. The current abbess was regarded as a mild disciplinarian, refined, courteous, but firm almost to obstinacy. A lady of pleasant and easy speech, with a memory stored with anecdotes. She was university-educated and a competent manager of the order's affairs. Long ago it was learned that if a leader was capable, conscientious, and devoted, the collective prospered. Thankfully, the Maidens of Saint-Michael had always been blessed with competent leadership. And though Claire disagreed with the course taken, she'd never doubted the abbess. Good thing. As this place harbored a great secret. And, when it came to that, no amount of clever scheming or economy of thought could counterbalance a bad leader. All who rose to be abbess had been the best of the best.

Herself included.

"Forgive us," one of the women said. "But it is hard to focus with Rachel dead."

"What would you have had us do?" the abbess said to the group, and seemingly straight to those who'd voted no a month ago. "Sit back and allow the panel to be revealed? To be studied by every art expert in the world, including the Vatican? And not with a steady eye and a magnifying glass. But with the clarity of electronic high resolution. Nothing would have escaped detection. All its secrets would have been revealed. Is that what you wanted?"

"We are dealing with a work of art that was created six hundred years ago," one of the maidens said. "Whatever secrets existed within it are long forgotten. Meaningless. To everyone."

"Not everyone," the abbess said. "The Vatican is always watching."

"We don't know that," came the challenge. "What we guard, what we protect, could well be one nobody cares about anymore."

Exactly what Claire believed too, and a sizable portion of the women staring at her felt the same way. Not quite a majority, as yet. But a surprising number. She'd long wondered if what they did still made sense, and Rachel's untimely death had brought her doubts into clearer focus. But she swept those doubts aside and, acting like the Vestal, said, "Whether the Vatican or anyone else cares is irrelevant. What we all swore to do is the important matter. The vow we took before God. That is what we are obligated to follow. Perhaps I missed something, but the last I looked none of us have been released from that duty. The *Just Judges* was gone. Now it's back. The threat was gone. Now it's back. Whether we personally agree or not, we must deal with that."

Her gaze bore in.

"I do not dispute you," one of the women said. "But I do dispute the necessity for us to have acted in the manner in which we did. Patience was the better course."

Many heads nodded in agreement.

And Claire did not disagree.

"What of our exposure?" one of the others asked. "Sister Rachel's body is within police jurisdiction. She can be identified."

"Thankfully, nothing came of their search of the convent in Ghent," the abbess said. "Yes, there is now a connection between the panel's destruction and us, but it's a tenuous one. Let's hope that the trail goes cold. All they have is the word of one man, as to what he may or may not have seen. And, yes, Rachel's identity could be learned, but that will take time."

"We have never been this vulnerable," one of the women noted. "It is quite disconcerting."

She agreed. And it was her fault.

"We can only hope that the Vatican is not vigilant," she said. "But, as the abbess has said before, we have to assume, whether we personally agree or not, that they are."

"Are we going to bring Rachel back?" one of the women asked. "She is a maiden and we have never abandoned anyone."

That duty traced itself all the way back to Joan of Arc, a maiden herself, whose remains were snatched from the smoldering pyre and brought back to the mountains where they'd remained since 1431.

So her duty was clear.

"I will bring her home," Claire said.

"And what of the electronic images?" came a question.

"I have dealt with those," the abbess said. "They are, right now, being obtained."

"Then what?"

"We shall destroy them," the abbess said, "bury our sister, and, hopefully, this matter will be at an end."

CHAPTER 30

Nick entered the Novotel Gent Centrum. Nothing shy about its décor, a bold modern splash of color atop white marble. Beyond a set of tall windows and glass doors at the far end he spotted an inner courtyard that accommodated a pool. He was taking a chance coming inside, but Kelsey had confirmed that the laptop was at this location and there was no way to electronically narrow that down any further. She'd checked on the internet and learned there were 117 rooms. But it wasn't necessary to find the computer. The plan had been to learn where it was headed.

He studied the spacious interior and decided on a location inside a lobby bar where he could watch the exits and elevators without being readily seen. He sat at a small table against the wall and kept his eyes focused. He was surprised by Kelsey's admissions, especially that she still loved him. Of course, it wasn't the love of a man and woman, husband and wife. But a connection still existed, one that she'd obviously wanted to rekindle.

And he was glad.

If friendship was all she could offer, then he'd take what he could get.

Two nuns entered the lobby through the front doors. Older

women. Dressed in the same gray dresses and veils as the other two with the laptop. More Maidens of Saint-Michael, the retired version. They calmly walked to the elevators and disappeared inside. He hustled over and watched the floor indicator stop at 3, then begin a descent.

Okay. He'd narrowed things down.

He was about to head up to the third floor when, across the busy lobby, Inspector Zeekers entered through the main doors accompanied by four uniformed officers.

He darted left and found the stairwell.

Zeekers and the other officers never saw him. They headed straight for the main desk, flashing badges and talking with the people behind the counter. He watched through a small glass window in the door. What was he doing here? It would not be long before Zeekers headed to the third floor. Kelsey had wanted to know why her prioress had betrayed her. Why the twelfth panel had been destroyed. And what was so important about the images she'd recorded. All excellent questions. Which Inspector Zeekers might or might not care to answer. But those nuns? They had answers.

He found his phone and reconnected with Kelsey. He'd ended their continuous call when he'd first entered the hotel.

"The police are here," he told her.

"I know. I called them."

He was shocked. "Why?"

"This is a matter for them."

He told himself to stay cool and not show irritation. She didn't know better. "I wish you'd run that by me first."

"What else would we do? They have my laptop. You have them. Let the police take over."

"Kelsey, I don't try to tell you about God. How about you let me handle the investigatory stuff?"

"I was only—"

No time to explain. "I have to go."

He ended the call and rushed up the metal risers two at a time. Before he reached the door for the third floor it opened and four nuns hastily entered the stairwell. The two from the market along with the two older women who'd just arrived. One held the laptop. Another carried two small knapsacks.

They froze and stared at him.

"Now, this is awkward," he said. Then he raised his hands in mock surrender. "I'm not your enemy. Okay?"

None of them said a word.

"The prioress told you the password, so you've surely discovered there are no images on that machine. I removed them."

He could see that admission drew their interest.

"I have them safely tucked away. So that cow is gone from the barn, if you get my drift."

He could see they did.

"We need to leave," one of the younger nuns said. "The police are here."

"I know. But that wasn't my doing. I'm here to help with that."

"We should trust him," one of the older women said. "We really have little choice."

The younger nun, the one with the bruise, nodded.

He pointed. "Sorry about that smack to the face."

"I'm not sorry for the kick to your gut."

He smiled. "No, I imagine you're not. Let me deal with the police. I'll buy you time to get out."

They still did not move.

"Or you can stay and take your chances with them," he added.

"All right," the one with the bruised face said.

"Head down to the underground parking garage," he said. "I saw a sign on the ground floor that pointed an arrow downward. I'll deal with Inspector Zeekers. He's with the General Directorate of Judicial Police. You people have attracted the big boys."

"Along with the United Nations?" the older women asked.

"It would seem so."

Apparently, he'd been checked out too.

He stepped aside and motioned for them to go.

They passed without a word.

"Oh, by the way."

They stopped and turned around.

"Here's my cell phone number."

And he rattled it off. One of the younger nuns produced a phone and entered the digits. His phone buzzed in his pocket.

"That's mine," she said.

He nodded. "Call me when you're ready to talk. I might be able to help contain those images."

They started to leave.

"Ladies," he said. "One more thing. That laptop is being tracked. It's how I found you. Leave it there. Let the police find it."

The younger nun nodded and the other woman laid it on one of the steps.

And they left.

He headed up to the third floor and exited the stairwell just as the elevator dinged and the car door opened. Zeekers and two of the uniforms marched off. He hoped the other two were stationed in the lobby and not watching the stairs or garage.

"Monsieur Lee," Zeekers said. "Sister Deal alerted us to your presence. The nuns are on this floor. Which you seem to already know."

"I followed them here but wasn't able to see which room they entered. I was trying to not be detected, until you arrived."

He was acting like he was in on the call to the police.

Zeekers nodded. "Sister Deal explained about the laptop and what you did. Let's see what these nuns have to say today."

The inspector led the way to a door marked "307" and used a key card to gain access. Inside was a spacious room with laminated furniture, a queen-sized bed, and a large bathroom. Views of Saint Bavos could be seen through the windows. But no people. No clothes or possessions.

"I don't understand," Zeekers said. "The hotel says this is their room. They checked in late last night." Zeekers motioned and one of the uniforms found a radio and asked what was happening at their location. "All clear," was the response. Nick caught the annoyance on the inspector's face.

Zeekers found his cell phone and tapped the screen. "Sister Deal, are you still tracking the computer?" He listened a moment, then ended the call. "She says it's still at this location."

"It's a big hotel," he pointed out.

Thankfully, the inspector wasn't pressing him on what happened, thinking him an ally. After all, he and Kelsey had led him here.

"Seal this floor," Zeekers said to the uniforms, "then search all the rooms."

The two men nodded and hurried off.

"This is all quite strange," Zeekers said to him.

"I agree," Nick answered.

In more ways than one.

CHAPTER 31

Bernat completed the arduous climb to the mount at Montségur.
He'd come early to make the trek. A pilgrimage of sorts. One he'd
made many times before.

The loose soil and pebbles along the way presented their usual
challenge. The steep rocky path wound up the cliff face through
stands of cypress and pine, fragrant in the spring air. The wind
had steadily increased, blowing with more gusto the higher he
went. Stops had been created at points along the way and he'd
lingered at one that offered a panoramic view of the forests
below. He'd studied the car park and spotted Andre, discreetly
placed to keep a watchful eye out for their visitor, who was
expected to arrive in an hour or so.

The castle ruin loomed above him, ferocious and unwelcoming.
Almost threatening. As if warning him not to come closer. The
mountain's sheer power and height had surely once proved the
citadel's best defense. Bringing a fully equipped army up here for
an attack would have been nearly impossible. No wonder a siege
mentality had prevailed.

The fortress itself was simple in design. A single postern, a
massive keep, walls reinforced by limestone rock surrounding a

long central courtyard. Once it had been home to several hundred. Now it seemed icy cold, nearly corpselike. Tour guides loved to link the fortress with the Cathars. And there was a connection, just not with this ruin. It was not the original stronghold. Instead, it was a seventeenth-century French border post destroyed during a war. The original castle had been razed in 1244, just after the Cathars surrendered the site.

He trudged toward an opening in the crumbling wall. A north wind whipped with no mercy, rushing across him as if angry. Scattered clouds overhead cast shadows. Once he was inside, the walls blocked the wind, offering a feeling of protection, but also one of isolation as nothing could be seen past the stone. A few other visitors had braved the climb and were enjoying the reverent ambience.

He exited the enclosed space through a doorway in the wall, finding a precipice, staring across an emerald-green valley that stretched for as far as he could see, ending at high peaks on the horizon. Patches of light swept across the hillsides. Above, a hawk rode the warm currents. The breeze whipped his hair. He wanted to stretch out his arms and ride the wind too. Where the other side of the *pog* from which he'd come was climbable, this part dropped in a sheer fall of over twelve hundred meters. As no barriers blocked any approach to the edge, it would be an easy matter to leap right off. The height and grand vista energized him.

Like always.

This was a holy place, despite the tour guides' lies.

And the perfect location.

To finally confront the devil.

"He is not my child," the priest said, voice rising. "Please do not say that again."

Bernat stood outside the rectory, beneath an open window. He'd followed his mother from their home, across the streets of Pau, to here.

She'd been upset all morning. When she'd knocked on the rectory door and entered he'd thought her need spiritual and almost left. But something had told him to be sure.

So he'd found the window.

He'd lived in Pau all ten years of his life, enjoying hikes in the nearby mountains and swims in the icy-cold lakes. All had been great until six months ago, when his father suddenly died, his heart giving out. His mother had taken the loss hard but, true to her good nature, she'd rebounded.

But what was she doing now?

"Why do you lie?" his mother asked in her soft voice. "Why hurt me like this?"

"I do not mean to hurt you. I am simply telling the truth. I have no child."

"But you do. I have kept this to myself all these years out of respect to my husband. With him now dead, it is time for you to know the truth."

He was shocked at what his mother had said.

It couldn't be.

"Do you deny what happened between us?" his mother asked. "How could you possibly?"

"Madam—"

"My name is Rene. You called me Rene when you took me to your bed."

"I prefer to keep this at arm's length," the priest said. "Madam, we have known each other a long time. I baptized your son. You have volunteered your services to this parish incessantly. I too have served this parish a long time. Never has there been even a hint of scandal associated with me."

"Because I kept quiet. I respected you. I respected the church. But I also cannot deny what happened between us. I . . . loved you. I still love you. How can you stand there and deny the truth?"

A long silence passed, and the sound of distant traffic could be heard. He'd walked down this alley between the rectory and the church many times. He attended school nearby and mass every Sunday. He'd passed this window day after day, never realizing that it opened to the priest. A man he'd both feared and idolized. All of his friends felt the same way. The black suit and white collar that swept into their classrooms from time to time, smiling, speaking to them for a few moments, then leaving. He was Father. The one who granted forgiveness in the confessional and Holy Communion at the altar. A man to be respected and obeyed.

But his father?

No.

His father was dead.

"While my husband lived," his mother said, "I vowed never to speak of this. And I never have."

"You should have continued to keep that vow."

His attention piqued.

An admission?

Bernat walked back through the ruin, toward the southwest and the side from which he'd climbed. The day was waning and the number of visitors dwindling. Precisely why he'd chosen this rural locale, along with its obvious symbolism, as the meeting spot. He stared out at the distant hills, the countryside filled with trees and pastures under a pale sun. Below, the car park remained nearly empty, Andre still in position.

He liked to imagine what happened here in May 1243 when a crusader army arrived below. Ten years of fighting had failed to end Catharism. The pope had threatened a renewed crusade with more deaths and persecutions. Cathars had steadily withdrawn to remote citadels, which began to fall one by one. The fortress at Montségur was last. Nearly impregnable. Rising three stories. Around its central courtyard stood workshops, storage rooms, and stables for

181

horses and mules. The crusaders laid siege and a few hundred Cathars managed to hold them off for nine long months. Finally, on March 16, 1244, they surrendered. Two hundred and twenty Cathars refused to renounce their faith and were burned en masse at the base of the *pog*, each one dying willingly in the flames.

The thought turned his stomach.

Greed, arrogance, hypocrisy.

The Holy Roman Church was guilty of all three.

Then.

And now.

"What would you have me do?" his mother asked the priest. "I have a son to raise. Alone."

"Leave here, and never broach this subject with me again."

"You deny your child?"

"I. Have. No. Son."

"You do. A fine young man named for my father."

"Rene."

No Madam? Much more personal. Bernat stood beneath the window mesmerized, angry, confused.

"Please," the priest said. "I am to be the new bishop of Albi. I will be leaving here soon."

"You can't go. Your son needs a father in his life. I recognize you cannot be that openly, but you could be that privately."

"I cannot. Not in any way. That boy means nothing to me."

"He is in many ways like you. I think you would enjoy getting to know him."

"Your son is yours to raise, as you see fit. He does not concern me."

"You are a cruel man."

"I am a Roman Catholic priest, about to be a bishop. I cannot have any children. It is unthinkable. Don't you understand that? You cannot be that ignorant."

His mother started to cry.

The sound broke his heart.

He ran around to the front of the rectory, up the steps, and opened the front door. He rushed inside and found the room with the open window.

"Bernat. My God. What are you doing here?" his mother cried out.

He wrapped his arms around her waist and hugged her hard. Tears dripped down her face. Like at the funeral.

"Did you follow me?" she asked.

He nodded.

Then he faced the priest.

Father Gerard Vilamur.

"Are you my father?"

"No. I am not. Please, never ask me that again. Now you both must leave."

Thirty-two years had passed since that day, and the memory had never left him. Nor would it ever.

Time to head back down.

The sinner would arrive soon.

This place had been the Cathars' last stand. Their final act of defiance. Where they'd been forced from reality and into a memory.

He'd come today to do the reverse.

And bring a memory back to life.

CHAPTER 32

Nick exited the hotel, leaving Zeekers and his uniformed officers there to keep asking questions. Eventually, they would check the security cameras and see a gaggle of nuns escaping through the parking garage. Thankfully, there'd been no cameras in the stairwell and, once clear of the building, those women would dissolve into the street crowd. He assumed they knew all about how to lose themselves. The computer in the stairwell had been found, which confirmed what Kelsey had said about the tracker and its location. Since it had only acted as bait, with nothing incriminating or damaging on the machine, it had been returned to him for delivery back to Kelsey. He found his phone and dialed the number the maiden had provided.

"You are Nicholas Lee, with UNESCO?" the female voice said, as the call was answered.

"That's me."

"What is your involvement here?"

"Sister Deal is an old friend."

"So this is personal?"

"Does that matter?"

"We're simply trying to gauge the level of official interest."

"You definitely have the UN's attention. But, right now, I'm the best friend you've got. Remember, I have the images."

"What do you want?"

"I want to know why you destroyed the *Just Judges*."

"Providing that answer is beyond my authority. I have to communicate with my superiors."

"Do that. I'll wait for your call. But, sister, don't take too long."

Ω

Kelsey could tell that Nick was irritated with her.

She knew him well. They'd spent three years together. And though they'd been apart for nearly a decade her instincts relative to him were right on. For some reason he hadn't wanted her to involve the police. Why not? This was all surely a matter for local law enforcement. The Ghent Altarpiece was regarded as a Belgian national treasure. Anything and everything concerning it captivated the public. Which was precisely why she'd made the call to the inspector, who'd seemed quite grateful for the information.

She stared at Nick's computer and the blinking blue dot.

Her laptop had left the Novotel Gent Centrum. With Nick? Or someone else? The Maidens of Saint-Michael?

There were hundreds of female religious orders of all sizes and beliefs that serviced countless people, charities, and organizations around the world. Her own was devoted to the poor, along with aiding churches and museums with the restoration of religious art. Quite a contrast in purpose. But it had all made sense. Until today. What was her prioress doing? Putting the needs of the maidens before the needs of her own order?

Every sister owed the prioress a duty of obedience. That was mandated. But respect? That was earned. And, until today, her prioress had possessed her unquestioned respect. But the deceit had ended that. Willful. Blatant. Offensive. Naively, she believed that everyone within a convent would be true and honest. The dedication and determination needed to maintain that rigid lifestyle demanded a certain degree of discipline, which almost eliminated the need for lies. How disappointing to learn that she'd been wrong, and that deceit played just as devilish a role inside the walls as out. And that realization cast a shadow of doubt. One she hadn't felt since before joining the convent.

She hated—

No.

Resented her prioress for casting that shadow.

She had to know more. She could not allow this to go unchecked. So she found the cell phone she'd been provided on arriving in Ghent and dialed her convent in France. She was connected with the presiding sister and explained the necessity to speak with the prioress. She had no way of contacting the woman directly.

Ten minutes later the cell phone rang.

"I know what you did with that laptop," she told her superior.

"And how would you know that?"

"We set you up and tracked the computer. You took it straight to the Maidens of Saint-Michael. I want to speak with you. Now. In person."

"I do not take orders from you," the older woman said.

"Fine. Then you can speak to the police."

Silence.

"All right. Where would you like to meet?"

Ω

Claire remained unnerved by the amount of conflict exhibited at the gathering. The maidens had seemed a nervous coalition of doves and hawks. She on one side, the abbess on the other. Rarely had they so deeply disagreed. But rarely had so difficult a quandary been presented.

The order traced its origins to nine women who formed themselves into an organized group sometime around AD 250. It happened nearby, in the region known as the Roussillon. Best guess was the village of Las Illas, about twelve miles away from the current motherhouse. They remained a loose, covert association, membership passed from mother to daughter, until the eighth century, when they petitioned the local bishop for permission to form a religious order. That charter still existed in their archives, along with a report dated November 10, 1009, which noted an abbey had been built "on the mountain by a group of women, consecrated by the Bishop of Elne in honor of the Blessed Virgin Mary and the Archangel Michael." The land had been donated by Count Wilfred and his wife who enriched and endowed the new group. Two years later Pope Sergius IV issued a papal bull that declared "from now on, no king, no prince, no marquis, no count, no judge, no bishop, no priest will take it on himself to commit any act of violence, invasion or subjugation in this convent or its outbuildings."

And none had for over a thousand years.

But threats had materialized every now and then.

By the twelfth century, women had been effectively subjugated in the church, the powerful abbesses and prioress gone, male monasteries rising in size and influence. Women were forbidden from the altar, school, and conclave, cloistered away in solitude and generally ignored. Which had allowed for an even greater level of secrecy among the maidens. The worst threat came in the early part of the fifteenth century from an unlikely source. A Belgian artist named Jan van Eyck was chased into the valley below the motherhouse by Moors who'd pursued him north across the border. He'd apparently been spying on them, something they took great offense toward. But they'd halted their attack once confronted with the *quebrantahuesos*.

Bone smasher.

The Vulture.

Le Vautour in French.

She gently caressed her left shoulder through her gray smock. The image had been tattooed into her skin two years after she took her final vows. After she was thoroughly vetted and schooled. After she was trained, saw the truth for herself, and took one more vow.

To *Veritas Vita*.

The truth, the life.

Sadly, the painter van Eyck had not respected their secrecy. Thankfully, though, he knew precious little about them, and the revelation he left within the Ghent Altarpiece was not discovered for centuries.

But it was discovered.

They'd hoped time would eradicate the problem, and to some extent it had. But the Vatican refused to allow it to fade away. The *Just Judges* disappearing in 1934 had helped, as it removed a vital element in the puzzle. But now the painting had reemerged. Should they have moved on it? No. Better to leave it alone, and hope the Vatican did the same. That was her position weeks ago and it remained her position. But all that was academic now, as the damage had been done.

Her phone buzzed.

She'd been waiting for a report. She answered, listened to what had happened, then told the maidens on the ground in Ghent, "We have no choice. Make contact with Lee again and find out what he wants. Reveal nothing. Learn what you can about the images. Above all, contain this disaster."

She ended the call.

A soft tap came to the door of her room.

Her abbess entered.

Claire explained about Nicholas Lee and his commandeering of the images and the additional copies, then said, "If he wants to help, let's use him until we no longer have to."

"I agree," the abbess said. "Sister Deal has also become more of a problem. I have it somewhat under control, but we need her contained."

She understood.

"With your permission, I'll take care of her myself."

CHAPTER 33

Archbishop Vilamur motored into the graveled lot at Montségur and parked the car, the ride from Toulouse a little less than two hours. He'd made the trek many times in the past, visiting and inspecting the various parishes that stretched to the south toward Spain. There'd been no choice but to respond to the summons. That video would be the end of him, and he needed to learn more before Cardinal Fuentes arrived. He'd come to believe that whoever was masterminding this whole endeavor was intent on a result different from simply exposing the sins of a sexual predator. If that were the sole object, then it would have already happened, without the additional drama.

He stepped from the car.

He'd dressed in hiking clothes. Nothing to indicate his rank or privilege. The jeans and boots he would wear occasionally when he took long walks in the countryside. It was important that he not be recognized. Thankfully, despite his exalted position, few outside the Catholic community readily knew his face. He wasn't sure what he was supposed to do next. So he simply stood in the fading afternoon sun and stared up at the *pog* and the citadel that crowned its summit.

190

He was not ignorant about what happened atop that needle of rock in March 1244. Fifteen years of revolt and repression ended when the Cathars there surrendered to the Albigensian Crusaders. Five terms were negotiated. Clause four provided that "all persons in the fortress would remain at liberty, and would similarly be subject to light penances only, provided that they abjured their heretical beliefs and made confession before the inquisitors. Those who did not recant would be burnt." Two hundred and twenty refused to recant. So the soldiers built a palisade of stakes and pales, heaping into it kindling, straw, and pitch. No time had existed to erect individual stakes. Instead, the defiant Cathars were simply shut inside the palisade, most walking in willingly, the sick and wounded carried to their fate. Fires were set at the four corners, which quickly raged. The only sounds were the crackle of the flames, the chink of weapons, the clergy chanting Psalms, and an occasional groan of misery.

Few cried out.

Nearly all of them left this world in silence.

The soldiers and executioners had backed away to avoid the heat and the pall of thick, blackish smoke. Those still remaining in the citadel high above had watched as the fires burned until there was nothing left but a raw, blackened mass, cindered to a crisp, the stench of burned flesh heavy in the spring air. Red embers lingered long into the night. How horrible that Christians could do that to other Christians simply because they disagreed on how to worship God.

But it happened.

Now bad things were happening to him, and something told him that the two events were connected.

He stood in the cool, late-afternoon air. From behind he heard footsteps and turned to see a younger man walking his way. Slim. Muscular. Black curly hair. Who stopped three meters away.

191

He decided to get to the point. "I'm here. What do you want?"

"I want nothing," the younger man said. "But he wants a great deal."

A finger was pointed his way.

He turned to see a man emerge from the trees on the trail that led up over a thousand meters to the ruin. Between here and there was the open space that had come to be known as the *Prat dels Cremats*, the Field of the Burned. Where the slaughter had occurred.

The man stopped.

"He's waiting," the younger man behind him said.

Vilamur was becoming irritated, unaccustomed to being ordered about. "Who are you?"

No reply.

"What am I expected to do?" he asked.

"Go to him and find out."

He turned back and stared at the figure standing about a hundred meters away.

With no choice, he started walking.

Ω

Bernat closed his eyes and allowed the ghosts that swirled around him to settle. He always felt different here. Though a lot of the stories about Montségur were more fiction than fact, embellished for the tourists, the reality was unchanged. Cathars died here on the authority of the Holy Roman Church. And though afterward the religion had not ended, it definitely diminished. It would take nearly eighty years before the last known Cathar Perfectus was executed in 1321. After that, no records of the Inquisition mention Cathars again.

They faded away.

Into the shadows.

Today, the entire Languedoc embraced them. But not as a religion. More a novelty. An idea. The word *Cathar* and its commemorative spirit seemed everywhere. On cafés, shops, real estate companies, menus, wine, you name it. Strange, really. The whole belief system was effectively annihilated seven hundred years ago. No physical traces remained. No art. Monuments. Chapels. Writings. Little to nothing. What the church labeled a failed heresy and slandered, libeled, and distorted, modern society had transformed into a romantic legend.

In recent years the Catholic Church had apologized for the way it historically treated Jews, the repeated use of violence under the guise of religion, the Inquisition, the disrespect it had shown toward women and minorities, even the rampage of crusaders through Constantinople in 1204. But never had it explicitly stated open and sorrowful regret for the Albigensian Crusade. True, in March 2000 John Paul II issued a general apology for, as he said, *all of the faults of the past.* But no specific mention of Cathars was included. You would think the systematic extermination of tens of thousands of people, Christians killing Christians, would merit at least one mention.

But not a word.

He could not change those omissions, but he could expose the hypocrisy of both the institution itself and certain members of the Roman Catholic Church.

Starting with the bastard walking toward him.

Ω

Vilamur studied the man waiting for him.

Tall, broad-shouldered, middle-aged, with a thick mane of chestnut hair, dressed in a long-sleeved shirt, jeans, and boots. He stood with both hands behind his back, ramrod-straight, near a stele that commemorated those long-ago victims. Its inscription an open slap to the church: "*Als catars, als martirs del pur amor crestian.*" Occitan for "To the Cathars, to the martyrs of pure Christian love." Along with a date. *16 March 1244.*

He marched across the grass, the wind whipping in from the north and carrying a chill. He told himself that he was the esteemed metropolitan archbishop of Toulouse, a sacred member of the Roman Catholic Church, entitled to respect. No matter what.

He stopped before the man. "Who are you?"

"You don't remember me?"

He'd never seen the face before.

"I own an auction house in Toulouse. Have you ever frequented it?"

"Never."

"That's a shame. We've sold some beautiful items."

"Your name?"

"Bernat de Foix."

"Am I supposed to know you?"

"You knew my mother. Rene Bellamy."

A name he'd not heard in a long time. One he hoped to never hear again. Now he remembered. "You're the little boy that day, in the rectory, when your mother came to see me?"

"I am. All grown up. I no longer carry the Bellamy surname. I had it legally changed to de Foix, out of respect to my mother and her family. That was her maiden name."

He could not care less.

"Are you proud, Father? And I don't mean that in the religious way."

"I told your mother then, and I tell you now, I am not your father."

"She's dead."

A part of him was glad. But he knew what to say. "I am sorry to hear that."

De Foix chuckled. "I seriously doubt that. Just one less witness to your sins."

"I am not your father," he said again.

De Foix reached into his pocket and removed a glass vial. "Prove it with a simple DNA test. If it comes back that you are not, I will give you Tallard's recorded confession and our business will be concluded. But, if it's positive, then you and I will have much to discuss."

"And how will I know the results you share are legitimate?"

De Foix produced another vial. "Two tests. One by me, the other by you to a lab of *your* choosing. I want there to be no mistake."

"Do I have a choice?"

De Foix shook his head. "None at all."

"What do you really want?" he asked.

"What every son wants. For his father to know he exists."

He doubted that. This man had gone to a lot of trouble to make this connection. And not out of any love or curiosity. "Did you kill Tallard?"

"I did not. That would be contrary to my religion."

He was shocked. "You are Cathar?"

"I am a Perfectus."

He shook his head. Idiots. Perfecti prostrated themselves before falsity and swore to no carnal intercourse, lies, or oaths. To them, having children was abhorrent. The extinction of the human race seemed their ultimate goal. They believed in reincarnation, living one life after another until they supposedly got it right. They called themselves Good Christians. Pure Ones.

What a joke.

But he wanted to know, "Why did you mention *les Vautours?*"

"To get your attention. And it seemed to have worked."

Not much of an answer, but he cautioned himself to not be too inquisitive and become trapped in his own lies, which would only make things worse. So he diverted things from himself. "You're a fool."

De Foix smiled. "I may be, but I am the fool who has you precisely where I want you."

That was true.

But now he knew his enemy.

CHAPTER 34

Kelsey opened the apartment door and invited her prioress inside.
She'd chosen here for their talk as the safest and most private place.
Home turf. Where she controlled the surroundings. What they were
about to discuss could not be seen or overheard by others. Before
today she and the prioress had enjoyed a cordial, friendly relationship that had stayed at arm's length. Never had she doubted the
older woman's wisdom, leadership, or loyalty. There'd been a great
element of trust.

Which had now been shattered.

They sat in the den and faced each other.

"I understand your anger," the prioress said. "But I had no choice."

"Why did you not just tell me? And ask?"

"I do not have to explain myself."

Her spine stiffened. "You can't be serious. That panel was in my
care. Entrusted to me. A restorer's number one duty is to not harm
what he or she is working on. Mine was destroyed. I was attacked.
You were part of that. I think you definitely need to explain
yourself."

The prioress kept silent and Kelsey allowed her a moment.

"After your call, I made one myself," the older woman said. "I have received permission to relay some confidential information to you. Hopefully, it will provide the explanation you need."

The two women waited in the dark.

They'd entered Saint Bavo's through the front door seven hours earlier, one of many who'd visited the church on April 10, 1934. They'd walked the nave, studied the elaborate rococo pulpit, then wandered through the chancel and its eight chapels. They'd lingered before Rubens' magnificent Saint Bavo Enters the Convent at Ghent, *which the great master called the most beautiful work he'd ever produced. Admired the organ, the choir, the high altar, and the statues of Peter and Paul. Toward the cathedral's closing time they descended to the crypt, the largest in Flanders, lined with exquisite frescoes. Their tour had been not only to admire the majestic interior but also to discover the best place to hide.*

They found a perfect spot and waited until midnight had passed before venturing back up to the nave. All of the maintenance personnel were gone. The coin boxes empty and hidden away beneath the votive candles. The doors were locked, the lights dimmed. The two women were dressed in black, their heads and faces covered with hoods for no one to see. The last thing they needed was to be recognized. The idea was to accomplish their task and leave quickly.

They walked through the nave to the Joos Vijd Chapel, named for the fifteenth-century first alderman of Ghent who, along with his wife, endowed the creation of the famed altarpiece. A padlock sealed its doors, but they'd brought tools and easily freed the lock. Everything about this seemed easy. No security. No guards. Not even barriers to keep visitors from actually touching the painting.

They entered the chapel.

The altarpiece stood about a meter off the ground, closed, its side panels folded inward shielding the main panel depicting the Lamb of God. A cloth draped over it aided with dust control.

Everything had been planned for weeks. Every detail accounted for.

One of the women removed the dust cover and opened the two side wings, which squealed on their hinges. The object of their visit hung at the bottom left of the open altarpiece. It had been carefully studied thanks to photographs taken by other women who'd visited the chapel, with the rest of the public, in recent weeks. Fifty years earlier, when some of the panels were on display in Berlin, they had been sewn through and cradled so that all of the painted surfaces could be shown simultaneously. Repairs had occurred, which made it easy for them to free the hinges and separate the two sides of the panel. There was no need to take the frame itself, so both paintings were pried loose, slightly damaging the olden frames but otherwise not affecting the other images.

They were not here to destroy.

Only to protect.

Both women wore gloves and were slow and methodical in their efforts. The idea was to leave not a shred of evidence that could be used to locate the thieves. Once free, they slid the two panels into burlap sacks, then reclosed the two wings of the altarpiece and re-draped the dust cloth. With the twelfth panel gone a portion of the main panel was now visible. Usually, that could only be seen when the wings were swung open. They each crossed themselves and muttered a quick prayer. Then they left a handwritten note, one designed to misdirect the authorities. Taken from Germany by the Treaty of Versailles. The idea being that this was some sort of act of revenge for the indignities suffered by Germany at the end of World War I.

Then they left the chapel.

"Those two women," the prioress said, "were Maidens of Saint-Michael, pledged to a sacred duty."

She was shocked. "Nuns stole the *Just Judges*?"

The older woman nodded. "That is correct. But something un-expected happened afterward."

She listened as the prioress explained how the two maidens left the cathedral through a side door. No way had existed to relock it, so their exit route would be easy to determine. Once outside they each cradled one of the large sacks and headed off in separate directions. The late hour helped. Few people were out in the cool night. Though by differing routes, their destination was the same. The convent of the maidens on the city's north side.

"They had planned it all so carefully," the prioress said. "Intentionally, they took the front and back of the twelfth panel so as not to draw attention to one side over the other. Unfortunately, once away from the cathedral, the two maidens were attacked and robbed of their panels. Neither was ever seen again. The maidens had received help in planning the theft from people they thought allies. Those men had other plans. They took both panels, then engaged in months of negotiations with the authorities, trying to garner a ransom. At one point, they even returned the panel of St. John the Baptist, as a supposed show of good faith."

Kelsey knew the story.

No ransom was ever paid. Police zeroed in on a Belgian, Arsène Goedertier, who claimed on his deathbed that he had stolen *Just Judges*. But his admission was met with skepticism. He had no real motive, no need for money as he was well off, and he lacked the physical capability to have even executed the theft. Then Goedertier died suddenly in late 1934.

"Copies of the twelve ransom letters were found in Goedertier's home," the prioress said. "The maidens investigated everything thoroughly, but they were never able to locate their lost sisters, find the *Just Judges*, or identify any of Goedertier's accomplices."

"Why did they steal it in the first place?"

"It contains a secret."

"About what?"

"To know that you will have to speak to others."

She was puzzled. "Who?"

"Sister Deal, since our formation, the Congregation of Saint-Luke has maintained a close relationship with the Maidens of Saint-Michael. Our prioress has always come from them. I am but one of a long line to make the transition. Until now, that relationship has been private. But what's happened here over the past few days has changed things significantly. The abbess of the maidens has been in contact with me. It is why I am here. I now know that the laptop you gave me contained no images. You and your acquaintance Nicholas Lee were clever in tricking me. But what you recorded on those images is threatening something that the maidens have guarded for nearly two thousand years."

CHAPTER 35

Nick ranked what he was about to do at the top of his you-gotta-
be-kidding list. He'd first deceived, then made a deal with a group
of nuns who were doing who-knew-what. The one indisputable fact
was that the *Just Judges* had been burned to a cinder by the same
nuns he'd successfully worked into a corner. It had taken them
nearly an hour to call back and arrange for a meeting. But call they
did, choosing home ground at the convent. Which was fine by him,
since he held all of the cards.

A cab dropped him outside the iron gates.

The day had turned warm, the late-afternoon sun beginning its
final act toward the west. He'd made a lot of progress in one day.
Far more than the police. Hopefully Inspector Zeekers would keep
chasing shadows and stay out of the way. He'd stopped by his hotel
and deposited Kelsey's laptop in his room. He hadn't called her
back, preferring to let that stew a little while longer until he could
figure out how best to handle her. She should be fine in her apartment. Time now to see just what in the world was going on.

He stepped through the gate, walked toward the convent's
front entrance, and knocked on the heavy oak slab. The door
was answered not by one of the nuns, but by a tall man with

piercing violet eyes and strong, lean features. The older woman from last night, the one who'd said she was in charge, stood off to the side beside another man. This one shorter, more rotund, with florid jowls hanging to each side of thick lips. The two men were dressed in differing trousers, shirt, and shoes, with jackets, but each sported a chain around his neck from which a cross hung.

Which had to be significant.

"You must be Nicholas Lee," the tall man who answered the door said.

He caught the concerned look on the older nun's face.

"And you are?" he asked.

"Friar Robert Dwight."

He pointed at the other guy. "And him?"

"My associate, Friar Paul Rice."

His gaze shot to the nun, asking with his eyes if she was all right. The older woman nodded. Not a hint of fear filled her eyes. Instead, she seemed on alert, watching, listening.

"I understand that you've come to speak with the maidens," Dwight said. "Instead, you will now speak to me."

"And what will we be talking about?"

"The electronic images of the *Just Judges* that, I'm told, you possess."

"And what's your interest?"

"If you please, I'll be the one asking the questions."

He wasn't sure about the arrogance but decided to let it pass. For the moment. He needed to find out what was going on, as these men's appearance had clearly been unexpected.

"Where is the laptop computer these women say you stole back from them last night?"

Now he understood. The good maidens were playing a shell game of pass the laptop. Smart. Which raised a question.

"Where are the others?" he asked the mother superior.

"They are not your concern," Dwight said.

"If you want those images, they're my concern. That's non-negotiable. And, by the way"—he pointed at the cross around the guy's neck—"what are you?"

"*Domini canes*," the older woman spit out, contempt in her voice.

"Forgive her," Dwight said. "She uses an old Latin pun, a nickname we were sometimes referred to. The master's dogs. The Hounds of the Lord. Which by the way, we take as a badge of honor."

"And who is *we*?"

"I am of the Dominicans," Dwight said. "The insult the mother superior hurled, her reference to hounds, draws on the story that Saint Dominic's mother, while pregnant with him, had a vision of a black-and-white dog with a torch in its mouth. Supposedly, wherever the dog went, it set fire to the earth. That vision was fulfilled when Dominic, and his followers, went forth, clad in black and white, setting fire to the earth with the Gospel. A hound is loyal, and we Dominicans have a reputation as obedient servants of the faith."

"And the cross around your neck?"

"Our symbol. Revealed here," Dwight said, "so the maidens understand that we are not a fraud."

He'd already underestimated one religious group, and he wasn't about to make the same mistake twice. So he calmly asked, "Where are the other maidens?"

Dwight motioned toward the corridor leading out of the foyer.

He headed in that direction, assuming that the others were in the hall he'd spotted during his first visit. Some sort of dining room and gathering spot. He entered and saw more of the older women, two he recognized from the hotel along with the two younger ones. All of them wore the same gray smocks and veils. Another man, with a cross around his neck too, watched over them.

"Satisfied?" Dwight asked him. "What did you think? They were in some sort of danger? I am a friar of the church, not a thug."

"That's open to debate," one of the younger maidens said, the one with the bruised face.

Dwight pointed a finger her way. "You should watch your words."

Actually, Nick thought, *you should watch yours. That woman can hurt you.*

"What are you doing here?" he asked Dwight.

"I've been sent to conduct an investigation."

Now he was intrigued. "By who?"

"The Vatican," the mother superior quickly said.

And he saw the concerned faces of the other maidens. This was apparently not a good thing.

"That's correct," Dwight said. "My mission is one of long standing. Perhaps, finally, we may know the truth, the life. *Veritas Vita.*"

"Is that supposed to mean something?" he asked.

"To you? No. But to these maidens. Absolutely."

Something major was happening here.

And bad.

"These women say you know where the laptop computer they managed to steal last night is located," Dwight said. "One of their own was killed by the police in the process."

This guy had some good intel. The question was, how much did he really know?

Nick tried to recall what he could about Dominicans from his grade-school exposure, as a Protestant, to Catholicism. Founded in the early thirteenth century by a Spanish priest named Félix de Guzmán, who came to be known as Brother Dominic. The order preached the Gospel, opposed heresy, and served as teachers at the forefront of medieval intellectual life. Some called them black friars because of the black cloak they wore over white habits. Also, they'd once sported a distinctive hairstyle. A tonsure. The scalp shaved smooth to a perfect bald cap. In books and movies they were always the scary ones in the dark robes who did all sorts of sinister things.

But that was fiction. Right?

Dwight reached into his pocket and found a cell phone. He tapped the screen then displayed it to him. On it he saw an image he recognized.

"That was taken from the left shoulder of the dead woman from last night," Dwight said.

"And how did you gain access to the body?" he asked.

"The church has many friends in Ghent," one of the friars said with an annoying grin.

"Do you know its significance?" Dwight asked.

"Not a clue."

"Perhaps I should be asking that question to the maidens here in the room." Dwight held the image up and displayed it to them. "Do you recognize this?"

No one spoke.

"I wouldn't think you'd admit to a thing," Dwight said. Then he motioned and the two other friars grabbed the younger maiden with the bruised face, the one who'd insulted Dwight. Nick and the other maidens moved to help, but Dwight displayed a gun, aimed straight at them.

They froze.

"Is that standard issue at the monastery?" he asked Dwight.

"It is today. Now, all of you, step away."

No one moved.

And he brought the gun level to make his point clearer, cocking the hammer back into place.

"Do as he says," Nick urged the women, and they collectively retreated.

But Nick held his ground.

"You too," Dwight said.

"What are you doing with her?" he asked.

"Finding out the truth."

Dwight kept the gun aimed and stepped toward the younger maiden. He grabbed her smock, pulling it back across her left shoulder, ripping buttons away and exposing the skin and bra strap. The other maidens gasped at the violation. But there, tattooed, like on the dead woman from last night, was a vulture.

A smile creased Dwight's thin lips. "*Les Vautours.*"

His French was terrible. "You're going to have to translate that."

"The Vultures," Dwight said. "These women are *les Vautours.*"

"And that is?"

"A thorn in the side of the church. But now we know they have existed, out in the open, right in front of everyone, as the Maidens of Saint-Michael. Finally, we have shed their disguise and located them. And that's all thanks to you, Mr. Lee. You caused quite a disruption in their operation last night."

Dwight motioned with the gun and the two other men released their hold on the maiden, who quickly covered the tear in the smock with her right hand.

"You will regret what you just did," the mother superior said.

Dwight chuckled. "You're an old woman. No threat to anyone."

"I'm not old," the younger maiden who'd been assaulted added.

"This is a lot of intimidation," he said to Dwight.

"Necessary, under the circumstances. These Vultures have been a problem for a long time. And you? They willfully destroyed a great work of art last night. Is it not your job to protect the world's treasures? Now, what about that laptop computer."

"Not going to happen."

He hoped his obstinance bought some brownie points with the maidens.

Dwight, though, only shrugged. "I don't really need those images any longer. I now know exactly where I have to go, and that's what I came to find out."

The friar motioned and his two cohorts headed from the room.

Dwight backed out, gun still pointed. "Please. Stay here until we are gone."

Nick's gaze scanned the room. Nothing from any of the women betrayed even the slightest emotion. They watched calmly as the Dominicans left.

One of the younger women stepped forward. A brunette, with an olive complexion. "Mr. Lee, I am Sister Isabel. My colleague, the one who was just violated, is Sister Ellen. We appreciate what you did."

"You're going to have to tell me what's going on. A woman died last night and a great work of art was intentionally destroyed. That piece of crap that just left here was right. It is my job to look after cultural treasures. What did he mean about knowing exactly where to go?"

The mother superior stepped forward and told the two younger women, "Make the call. Now."

Sisters Isabel and Ellen fled the room.

He faced the older woman. "Are you going to talk to me?"

She nodded. "I am. And you are correct. Nothing about this is good."

CHAPTER 36

Vilamur entered the rectory.

On the drive back to Toulouse from Montségur he'd processed everything. Why this? Why now? Just when everything was falling into place. After all the years that had passed, Bernat de Foix appears? *Do not be deceived. God is not mocked, for whatever one sows, that will he also reap.* Galatians 6:7. Quite apt. And Cathars. Back? Existing? How was that possible?

He'd meant what he'd told de Foix. Cathars were pedantic fools, who regarded the Holy Roman Church, much the same as everything else, as evil, allied to the wrong god. Like there were two different gods? Really? Polytheism had been gone for a long time.

But so had Cathars.

The idiots rejected the entire material world, considered having children offensive, and regarded the church as satanic. For them, anyone who attached great value to things was, at best, mistaken, and, at worst, a disciple of the devil. Sadly, the church of the thirteenth century had certainly provided more than enough support for that conclusion. Popes, cardinals, bishops, and priests of that time all lived in great luxury. They said one thing and did another, elevating hypocrisy into an art form. Even worse, the church had openly encouraged the worship of material objects such as relics and venerated the cross. And for good reason. Both were revenue producers. Cathars liked to quote Matthew. *Watch out for the false prophets who come to you in the guise of lambs, when within lurk voracious wolves. Only their fruit will tell them apart.*

Hence the label the Cathars created for papists.

The Church of Wolves.

And there was much truth to those assertions.

Just like there was to him being Bernat de Foix's biological father.

He'd known Rene. A beautiful woman with curly auburn hair and a bosom he'd greatly admired. She'd been one of his parishioners in Pau over forty years ago. He'd served that parish a long time and there'd been many women. Ten? Twenty? Hard to say. All of them had been married since, after all, those were the safest to pursue. Something about the white collar attracted them. Not a one had ever been forced to do a thing contrary to their desires. All grown adults. Nearly all with children. And when it came time to end things, they all ended easily.

Except for Rene.

She'd birthed a child.

And kept that to herself for ten years.

Amazing.

When the worldwide revelations of clergy sexual abuse were first exposed he'd worried that something from his past might resurface. But nothing had. Whatever happened was long over and none of the women involved wanted any attention brought to it.

He'd chosen them carefully.

Rene had seemed the perfect example.

She'd worked at a local department store. A devout Catholic, active in the church, who regularly took confession. That was where he'd learned about the unhappiness in her marriage. A simple matter from there to lure her into his bed, her vulnerability easy to exploit. Their relationship had been a long one, more so than the others. They'd both seemed to enjoy it and, for a while, he'd devoted himself solely to her. But the inevitable end came and he moved on. She'd taken it fine, just like all of the others, and never created a problem. But what were they going to say? None really wanted to leave their husbands. They just wanted a diversion, the attention, the pleasure, for however long it might last. Then Rene had come back.

With a ten-year old son.

He and Bernat de Foix had swapped saliva samples, each depositing damp swabs into their respective glass vials. But he had no need for a DNA test. He knew then and now.

That man was his son.

"What do you want from me?" he'd asked de Foix, before leaving.

"A great deal, Archbishop. A great, great deal."

None of that had sounded promising.

He assumed de Foix would run the DNA test, not quite as sure about parentage as he wanted him to believe. That should buy a day, maybe two.

Then what?

"You have a visitor," the housekeeper said, interrupting his thoughts.

He stood in the rectory's foyer.

The older woman had been with him a long time and they got along reasonably well. He'd always made a point to never alienate, abuse, or sleep with his staff. They were vital to an orderly progression of things. Parishioners came and went. Diocese employees stayed around a long time.

"Who is it?"

She told him.

And he headed straight for his office.

211

* * *

Hector Cardinal Fuentes rose from the chair as he entered the room. "Archbishop Vilamur, it is a pleasure to meet you."

"Eminence, I thought you said you would be here tomorrow."

"The opportunity presented itself to come immediately, so I took it."

No way that fortuitous occurrence was going to be good for him.

Fuentes was a husky man with bearish shoulders, a thick chest, and meaty arms. He had a broad nose and a heavy shelf of thick eyebrows under close-cropped auburn hair. Well groomed, the face, the eyes, the creases in the skin all conveyed a perpetually intense look, which, he assumed, fit this man's mood more often than not. Cardinals by and large were an aloof group. There were only 221 on the planet, 128 of them below the age of eighty and eligible to elect a pope. Fuentes appeared to be one of the younger ones. Mid- to late sixties, possibly. The question for the moment, though, was what was he doing here? And what did he want?

They both sat in chairs, facing each other.

Fuentes, like himself, was dressed casually in trousers, shirt, and jacket. No ring. No cross. Not a thing that identified him as a prince in the Holy Roman Church. Which also raised warning flags.

"You look like you've been hiking," Fuentes said.

"I had to travel to the south to see about things. I decided a walk in the mountains would be good."

"Was it?"

"Delightful."

"I love the outdoors. Unfortunately, I don't get to enjoy it much anymore."

He decided to get to the point. "What brings you here? And why all the interest in what happened to Father Tallard?"

"Let me be clear. I care nothing for that deviant priest. You were correct. Whoever killed him did the world a favor. But that video confession is something that interests me, along with Cathars and *les Vautours*. Two subjects I have long been fascinated with."

He now knew that all of the information anonymously sent to him had come from Bernat de Foix, who apparently was incredibly well informed about something important enough to stir the Vatican.

"Will you be explaining why you have such an interest in those two subjects?" he asked, keeping his voice controlled. "Or will I be working in the dark?"

Fuentes grinned and motioned with his hands. "That is precisely why I am here. But first, Archbishop, is it possible to have some dinner. It is nearly 6:00 p.m., and I have neglected to eat since this morning."

He'd spent his entire clerical life dealing with people. Some priests focused entirely on their parishioners, ignoring ambition, intent only on human relations. Others were more aloof, keeping their distance, directing their attention toward the politics of religion rather than its substance. He liked to navigate a middle-of-the-road approach, interested in parishioners but always conscious of the lay of the land around him. Always looking for the next fork in the road. Which explained his rise from priest, to monsignor, to archbishop, to metropolitan archbishop, to, he hoped, cardinal.

Be careful, he told himself. *Be really, really careful.* He'd drawn Rome's interest, and the man sitting before him had the pope's ear. A word from him could make or break. Something here, in Toulouse, had grabbed Fuentes's attention. So he could be either a help or a hindrance. And he'd learned long ago that hindrances ended up with nothing.

"I'm sure the cook is preparing my dinner as we speak," he said. "I will make sure there is plenty for two."

"That is most kind of you. But perhaps we could go out to eat. I would so like to see Toulouse again. It has been a long time since I visited."

Okay. Plan B. "I will make us a reservation."

"I will also need a place to stay."

He knew the correct response. "I have five bedrooms. Pick whichever one you desire."

"Again. Most kind."

Like he had a choice.

Fuentes pointed a stubby finger. "I was told by those who know that you are a good man to have on your side. The pope himself is aware of you. But let me make something clear. Your cooperation here will have a direct bearing on whether you remain in good favor."

As if he did not already know that.

"Be assured, Cardinal Fuentes, you will have my undivided attention."

CHAPTER 37

Nick and the mother superior retreated to a small office not far from the dining hall. There, behind a closed door, the older woman faced him.

"There are many, many religious organizations," she said. "Each has its own purpose. Its own meaning. They cover everything and anything. The one common denominator, though, is an unwavering devotion to the particular duty, or duties, they select."

"And what is the duty of the Maidens of Saint-Michael?"

"To serve the poor and help the disadvantaged. Along with another, more sacred responsibility." She paused. "To protect a secret."

"Are you *les Vautours*?"

She nodded.

"Why are the Dominicans focused on you?"

"The Vatican has been seeking us for a long time. But we've managed to evade them at every turn, which was no small feat. Our luck, though, has finally run out."

"Do you have a vulture on your left shoulder too?"

"I led the maidens for fifteen years," she said. "I did my best, as have all of the other women who came before and after. I know the current abbess would vehemently disagree, but I'm trusting you. You seem like a decent person. I was told about what you did at the hotel, helping with the escape. With the Dominicans at our door, I have no choice, Mr. Lee. We need your help. Please don't make me regret this."

"How about you answer my question."

"I have a vulture on my shoulder. As do all of the maidens. It is placed there after taking an oath. It reminds us of our duty."

"Which is?"

"To guard the truth."

He could see that she meant every word. This was no fanatic. Or dreamer. Whatever was involved seemed deep-set, reverent.

"Trusting outsiders has proven a problem for us in the past. That's why we deal with things ourselves, in our own way. The truth we protect is not something the Vatican supports. Quite the contrary. Many popes have preferred that it go away, which has placed us at odds with Rome for centuries. But this is the first time that they have ever been able to positively identify us."

He understood. "Because of me? And what happened last night?"

She nodded. "It was an unprecedented breach of our security. You heard Friar Dwight. He knows where to go now. He doesn't need those images you guard. They are irrelevant now. The path straight to us has been brightly illuminated."

"Where will they go?"

"To our motherhouse, in southern France. They came here first. To be sure. Now they are."

"It would help if you'd stop talking in riddles and tell me the situation."

He could see the older woman was conflicted. A part of her seemed to want to talk, while another part, one trained and hewn from years of experience, cautioned silence.

Finally, she said, "Do you know much about Jan van Eyck?"

"Only that he created the Ghent Altarpiece, finishing what his brother started."

"He did just that. But he also went a step further."

In late spring of 1428 Jan van Eyck found himself along the border with Spain and the Languedoc. He'd been sent south from Burgundy by his patron, Philip the Good, on a reconnaissance mission to map mountain passes. Philip was then in a state of civil war against the French dauphin, blaming Charles for the murder of his father, John the Fearless. Charles saw Philip's Burgundian state as a serious impediment to the expansion of French royal authority. Finally, in 1420, Philip formally allied himself with Henry V of England against Charles. In 1423, the marriage of Philip's sister Anne to the Duke of Bedford, regent for Henry VI, further strengthened the English alliance.

During all of those conflicts van Eyck engaged in covert missions for Philip, using the guise of an artist to make detailed observations. He was nearly the perfect spy and Philip had been thrilled with the results. So much so that in 1428 he dispatched van Eyck to the south and the cursed Languedoc, a place that had been a thorn in the French monarchy's side for a long time. Philip planned to sow further discontent for Charles by stirring up the south. Van Eyck completed his mission but was discovered by Moors and chased over the border into the Pyrénées, where he happened upon a mountain convent. Women the Moors would not defy. Women who bore a strange name.

Les Vautours.

He spent a week with the Maidens of Saint-Michael, marveling at their closed community and making friends. That friendship was tested in 1431 when Joan of Arc was burned at the stake. By a stroke of good fortune van Eyck's patron, Philip the Good, had been the one who captured and sold Joan to the English. During her four-month trial the maidens reestablished contact with Jan van Eyck. Their first desire was to effect a rescue. But when that became impossible, it had been van

Eyck who aided them in retrieving Joan's ashes. Those were taken south, to the mountains and the motherhouse, where they were reverently buried in what was known as the Chapel of the Maiden.

"Joan was one of us," the mother superior said. "She was so young. A mere postulant, who left the motherhouse and ventured north, thrusting herself into the Hundred Years' War. But we revere her and, from 1431 onward, we wore gray smocks in honor of Joan, who wore one to her death. And if that had been the end of the story, all would be good. But there's more. Jan van Eyck betrayed us."

He waited for her to explain.

"For reasons known only to him, after helping us secure Joan's remains, he included a way to find them on the Ghent Altarpiece," the mother superior said, "which he was working on at the time. A map, if you will. Cleverly presented. Hidden. But there nonetheless. We became aware of that sometime in the late fifteenth century, but it never grew into a problem until 1934. That was when the Vatican first learned of the connection between the altarpiece and *les Vautours*. How? That's unknown, but we were able to steal the *Just Judges* before any detailed examination could be made."

"The maidens stole the *Just Judges*?"

"We did."

"But there were other copies of the altarpiece," he said. "Several, in fact, around Europe."

"That's true, but none contained the detail of van Eyck's original. How could they? The dirt and grime on the panels was extensive, masking so much. Any artist trying to make a copy would be hampered. It was not until recently, when the latest restoration was performed, that all was revealed in its original glory. I'm sure those copies were examined after 1934 by the Vatican, but they led nowhere."

He was puzzled. "This is about the ashes of Joan of Arc?"

218

"No, Mr. Lee. It is about something far greater, something far more important. Something the Vatican and the maidens vehemently disagree upon."

He'd definitely stumbled into something significant. Maybe even extraordinary, involving far more than the willful destruction of a national art treasure. His job was to investigate, so that's what he planned to do.

A knock came to the door, which opened, and Sister Ellen entered. "Excuse me, Mother Superior, but the Vestal wants to speak with Mr. Lee."

He accepted a cell phone.

"My name is Claire," the voice said in his ear. "I believe you were in my room last night."

"I was."

"I assume you're not going to go away?"

"I can't. Not now. But I'm not the police. I'm not the Vatican. My focus is protecting cultural heritage. Something was lost yesterday. Help me understand why, then maybe I can walk away."

"I have many issues to consider. Not the least of which is my friend, lying dead in the local morgue. Whose body, I am told, was disgracefully photographed by the Dominicans."

"I'm sorry about that."

"We need to free her from there," Claire said.

An idea occurred to him. The images he possessed were no longer a bargaining chip. So if he was going to keep making progress with these women he had to gain their trust. The mother superior had started the ball rolling.

"What if I could get her body back?" he asked.

"That would be most appreciated."

She paused.

"In many ways."

CHAPTER 38

The village of Las Illas sat niched against the Pyrénées, in a swath of mountainous terrain that lay at the fringe of what would one day be called France. The only road leading to it was lined with tamarisk, an occasional almond tree, and plenty of silver poplars whose white leaves shook against the blue sky. It had existed for over fifteen hundred years, once an important settlement, a place where Hannibal had encamped after crossing the Pyrénées in 218 BC. Its small cathedral was classic Romanesque. A fortified church, built of solid masonry, with the narrow-est of loopholes serving as windows. The town was one of the earliest Christian strongholds west of Rome and, up to AD 600, housed a bishop. By 1200, it had dropped to the status of a mere parish, its church inside cruelly denuded and gaunt, all of the silver and gold sold off long ago. One treasure, though, had been spared. It occupied a side chapel without windows, which cast it in shadow and made it hard to see.

An altarpiece. Painted on wood, representing Saint Michael.

On the morning of June 9, 1210, a small contingent of soldiers ap-proached the town's outer walls. The main attack force was over a hundred kilometers away, ravaging the Languedoc, rooting out heretics, killing Cathars. The Albigensian Crusade was proceeding, town after town falling. This group was a special contingent selected by the Dominicans to carry out a clandestine operation under direct orders from the pope. They'd broken from the main army and traveled south, staying off the roads, making their way past the forested foothills and up into the mountains.

Waiting for them on the path ahead stood a man wearing a faded bonnet. He had a lean face, close-shaven like a priest, with a blue jowl and a long chin, the eyes small and deep-set. One of those inscrutable Spanish faces that suggested much and told little. He was clearly aged, but walked with a springy step, shifting on his feet like a cat. They'd been warned about him. Half priest, half villain, superstitious, devout, a man who would knife anybody for a silver coin. No surprise that he was the first to greet them.

"We are here for les Vautours," one of the soldiers called out.

The old man waved them off. "Leave. Now. You are wasting your time."

None of them were in the mood for defiance. They'd experienced enough of that over the past few months, and their response had always been the same.

"Deal with him," the Dominican who'd come south with them ordered.

Two of their number drew swords and advanced, skewering the old man.

The body dropped to the dusty road.

The contingent proceeded ahead through the open gate, into a small central square. The people here existed in relative isolation, belonging to nobody but themselves, the long uphill trek more of a barrier than a link with the outside world. Living here with the wind, and the menace of the rocky heights, it was easy to understand how the residents became comatose, shut out, buried into themselves.

Unafraid.

"Move out," the Dominican said, "and bring everyone you find to the church."

Kelsey sat still in the chair, listening to her prioress. "Did they find anyone?"

"The locals had seen the soldiers coming, so most had hidden themselves away. They managed to find one woman, whom they dragged screaming from her children. They cut off her ear and tossed it in the main square, with an announcement that if the villagers did not surrender themselves, more parts of her would be severed. An hour later they cut the other ear off. Still, no one appeared. They were about to cut her hand off when the residents surrendered. Each was questioned. None provided a shred of information. So the women were raped, then everyone was slaughtered."

She was shocked. "What were they after?"

"The Chapel of the Maiden," the prioress said. "The women of Las Illas had once been *la garde d'honneur*. The guard of honor. Protecting it. But the crusaders were ill informed since, by the time they arrived, that duty had long passed to others."

Now she understood. "The Maidens of Saint-Michael?"

The older woman nodded. "They became the guardians."

"Of what?"

The Gospels of Matthew, Mark, Luke, and John, which lay at the heart of the New Testament, were all penned by the beginning of the second century after Christ. Mark and John's accounts were silent as to Christ's birth. For them Jesus existed only as an adult, his adolescence never discussed. Mary was mentioned only in passing in one line of Mark. Luke and Matthew dealt with Christ's birth and referenced Mary, but neither delved into her origins or subsequent life. Instead, she appears as a woman, ready to accept the virgin birth as the wife of Joseph. In none of the Gospels was Mary ever a constant companion of her son. In fact, mentions of her were rare. Mark, Luke, and John recounted the crucifixion with no mention of Mary. Only John placed her at the foot of the cross, and the apostle Paul never named her in any of his famed letters.

The Council of Nicaea in 325 started the notion of Mary being a virgin, enthroned beside the Lord as a bridge between heaven and earth.

It also bestowed upon her the title Mother of God. Theotokus in Greek. A fragment of a prayer found from then on papyrus proclaimed, Mother of God, hear my supplication, suffer us not to be in adversity, but deliver us from danger. Thou alone. *The logic became easy. If Christ was God, then Mary was the Mother of God. The great theologian Saint Augustine reinforced this notion when he wrote that no one, save for Mary, had been born without sin.*

She alone was pure.

For biblical support they looked to Revelation. Chapter 12. And there appeared a great wonder in heaven, a woman clothed with the sun, and the moon under her feet, and upon her head a crown of twelve stars. And she being with child cried, traveling in birth, and pained to be delivered. *Further chapters noted that the child was to rule all nations, caught up unto God and to his throne, equating that with Christ, the crowned woman his mother.*

By the fifth century divisions had arisen within Christianity that questioned whether Christ had been born of a woman, and whether any woman was worthy of such an honor. Some argued that divine nature cannot be born. It can have no mother. Mary may have been a good pious woman, but she was not the queen of heaven. The betrayal of Eve in the Garden had not been forgotten, Mary regarded as Eve without the fall— a figure from the past, just another part of Christ's evolving story.

Nothing more.

The oldest surviving reference to her childhood was found in the Protevangelium, *a second-century text possibly written by James of Ephesus. By the sixth century that account was deemed apocryphal, not part of official church dogma, a mere story, but it remained popular, providing Mary with a rich detailed life befitting her status as the supposed Mother of God. As time went on the account provided church theologians with fodder for the creation of a full-fledged Marian legend. Supposedly, she was born into a devout Jewish family in Galilee. Her parents were Joachim and Anne, whom Catholic tradition says angels visited separately to inform them that Anne was expecting Mary. By the time Mary was twelve, she was engaged to Joseph. It was during her engagement that she learned, through another angelic visitation, of the plans God had for her to serve as Christ's mother. She responded with faithful obedience, despite the obvious challenges.*

Matthew wrote that Mary and Joseph raised Christ, along with their other children. Protestant Christians think that those children were Mary and Joseph's, born naturally after Jesus, and after they formally consummated their marriage. But Catholics thought that they were cousins, or Mary's stepchildren from Joseph's former marriage to a woman who had died before he became engaged to her. Catholics fervently believe that Mary remained a virgin her entire life.

By the Middle Ages, Mary had been allocated five holy days. Her cult of worship became rooted, flowing from the crusades, encouraged by contact with the Byzantine church, which had long idolized her. New art, poetry, and the romanticism of women helped with her elevation. The rise of monasticism also played a part. Mary became the heavenly helper to the vowed celibate, male or female. Eventually, Catholic teachings said that the quickest path to Jesus was through Mary, as he always did as his mother asked. She was planted above the angels, equal to her son, in a class by herself, accorded the title Blessed, which acknowledged her exalted state as the greatest among the saints. Those teachings also made it clear, though, that Mary was not divine. Any prayers were not answered by her, but rather by God through her intercession.

Five sacred dogmas regarding her emerged.

Her own Immaculate Conception, making her free of original sin. The Annunciation from the Archangel Gabriel. Her status as the Mother of God. Her perpetual virginity. And her final bodily Assumption into heaven.

The first and last of those became the most troubling.

Early on theologians purged Mary of personal sin, even the original sin that required baptism to eliminate. How? She was the Mother of

God. Potuit, decuit, fecit. *It was possible, it was fitting, therefore it was done. But for centuries theologians debated that point. Some argued that if Mary was free of original sin at her own conception then she would have no need of redemption, making Christ superfluous. Others reasoned that Christ was Mary's personal redeemer, his birth and presence shielding her from original sin.*

Her Assumption into heaven became equally problematic. Matthew wrote, Truly, I say to you, there are some standing here who will not taste death before they see the Son of Man coming in His kingdom. *Theologians took that to mean that an assumption was possible. Dead-yet-not-dead. Gone-yet-not-gone.*

But nothing seemed clear.

So the church stepped in to erase all doubt.

In 1431 the Council of Basel declared Mary's Immaculate Conception as a pious opinion consistent with faith and Scripture. During the Council of Trent, held in the early 1500s, she was exempted from the universality of original sin. In 1571 Pope Pius V set out an elaborate celebration of the Feast of the Immaculate Conception, to be held on December 8 of each year. In the sixteenth and seventeenth centuries the Habsburg monarchs, who dominated Europe, demanded that the papacy elevate the immaculate conception to official dogma. Finally, in 1854 Pope Pius IX issued a papal bull, Ineffabilis Deus, *that officially proclaimed Mary's Immaculate Conception. He found support for the event in the ark of salvation, Jacob's ladder, the burning bush at Sinai, the enclosed garden from the Song of Songs, and other biblical passages. Particularly Genesis 3:15. The most glorious Virgin was foretold by God when he said to the serpent,* "I will put enmity between you and the woman."

Kelsey sat silent as her prioress told her things, most of which she already knew. The study of the Virgin Mary was mandatory for all novices in the Congregation of Saint-Luke.

"Then," Kelsey added, "having completed the course of her earthly life, as a divine gift to her as the Mother of God, her body and soul were taken up into the glory of heaven. That's what Pius XII proclaimed in 1950."

"And that bold declaration was backed up by papal infallibility," her prioress said. "The pope is never wrong when it comes to dogma, and Pius' *Munificentissimus Deus* was just that. He emphasized Mary's unity with her divine son and, as his mother, she is the mother of his church, which is his body. She is the new Eve, a term he used three times, making Christ the new Adam. Her ascension was the final bodily resurrection promised to all Christians. So she was received into heaven, the recipient of corporeal glory."

The older woman paused.

"But, Kelsey, what if Pius XII was wrong?"

CHAPTER 39

Bernat had felt at peace being back near Montségur. He'd lived his entire life within the Languedoc, born and raised in the mountains toward the west, but growing into a man in Toulouse. He'd always made a point to stay near Gerard Vilamur, never allowing the way-ward prelate to venture too far out of range. For a while Vilamur had been a few hundred kilometers to the north in Albi, serving as bishop. But an elevation to archbishop and a return to Toulouse had proven ideal.

He'd worked hard establishing his auction house as one of good repute. Other houses, those with grand international reputations, always possessed larger and more valuable inventories. They also produced steady, astronomical sales. They were leaders in fine arts and in bringing lost treasures back to light, their collections making headlines and appearing in publications for museum and gallery professionals, artists, and historians. Places like Sotheby's, Christie's, Beijing Poly International, and Heritage. His business occupied the next tier down. One that focused on regional art and estate sales, branching out into real estate and racehorses. He'd never realized such a robust market existed for the sale of horses bred to run. But there he'd made a respectable fortune and was known throughout Europe as the man who could find a winner.

He was blessed with an eye for business and made even more money with smart investments in banks and wineries. True, this world, and all its physical attributes, was evil and he would eventually flee it. But this also wasn't the thirteenth century and Catharism had adapted to the times. Being nearly wiped out brought about a few changes in doctrine. Physical things were still evil, but some were necessary tools, needed for both existence and survival.

Like money.

The trick was not to allow that evil to consume you and to eventually shed yourself of it all.

Personally, he did not collect what was valuable or what might accrue in value through the years. His eye was drawn only to what spoke to him. Yes, he possessed the requisite amount of paintings and sculptures that could always be sold for profit. But the vast majority of his personal art collection related to the Languedoc, created by local artists, reflecting its long history of expression and repression. Becoming involved with the restoration of the *Just Judges'* reproduction had been conceived as a way to finally bring him onto the world stage.

He and Andre had left Montségur and driven north about twenty-five kilometers, enjoying dinner in Mirepoix, with its magnificent arcaded square, bordered by houses dating from the thirteenth century. It had been a Cathar stronghold until Simon de Montfort captured it in September 1209 and gave it to his most loyal lieutenant.

How utterly arrogant.

Darkness had come during the meal, which they'd enjoyed at one of the outdoor cafés. Then they'd driven west from town, toward Foix, venturing off the highway into the thick woods where a bonfire burned. Gathered around were about thirty men and women, all dressed in black robes. Each was a Perfectus who served a community of believers. They existed in secret and kept their identities and beliefs within the Cathar community. Recruits, like Andre, appeared from time to time, and each was dealt with individually. Thankfully, modern society allowed a huge amount of religious freedom and few cared anymore what people worshiped, so long as those beliefs were not forced onto others. Not all that dissimilar to the Languedoc before the crusaders arrived.

Once every three months the Perfecti gathered at different spots across the region to talk, pray, and communicate. When together they formed the Elders and made decisions relative to their ever-evolving religion. Being a Cathar came with rewards in the form of peace and solitude, a contentment that few in the world experienced. That was one of the reasons he'd been drawn to it, which helped with his inner demons. The other was its juxtaposition to the Catholic Church. A direct counter to Rome in every single way that mattered.

And that really appealed to him.

"This is an opportunity for you to meet others," he said to Andre as they both donned robes. "Your first as a Perfectus. Some you know, but circulate around and introduce yourself to those you don't. These are your peers now."

Andre nodded and walked off.

He headed beyond the fire to an older man sitting alone in the dark on one of the wooden benches beneath the trees. The land for nearly a kilometer in every direction was owned by a believer, so the gathering was assured privacy. He walked over and sat on the bench beside Raymond Barbe, the oldest living Perfectus. How old? Nobody really knew. Most guessed ninety to ninety-five.

"I made contact today." He spoke in Occitan, which they both understood.

"What was it like?" Raymond asked, the voice rough and gravelly, as if it hurt to talk. "How did it feel to face him again?"

How had it felt? He'd come to despise Gerard Vilamur, a man who for all his righteous correctness was nothing more than an arrogant hypocrite who preyed on vulnerable women.

"Strange, actually," he said. "All that anger, which I've been amassing for thirty-two years, was instantly replaced by an immense satisfaction. A feeling that I had him right where I wanted him."

His mother never remarried, raising him alone, then dying of breast cancer before making it to age sixty. To her final breath she never said a foul word about Vilamur.

"He's your father," she told him, struggling to breathe. "Find him. Make him accept you."

"He said he never wanted to hear from us again. He denied everything. He was cruel to you."

"I loved him, Bernat. God help me, but I did. I still love him."

"But what of your husband?"

"I loved him too. Only differently."

Incredibly, in her mind, what happened between her and Vilamur had always seemed her fault. Unhappy in her marriage, she'd tempted a priest and caused *his* fall from grace. Not the other way around. The burden of raising a child on her own became a sort of penance for that perceived sin, which she'd accepted with the grace of a fool. He'd loved her as a son should love his mother, but the older he became the more he realized where the fault lay.

"The one who does what is sinful is of the devil, because the devil has been sinning from the beginning," he said.

Raymond smiled. "The Gospel of John is always instructive. Here's some more. *You belong to your father, the devil, and you*

230

want to carry out your father's desires. He was a murderer from the beginning, not holding to the truth, for there is no truth in him. When he lies, he speaks his native language, for he is a liar and the father of lies."

"That he is. And now I have that cheat and liar precisely where I want him."

"Don't get ahead of yourself."

Good advice.

He owed this old man everything. Fifteen years ago, Raymond had been his *socius* when he'd ascended to the Perfecti. True to the name, the old man had been a comrade who shared both his labors and his hardships. He'd confided in Raymond and told him the truth about himself. Together, over the years, they'd formulated the plan he was now implementing. Raymond had been the one to tell him about *les Vautours*.

"The Holy Roman Church has always been interested in them. Trust me on this. That curiosity dates all the way back to our time. Before the crusade."

"Do you know why?"

"I was never told. Only that the group had caused the church many problems and they wanted to eliminate them while they were eliminating us."

So he'd included a reference in his second communication with Vilamur simply as a misdirection since he could not then reveal the real reason for the extortion, not until they were face-to-face. He wanted to watch the reaction for himself. But it had not been much. Vilamur had stuck to his lie. Which he could, for a few days more.

"I'm having the DNA test run," he said. "I'll be taking the samples to a lab tomorrow."

"That will be the incontrovertible proof," Raymond said. "Then, and only then, will you have him where you want him."

Fifty meters away the bonfire continued to burn and the Perfecti were mingling among themselves all around it.

"It's good to see them all together," Raymond said.

That it was.

"The sinner priest is dead?" Raymond asked.

He nodded. "Gone to hell, where he belongs."

Killing had never been part of Cathar doctrine. But allowing a predator like Tallard to continue to live seemed even worse. So they'd compromised and outsourced the task. Good thing he could afford to hire the right people.

"Andre is proving to be an excellent recruit," he said.

"That is good to hear. I feel for him. He endured a lot. We need more like him."

"I'll make sure we get them. There is another problem."

And he told Raymond about what happened in Ghent.

His old friend was shocked. It had been Raymond who told him about the original *Just Judges* being hidden beneath the reproduction.

"*Why are you telling me this?*" he asked.

"*You are my dear friend. That masterpiece has lain hidden for a long time. You should be the one credited for its rediscovery. That will help your business immensely.*"

Yes, it would.

And he'd appreciated the inside information.

"*Are you sure that the original is there?*" he asked Raymond.

"*Nothing is a certainty, besides death. But I have no reason to believe that what I know is false.*"

And Raymond had explained that the creator of the reproduction, Jef Van der Veken, lived to the age of ninety-two, dying in 1964. Van der Veken had continued to ply his trade as an art restorer, copyist, and forger after 1945 until blindness forced him to stop. His son-in-law, Albert Philippot, an artist too, gradually took over his tasks. It had been Philippot who oversaw the 1950 restoration of the Ghent Altarpiece.

"*His father-in-law confided in him that the original lay beneath,*" Raymond said. "*He'd been involved with the 1934 theft. But when his co-conspirator died of a heart attack he was left with the* Just Judges. *When he was asked to create a reproduction for the cathedral he used the opportunity to hide the original back in plain sight. Quite brilliant, actually. During the 1950 restoration, Philippot confirmed that fact for himself, but told no one.*"

"*Why would he keep that secret?*"

"*He was one of us.*"

"*Cathar?*"

Raymond nodded. "*A Perfectus. He hated the Roman Catholic Church and loved his father-in-law. To hurt the one and protect the other, he kept Van der Veken's secret. Before he died in 1974, he told me. We were friends for a long time. Now I'm telling you. Use this opportunity and bring it back to life. Make a name for yourself.*"

Which was precisely what he'd done.

"I worry about you, Bernat," Raymond said.

He smiled. "And I appreciate your concern. You have been more than good to me."

"It's curious why someone would destroy that panel, but perhaps the images of it might still be enough for you to garner some recognition."

They'd timed the attack on Vilamur to happen while the *Just Judges* made its reemergence. A one-two punch. Acclaim from one direction. Satisfaction from the other. The cathedral curator had told him a few days ago that a press conference would happen shortly when the world would be told what had been found. The attack might well alter that timetable. He was still waiting on the curator to forward Sister Deal's images.

"Careful, my friend," Raymond said. "The barrel regarding the church and Vilamur has been jostled. You have no idea what might spill out."

"It doesn't matter, I'm way ahead of them."

Raymond shook his head.

"That's what our ancestors, who once filled these woods, thought too. But a papal army came and look what happened to them."

CHAPTER 40

Vilamur strolled with Cardinal Fuentes down the streets of Toulouse. They'd enjoyed dinner at his favorite restaurant, sitting at his usual table, the meal interrupted several times by parishioners stopping by and extending him greetings. Here, in the heart of the city, he was well known. But he'd always made a point to be visible, accessible, making sure that his was the face of the diocese. At Fuentes's request he'd kept the cardinal's identity confidential, introducing him with another name, explaining he was a friend from Spain visiting for a few days. He assumed that the cardinal, unlike himself, kept a much lower profile.

"Let me see if I have my history correct," Fuentes said as they walked. "St. Saturnin was the first bishop of Toulouse. Supposedly, he was the son of Aegeus, king of Achaea. He lived in the first century and some chroniclers have described him as one of the seventy-two disciples of Christ, placing him at the Last Supper. Quite an honor. Peter himself supposedly consecrated him a bishop. But who knows if any of that is accurate?"

He agreed. There was simply no way to know what happened that far back, as few records had survived.

"But," Fuentes said, "like with most of the important people from that time, his death had greater significance than his life. Strange how that is."

Yes, it was.

"Supposedly, Saturnin lived here, in Toulouse. Each day, to reach the local Christian church he had to pass by the Capitole. The pagan priests had an altar there and they began to blame the silence of their oracles on his regular appearances. So one day they seized him and tied his feet to a bull, which dragged him about the town, killing him. How am I doing?"

"Quite well, Eminence."

Fuentes stopped walking, clearly pleased with himself. "Where the bull stopped and the rope broke, Saturnin lay dead. Two Christian women gathered his remains and buried them right there. Which, if I'm not mistaken, is somewhere here, on this street. Correct?"

He nodded. "That's why it is named the Rue du Taur, street of the bull. The church of Notre-Dame du Taur, right over there, is regarded as the place where the bull stopped. The saint's bones were there until the basilica was built farther down that way. We recently completed a renovation of the tomb. I reconsecrated it this morning."

"Ah, that's right," Fuentes said. "I saw a news clipping from one of your local papers. I did some reading on the flight over from Rome. After all, I do head the Pontifical Commission for Sacred Archaeology. So I should know these things. Right?"

He knew the correct answer. "Of course."

They kept walking and entered the plaza before the basilica, lit to the night. People milled about in every direction.

"Archbishop," Fuentes said. "As I mentioned on the telephone, it's important that you tell me exactly why you were provided that email referring to les Vautours. Why you? Why now?"

He did not know what to say.

"And, please, do not lie or try to say it was all because of Father

Tallard. The truth I can deal with. I can even be helpful. But lies? That will bring you nothing but misery from me."

That he believed. So he decided to take a chance. "I have a son."

If Fuentes was surprised, the man showed not a hint.

"Conceived when you were a priest?"

He nodded. "He's a grown man now and had Father Tallard killed. He's using the fact that Tallard told me everything, in the confessional, about his past sexual deviancies, as blackmail on me and the church. He's the one who sent the video to me."

"What does he want?"

"I don't know. I met with him earlier and learned little. Right now, he just wants DNA tests."

They were standing off to themselves. No one within twenty meters. He sensed that Fuentes had maneuvered him here on purpose, wanting this conversation in public. Perhaps as a way to further assert control since, after all, what could he do in opposition? Walk away? Get angry? Raise his voice? Create a scene? Hardly.

"This supposed son of yours knows of *les Vautours?*"

"Apparently so."

"Do you have any idea how?"

He shook his head. "Today was the first time I've seen him in over thirty years. I probed, but he offered nothing."

"I would like to speak to him."

"He's also Cathar."

That brought a momentary reaction to the stone face. "So he hates you *and* the church?"

"Apparently."

"There is no doubt?" Fuentes asked. "He is your son?"

"His mother confronted me with that fact long ago. I knew then that she was telling the truth."

"Where is she?"

"He told me she was dead. I have not seen her in a long time."

"How many women were there?"

No sense lying. "Quite a few. But none ever presented a problem, save for her."

"And your son now has your DNA."

He shrugged. "No one witnessed what we did but the two of us. Deniability still exists. But I doubt all he wants is to establish parentage. He had a man killed just to gain my attention. He's after something else. Something bigger."

"That's quite obvious. Any idea what?"

"Probably to expose me as a lying, cheating hypocrite and the church as the protector of sexual predators."

"My thoughts exactly. Double revenge. But the mention of the Vultures? That's the puzzling part of this."

He realized that he would not be the first cardinal with a questionable past. Truth be told, most of them harbored more than one secret. But the problem was more acute. He *wasn't* a cardinal.

Not yet.

"The Pontifical Commission for Sacred Archaeology was created to watch over and protect the ancient cemeteries beneath St. Peter's Basilica," Fuentes said. "That is our primary obligation. But we also have a duty to safeguard the oldest memories of the first Christian centuries, wherever that might be. That grants me a fair amount of latitude. Do you play golf?"

He shook his head.

"A shame. It's a wonderful game. Quite relaxing. There are out-of-bounds markers all along the course defined by white stakes. Places you cannot venture without a penalty stroke. The commission's markers are spaced out too, but quite wide, offering plenty of room for me to play."

He was a bit frustrated with all the hedging. "Eminence, I've been painfully honest with you. Could you extend me the same courtesy?"

Fuentes smiled. "Since 1852, only nine men have headed the pontifical commission. The tenure for each was long. All competent individuals who performed their job with skill and dedication. I was appointed by the last pope and kept in the job by the current one. With your help, Archbishop, we are going to finally solve a mystery that has plagued the church for a long, long time."

Now he was intrigued.

Fuentes motioned. "Let's walk and enjoy this marvelous evening. Along the way, in return for your honesty, I'll tell you something that few on this earth know."

Chapter 41

Kelsey was unsure what to make of all that was happening. Her emotions had spanned a wide spectrum. First anger toward her prioress, then amazement, distrust, confusion, and finally curiosity. The comment *What if Pius XII was wrong* had definitely intrigued her. Which had surely been its purpose. But her superior had declined to elaborate any further, saying that they were needed across town and all would be explained then.

"*And pack your things,*" the prioress said. "*You won't be returning.*"

They'd both left the apartment and headed out on the streets. She wanted to call Nick and tell him she was leaving but the prioress had insisted that she surrender her phone. She'd first donned the dark-green smock that all the sisters of Saint-Luke wore, but her prioress had told her to change back into street clothes. She rarely wore her habit while on assignment. It was just easier to look like everyone else than to explain her presence. But she'd thought the assignment over, time to re-don her uniform.

"Where are we going?" she asked, a bit irritated at the silence.

"Sister, somewhere along the way you've lost sight of the fact that I'm your superior. I don't have to explain myself."

"You lost my unquestioned allegiance when you lied to me."

"I never lied. I simply withheld the entire story. And, by the way, you lied too. I asked if there were copies of those images and you said no."

"There were no copies. Just my original file."

"Moved somewhere else. Now who is splitting hairs?"

She desperately wanted to make sense of things, but realized that the prioress was only going to tell her the barest minimum.

"We are going to meet some people who can answer your questions," her prioress suddenly said.

"Thank you. For telling me."

They were headed away from Saint Bavo's, past a row of local landmarks, strung together like rides at Disneyland. First the Belfort, the ancient bell tower lit to the night. Then the Stadshal, an odd-shaped canopy that stood at nearly the center of town. And finally two churches, the first dedicated to St. Nicholas, the second, across the river, to St. Michael. She'd walked by here many times over the past few weeks, enjoying the sights. One of the things she truly missed from before taking her vows was unlimited human interaction. Living within a convent came with limitations. Some she liked, others not so much. Being on assignment offered her the freedom to interact at will. She'd always been a social animal, unlike Nick who leaned more toward being a loner. That was another thing that had made them great together. Their strengths and weaknesses had complemented the other's.

"Prioress, I'm sorry for my impertinence," she felt compelled to say. "But this situation is extraordinary, to say the least."

Which seemed like an understatement.

"I am telling myself," the older woman noted, "that this is indeed a difficult situation. For us both. So I am trying hard to ignore your disrespect."

There were definitely difficult aspects to a religious life. But most were not all that different from the nicks and bumps that came in

241

all walks of life. Marriage. Career. Family. Raising children. All of it was hard. For so long she'd wanted a sign to tell her that if she joined a convent everything would be okay. Life would work itself out and she'd finally be content. But no such divine message ever came. So she'd ignored the voices inside her head and procrastinated for years. It took an impending wedding for God to finally acquire her undivided attention.

She loved the convent and living with the sisters. She missed her family, but they visited at least once a year. Either she flew home to the United States, or they came to Europe. Thanks to her restoration work she'd had the opportunity to meet all types of people and learn from them. She'd been fortunate to be part of some really fascinating projects. It seemed her place to help bring back what had been lost. Which was why the destruction of the twelfth panel had struck her so hard.

She knew several published writers in the art field and the number one question they always heard was, *Where do you get your ideas?* For a nun there were three equally common topics for questions. The first was superficial. Why do you cover your hair? Or why wear black robes? Why do you have knots in your belt or a cincture at your waist? The second dealt with practicalities, like what do you do all day or how do you support yourself? The third was the most intriguing. Why are there monks and nuns at all? What purpose do they serve? What good do they do? Those were the questions she'd posed to the woman who'd come to see her from the Congregation of Saint-Luke. The woman who provided her with answers that made sense and who eventually brought her to the convent. She was gone now, God rest her soul, having died five years ago. Liver cancer. Kelsey missed her. Especially right now. That woman had never, ever lied to her.

They turned off attraction row and headed down a quiet side street. She'd walked here before too. The route led to the central

242

train station. Ahead she spotted the neoclassical building for the old law courts. It sat directly adjacent to the river, a low wrought-iron fence the only barrier from a small parking lot down to the water. Her prioress led the way toward a vehicle that sat idling near the iron fence.

The doors opened and two women emerged.

Both dressed in jeans and shirts.

They approached.

"It's good to meet you," one of the women said. "I'm Sister Ellen. This is Sister Isabel. We are Maidens of Saint-Michael."

No surprise really. As these women were the only ones with answers.

"What happened to your face?" she asked Ellen.

"An unexpected fall. It looks worse than it is."

"Sister Kelsey," her prioress said, "the maidens are here, in Ghent, performing a sacred duty."

"Did that include the willful destruction of a national treasure?"

"It did," Isabel said.

She was fascinated. "Why?"

"Sister Deal," Ellen said. "We would not have done such a grievous thing if it was not vitally important."

"You're talking like terrorists."

"They are anything but," the prioress interjected.

"Believe me," Ellen said, "we regretted having to burn that panel. But there were good reasons for it."

Kelsey shook her head. "A woman died."

Ellen nodded. "Rachel. She was our friend."

She saw the pain in both women's eyes, which eased her anxiety a bit.

"Why not just come to me?" she asked. "Explain the problem." She pointed at her prioress. "Or go to her, as you're doing now. Why all the subterfuge?"

"We had no choice," Isabel said. "None at all."

She stayed defiant. "I have high-resolution images of that entire panel. Burning it was useless."

"We are aware of that," Isabel said. "But your images are no longer an issue."

"What is?"

"Monsieur Lee."

That raised red flags inside her. "Is Nick all right?"

He hadn't called her back since much earlier when she told him about summoning the police. Since then she'd been consumed with her prioress and now with these two. She needed to talk to him.

Now.

"I want my phone back," she said to the prioress.

"I can't do that."

"Then I'm leaving."

She turned.

Isabel lunged toward her, one arm wrapping her neck, the other bringing a cloth to her face. A sickly-sweet smell invaded her nostrils, reminiscent of cleaning day at the convent or a visit to the hospital.

Her head began to spin.

Isabel kept a firm hold. She tried to resist but her muscles would not react. The world winked in and out.

Then vanished.

CHAPTER 42

Claire was back in Belgium.

She'd been driven north from the mountains to Toulouse and caught the only nonstop flight from there to Ghent. Normally, maidens shunned air travel, preferring car or train. Less expensive and less noticeable. But there were exceptions to that rule, especially when time was of the essence. Like here, over the past two days.

Nick Lee's offer to help retrieve Sister Rachel's body could not be refused. They desperately wanted to return her to the abbey for a burial befitting a maiden, especially one like Joan of Arc herself, who'd made the ultimate sacrifice. She'd been at a loss as to how that could be accomplished without risking even greater exposure, but their new ally had assured her he could make it happen. And, to fix this mess, she'd accept help from wherever it might be offered.

She'd taken a cab from the airport and caught up with Sisters Ellen and Isabel, directing them, on orders from the abbess, to take control of Sister Deal. While that happened, she would connect with Nick Lee. He'd been told to wait for her in the Groentenmarkt which, long ago, had been Ghent's main vegetable market.

A nineteenth-century water pump still filled its center, a high obelisk atop a square pedestal. Bordering the cobbled square were a variety of specialty shops selling things like high-end chocolate, sweet cuberdons, and tangy Tierentyn mustard. She was familiar with Oud Huis Himschoot, the oldest bakery, which produced some wonderful bread.

She'd dressed in pants, a dark blouse, jacket, and comfortable shoes with laces. She'd left the *fleur-de-lys* necklace off, nothing indicating that she was a maiden other than the tattoo on her left shoulder. The ability to blend in was one of the things that had long aided their effectiveness. But she could not help feeling a little exposed.

The cab dropped her near the square and she walked right over. She'd been texted a picture of Nick Lee found on the internet, so it was easy to find him near the fountain.

"I'm Sister Claire," she said, introducing herself.

And she took measure of her adversary.

Medium height and build. Brown wavy hair cut in a boyish fringe that definitely made him look younger than mid-thirties, which was most likely his age. Clean-shaven, the face as yet not sheathed with any fine lines from age. And the eyes. A pale gray. Warm. Playful. Engaging. She told herself to be careful. This man was physically attractive, forceful, quick-witted, and surely charismatic, the type who gave just enough of himself to inspire trust, dropping the other person's guard. She'd tried to learn what she could about him, but the UN and UNESCO websites mentioned little to nothing.

Which made her wonder. "Who exactly do you work for?"

Nick produced a badge from something called the Cultural Liaison and Investigative Office. "We deal in the loss or destruction of cultural treasures for member states. Belgium and France are members."

"I would imagine you have precious few powers to go along with that badge."

He grinned. "It gets me by."

She supposed it did. He was definitely competent and resourceful. After all, he'd gotten the better of her. She'd thought about how to handle this situation on the trip north from Toulouse. Everything was in motion. Fluid. Changing by the minute. Police were involved. A convent violated. Dominicans had arrived. It was only a matter of hours before all of them appeared in southern France. Isabel and Ellen had reported how Lee had helped them with the police and the Dominicans. So she'd decided on conciliation and diplomacy, until a more definitive course became evident.

"You followed me last night?" she asked.

He nodded. "I tailed your accomplice and watched as they shot her, then found a boat and kept close to you."

"And broke into a convent. That will look good on your résumé."

"You do what you have to do. Right?"

She smiled. Right.

"Your minions are tight-lipped," he said to her. "They told me to come here, and you would explain everything."

"Can you obtain Sister Rachel's body?"

"That depends."

"On what?"

"Whether I want to help or not."

"I have to tell you, Mr. Lee—"

"How about you call me Nick?"

"Going to a first-name basis isn't going to change things between us."

"I didn't realize there was an *us*."

She caught herself. There he went again. Drawing her in. Engaging. "Do you use that charm often?"

"All the time."

She smiled. "All right. Nick. As I was saying, I have little room to negotiate."

"You destroyed a Belgian national treasure. I'm assuming there was a really good reason for that. At the moment, the police are not on your trail. Only me. We can keep it that way. The Dominicans, though, seem laser-focused on you."

"They are, but we will deal with them, as we have in the past. You, though, are another matter. I came to listen to what you propose."

But she wondered how he would react if he knew that Sister Deal was being taken as they spoke. What was their connection? Friends? Family? Who knew? The mother superior had reported that it seemed there was something familiar between them. But asking would only arouse suspicions.

"Rachel was a friend," she said. "A close friend. How do you plan to retrieve her body?"

"You left her to face those police alone."

Yes, she had. The reminder of which she did not appreciate. "At the time, securing those images was more important. Rachel knew that. She did her duty. And I had no choice."

"We all have choices."

"I wish that were the case. Unfortunately, it's not here. Of course, no one, Rachel included, thought they would shoot her."

"Those cops were fired up and hot. That never ends well. Where are you from? I hear Cajun in your voice."

"Louisiana. Born and raised. But I've lived overseas a long time."

"If I get your friend's body back, are we going to talk about why all this was necessary?"

"I can't promise that."

"At least you're honest. But I want you to know that, if you can convince me, I'll help get the heat off you."

A cautious atmosphere had sprung between them, as if neither believed a word the other said. They were definitely fencing, and she doubted he could deliver on that promise, especially with the Vatican and the Dominicans, which represented the greatest threat. But she wasn't going to tell him that. "Do what you promised and we'll talk."

He grinned. "I get it. And it's okay. I don't trust you either. But neither one of us has a choice. We seem stuck with each other."

True.

For now.

CHAPTER 43

Mary first appeared in the art of Roman catacomb paintings, though it was hard to know for sure since the images of a woman, cradling a baby, were rough and blurred. By the fourth century after Christ her skin became dark, with heavy features, typical of the Mediterranean region. Usually she was depicted as praying with arms raised to heaven. With the rise of the Byzantine Empire she changed to an august, pale, blue-clad figure, hooded and haloed, their patroness in both war and peace. By the Middle Ages her features were firmly established as European, her skin always a milky white.

Marian worship existed nowhere in the church's origins or in the teachings of the apostles. There was no Immaculate Conception, Annunciation, or Assumption into heaven. She was not the mother of the faithful, the interceder with Christ. The Gospels themselves never described what she looked like and never mentioned where she lived. No ages were listed. She played no part in Christ's ministry and no role in establishing Christianity. Yet she became the second Eve, bestowed by popes with divine power though she herself was not divine. Protestants generally rejected Marian devotion. For them, Christianity was all about one person. Sure, there were supporting players, but nothing ranked with the Son of God.

Even more puzzling was what happened to Mary after the crucifixion.

She was not present when Christ's empty tomb was discovered. Nor was she there at his Ascension into heaven or at Pentecost when the Holy Ghost divinely inspired the apostles. She was never visited by the risen Christ, though he did appear to the disciples and Mary Magdalene. There was but one reference in the Gospels.

John 19:25–27.

Near the cross of Jesus stood his mother, his mother's sister, Mary the wife of Clopas, and Mary Magdalene. When Jesus saw his mother there, and the disciple whom he loved standing nearby, he said to her, "Woman, here is your son," and to the disciple, "Here is your mother." From that time on, this disciple took her into his home.

The disciple whom he loved.

A cryptic reference that appeared two other times in John's Gospel. That mysterious man was mentioned with the same five words as being at the Last Supper, his head resting on Christ's chest. Then again when the risen Christ appeared to the disciples on the shores of Lake Galilee. Who was this person? No one knows.

But he supposedly cared for Mary the rest of her life.

Eventually, Ephesus, in Turkey, became the center of her worship. Supposedly the disciple whom he loved took Mary there. By the fifth century a basilica had been erected there in her honor. Centuries later a house was recognized as belonging to her and venerated.

But no mention of her grave appeared.

And though relics of saints flooded churches, other than a garment and a few supposed drops of her milk, nothing of her was ever found.

"You speak strangely of the Blessed Virgin," Vilamur said to Cardinal Fuentes.

"I speak honestly. Catholicism wanted Mary to be a woman who never sinned. Never did a thing wrong in her life. Birthed children, but was still a virgin. They went to those extremes for good reason. They needed a goddess, and the worship of her proved quite lucrative."

He realized that everything associated with Mary had been manufactured early on, seizing on the wants and desires of the faithful since the adoration of pagan goddesses had been so prevalent. Christianity was then a male-dominated religion. Mary added a new dimension, one that quickly gained traction. She aided with the recruitment of new followers and opened the purses of the existing faithful. She acquired her own prayer, the Ave Maria, along with a rosary. Eventually, she established an autonomy—not a god, but more than a saint—*blessed* the term appended to her. She became the voice of heaven and even appeared on earth from time to time. At Guadalupe in Mexico. Czestochowa in Poland. Lourdes and La Salette in France. Fatima in Portugal. Beauraing and Banneux in Belgium. Medjugorje in Bosnia. And many other places, some recognized by the church, most not. Always to the poor or the downtrodden, leaving cryptic messages to decipher. Hundreds of churches, cathedrals, and basilicas around the globe were still, to this day, dedicated to her. A myth that became a reality. One that was never widely debated, or ever challenged.

Just adored.

"Why are you telling me this?" he asked Fuentes.

They still lingered in the square before the basilica, under one of the overhead lamps, the hour approaching 10:00 p.m. Fewer people were now moving about in the darkness, nobody paying them any attention.

"What do you know of the Virgin's grave?" Fuentes asked.

Quite a bit actually.

Eastern Christianity taught that Mary died a natural death, like any human being. Then her soul was received by Christ and her body resurrected on the third day into heaven. The Roman Church went a step further, teaching that Mary ascended into heaven in full bodily form. But had she died first? That point was never resolved until 1997 when John Paul II decreed that Mary had in fact died before ascending. But how would the pope have known that? Easy. It was all a matter of faith. Aided by the fact that no one knew where Mary's tomb lay. Some said in Gethsemane, others in the Valley of Jehoshaphat, and still more thought she was laid to rest in Ephesus.

He told Fuentes what he knew.

"An old account said Mary was buried somewhere in the valley of Jehoshaphat and, lo and behold, a tomb was found there in the sixth century. After the crusades, in the twelfth century, so many pilgrims flocked to that tomb that the Church of the Assumption was built to take advantage of their presence. But after Pius XII declared her Assumption we abandoned the site to the Orthodox churches."

Which made sense. "You could not on the one hand say Mary was brought into heaven, body and soul, then, on the next, have a church standing at her grave."

"No," the cardinal said. "We could not. In 1950, prior to Pius XII's decree on the Assumption, the church sent an archaeologist from the Vatican Museums to investigate that tomb. Relics supposedly found there turned out to be sheep's bones. Not a shred of evidence existed that the site was associated with Mary. You would think that conclusion would have been welcome. No bones. No body. Exactly what the church would have wanted. But the Vatican, in its usual infinite wisdom, promptly ordered that archaeologist, on threat of excommunication, to discontinue his work and never publish or speak of the tomb again. Being the good Catholic that he was, that man complied."

"I never knew that."

"It was not something we broadcast. And then there were the secret archives."

Vilamur smiled at the label. The press loved the term *Vatican Secret Archives*, which were no secret at all. They'd been open to the public since 1883. The real secret was their organization and condition. They were once a total mess, and it had taken the last forty years to bring a measure of order to the collection.

"Information was found there in 1934," Fuentes said. "Old information that had been known, then lost, then refound. It was a copy of a text that detailed Mary's life after the crucifixion. *The Testimony of John.*"

He'd never heard of it.

"An ancient manuscript. Quite informative."

"Authentic?"

Fuentes nodded. "Without question. It was recovered during the Albigensian Crusade from an old church in the Roussillon. Experts all agree it is from the fifth or sixth century. It states that it's a copy of a much older manuscript from the first century. Is it true? Factual? Accurate? Impossible to say. But according to its text the Blessed Mary lived to the age of seventy-four and was interred, after dying, *according to contemporary custom.*"

"Why has no one heard of this text?"

"It was sealed away. Only available to popes."

"And apparently you."

Fuentes nodded. "The pontifical commission head has been traditionally made aware of the manuscript. But there's a reason for that."

Which he could hardly wait to hear.

"The account is quite specific," Fuentes said. "Mary left Jerusalem and, for a time, lived in Ephesus. Then she left there and traveled east, on a pilgrimage, eventually ending in southern France, where she died near a town called Las Illas." Fuentes paused. "And was buried there."

"I know that village. I've been there."

"I was hoping that might be the case. I will need your knowledge of that area."

He was curious. "For what?"

"Popes are fools."

The sudden shift in topic surprised him. Truth? Or this man's way to catch him off guard and ferret out a bad apple? Especially one about to be elevated as cardinal?

"I don't agree," he immediately said.

Fuentes stared at him. "This is not a test, Archbishop. I am being honest, as you have been with me. Popes are imperfect men who hide behind their own self-made image. They do what is necessary at the time, for the good of their church. And make no mistake, while they live the church is indeed *theirs*. It molds and conforms to their thoughts, their likes, their dislikes. Pius XII declared in 1950 that *the Virgin Mary, having completed the course of her earthly life, was assumed body and soul into heavenly glory*. Quite a bold pronouncement. *Body and soul*. Pius simply ignored *The Testimony of John*, saying it was unproven. And since no one beyond a handful of people knew of the manuscript's existence, he could do that with impunity. Nearly fifty years later John Paul II ignored it too and clarified one point. *Having completed the course of her earthly life* meant she died. But he did not refute what Pius had said about her body and soul being assumed *whole* into heaven. All of that remains dogma, backed up by papal infallibility, to be believed by 1.2 billion Catholics, nearly 18 percent of the world's population, on threat of excommunication. But, unfortunately, they were both wrong."

He was shocked.

"The Virgin Mary lived and died and was buried here, on this earth," Fuentes said. "Her grave exists and it is being guarded, as it has for nearly two thousand years, by a group that calls themselves *les Vautours*. They are mentioned and described in detail within other accounts we have in the archives. Now do you see why this is so important?"

He did. "Being wrong is one thing. But a pope being proven wrong? That's quite another. Not to mention the theological implications. If the church was wrong about that, what else falls into that category? Holy Communion? Confession? Its stance against homosexuality? Abortion? Priestly celibacy? Every concept and view will come into question."

"We are not strong enough to withstand all of that. We live in a world of instant communication to every corner of the planet. Many will take delight in our arrogance and conceit. And if the faithful stop believing in dogma, stop relying on the church for absolute guidance, then it is all over."

Okay, he got it. This was important. At least to Fuentes. And maybe to the pope himself. "What do you want me to do?"

"I need you to tell me everything you know about this son of yours. Then we are going to determine if he is a person in the know, an opportunist, or a fraud. After that, we will deal with him."

"And the Vultures?"

"I plan to deal with them too."

"Can I ask how?"

"What should have been done long, long ago."

He waited.

"I will silence them."

CHAPTER 44

Nick entered the nondescript building on Ghent's southern edge that served as the local morgue. It sat next to a police substation that was busy with activity. He'd learned the location thanks to some recon work from CLIO's New York office. They'd provided him with not only the location, but also a schematic of the building. How they'd managed that? No clue. But he appreciated the extra effort.

They'd driven over in the vehicle he'd earlier secured, also with New York's help. A small Mercedes coupe that was now parked a block over on a quiet side street. From the intel he'd been provided with there were two ways in and out. One served as the main entrance for the public off the street, the other a service dock in the rear. That was most likely where bodies were brought in and out, beyond a chain-link fence that provided a measure of security and privacy. He had to assume there'd be cameras. Nowadays, in facilities like this, there was always a camera somewhere.

So he'd decided on using the front door.

Straight in.

Where any visitor would go.

The late hour should help, and hopefully the facility was sparsely staffed, but the cops next door were an issue. Once inside, he saw that no one waited behind the front desk. A closed door led from there into the bowels of the building.

"Check it," he said to Claire as he watched for anyone else who might enter behind them.

She moved toward the door and tested the knob.

Open. So far so good.

He nodded and they both headed through and into a dimly lit corridor. Everything smelled of formaldehyde. Claire made sure the spring-loaded hinges did not cause the door to slam back into the jamb and alert anyone. He hadn't said a word about that. She just did it instinctively. Impressive. Three closed doors lined the corridor with another at the far end. She tried all three. Locked. No cameras were in sight here. Good. He headed for the door at the far end.

Which opened.

Inside was the refrigeration room, two walls lined with latched stainless-steel doors for body compartments. He wondered where the attendants were. From the look on Claire's face she was thinking the same thing.

Then he heard it.

A door opened, then closed.

Footfalls.

Approaching.

He nodded to Claire, who assumed a position behind the door. He stood in the middle of the room and waited.

The door opened.

A bearded young man entered, eating a sandwich. His eyes immediately locked on what was surely the only strange thing, to him, in the room. The guy said something in Flemish.

"English?" Nick asked.

"Who are you?"

"No one told you?" he asked, adding surprise to his voice.

"No one told me anything."

"I'm here for the woman shot last night. I don't have a name. Caucasian. Blond hair, cut short. Face bruised from slamming the pavement. Multiple gunshot wounds."

"I know who you mean. But nobody told me her body was being moved. I am going to have to—"

Claire pounced, wrapping her right arm around the man's neck and clamping her left hand tight to the right wrist.

A choke hold?

She applied pressure until the sandwich slipped from the man's grip.

"Are those taught in the convent?"

She released her grip and helped the man's limp body fold to the floor. "We never use lethal force." She stood. "I wasn't sure where you were headed with the double talk. We don't have time to be subtle."

Apparently she had little faith in him. "How about we find Sister Rachel and get out of here. There could be more people working tonight. And we can't choke 'em all." He paused. "Or can we?"

She ignored his jab and they checked the refrigeration compartments one by one, finally finding Sister Rachel. She lay inside a black body bag on a stainless-steel tray. Sister Claire crossed herself and recited a prayer. He stood reverently and allowed her the moment. They'd only zippered back enough to expose the pale head on the naked body.

But the tattoo was visible.

The plan had been to get the body out, then leave Ghent and connect with Sisters Ellen and Isabel, who would be waiting out of town. From there, Sister Rachel would make a journey out of Belgium and back to France. About a twelve-hour trip. Thankfully, there were no border checks between European Union nations. A free flow of commerce, which these maidens planned to take full advantage of.

Claire crossed herself again, signaling she was finished.

He zippered the bag shut and looked at her.

Tears seeped from her brown eyes. "She should not have died."

He agreed. But he had to ask, "Was it worth it?"

She glared at him. "To her it was, and that's what matters."

"You people are quite cavalier about death."

"Not in the least," she shot back.

"That's not the way it looks from here. I watched this woman die. She tossed that laptop down and then stood there and took the bullets. Maybe she thought they wouldn't shoot? But when they did, she just stood there." He paused. "To give *you* time to get away."

The tears increased. He wondered how often this woman cried.

Not all that much, he imagined.

"You do know," she said, "that I fully realize all of that. I was her superior. I sent her in there. I was responsible for her."

The voice cracked but stayed firm.

"Whatever is going on here, I hope it's worth it."

Her eyes drifted back down to the body bag. "It is."

"We need to go."

She swiped the moisture from her face and nodded.

He reached down, gripped the bag, and lifted it, draping the corpse over his right shoulder. Not the most respectful way to carry the dead, but they had no choice. He had to hope that there was a path away from the building where darkness could be their ally. They certainly could not traipse out the front door and risk being seen by the police next door. A second door led out of the room, which Claire opened to reveal a larger space with stainless-steel tables where autopsies were surely performed. Glass-fronted cabinets lined the walls holding supplies and instruments. He found what he wanted across on the other side. The door out. Heavy metal with a small wire-meshed glass window.

They headed for it.

Then he spotted trouble.

A camera in the far corner, with a red dot signaling it was on.

Claire saw it too but said nothing. Instead, she yanked open the door and they rushed out into the night.

An alarm sounded.

Loud.

No way they could make a discreet retreat now. And no way they'd make it to the car parked a block away. He spied another vehicle just past the small loading dock. "Go and see if there are keys on that guy."

She did not hesitate and disappeared back inside. He descended a short set of steps and headed for the vehicle, which was unlocked. No surprise considering it was parked inside a fenced enclave with a police station a stone's throw away.

The alarm kept wailing.

Claire rushed out the door, displaying a set of keys. The vehicle was an older Volvo, a compact with four doors, messy on the inside with clothes and other stuff scattered everywhere. He carefully laid Sister Rachel across the back seat atop what was there.

"I hope those are the right keys," he said.

She tossed them and he saw the black chuck of plastic attached to the ring with "Volvo" etched on it. "We've got company coming this way. I pushed those tables against the interior door to slow them down."

They both hopped into the car.

He settled behind the wheel and inserted the key end of the fob. Which fit.

The engine roared to life.

He depressed the clutch and slammed the gearshift into reverse, spinning the car back and out of its parking spot. The outer door to the building burst open and several uniforms emerged. He watched them through his side window and saw no weapons.

Thank goodness.

He floored the clutch and shifted into first gear, spinning the wheel and accelerating straight for the fenced double gate, chained shut at its center. No fancy electronics there. Just old-fashioned locks and key.

He shifted from second to third, adding speed.

"Hold on," he said.

And he powered through the gate, exploding the two fenced panels outward.

"You told us you could handle this," Claire said. "We thought that meant you would be using your UN credentials."

He whipped the car sharply to the right and his headlights swung out across the silent narrow street. It would only be a matter of seconds before the police gave chase. "You never gave me a chance to handle it." He came to an intersection. "Any idea where we go?"

"Give me a second."

She produced a phone and started tapping.

In the rearview mirror he saw flashing lights, headed their way.

And he sped ahead.

CHAPTER 45

Bernat was back home in Toulouse, having driven there from his trip south to Montségur. He owned a large five-bedroom, art nouveau home with mosaic floors and stained-glass windows. When he bought it the attic was unfinished. He converted it into a stylish office where he spent a lot of time. He should be sleepy, but his brain reeled with thought after thought, and his focus was on the computer screen before him.

The curator for the Ghent Altarpiece had sent an email explaining that Sister Deal had not forwarded the images, as instructed. Disturbing. But the curator assured him that this would be corrected. He'd been scheduled to see the totally revealed *Just Judges* next week, before any news conference and public announcement. But with the panel in ashes the images were all that remained of a medieval masterpiece, and the only way to perhaps salvage some element of notoriety from his investment.

The wallpaper on his screen showed the entire altarpiece, stretched flat, the panels fitted properly together. He'd downloaded the high-resolution image a few months back. Each of the twelve panels carried a label, a reference relevant to the images they depicted: "Adam," "Left Choir," "Virgin," "Deity," "John the

263

Baptist," "Right Choir," "Eve," "Knights," "Adoration of the Holy Lamb," "Pilgrims," "Hermits," and the one he was now staring at, "Just Judges."

Of course, it was Van der Veken's reproduction. Ten men atop horses on a pilgrimage toward the center panel and the Holy Lamb. They were meant to represent the secular world—learned, noble, knightly, mercantile—and a lot of debate had ensued over the centuries as to the faces depicted. The general consensus was the blue-robed man atop the white horse in front was Hubert van Eyck, his brother Jan right behind him in a dark-brown robe and a hat trimmed in fur. Sadly, now only in images would the altarpiece ever be displayed in all of its original magnificence. The physical, original *Just Judges* was gone. Two weeks ago he'd thought that he'd be part of reuniting the last missing part of van Eyck's masterpiece.

Now it was only a partial victory.

The curator indicated in his email that he was still planning a public announcement. The *Just Judges* had been found. A crime of long standing had been solved, though a thousand new questions remained unanswered. The idea was to generate worldwide interest in the altarpiece and alert the public to the crime. He liked the sound of it all. Every bit of that publicity would spill over to him. How could it not? And he should still be able to reap ample benefits. The curator wanted him there, on the podium, beside him when the announcement was made. The press conference was scheduled for 1:00 p.m. About twelve hours away. The cathedral was sending a private plane to ferry him back and forth, which he appreciated. He was planning on allowing Vilamur to stew for most of the day anyway. No need to rush a thing. He had all the time in the world to make that man's life a living hell.

Maybe even enough that the bastard would end his own life.

Suicide among clerical sexual predators, both male and female, was common. He'd researched the issue in detail. Good thing many of them chose death since the recidivism rate, due to their rabid narcissism and inability to feel a speck of remorse, was sky-high. Cathars took a different approach to death. No fear. Instead, a welcome act that freed them from the physical world. They even had a particular practice relative to it. The *endura*. It came from the Occitan word for "fasting." Toward the end of their life, believers would take the *consolamentum*, achieve Perfectus status, then starve themselves to death. This had been quite common in the thirteenth century to avoid falling into the hands of the inquisitors. Why hang around in hell, when freedom on the other side was within easy reach? Catholics regarded suicide as a great sin. The idea of a *good end* was a concept peculiar to Cathars. When parting from each other Cathars never said *goodbye*, or *God be with you*. Instead, they used the more specific *May you come to a good end*. No such one came to Father Tallard. He died the disgusting sinner that he'd been his entire adult life.

Any regrets?

Not a one.

His encounter with the archbishop still unnerved him, and Raymond Barbe's question about how he'd felt was a fair one. He'd wondered for a long time what it would feel like to finally be back in Vilamur's presence. His *biological* father. The man who'd raised him, whom he'd thought to be his father in every way, had been a gentle soul who died far too young. Aside from her indiscretion with Vilamur, his mother had lived an otherwise exemplary life, also dying young. She had, though, drifted away from Catholicism, eventually discovering Catharism, which offered her a measure of comfort and peace. She'd achieved Perfectus status just before dying. He'd followed her into the religion, trying to find his own inner peace. He hated that he carried any of Vilamur's DNA inside him. The hypocrisy of the man's life, along with the evil of his religion, disgusted him.

The Catholic Church had murdered more people during the past two thousand years than any other institution devised by man. It systematically suppressed knowledge and fought scientific progress. Across time, at one point or another, it had actively supported slavery, racism, fascism, and sexism. It published the *Hammer of Witches*, detailing how to torture and murder innocent women. It jailed and burned scientists at the stake in a futile attempt to keep the masses ignorant. It terrorized Jews and Muslims for centuries, torturing and murdering during the Inquisition and crusades, all in the name of a supposedly loving God. It ignored eyewitness accounts that Jews were being slaughtered by Nazis. It systemically covered up tens of thousands of cases involving sexual misconduct by priests. It even had the audacity to absolve fault that had not yet been committed, thanks to indulgences bought with wealth.

John Paul II's apology in 2000 for all of the *sins committed by the church* seemed laughable.

"They will pay," he muttered.

He realized that the video sent to Vilamur was a two-edged sword. Not only did it incriminate Tallard as a sexual predator and Vilamur as an accomplice after the fact, it linked him to Tallard's death. Could Vilamur go to the police? Possibly. But he would never. The last thing the archbishop wanted was for the authorities to be involved. The resulting publicity would be uncontrollable. No. This was going to be a private affair. He doubted the bastard would even run a DNA test.

Vilamur knew the truth.

He'd known it thirty-two years ago when his mother first confronted him. And he'd seen it earlier when Vilamur's mouth said one thing, but the eyes another. They were related. No question. But the test would provide incontrovertible proof that Vilamur could never deny.

Which gave him a day or so.

And before he destroyed Vilamur, he wanted the bastard to witness his greatest triumph. He stared at the computer screen.

The *Just Judges*.

Apt.

As he was about to be.

CHAPTER 46

1:20 A.M.

Kelsey woke.

She was lying in the dark inside a confined space. Her hands were bound behind her back, her mouth taped shut. Not good. And she was moving, the compartment vibrating. A trunk? Yep. She was inside the trunk of a car, motoring down a relatively smooth road.

Her prioress had betrayed her again.

Her head was foggy, and she recalled smelling something strange then blacking out. She tested the bindings on her hands and feet. Solid. No way to get free. She did not like the confined feeling and told herself to calm down. Stay still. Breathe through her nose.

Then she kicked the side of the compartment.

Repeatedly.

The car began to slow.

Then came to a stop.

She heard doors open and close then, a few moments later, the trunk lid raised. In the light that came on inside the compartment she saw the faces of the two maidens from earlier, Sisters Ellen and Isabel. They helped her out and unbound her restraints. She peeled the tape from her mouth and wanted to scream but realized that the effort would be fruitless. Besides, she wasn't going to show these women that she was scared.

Despite the fact that she was.

Sister Ellen faced her. "We're willing to have you ride with us, inside the car, if you promise to behave."

"Why should I?"

"Because," Sister Isabel said, "we are not your enemy."

"You have a terrible way of showing that."

"We had no choice," Ellen said. "You gave us no choice."

"And how did I do that?" The fog had fully lifted from her brain. "Where are you taking me?"

"To a safe place."

"That's not an answer."

"*Haec est speciosior sole et super omnem stellarum dispositionem. Luci comparata invenitur prior. Candor est enim lucis aeternae et speculum sine macula dei maiestatis.*"

Sister Ellen delivered the Latin with perfect inflection.

Kelsey instantly knew what it meant. She'd studied Latin.

She is more beautiful than the sun and excels every constellation of the stars. Compared with the light she is found to be superior. She is in fact the reflection of the eternal light and the immaculate mirror of God's majesty.

And she recognized its significance.

Above the center panel of the Ghent Altarpiece were three other panels. One depicted God enthroned, which she'd shown to Nick. Another displayed John the Baptist, and the third was the Virgin Mary. In the halo that surrounded Mary's head, Jan van Eyck had painted an inscription.

The words that Sister Ellen had just repeated.

"Your Latin is excellent," she said.

"I'm specially trained in it. You know what I am referring to?"

STEVE BERRY

"Of course. It's how van Eyck described the Virgin Mary. The words are from the Book of Wisdom."

They were way beyond Ghent, somewhere in the countryside. The velvet sky overhead shimmered with stars. No moon tonight. Few sounds. She was alone with two Maidens of Saint-Michael, who obviously were much more than met the eye.

"Sister," Isabel said. "Would it be all right if we called you Kelsey?"

She decided, *Why not?* "Okay."

"Kelsey, you stumbled onto something the Vatican has wanted to find for a long time."

"The *Just Judges?*"

They both nodded.

"It's been gone since 1934," Ellen said. "For you it's a wondrous piece of medieval art from a grand master. For us, for the Vatican, it's much more. Your revelation has now started a race, one that has lain dormant for a long time. But the race is most definitely on."

She could see that this was no joke. These women were serious.

"A race for what?" she asked.

"Veritas Vita."

The truth, the life.

"That's on the altarpiece too," she said.

"We know. We would like you to come with us. Voluntarily. No pressure. You come because you want to come. Once we arrive at our destination, all will be explained."

"And if I refuse?"

"You're coming anyway. Only there will be no answers provided to your questions."

Good to know. "Why me?"

"We need your expertise," Ellen said. "Concerning the altarpiece."

"Who said I was an expert?"

Ellen smiled. "Your prioress. She said you spent several months

270

preparing for your work on the *Just Judges* by studying every-thing available. We need that knowledge, along with your artistic skills."

She was now more perplexed than angry. Intrigued, rather than repulsed. And what choice did she have? Apparently, both her prioress and these maidens had already concluded that she would help. So why disappoint them?

"All right. I'll do what I can." But, "I want to talk to Nick Lee."

"It's not necessary," Ellen said. "Our Vestal is with him now. She'll advise him that you're safe."

But she wondered.

Was she really safe?

CHAPTER 47

Nick worked his way out of Ghent, maneuvering the Volvo beyond the narrow streets and out onto a dark rural highway.

"They're still on us," Claire said from the passenger side.

A police car with lights flashing filled his rearview mirrors.

"Where are you going?" she asked.

"Anywhere. Just trying to lose them."

"Stealing this body was a bad idea."

Like he needed to be told. "I don't recall you having a better one."

"My abbess is not going to like this at all."

"Neither is my boss."

"She specifically told me to not mess this up. No more attention."

The police car behind them certainly qualified as such. He'd learned that his UN credentials could open a lot of doors, but they also were fairly useless once he broke the law. And he'd definitely done that. Pretty much a firing offense, according to the rules of engagement he was bound to observe, but a certain amount of law-lessness was tolerated depending on where in the world he found himself. Unfortunately, Belgium was not one of those places where free passes would be granted.

They were speeding through the countryside, trees lining both sides of the dark two-laned highway. No other cars had been in sight besides the one in pursuit. The road ahead was a straight line, so he swerved into the opposite lane and eased off the accelerator, allowing the police car to flash past.

Tires squealed.

They caught up with each other, now nearly parallel.

"Hold on," he told her.

He inched closer to the blacktop's edge on his side, which he used to maximum advantage, whipping the steering wheel to the right and slamming Claire's side of the car into the police vehicle.

Metal grated.

The steering wheel slipped from his hands.

The car rebounded with the left-side tires wobbling on the pavement's edge.

$$\Omega$$

Claire focused out the front and back windshields trying to assess things. The jar from the impact had rattled her bones, but Nick Lee seemed to know what he was doing.

They sped ahead.

The police car had been pushed to the edge but remained on the highway. She turned back and stared through the rear windshield. The car had swung back into their lane, now racing toward them.

"They're coming," she said.

Nick jammed the accelerator to the floor.

The police car smacked into their bumper.

Apparently, they had not taken kindly to his sideswipe.

The combination of speed and impact sent them surging forward, her body held in place thanks to the shoulder harness. Sister

Rachel, though, was unrestrained. The body bag flew off the rear seat and settled onto the floorboard.

With a thud.

She hated the indignities that poor woman was enduring.

Ω

Nick sawed hard on the wheel as the Volvo banked around a tight turn, tires screaming. The police car was using its horse-power advantage, closing the gap, jolting them hard again as the bumpers kissed.

The cop was determined.

He'd give him that.

Their pursuer angled left and moved up alongside in the opposite lane. He gave the Volvo more gas and increased speed. The police car jerked back and regained its equilibrium, its front grille visible in the mirrors from his taillights. The road ahead vaulted up then turned sharply. The police car dropped back, then closed again. They crested the hill and the Volvo's wheels left the pavement for an instant. He kept a tight hold on the wheel, fighting not to lose control.

They skidded around another turn.

Trees continued to be packed tightly along the pavement edges providing little room to escape. He poured on the power, a turn coming on fast. The tires slid right and he twisted the vehicle off the soft bumpy shoulder, back on solid asphalt, compensating for the slide that came from the sudden changes in speed, drag, and hold. A glance in the mirrors showed the patrol car to his left. What the hell was the guy doing? No telling what was coming up around that curve in the opposite lane, the one the cop had decided to use.

And they were both going way too fast for the turn.

The shattering of a horn sent a wave of thunder through the car as another vehicle appeared in the opposite lane, headed straight for the patrol car.

Nick hit the brakes.

Tires grabbed pavement.

They slowed, but the patrol car kept going into the turn.

Way too fast.

But he'd given them room to come back over into the proper lane. The cop seemed to realize the mistake and tried to brake while veering right. The car's rear end fishtailed in a 180-degree spin. Tires slid along the dry asphalt, smoke billowing up from the friction. Nick slowed and watched as the patrol car slid from the roadway. Thankfully, the trees had ended and nothing but an open field stretched out into the darkness. The car kept spinning, dirt corkscrewing up like a twister.

Finally, it came to a stop.

As did he.

The car sat out in the field, its lights still on. Nick heard power being added to the idling engine. The rear tires spun freely, obviously mired down in loose soil, unable to gain traction.

"Are they okay?" Claire asked.

"Looks like it."

He hit the accelerator and they sped away.

Half an hour later he eased the Volvo into a closed gas station, not a light on anywhere. It was really late and he was tired. They were south from Ghent, deep in the Belgian woods. No more police had appeared, the one vehicle their only pursuer. Still, they needed to ditch the car and find some other transportation. Surely the make, model, and license plate had been communicated across the airwaves.

Like the old saying went, *You can't outrun the radio.*

He stepped out and ran his hands through his hair, trying to shake the cobwebs from his eyes. Adrenaline had been keeping him going, but the rush was fading. He liked to say that he received his fears from his father and his audacity from his mother.

Both had just come into play.

Claire followed him out into the night, then opened the rear door and began to move the body bag from the floorboard back onto the rear seat. He opened the other rear door and helped. They settled the corpse back down, safe and sound.

"Where exactly are we going with this body?" he asked her.

"To our motherhouse. We have a burial ground there."

He knew that location. Southern France. Near the Spanish border.

They both closed their rear door.

"I'm going to call Sisters Ellen and Isabel," Claire said. "And arrange for us to meet them."

"I have to make a couple of calls too," he told her, pointing off to the left. "From over there."

He walked off, about a hundred feet away from the car, and dialed Reynaldo's number in New York. His boss answered and he apprised him of what he'd done.

"I assume there's a good reason for what you did?"

"This is bigger than I thought," he told Reynaldo. "I had to gain these nuns' confidence."

"I get that. But you broke a lot of laws. Maybe you've forgotten, but the UN has to respect its member states' autonomy. The Belgians are not going to be happy with any of this."

"I had no choice."

"Nick, there are always choices. You just chose the easiest one, and now I have a huge diplomatic mess to clean up."

He hated placing Reynaldo in such a difficult situation.

"And let's not forget," his boss said, "that you used this office to gather information and get a vehicle that facilitated the theft. We are an accessory. That means my ass is on the line now too. What's really going on there? You've taken chances before, but those were in war zones with few rules. Never like this."

If he revealed anything about Kelsey he knew Reynaldo would order him back to Paris. No question. So he abbreviated the explanation.

"I'm just doing my job. A Belgian national treasure was destroyed. I'm trying to find out by who and why. Stealing that body was the fastest way to get answers."

"Nick, listen to me and listen good. I'm giving you forty-eight hours. That's all. If you don't have anything concrete by then, get your ass back to Paris. Am I clear?"

"Crystal."

"And, Nick, don't make me regret that I even gave you two days."

He stood under the branches of a spanning tree, just beyond the gas station. "I won't. And I'm sorry about putting you in a bad spot."

"Just do your job. Without all the drama."

He ended the call and had one more to make.

To Kelsey.

She had to be wondering what happened to him. Sister Claire stood off on the other side of the parked car, talking on the phone too. They'd both retreated in opposite directions for privacy.

He punched in Kelsey's cell phone number.

The phone rang several times.

He allowed it to keep ringing, realizing she was probably sleeping. Finally, a voice answered.

Not Kelsey.

"Who is this?" he asked.

"I am Sister Deal's prioress, Mr. Lee. I have Kelsey's mobile phone and the caller identification named you."

He was concerned. "Is Kelsey all right?"

"She is fine."

Nothing more was offered. "Where is she?"

"She is safe. Don't concern yourself."

But he was concerned.

"I will be destroying this phone when this call is ended. There is no need for you to communicate with Sister Deal any further."

"Coming from the woman who sold her out."

"I did what was necessary. Sister Deal understands that. You should too."

And the call ended.

He'd turned away from the parked car, facing the tree, trying to keep his voice down. When he turned back toward the gas station the Volvo suddenly sprang to life, the engine roaring, lights on.

It sped away.

Sister Claire had abandoned him.

CHAPTER 48

Kelsey decided the best tack was a cooperative one. These two women needed something from her and she was curious as to what that might be. Besides, she didn't want to be stuffed back into the trunk so it seemed better to just get along. The two maidens' attitude had definitely softened and for two hours they rode in relative silence. She had to keep telling herself that these were daughters of Christ. Pledged to a religious order and a life of love and peace. She wasn't exactly sure what kind of religious order they belonged to but, from all she knew, the Maidens of Saint-Michael were well respected. Still, there was the matter of the *Just Judges*. Stolen by the maidens. Then the Chapel of the Maiden. Which, according to her prioress, the maidens guarded.

What was that?

A phone buzzed in the front seat and Sister Ellen answered. The conversation was short and, when she ended the call, Ellen turned back to face her. "I've been given the okay to further involve your help." Ellen produced a MacBook Air. "I'm going to set up a personal hot spot through my phone for this computer. We need you to access your images. And before you object, we don't want you to download them. They are actually not all that important to us any longer. Just access and compare your images of the fifteenth-century original to the copy of the *Just Judges* finished in 1945. We need to know if there are any differences."

"Of course there are," she said. "The copyist added the picture of the then Belgian king Leopold, along with a few other subtle changes. That's a well-known fact."

"Of course, we know that. We're interested in any other changes that you might find that seem significant."

A strange request, for sure, but one that definitely piqued her artistic curiosity. So she nodded and said she would do it. Ellen worked with her phone a few moments, then the laptop, finally handing it back over the front seats.

"It's online now. I'm trusting that you will not contact anyone by message or email."

"I won't. You've spurred my interest, so now I want to find out if there's anything there."

She accepted the computer and typed in the web address Nick had provided her. Thank goodness it was easy to remember. She then entered the password they'd both settled upon—the month and date they first met twelve years ago—and gained access into the secure site. She manipulated the touchpad and found a separate image of Jef Van der Veken's 1945 reproduction of the *Just Judges*, the one painted above the original, filling the right side of the screen with it and the left with her own image. Amazing how modern technology made that so easy. Years ago the analysis would have required both to be physically stood side by side. It would have then taken days with eyes straining through magnifying glasses to make any meaningful comparison. Now she could complete a survey in minutes, all thanks to ultra-high resolution that missed absolutely nothing.

She studied the original *Just Judges* panel.

The detail was extraordinary.

The embroidery in the cloaks. The intricate metallic designs in the gold medals wrapping one of the horses' necks. Skin creases in the faces. Even individual strands of hair in the manes could be seen. The lips, eyes, and noses of all the men were in perfect proportion. Incredibly, a small reflection could even be seen in one of the animal's eyes.

She'd done a good job in removing six centuries of grime. Thankfully, the overpaint had done little to no damage to the original. It seemed to be all there. She was still baffled by its theft in 1934 and subsequent overpainting in 1945. What was the point? Something told her that the two women in the front seat might have the explanation. Another reason to be a good girl and get along.

She rubbed her eyes.

The hour was late and she was beginning to lose steam. So far fear and anger had given her a second and third wind. She recalled something she'd read once about the altarpiece. *Van Eyck was clever. So we must be equally so in deciphering what he did.* She decided to start in the upper left corner, keeping the two images side by side, slowly scrolling down each one, bit by bit, looking for inconsistencies. Had Jef Van der Veken's copy been inexact?

Apparently so.

Or so these women thought.

She examined the left half of both panels, finding everything identical between the original and the copy. Back to the top right corner and she started down. The buildings in the distance were like all of the others in the remaining panels. Fantastical. Unreal. Only a few bearing any resemblance to actual places. She passed over the top of the grassy cliff and moved down its rocky face, where van Eyck had included tiny petaled white flowers sprouting from the outcrops.

She found the men on horseback again.

One bearded, dressed in an orange-colored fur hat, the man in front of him clean-shaven in brown robes and another fur hat. One looked Middle Eastern, the other European. Between those two rode another beardless man in green robes, with a silver-and-blue fur hat. A gold chain draped his neck from which a ring hung.

Then she saw it.

The faces between the original *Just Judges* and the copy were

definitely different. Van der Veken had changed them. But something else stood out. About halfway down the right side of the panel.
She stopped scrolling and checked again, comparing the images.

Definitely. No doubt.

The paintings were different.

The overpaint had left something out.

Something quite clearly there—

In the original.

CHAPTER 49

Fuentes could not sleep. But why would he? Everything was dropping into place. Finally. He'd been a cardinal a long time and had learned a lot about his colleagues. In the beginning, long ago, they were mere assistants of the pope. But by the twelfth century they were the sole means of anyone becoming pope, which provided them with extraordinary power and influence. Today, they controlled the church's theology, its inner workings, and were in total control of all priests, bishops, and archbishops, second only to the pope himself. But they were a peculiar lot. Easily influenced. And happily led. Thankfully, few among them ever aspired to be pope, looking to others for leadership.

Which he intended to provide.

He sat upright in the bed and stared at the iPad in his lap.

Then he tapped the screen a few times and opened the file.

After Christ's Ascension Mary lived for three years on Mount Sion, for three years in Bethany, and for nine years in Ephesus. During the fifteenth year after our Lord's death Mary left Ephesus and, with others, myself included, climbed into a boat, launched onto the sea at the mercy of the elements. By divine guidance we followed the northern coast of the great sea, heading ever eastward. Her journey ended in the Provincia Romana, in a region known as Volcae where she stepped ashore at Narbo. From there she journeyed inland, toward the mountains, where she settled to live out her days in repentance.

Mary's home occupies a hill, to the left of the road, some three and a half hours by walk from the sea. Narrow paths lead southwards to another hill near the top of which is an uneven plateau, some half-hour's journey in circumference, overgrown, like the hill itself, with trees and bushes. It is a lonely place but has many fertile and pleasant slopes as well as rock-caves, clean and dry and surrounded by patches of sand. It is wild but not desolate, and scattered about it are a number of trees, pyramid-shaped, with big shady branches and smooth trunks.

Several Christian families and holy women traveled with us from Ephesus. Some made their homes in caves or in the rocks, fitted out with light woodwork to craft dwellings. Some built fragile huts or tents. All had come to escape persecution, which many who worship Christ have come to endure. Their dwellings are like hermit's cells and, as a rule, they live a quarter of an hour's distance from each other. The whole settlement is like a widely scattered village. Mary's house is built of rectangular stones, rounded or pointed at the back. The windows are high up near the flat roof. The house is divided into two compartments by a hearth in the center. To the right and left of the hearth doors lead into the back part of the house, which is darker than the front and ends in a semicircle. It is all neatly and pleasantly arranged. The walls are covered with wickerwork and the ceiling is vaulted. Its beams are decorated with a mixture of paneling and wickerwork and ornamented with a pattern of leaves, all of it simple and dignified.

The farthest corner of the room is divided by a curtain and forms Mary's oratory. In the center of the wall is a niche in which has been placed a receptacle, like a tabernacle, which can be opened and shut by pulling at a string to turn its door. Inside lies a cloth which has the impression that it was the one with which blood was wiped from all the wounds in Our Lord's holy body after it was taken down from the cross. At the sight of the cloth I can see the manifestation of the Blessed Virgin's motherly love in her eyes.

Fuentes stopped reading the account.

He'd read it many times before but, given what was happening, he felt a refresher was needed.

The Testimony of John.

Dated to the fifth century. A copy of a far older original from the first century. Being a copy immediately raised questions of reliability. Was it complete? Edited? The document had been part of the Vatican archives for a thousand years. Several investigations had occurred into its authenticity and each one had stamped it real. But the time lapse between the events themselves and the surviving copy had always cast a shadow of doubt. So much so that the church had ignored it, and forged ahead, creating its own Mariology and bestowing upon Mary an untarnished life and a magnificent end.

Something John had not been so willing to give.

Now I will tell of the death of Mary. It happened in year fifty-two after Christ's birth. There was great grief and mourning in her house. The local women came and dealt with her final needs. She lay still, as though near death, completely enveloped in a white coverlet. The veil over her head was arranged in folds across her forehead. In the last days of her life she took no nourishment except a spoonful of juice which one of the women pressed from berries into a bowl near her bed. She lay pale and still. Her gaze was directed intently upwards. She said no words to anyone and seemed in a state of perpetual ecstasy, radiant with longing, which seemed bearing her upwards. My heart longed to ascend with hers to God.

On the final day I anointed her face, hands, and feet with holy oil. The women recited prayers. Her face was radiant with smiles, as if in her youth. Her eyes stayed towards heaven in holy joy. I imagined a marvelous vision where the ceiling of the room disappeared and I saw through the sky into the heavenly Jerusalem. Two radiant clouds of light sank down, out of which appeared angels. Between these clouds, a path of light poured down upon Mary. I wanted to see her arms stretched out in infinite longing, her body, all wrapped up, rising so high above her bed that one could see under it. I wanted her soul to leave her body, like a little figure of infinitely pure light, soaring up to heaven. There, the angels would meet her soul and separate it from her body. My gaze would follow her soul as it entered the heavenly Jerusalem to the throne of the most Holy Trinity. There she would take her place with God and her Son, who would receive her with divine love. They would place in her hands a scepter with a gesture towards the earth, as though indicating the power which He had given her. But that would be only a dream. Instead, when I once more looked I saw the body lying still on the bed. Her eyes were closed, her arms crossed on her breast. The women knelt round praying. She had died just after the ninth hour in the nineteenth year after Christ's death.

She was laid to rest nearby, about a half an hour's journey through the trees. The cave was not as spacious as Christ's tomb and hardly high enough for a man to enter upright. The floor sank at the entrance, and then one saw the burial-place, like a narrow altar with the rock-wall projecting over it. A hollow had been made in the shape of a wrapped-up body, slightly raised at the head.

Inside Mary's house the women prepared the body for burial. They brought with them cloths, as well as spices to embalm. They all carried little pots of fresh herbs. The house was closed and they worked by lamplight. The women freed Mary from her deathbed and laid her body inside a long basket piled up with thick, roughly woven coverings. Two women then held a broad cloth stretched above the body, while two others removed the head-covering and wrappings, leaving the body clothed only in a long woolen robe. They cut off Mary's beautiful locks of hair to be kept in remembrance. Then two women washed the holy body with sponges. They carried out their task with great respect and reverence, washing with their hands without looking, for the cloth which was held over the body hid the dead flesh from their eyes. A fifth woman wrung out the sponges in a bowl and then dipped them into fresh water. Three times the basin was emptied into a hollow outside the house and fresh water brought in. The holy body was dressed in a new robe, then reverently lifted onto a table where the grave clothes and swaddling-bands had been arranged for use. They wound them tightly around the flesh from the ankles to above the breast, leaving the head, hands, and feet free.

She looked like a child in swaddling clothes. A transparent veil was folded back from the face, which shone between bunches of herbs. On her breast was laid a wreath of white, red, and sky-blue flowers as a token of her virginity. The women gazed on the beloved face once more before it was finally covered. They knelt, shedding many tears in farewell as the lid was placed onto the wicker coffin. Dusk had arrived by the time they left the house and headed for the tomb.

He lay in the bed, staring at the iPad, the room illuminated only by the light from the screen. *The Testimony of John* had long been translated into Latin, Italian, and English. It had also been suppressed, locked away in the sealed archives, accessible only by permission of the pope. Which had been granted to a precious few. All inside the Vatican. Himself the sole one at the moment so privileged.

With all his heart he knew that every word of the account was true.

Those early church fathers had not been overly bothered by what the masses thought. They were blessed with a largely illiterate and frightened populace that could, and was, easily controlled. A healthy mixture of fear and fantasy worked wonders. If anyone questioned anything they were branded a heretic, tortured, then burned at the stake. Needless to say, opposition voices were few and far between.

That was not the case today.

Opposition had a multitude of tools available to it that could wreak havoc. Radio. Television. Texting. Social media. The internet. The press in general. You name it. All bad. And uncontrollable.

Which made him wonder once again. What would he do if he truly found what he sought?

His cell phone vibrated.

He lifted the unit and recognized the number. He'd been waiting for a report. He answered and listened for a few moments.

Then made a decision.

And issued orders.

CHAPTER 50

Vilamur opened his eyes.

Someone was knocking on his bedroom door.

He glanced at the nightstand. The clock read 2:07 a.m. He'd been asleep for nearly three hours. After he and Fuentes returned from dinner and their walk, they'd both retired for the night, the cardinal in one of the guest rooms on the third floor. No staff stayed over in the rectory. Once they left each evening he was alone in the spacious house, which had been home to the archbishops of Toulouse for nearly half a century.

He rose from the bed and slipped on the bathrobe draped at its end. He liked to shower, shave, and dress before the staff arrived, preferring not to have an audience to his daily ritual. He stepped across the bedroom, night-lights illuminating the way, and opened the door. Fuentes stood in the dimly lit hall, fully dressed in street clothes.

"You're needed downstairs," the cardinal said to him.

"Let me dress."

"No. The robe is fine."

Okay.

He followed Fuentes to the staircase and down to the ground

floor. Waiting in the foyer were two men. One was tall, with dark hair, violet eyes, and a lean muscular build. The other was short and stout with a light dusting of brown fuzz atop a round head. Both were dressed in trousers, shirts, and shoes, with light jackets. Each sported a chain around his neck from which an ornament hung.

The Gyronny Cross.

The heraldic arms of the *Ordo Praedicatorum*, the Order of Preachers.

Dominicans.

"This is Friar Robert Dwight," Fuentes said, introducing the tall man. "And Friar Paul Rice." Shorter, with gray eyes.

No hands were offered to shake, which was fine by him.

Fuentes motioned and they all walked back to the study. The cardinal switched on one of the lamps. "Archbishop Vilamur, the situation has changed."

Obviously, something was up.

He listened as Friar Dwight explained about what had happened in Ghent, Belgium. A lost work of art had been found, then burned. The *Just Judges*. Part of the famed Ghent Altarpiece. Stolen in the 1930s, but recently rediscovered during a restoration. The Maidens of Saint-Michael had burned it. They were, in actuality, *les Vautours*.

Really?

He was familiar with the maidens. Headquartered to the south, in the mountains, near the Spanish border. He'd visited their motherhouse several times. Knew the current abbess. Nothing exceptional about her or them. One of many convents located within his archdiocese, each a quiet, innocent place.

"You're saying that the Maidens of Saint-Michael actively attacked and burned a panel of the Ghent Altarpiece. And that these nuns are the Vultures?"

Fuentes nodded. "That is exactly what he's saying. Regrettably, one of their own was killed in the process, but that has allowed us to finally locate them. And, most fortuitous, here they are, right in your archdiocese."

He did not know what to say.

"They also have acquired some assistance from the United Nations," Dwight said. "A man named Nicholas Lee, who is actively involved with them."

"Let me see what I can do to end his involvement," Fuentes said. "We have a presence at the UN."

He wondered why he'd been woken and included in this conversation. Fuentes could have easily done this without him. But he recalled what the cardinal had said earlier about what would happen once the Vultures were identified.

"Do you still plan to silence them?" he asked.

"I do," Fuentes said. "And immediately. I'll supervise the incursion."

Incursion? "Are you planning a war?"

Fuentes's eyes zeroed in. "I'm planning on dealing with a group that has shown nothing but disrespect to Rome for centuries. I'm planning on teaching them a lesson, one they will never forget."

He could see that the Spaniard was serious. Still, he wondered, "Why am I involved?"

"Because," Fuentes said, "you could prove helpful in dealing with the maidens. They are subject to your temporal authority. Also, we must deal with Bernat de Foix. It seems that your blackmailer was also involved with the *Just Judges*." The cardinal pointed to Dwight. "Explain it to him."

"De Foix funded the restoration of the *Just Judges* reproduction. To his good fortune, the restorer discovered the hidden original beneath that overpaint. We have to wonder if that was coincidental or intentional."

He was wondering the same thing.

"Also," Dwight said, "the restorer created electronic images of the original panel."

"Which are now irrelevant," Fuentes added. "Prior to yesterday they were invaluable. But now we know where to find *les Vautours* so it doesn't matter if they are revealed and studied by others. But de Foix? He's a separate issue altogether. On several levels. One we must deal with tonight."

"What do you mean *deal with*?" he asked.

"We've gathered as much information as we could, in the short time we had to prepare," Friar Rice said. "But we know a lot more about de Foix than we did a few hours ago. Him being involved with the discovery made in Ghent, funding the restoration, could be significant. It might be connected to what is happening here with you, Archbishop."

"And he might know nothing at all," Vilamur said, a touch of irritation in his voice. "He might just hate my guts."

Fuentes shrugged. "Quite true. It's hard to know for sure. But he did specifically mention *les Vautours* to you, which is a rather obscure subject, so it's not that far-fetched to think he could know more. He is definitely schooled in your personal problem with him."

"*Our* problem, Eminence," he said.

Fuentes nodded. "Quite right. Our problem."

"And they are also here to deal with that?" he asked, pointing at the two friars.

Dominicans. In Toulouse. Ironic, since this was where the order began. Its founder, Félix de Guzmán, had dedicated himself, and his followers, to the reconversion of the Cathars. The friars played an integral role in the Albigensian Crusade, effectively leading the attack. In 1206, Dominic founded a convent near Toulouse. Then, eight years later, he added another order for men. Vilamur had studied that time period. A lot of irony existed then.

294

Some historians had even postulated that the Dominicans were a blatant attempt by the church to copy Catharism. Friars traveled around the Languedoc in pairs, like Perfecti, dressing simply in sandals and plain habits, avoiding the ostentation of other church-men and preaching poverty. They spoke in the local language in order to be understood, a practice the Cathars began. Even now, Dominicans still wore black robes, almost identical to the habit of the Perfecti. Celibacy itself might have been hurried into dogma in the twelfth century as a reaction to the Cathars' aversion to sex.

Like with here, far too many things to be coincidental.

"Within the Dominicans," Fuentes said, "there are specialized cells, friars who are trained and devoted to a particular expertise. These two are part of the *Ad Designandum Hastam*. The Point of the Spear. For centuries that cell has been called upon to deal with problems in ways that may seem...unconventional for the church. But the desired results cannot always be accomplished solely by talk or prayer. There are times when more definitive measures must be taken."

Good to know. And also disconcerting.

"Please, wait outside," Fuentes said, and the two friars left the study. The cardinal faced him. "Archbishop, our pope is dying."

Had he heard right? That couldn't be. "He was only elected a short while ago."

"He has a tumor in his brain that will kill him within the coming months. Only a handful of people know this. Now you are one of them."

He was shocked. "Why me?"

"Because I intend to be the next pope."

Now he understood. "And you have the advantage of being able to get ready for the next conclave."

"Exactly. I have many friends, but I will need more within the

College of Cardinals in order to be elected. Friends of unquestioned loyalty."

"And ones upon whom you know a great secret."

"Precisely. Trust can be so fleeting. But, as you said, this is *our* problem. And I intend to solve it. I also have to know that whoever I choose to bring within my confidence will participate in the conclave with great zeal."

He knew the right answer. "That would be me."

Fuentes smiled. "I thought as much. Which explains why we are here, in the middle of the night, speaking to each other. I will deal with Bernat de Foix. Together we will deal with *les Vautours*. And, after that, you shall become a cardinal."

"And perhaps also garner a worthy appointment to the Curia, once you are pope?"

Fuentes never flinched at his greed. "I would expect no less for you."

Message sent. And received. The extortion ran both ways.

"I did not ask before," Fuentes said, "but I will now. Do you still have Father Tallard's video that was sent to you?"

He shook his head. "Deleted."

"All right. We will need to also retrieve it from de Foix. Friar Rice is an expert with computers. Get dressed, Archbishop. We are going to face your demon. Then we will face mine."

CHAPTER 51

Claire kept driving, like a robot, her mind numb, her body reacting automatically to the road and traffic. She was well out of Belgium, now into northeastern France, headed south at a good pace. Hopefully, there'd be no more police. It was important that she return to the motherhouse with Sister Rachel's body. She'd stopped a few hours back for gas and a bathroom, shielding the body bag with a lot of the clothes and other stuff that littered the back seat. She'd have to stop again along the way, but thankfully the black body bag was fairly innocuous among the litter. Still, she'd have to be careful. Ellen had called and confirmed that Sister Deal was in their custody and had agreed to cooperate. So she'd given the okay to provide her a laptop so the images could be compared.

They needed that expertise.

To be sure. To know if the old stories were indeed true.

If and when they dealt with the current threat, depending on the outcome, those images could present a more lasting problem. But first things first. She checked her watch: 2:25 a.m. She reached for her cell phone and tapped the screen at the top of her favorites. The call connected and the abbess answered almost immediately.

"I should be there a little past noontime," she reported. "It was not exactly what I envisioned, but Lee got the job done. Hopefully, he'll give up and move on."

The plan all along had been to use Lee to the point where he was no longer needed. Then ditch him. Which she'd done.

"What does *not exactly what I envisioned* mean?"

"The police were involved, but we eluded them."

"Are you sure? Were you identified?"

"I don't know."

Silence filled the phone.

"It's so easy for you," she said. "There. Safe in the abbey. Judging. It's really different out here."

"I worked the field for many years, without any problems."

"But did you have any challenges?"

More silence.

"I didn't think so," she said. "Look, I realize the Dominicans have changed everything. But I'm just a schoolteacher from Louisiana who answered the call in her head, and now finds herself at the epicenter of a storm that has raged for centuries. I'm doing the best I can."

"But you keep falling short. Focus on the task," the prioress said. "We can debate all this later."

And the call ended.

Damn that woman was obstinate.

She was hungry and made a note to stop at the first opportunity that food was available. The car needed more gas too. A road sign indicated that Reims was twenty kilometers ahead. She'd purposefully avoided any roads through or around the snarl and blare of Paris, staying east in the French countryside, her intended route moving from Reims to Dijon to Lyon to Montpellier, then Perpignan and west into the mountains. Four-laned autoroute nearly the whole way. Another sign indicated that a service area was coming up soon.

Unlike back in the States, none of the commercial establishments were off the exits. Instead, they were built between the four lanes where drivers from either direction could make use of the gas pumps, food, bathrooms, and rest areas. They came at regular intervals and she'd make a stop at the next one parking the car off to the side, away from any bright lights. At this late hour there should not be too many people around. It seemed that everything she'd devoted the better part of her adult life to would come down to the next day or so.

"You will not have died in vain," she said to Rachel in the back seat.

And she meant it.

Women had been living in the abbey atop Mount Canigou for over a thousand years. Each was the successor to other women who'd assumed a duty starting around AD 50. Those first few had buried the Blessed Virgin in a place only they knew, and then assumed stewardship over the tomb, passing their guardianship down from mother to daughter. They'd survived countless wars, the Albigensian Crusade, the French Revolution, and repeated attempts by Rome to discover their presence. Eventually, they evolved into a religious order, which made their task much easier, and for over a thousand years the maidens had performed admirably.

Only a tiny portion of those who attempted to join were allowed to stay. The *most dedicated and determined*, she'd been told. Women who freely swore allegiance to God and the Virgin. Every single person who'd done that was recorded in the Books of Honor. Volume after volume that noted the date of final vows and date of death. Rachel's entry would now be amended to add her date of death, then she would be afforded her final rites, as had been extended to maidens all the way back to Joan of Arc and before. Claire had presided over many such solemn occasions. But all of those maidens had died from natural causes.

This was different.

She muttered out loud three Hail Marys and asked for strength.

Catechism declared that through that prayer a person *rendered to God the highest praise and most gracious thanks, because He bestowed all His heavenly gifts on the most holy Virgin. Never be afraid to earnestly implore Her help and assistance as She is most desirous to assist.* As a Christian, a practicing Catholic, and a daughter of Christ she believed that to be true.

But as a maiden—

Sworn by oath as a *Vautour.*

She had her doubts.

CHAPTER 52

Bernat was dragged from the car, his hands bound behind his back, his mouth taped shut. Two men had burst into his bedroom, roused him from a sound sleep, then forcibly removed him from his house. In the past, living outside of Toulouse amid the woods had been a blessing. He enjoyed the solitude. But now that refuge had turned into a liability, as there was no one around to see what was happening. He'd never alarmed the house or equipped it with cameras either.

There'd never seemed a need.

After all, it was nothing but physical objects that carried only a minimal amount of value. Eventually, he would shed himself of them all.

The best he could determine they were an hour to an hour and a half south of Toulouse, in the Pyrénées foothills. Darkness enveloped everything in thick shadows, the black sky overhead teeming with stars. His captors were two men, one tall, the other short and stout. They'd not said a word on the trip from his house, nor could he speak thanks to the gag. He was still in a state of shock and surprise. Never had he been so violated. He was unsure as to the men's identity or affiliation, except for one thing.

The Holy Roman Church.

It had something to do with them.

Ω

Vilamur waited among the trees, watched as the car came to a stop, and Bernat de Foix was pulled from it. He and Cardinal Fuentes had come straight here from the rectory while Friars Dwight and Rice retrieved de Foix. He was unsure just exactly what was happening and what was going to happen, but he appreciated all of their efforts.

Desperate problems mandated desperate measures.

De Foix was bound and gagged. Not the cocky son of a bitch who'd sent threatening e-messages and summoned him to Montségur.

"Are you ready to face your son?" Fuentes softly asked.

"I'm ready to be rid of him."

Ω

Bernat caught movement in the darkness and saw two people walking toward him through the trees. They came to within a couple of meters and, with eyes adjusted to the dark, he saw that one of the men was Vilamur.

"Monsieur de Foix," the other man said. "I am Hector Cardinal Fuentes. I've come from Rome to deal with you."

Friar Dwight ripped the tape from his mouth.

"This is outrageous," he blurted out.

"I agree," Fuentes said. "The murder of Father Tallard, though perhaps deserved, is outrageous. The extortion you have attempted relative to Archbishop Vilamur is, without question, outrageous. Your chosen religion is most definitely outrageous."

What had Raymond warned? *Careful, the barrel has been jostled, and you have no idea what will now spill out.*

No kidding.

"What are you doing here?" he asked the cardinal.

"Why did you mention *les Vautours?*"

"Is that what this is about?"

"Please answer the question."

"I was told to use the reference in order to get Vilamur's attention. Beyond that, I know nothing."

"By who?"

He hesitated. No way he was going to involve Raymond Barbe. One Perfecti never implicated another. Not eight hundred years ago. Not now. Not ever.

"How about you go—"

Fuentes held up his hand. "No need to resort to the profane. I understand. You do not wish to say. I can only assume it was one of your Cathar companions. Possibly another Perfectus."

He said nothing.

"The Cathars knew *les Vautours,*" Fuentes said. "They were… kindred spirits. Rome wanted them both destroyed. It sent a crusade to accomplish just that. It seems the church failed in both endeavors." Fuentes paused. "But all that failure has brought us here."

He wanted to know, "Is the archbishop allowed to speak? Or does he just do as told?"

"This man is your father," Fuentes said. "You went to a lot of trouble to garner his attention."

"I still have Tallard's confession and a video of the archbishop leaving the priest's house."

"Not anymore," the shorter friar said.

"Friar Rice," Fuentes noted, "is an expert with computers. The Dominicans have fully embraced modern technology. Tell us what you were able to accomplish."

"I erased the video and text messages sent to the archbishop from Monsieur de Foix's computer and phone. I then accessed his cloud server and deleted them from there too. I also deleted a second video of the archbishop leaving the dead priest's house. Then I altered the registries to eliminate all references to them. They no longer exist. Anywhere."

"No password?" Fuentes asked.

"There was. A complicated series of letters and numbers, but Monsieur de Foix kept them written down on a piece of paper taped under his desk drawer. Not all that imaginative."

Bernat's mind raced. The video of Vilamur at Tallard's house, which Andre had captured. He'd told the younger man to delete it once sent. Maybe he'd not done so, and a copy still existed.

"Seems you've been quite the busy man," Fuentes said to him.

Bernat motioned with his head toward Vilamur. "He's a sexual predator, as dangerous as Tallard. You criminally violated every one of those women, including my mother."

Vilamur started to speak, but Fuentes held up a hand. "This is no longer about the archbishop."

"It is entirely about that bastard," he spit out.

"This is about the Vultures."

"Then you're wasting your time. I know nothing of them. I was told they would get your attention, and that information proved correct."

"I agree," Fuentes said. "You absolutely have my attention."

CHAPTER 53

Kelsey continued to study the twelve panels for the altarpiece.
Thanks to computer imaging she was able to lay them out flat on
the screen, side by side, in perfect proportion, as Jan van Eyck
initially created them. But since 1934 the work had not been
complete. Here, on her screen, for the first time anywhere, was
the actual, cleaned, restored *Adoration of the Mystic Lamb* in all its
glory. What a sight. And by comparing the original *Just Judges* from
the fifteenth century with the 1945 reproduction she'd noticed
something.

Small. Relatively insignificant.

Or was it?

The *Just Judges* displayed ten men on horseback. Who were
they? Art historians had debated that for centuries. Were they
burghers from van Eyck's time? Other princes? Dukes? The only
thing experts seemed to agree upon was that two of them were
the van Eyck brothers. The one most prominent, in the center,
wearing a blue cloak and ermine hat, striding on a white horse
was Hubert van Eyck. Right behind him in a brown robe and
another fur-trimmed hat was Jan. No reliable images of the van
Eycks actually existed, though many historians think Jan added

his face to several of his private commissions. Still, the general consensus was that the van Eyck brothers were there, part of the *Just Judges.*

What she'd noticed on the original, under high resolution, was that two of the ten faces were identical. Which was not the case in the reproduction. All ten faces were clearly different. From what she'd read about the reproduction, Jef Van der Veken changed some of the faces, adding in contemporary public figures from his time, including Belgian's then king Leopold. From a close look at the reproduction she saw that was indeed the case. The ten faces were all different. But on the original, eight were different, and two were the same. When Van der Veken created his reproduction, it would have been hard to determine much detail in the faces, given the amount of dirt and grime that had invaded the panels by the 1930s. So when Van der Veken painted over he just fashioned the faces as he pleased. It was, after all, intended as a mere reproduction.

The car kept speeding down the highway, Sisters Ellen and Isabel in the front seat, not bothering her.

No way existed to contact anyone. No email accounts were associated with the laptop. Same with text. No icon led to any texting platform. But she did not feel the need. She was no longer afraid or angry. Instead, she was interested and engaged.

She focused on the two identical faces from the original *Just Judges.*

Both were clean-shaven, and one wore a green robe with a silver-and-blue fur hat. He was facing ninety degrees to the right, his gaze across, straight toward the center panel. Both hands were visible, the left empty, the right holding a short stick balanced atop the index finger, held in place by the thumb. It pointed in the direction the face was looking.

To the right.

The face was the same as the image behind Hubert van Eyck. The one generally believed to be Jan van Eyck.

Why had Jan included himself twice?

Her gaze followed the pointer in Jan's hand across to the adjacent panel, the one known as *Knights of Christ*.

She clicked and enlarged the image.

Nine people on horseback.

Several wearing crowns denoting kingship. The lead figure sported silver armor, holding a banner pole in one hand and a shield in the other. It was the same figure she'd shown Nick, pointing out the strange words that appeared within the red cross atop the shield. She knew the story of this figure. The neutral face, not male or female. A laurel encircling the head. The decidedly feminine touch to the armor.

Most art historians said this was Joan of Arc.

Entirely possible given that Jan van Eyck had a connection to her. His benefactor, Philip the Good, the Duke of Burgundy, had been the one to both capture and turn her over to the English. She was executed in 1431. The altarpiece was completed in 1432. If the two faces on the *Just Judges* were Jan van Eyck, then Jan had painted a pointer in his hand that was aimed straight at Joan of Arc.

With her finger, Kelsey kept going in a straight line beyond Joan, off the *Knights of Christ* and onto the larger main panel. The path took her finger across a hedgerow that filled the painting's upper left quadrant. Toward the center the bushes dipped, forming a distant valley, before rising ever skyward toward the Holy Ghost who shone down on the entire scene. The valley seemed a blue-gray smudge, far off in the distance, misty and foreboding. But high-resolution imaging allowed her to enlarge the area and, as she did, something remarkable formed out of the blur.

A building.

Distinct. Unusual. Multistory, with several wings, stepped gables, and a conical tower. It seemed to fill a promontory high among the trees, off to itself, quiet and alone. Surely it had been noticed before, since the minute details of the altarpiece had been analyzed to death. It had most likely been dismissed as just more of Jan van Eyck's realism, part of a thousand other miniature details he'd included. But no one, other than she, since 1934, had been privy to the original *Just Judges* being a part of the altarpiece.

Was all this nothing more than coincidence?

Something told her no.

Jan van Eyck had left that trail intentionally.

"Has your order always been called the Maidens of Saint-Michael?" she asked the two women in the front seat.

Sister Ellen turned back to face her. "Not in the beginning. They were the Sisters of Saint-Michael. That all changed in the mid-fifteenth century when they adopted the moniker of *maiden*."

"Did that have anything to do with Joan of Arc?"

She asked because of the nickname Joan subsequently acquired after her death. *La Pucelle d'Orléans*. The Maid of Orléans.

"It did," Isabel said. "She was one of us, a postulant, who left the motherhouse during her training and did great things. She died far too young. But we drew strength from her martyrdom. So, with her vindication in 1456, our name was changed to honor her."

After 1431 Joan's negative image changed. Apparitions began. Miracles attributed to her happened. Imposters flourished. She was no longer deemed a heretic. Instead, many began to call her a saint. For Charles VII, time had draped a taint of illegitimacy over his anointing, since Joan had played a key role in making that happen. If she was a heretic and sorceress, as the tribunal had decreed, had the king gained the throne by using her powers—which, by default, made him a heretic too? That question kept being raised. So much so that, in 1450, Charles ordered an investigation into her conviction. Five years later the pope joined the effort, urged on by Joan's mother, calling for the tribunal's original verdict to be overturned.

Which happened in 1456.

The original tribunal was declared tainted with fraud, iniquity, and contradiction, manifest with errors of fact and law. Joan's conviction was deemed null, invalid, worthless, and without effect. She was washed clean of all sin. And ultimately made a saint.

"There was a grand celebration in Orléans after her vindication," Ellen said. "Our response to that was to change the name of the order. We became maidens. Why do you ask?"

"Simply curious."

But she wondered. Was there more to that story? If so, she

doubted these two women would be sharing it. She needed to speak to whoever was in charge.

"Have you found anything?" Ellen asked.

May God forgive her.

"Not yet. But I'll keep looking."

CHAPTER 54

Fuentes assessed Bernat de Foix.

Master Dati of the Dominicans had provided some background information. De Foix was a successful businessman with a reputation for fairness and honesty, two traits essential for someone owning and operating an auction house. No criminal record. No bad publicity. Nothing negative. Except that he was clearly a deeply troubled man.

"I thought Cathars detested wealth and all things of this world?" he asked de Foix.

"I thought priests were to be celibate."

Fuentes smiled. "As did I. Did you have Father Tallard killed?"

"The world enjoys one less predator."

He took that as a yes. But he wondered, "Cathars do not kill."

"I killed no one."

"You just ordered it done. Same thing."

"No. It is not."

"So then you would say that Pope Innocent III, who ordered the Albigensian Crusade, bears no responsibility for the tens of thousands who died?"

De Foix said nothing. But the logic was impeccable.

It was indeed the same thing.

He pointed a finger. "You may have violated the *consolamentum*."

"You know of our practices?"

"I've studied Catharism. Of course, I believed it to be in the abstract, that the religion no longer existed. Yet, here I am, face-to-face with a Perfectus. Your salvation from this evil world may now be in jeopardy."

But he saw that de Foix did not care. All he wanted was the ruin of Gerard Vilamur, and he was willing to risk his soul to get that.

Impressive.

And telling.

"Why did you choose to sponsor the restoration of the *Just Judges* reproduction?" he asked.

De Foix cast a curious look. "What does that have to do with anything?"

"Please just answer the question."

Fuentes had to gauge for himself whether the act was intentional or merely a fortuitous event.

"I thought it would gain me some notoriety. The cost was relatively low and the amount of publicity high."

"Another of those things your religion deems evil."

"We've adjusted."

He chuckled. "I suppose you have. Did you know the original lay beneath the reproduction?"

"I had suspicions."

"From other Cathars?"

No reply.

But that was okay. He was convinced that this man knew nothing of the *Just Judges'* significance. Nothing of Jan van Eyck, Joan of Arc, or the Blessed Virgin.

Nothing of *les Vautours*.

Just a vengeful opportunist.

Perfect.

Exactly as he'd hoped.

Ω

Bernat was feeling uneasy.

True, these were men of the church, but his kidnapping and their treatment of him seemed more in line with mobsters than prelates. Nothing all that unusual, if history was any teacher. Surely, Cathars from long ago had thought the same thing about an invading army storming the countryside, pillaging and plundering, destroying everything and everyone in its path, all in the name of God.

Cathars had it right.

This world truly was evil. Everything in it tainted by evil. It was a place to escape from, to leave behind. How many times had he come and gone before? How many other lives had he experienced? Impossible to say. He'd intended for this to be his last since he'd accepted the *consolamentum* and was now a Perfectus. But the cardinal could be right. Innocent III was as guilty of murder as every one of the crusaders. No difference. And the same was true for him. He would have to start the *consolamentum* all over. But he flushed those troubling thoughts from his brain and refocused on the more immediate problem.

"You're a prince of the church," he said to Fuentes. "What are you going to do about Vilamur? He's a criminal. A disgrace."

The cardinal faced Vilamur. "What do you say to that, Archbishop?"

"I categorically and explicitly deny everything he says in its entirety."

"You see, Monsieur de Foix, the archbishop maintains that you are a liar."

"I have proof."

"Not anymore," one of the other men said. The tall one. "We removed all of the files and information on the archbishop that we found in your study. And we found this." The man displayed the glass vial with Vilamur's saliva. He'd planned on taking it to the DNA laboratory when he returned from Ghent. "You have nothing."

"And I doubt that you have discussed this with anyone, other than the one compatriot," Fuentes said. "Friar Rice, what was the name you found on the email?"

"Andre Labelle. He sent the video of the archbishop leaving Father Tallard's house, with the body inside. We can only assume he recorded it."

"Other than this Monsieur Labelle," Fuentes said, "and perhaps a few within the Cathars, I doubt anyone else knows anything."

This man was both perceptive and thorough. What had he stumbled into? What was happening here? Something far more than Vilamur's adultery.

"Tallard is still dead," de Foix spit out. "There will be an investigation."

"Actually," Fuentes said, "there will not. That body has been removed and disposed of, the house thoroughly cleaned. No one will ever see that pedophile again. The authorities will simply think he fled. A warrant will be issued for his arrest, and that will be the end of it. The men you hired to kill him will, of course, never say a word."

Every detail had been addressed.

Which made him wonder.

What were they going to do with him?

Ω

Vilamur was exercising the patience that forty years of wearing a white collar had taught him. True, he'd once engaged in multiple sexual affairs with a great deal of women. But he quit all that a decade ago. Not even a rumor of his amorous exploits had ever surfaced. He'd thought all that a thing of his past.

But that was not the case.

So he wanted to make clear to de Foix, "This ends here. You can't go any further with whatever you had in mind."

"I can still ruin you," de Foix said. "The allegation alone is enough. I read that you're being considered for a cardinal. So much negative publicity will surely end that."

He glanced over at Fuentes. Hard to gauge the man's eyes or features in the dark. But what de Foix had just said rang true. The time was approaching 4:00 a.m. Dawn less than two hours away. Which meant daylight. People. Witnesses. Trouble.

Wherever this was going, it better get there fast.

"Archbishop," Fuentes said. "May I have a word with you. In private."

$$\Omega$$

Fuentes had come to France to find answers.

And he had.

Now it was time to make the hard call, the type that bishops, cardinals, and popes had made for centuries. The church had not survived for two thousand years by being weak or stupid. Instead, it was smart and strong. True, the Holy See no longer fielded an army or engaged in open warfare. But that did not mean battles were not fought. And he was now faced with one of long standing.

Prior to 1852, the Holy Inquisition had dealt with the problem of *les Vautours*. But it made little progress. Once the Pontifical Commission for Sacred Archaeology came into existence, the matter was transferred there. Over the course of the last 170 years the eighteen predecessors in his job had generally ignored the Vultures, arguing that it was better to let a sleeping dog lie. But none had been presented with the golden opportunity that had dropped into his lap. Archbishop Vilamur's problem had, at first, seemed the most promising lead. But events in Ghent had played out better than expected. The trail now seemed clear. He knew precisely where to find the Vultures. Which meant the matter of Bernat de Foix was more an annoyance. One he had no time to indulge.

He wanted to be pope.

Nothing and no one else mattered.

Ω

Vilamur walked with Cardinal Fuentes away from de Foix and the two Dominicans into the blackened trees. A day ago he was a relatively unknown metropolitan archbishop who wanted to be a cardinal, one of many other bishops around the world with the same ambition. Now he was the confidant of a man actively seeking to be pope, one who apparently commanded Dominicans.

Talk about good fortune.

What a difference a day made.

"It is sad but true that, throughout our history, violence has been a part of the church," Fuentes said. "Pope John VIII was poisoned and clubbed to death by his own clerics. Stephen VI imprisoned and strangled by other prelates. Leo V murdered on orders of Pope Sergius III. John X imprisoned and eventually smothered to death. Benedict VI, killed by a priest on orders from an emperor. John XIV's life ended by an antipope. Not to mention the many crusades, inquisitions, and wars popes waged for centuries where millions died. You know all about that, though, thanks to your thesis."

Yes, he did. But he had to know, "Are you equating me with those dead, corrupt popes?"

"Let us be frank, Archbishop. Those popes I just mentioned were horribly corrupt. They abused their position. You, of course, also abused your position. You took advantage of women. You violated your oath of celibacy. You *are* corrupt. I also want to point out what other Catholics, when faced with similar corruption, chose to do."

He understood. They killed.

"Please know that I did not come here to judge you," Fuentes said. "None of us are free of sin. But I also do not want you to become unmindful of the seriousness of your past actions."

"I don't need to be reminded."

"I think you do. And you also need to grasp the degree of salvation I am extending toward you."

"Which will not be free."

"Not in the least. There will most assuredly be a conclave sometime in the next twelve months. If granted a cardinal's hat, you will be eligible to participate and vote. Once you reach the age of eighty, in three years, you will lose that vote."

"But you will be pope by then."

Fuentes nodded. "And you can work within the Curia, for as long as you desire, well past the age of eighty. In a position befitting your status."

"As a cardinal whom you own."

"That's a crude way of referring to things. But accurate. If it is any comfort, you will not be alone."

Which was no comfort.

He'd dreamed about his elevation for many years, wondering what the moment would feel like. To be there, in St. Peter's Basilica, at a consistory, where his selection would be decreed in the presence of all the remaining cardinals. He would swear allegiance and be presented the ring, scarlet zucchetto, and biretta by the pope.

What a glorious moment.

"Archbishop. No. Gerard. Might I call you that?"

"Of course, Eminence."

"Gerard, thankfully, the Dominicans have always been there when the church needed them. They were here, in the Languedoc, during the Albigensian Crusade. They were there during the Inquisition, Reformation, Counter-Reformation, and every other challenge we've faced during the past eight hundred years. The Point of the Spear is their elite. The ones called upon for the most difficult tasks, the ones that try our consciences and keep us awake at night. I'm fortunate that the current head of the Dominicans is a close friend and understands the gravity of this situation." Fuentes paused. "And the importance of me being the next pope."

The Spaniard gently laid a hand on his shoulder. "Let me tell you a story. I like stories. They help bring things into clearer focus. I once knew a shop owner in Barcelona who had some puppies for sale. A young boy came into the store and wanted to buy one of them. Their price was ten euros, which the boy had. 'Can I see the dogs?' the boy asked. And out of the kennel came a large mother with five tiny balls of fur following. One of the five lagged considerably behind, limping as he walked. 'What's wrong with that little dog?' the boy asked. The shopkeeper told him, 'He has no hip socket. He'll always be lame.' The boy smiled, pointed, and said, 'That's the one I want to buy.' The shop owner was surprised and told the boy the dog wasn't worth the price. 'He's never going to be able to run and jump and play with you like the other puppies.' But the boy was adamant. 'I want that one.' Then the boy rolled up his pant leg to reveal a badly twisted, crippled leg supported by a metal brace. He looked up at the shop owner and said, 'I don't run so well myself, so the little puppy will need someone who understands.'"

Fuentes pointed. "You're my little puppy that I want to buy, and I will understand, too. Neither of us is without fault."

He realized that his own sins had backed him into a corner with no way out, save for the man standing next to him. To be a cardinal he had to sell his soul. But at least Fuentes was making it easy.

"What are you going to do with de Foix?" he asked.

"There is no choice."

No, there wasn't.

"That man is not going to stop," Fuentes said. "He can, and will, make your life a living hell. And he's right. You will not be given a red hat."

"And I will, most likely, also lose my archdiocese."

Fuentes nodded.

He did not hesitate. "Do what you have to do."

"You know what that means?"

"Of course. Do it."

The sale had just been finalized. His soul was gone.

"The Italians have a term. *Fiducia*. Their bond of trust," Fuentes said. "You and I will now have that too."

The cardinal extended a hand, which he shook.

He realized that his actions, swift and natural, with no hesitation, governed by reasoning and convenient rationalizations with zero quarrels of right and wrong, came with a name.

Amoral.

Fuentes motioned and they walked back through the trees, closer to where the others stood. The cardinal waved and Friar Dwight walked over to them.

"Make sure Bernat de Foix joins Father Tallard," Fuentes whispered to the Dominican. "Neither should ever be seen again."

CHAPTER 55

Nick stood at the base of Mount Canigou. Perched upon a rocky pinnacle thirty-five hundred feet up sat the motherhouse of the Maidens of Saint-Michael. A narrow single-laned, paved road wound a path up the mountain through stands of old-growth oaks, the cool midday disturbed only by a distant solitary church bell. The sole way to get up there was to walk. The idea, as had been explained in the nearby town, was for the arduous trek to allow the visitor to gradually leave the world below behind. There was a vehicular road, a bit wider and paved also, but it was on the other side of the mountain and sealed off, used only by the convent to bring up supplies.

It bothered him that he hadn't been able to speak with Kelsey. But he had to remind himself that she was part of another world now, one with its own ways and rules. Both of which he had to respect. At least she was safe, out of harm's way.

He'd contacted Reynaldo after Sister Claire had fled and explained the situation, accepting full responsibility for his own gullibility.

"This is turning ridiculous," Reynaldo had said. "Perhaps we should end this now."

"You said I could have two days."

320

"That was before you allowed a nun to get the better of you. The Belgians are going to start screaming shortly. Getting you out of there seems like a good idea."

"Something big is happening here."

"You don't know that."

"I'm here, on the ground, doing my job. I'm telling you that there's something here to discover. Something I need to follow through on."

They'd gone back and forth and finally Reynaldo had agreed to honor the two days. But it was clear that he owed his boss a big one. Less than an hour later a NATO chopper found him and he was flown south to Perpignan, where he'd obtained ground transportation and driven the hour west toward the mountains, to the motherhouse, where Sister Claire was headed with the body. Which meant she was most likely going to use the other way up. Fine. He'd allow her that. He just needed to be up there by the time she arrived.

He checked his watch.

That should be soon, if not already.

Assuming she'd driven straight through.

Which was a safe assumption.

He'd managed to grab a little sleep on the flight south, having long ago mastered how to rest in snatches of no more than an hour or so. He'd bought a couple of sandwiches and a bottled water before heading over from town to the abbey. The guy at the local café told him the hike up would take about an hour. *Hope you have strong legs.* And now, staring up at the start of the inclined journey, he could see that the man had been right.

That was a long climb.

But what the hell?

He could handle it.

Or could he?

* * *

"Come on, Nick, let's go," Charlie Minter said.

They were on an adventure. Nick, Charlie, and Marvin Royster. Three twelve-year-olds in the hills outside Colorado Springs. Hiking. Packs on their backs. Boots on their feet. They'd done it many times before, one of the perks of living in such a wonderful place. The three had grown up together, their parents close friends. Today they were explorers, following a trail above the timberline, jagged layered peaks capped with snow in the distance, only sunshine and green valleys in between.

A beautiful Saturday afternoon.

They were headed to the tunnels. Originally carved out to transport ore through the mountains, most were boring and unimportant. But one carried a legend. It was said that a wagon full of children had once been trapped there when the tunnel collapsed. So much damage had occurred that the entrance had been sealed, leaving the wagon where it sat with the bodies, trapping the spirits inside for all of eternity.

A good ol'-fashioned local ghost story.

"My brother told me," Charlie said, "that hikers have heard laughing inside the tunnel. He swears ghosts are there."

Nick had heard the same thing from his older brothers. But he wondered how much of that was true, and how much was just them trying to scare him.

"My dad told me," Marvin said, "that some people who've gone inside have been scratched by the ghosts. There are voices and all kinds of weird things goin' on there too."

They'd heard so many stories that they decided to go see for themselves.

Hence the adventure.

The hike took about half an hour, the trail more like a narrow dirt road, well defined with directional signage. No danger of getting lost. He spotted Beaver Lake off toward the west, its mirrored surface a shiny silver blue. Ghosts were said to dwell there too. He'd read about a battle between the Cheyenne and Utes near its shores. Indians fighting Indians. Women and children had taken to rafts trying to escape the carnage by floating out on the lake. A storm had struck and they were all lost in the water. People said the lake was haunted by those who'd drowned, but he'd never heard or seen anything there.

They were following the trail ever upward, the inclined path passing right by the haunted tunnel entrance, large and wide, plenty of room for a horse-drawn wagon to go inside.

Nick had not expected that.

"My dad told me that they opened this up years ago," Charlie said.

Nick was not as sure as he once was about the stories being false. Maybe there was something to it? "You think we ought to go inside?"

Marvin shook his head. "I'm not sure."

Charlie slipped his backpack off. "You're not scared, are you?"

"I'm not scared," Nick felt compelled to say.

And Marvin agreed. "Me neither. Let's go in."

"Not yet," Charlie said. "I brought some protection."

His friend unzipped the pack from his back, reached inside, and removed a gun.

"Wow," Marvin said.

Nick's eyes went wide too. "Where'd you get that?"

"My dad. He keeps it hidden, but I know where. I figured we might need it."

"Against a ghost?" Nick asked.

"We don't know what's inside there," Charlie said.

Nick had never touched or seen a gun up close. His family was not into them. This one was big and black, and looked heavy.

"It's a Colt," Charlie said, gripping the stock with both hands. "Like in the westerns." Charlie raised the gun and pointed it at a tree. "We're ready now for whatever's in there."

It happened fast.

So quick that Nick never realized until it was far too late.

Marvin reached for the weapon, saying he wanted to hold it. Charlie resisted, swinging the gun around and yelling no. The arc of his pivot pointed the barrel, only for an instant, straight at Marvin, but long enough for the trigger to accidentally be pulled.

The bullet plowed into the young boy's chest.

Then exploded out from the back.

Nick could still see the blood spray from the exit wound and the look of fright in his friend's eyes, then the body folding to the ground, as if in slow motion. Charlie had stood there, in shock, before tossing the gun aside and running away. Nick had been in shock too, but quickly ran over to Marvin, hoping he might be okay. He'd shaken his friend, trying to rouse him, but nothing happened. Color drained from the face. No breathing. No movement. Nothing. Only lots of blood. He'd seen only one dead body before that day, his grandfather's at the funeral, and the ashen shade that quickly appeared reminded him of that corpse.

Marvin Royster was dead.

The gun had been an M1911, more popularly known as a Colt 1911, a single-action, semi-automatic, recoil-operated pistol, chambered for a .45-caliber cartridge. Standard issue for the US armed forces from 1911 to 1985. Widely used in World War I, World War II, the Korean and Vietnam Wars. Charlie's father had served in Vietnam and kept the weapon both as a memento and for protection. He'd also filed down the trigger, as was common with those who'd served, reducing the amount of pressure needed to pull it. Something his twelve-year-old son would have never known, or understood.

A horribly tragic accident.

Nick kept walking up the path toward the abbey.

He still hadn't seen the motherhouse, which was much farther up. He also hadn't passed anyone else going either up or down.

No surprise there, as a placard below had indicated that the abbey was closed for the day. He was eating his sandwiches, drinking the water, and thinking back.

It always happened when he hiked.

He ultimately joined the army, became an MP, then went to work for the FBI. Guns had been a part of all his training. He knew how to handle a weapon and was a pretty good shot on the range. But truth be known, he hated them. One killed his friend Marvin Royster, which his other friend Charlie Minter had to live with until the day came years later when Charlie took his own life.

With a gun.

So far, he'd never drawn a weapon in the line of duty. And he only carried one when absolutely necessary. Reynaldo had authorized that he be armed and a weapon had been waiting in the chopper. A semi-automatic pistol with two spare magazines. But he'd left them all there. What awaited him at the end of this path?

Impossible to say.

But he wasn't going to shoot anybody.

CHAPTER 56

Kelsey had managed to tumble in and out of sleep, her mind roaming unrestrained. When she woke for good, Sister Ellen was driving with Isabel in the passenger seat and it was daytime. The dashboard clock read 12:20. She'd been out awhile. Amazing, really, considering the situation. The computer still rested on her lap. Outside the car windows she saw trees and mountains.

"Where are we?" she asked.

"Not far from the motherhouse, in southern France," Isabel said. "You slept a long time."

"I was more tired than I realized."

They'd made a stop hours ago, before she fell asleep, for food and a bathroom, which she'd appreciated. What she'd discovered within the original *Just Judges* panel still filled her brain. Was she right? Were the two faces the same? Pointing the way to a building?

It might never be clear why Jef Van der Veken painted over the original *Just Judges* and handed it off as a reproduction. Had he been part of the theft? After the suspected thief died of a heart attack in late 1934, had he been stuck with the panel and, so as to not be implicated, painted over and returned it, thereby preserving the original masterpiece and not implicating himself?

That made the most sense.

Then there was the poem Van der Veken painted on the back side. *I did it for love. And for duty. And to avenge myself. I borrowed from the dark side.*

Considering what she now knew, that seemed like a confession.

But none of those whys really mattered anymore.

The fact remained that the original had existed, she'd photographed it, and, most important, two of the faces were identical, something Van der Veken might not have even noticed given the original panel's horrendous condition at the time. No way those two faces being the same was simply a fifteenth-century mistake. Jan van Eyck didn't make mistakes. And, another fact, no other character on the altarpiece held anything like a pointer.

That was a message.

From long ago.

But for, or to, what?

Something told her the Maidens of Saint-Michael knew it all. Which was another reason why she'd decided to cooperate.

She wanted those answers.

Nick had to, by now, be wondering what had happened to her. Perhaps he contacted the convent or confronted the prioress? Either way he would learn nothing. How she wished he was here. She was in way over her head and the only person she trusted completely, in all the world, no questions asked, always and forever, was Nick. They might not be able to be husband and wife, or lovers, but they could be man and woman, friends.

And she definitely needed a friend right now.

They were off the main autoroute on a two-laned regional road that wound a path at the base of the mountains. The tires hummed a steady whine on the seamless asphalt. Sister Ellen slowed at a driveway protected by a heavy iron gate. Thick-trunked trees guarded both sides, along with a deep ditch that drained the road.

No way to drive around the gate. Ellen stopped the car and Isabel tapped on her phone.

"It's electronically controlled," Ellen said. "From the mother-house."

The gate began to roll to one side.

Apparently, they were expected.

Ellen drove through and navigated a switchback that zigzagged upward along the steep incline. It had been cut from the rock and paved with concrete, most of it cracked and potholed. Clearly it had been there awhile. The turns were tight and nerve-racking, barely enough room for the car to make the climb. But Ellen handled the challenge with expert precision.

"You've done this before," she said to Ellen.

"Once or twice."

"She's the best," Isabel said. "We all have to do it at one time or another."

"I actually prefer to walk up from the other side," Ellen said as she spun the wheel tight to the left and took another sharp curve.

She was beginning to like these two women, despite the fact that they'd assaulted and drugged her. For so long her entire life had been confined to the women in her convent. Sure, she still had her mother, father, and two brothers who all lived back in the United States. But contact with them was limited to a visit once a year, social media, and an occasional FaceTime call. They were all devout Catholics and respected the choice she'd made in life. No problems on the home front. Her closest friends all lived at the convent, with a few more added from the outside assignments she'd managed to snag along the way. That was another reason why she'd decided to contact Nick. She needed a different kind of friend. One who knew her from before, and one that she could count on no matter what.

The road began to level off and they came to its end. Three other vehicles were parked in a small graveled clearing ringed by trees. One of them a Volvo with Belgian license plates. They stepped from the car out into cool mountain air, warmed ever so slightly by bright rays of sunshine that filtered through the leafy canopy.

Sister Ellen retrieved the laptop from her. "Nothing there?"

Enough with the lies, she decided. "I wouldn't say that."

The admission grabbed the two women's attention.

"What did you find?" Isabel asked.

"I'll tell that to the person in charge. I have some questions of my own."

"I'm sure you do," Ellen said. "But today is not the day for answers."

She wondered about that comment, but let them know, "I seem to have nothing but time."

"I wish we could say the same," Isabel said.

She did not like the sound of that declaration.

Ellen motioned and they started walking from the clearing, leaving the gravel for a concrete path through the trees. To the left and right everything seemed groomed, the underbrush trimmed and sculpted in a calculated way. Flowers everywhere. Violas, hepaticas, violets. All natural, wild, yet controlled. She wondered if it was some sort of metaphor for the maidens themselves. They crested a small rise and several buildings came into view, snuggled tight among the towering trees across the ridge.

"The building there to the right is our visitor center," Ellen said. "We have people come daily for tours and we accommodate hikers who stop by from time to time. The farthest brick building was once a stable. Now it's a gymnasium."

"Which your members surely make good use of," she said.

Isabel smiled. "That we do."

She spotted an arched, stone gate spanning a paved road that led to another graveled car park beneath the trees. The last building seemed the abbey's main structure. Multiple wings. Stepped-gable ends. Conical tower. Slate roof. Its exterior was heavy hewn stone held in place by thick mortar, pierced by mullioned windows, their spacing perfectly calculated, the thickness of the walls evident from the recesses. Everything cast a rich blue-gray color, deep, soft, pastoral. It sat on the edge of the summit, open sky framing out the far side where the ridge ended and a gorge stretched to a rock face in the distance. Nothing appeared happenstance, all seemed the result of thought and knowledge, the whole thing a mastery of space, expression, vigor, and movement. She'd always thought that, of all the arts, architecture was the most aesthetic, the most mysterious, and the most nourished by ideas.

"Our motherhouse," Isabel said.

She'd seen it before.

Everything minus the white cherry tree out front in bloom. Though there'd been additions, the basic structure was the same as what had been painted in the fifteenth century on the altarpiece.

The building Jan van Eyck had pointed toward.

And the number of her questions—

Just multiplied.

CHAPTER 57

Claire knelt on the crypt's hard stone floor.

She'd arrived back with Sister Rachel about two hours ago. The maidens had reverently carried the corpse from the car to the abbey. Usually the entombment of a deceased maiden involved two days of prayer and mourning. But they did not have the luxury of time.

So everything was accelerated.

What had happened dated back to the beginning, the same ritual performed on every maiden. The naked corpse was laid onto a long oak table. Two maidens held a dark cloth stretched above the body, while two others washed the flesh with sponges. They carried out their task with great respect and reverence, without looking down, as the cloth held over the body respectfully hid the corpse from view. A fifth maiden wrung out the sponges in a bowl, then dipped them into fresh water. The body, once wrapped in a white linen shroud, was dressed in a freshly pressed gray smock, a veil set in the hair. Then the body was placed into a coffin made of wicker. On the breast was laid a wreath of white, red, and sky-blue flowers, as had been done long ago with the

331

first maiden. The coffin was brought down below the abbey into the church. The space was one of the oldest on the site, first dug from the surrounding rock and soil over a thousand years ago. Huge stone pillars, like tree trunks with branching arms, lost themselves in the shadowy canopy overhead. A series of low vaults and arches, each about three yards high, broke the space up into sections. There was no decoration, no frescoes, sculptures, or stained glass.

All of the other maidens had now gathered, on their knees, heads bent in prayer, a collective silence bonding them together. After a few moments the abbess began, and the others joined, in singing the Ave Maria. Not Sir Walter Scott's original words scored for piano by Schubert, but the lyrics that came straight from an ancient prayer.

> *Hail Mary, full of grace, the Lord is with thee.*
> *Blessed art thou among women,*
> *and blessed is the fruit of thy womb Jesus.*
> *Holy Mary, Mother of God, pray for us sinners,*
> *now, and at the hour of our death.*

The soulful melody made her heart swell.

Something about the soothing notes drew her closer to God. She never tired of hearing it sung, but wished it was under better circumstances. Twenty-one of the twenty-six maidens were back at the motherhouse, including Rachel who would soon be interred deep within the earth. Only five maidens were not present. Two were assigned lookout duty on the main northern entrance, one watching the car park and pedestrian road, the other the rear that accommodated their own vehicles, where the stolen Volvo she'd taken from Nick Lee sat parked. Two more were off-site, returning with Sister Deal.

Tours and public access had been canceled for the next few days. No reason was given, as none was required. This was private property, and it was a privilege for anyone to be allowed inside. The last time a threat of this magnitude occurred was late 1944, when the Nazis rolled through. For most of the war the Languedoc had been part of Vichy France, unoccupied by the German invaders. But toward the end Hitler took control of southern France and resistance activity soared. *Les Vautours* had done their part, trying to undermine the concentration camp at Rivesaltes, near Perpignan, with four maidens dying in the effort.

The abbess knelt with her head bowed in prayer. Claire knew this had to be especially painful for her.

Losing a sister.

And on her orders.

She hadn't been in favor of the attack in Ghent, but followed her vow to obey her superior. If she'd only been more careful and not allowed Nick Lee to track her they would not be in the mess they currently faced. So this was partly her fault too.

The song ended.

Silence reigned.

It was important that Rachel be laid to rest before the trouble began. She deserved that. Would the Dominicans come? Absolutely. No question. Since, for the first time, they knew exactly where to go. No more secrecy. No more guessing. All had been revealed.

The future of everything was on the line.

The abbess crossed herself and stood, stepping to the front of the underground chapel before the plain stone altar where Rachel lay in her wicker coffin. "It is important we speak as a group before we take our sister to her grave."

Claire and the others looked up from their prayers. The abbess' face was a bland mask of concern, the eyes exuding a power, determination, and strength of purpose they'd all come to expect. No fear. No doubt. Just resolve.

"I am not unmindful of the dissension that exists within our ranks. We are divided on what we have done. But I ask that you put all that aside. We will soon be challenged, and we cannot allow Sister Rachel to have died in vain."

No one spoke.

Claire heard movement behind her and turned to see Ellen and Isabel escorting Sister Deal into the church.

"Thank you for coming," the abbess said to Deal.

"Did I have a choice?"

Claire stood and faced the newcomer. "None of us has a choice any longer. Thanks to you and Nick Lee."

"You broke into my workshop, set a masterpiece on fire, attacked me, and stole my computer. And this is my fault? Nick's fault?"

No one replied.

Sister Deal pointed toward the altar and the wicker coffin. "Is that the woman who died?"

"It is," Claire said. "Nick helped us retrieve her."

"You've met Nick?"

Claire nodded. "He and I worked together."

"Who are you?"

"Sister Claire."

"Where is Nick?"

"I left him in Belgium."

"Left him where?"

Deal's voice had risen.

"It doesn't matter," Claire said. "Through whatever twists of fate, the two of you managed to take advantage of my mistakes and expose us, something that has not happened in over fifteen hundred years."

"And the *Just Judges* panel was vital, because it pointed straight here?"

"How do you know that?" Claire asked.

Deal told them what she'd discovered on the ride south.

When she finished, Claire said, "Jan van Eyck visited this site in the spring of 1428. He'd been on a spy mission into Spain. At that time there was no defined border between what would eventually become Spain and France. So we marked our land, which then extended down into the valley, with a symbol that the Moors understood."

She stretched back the left side of her smock and displayed the tattoo.

"A vulture," she said, "which we had long adopted as our symbol."

"A strange choice," Deal noted.

"Not really," Claire said. "They are quite formidable. Live solitary lives. Have few enemies. And never kill a thing. That's us. We carved them into tree trunks. The Moors respected us. We'd nursed several of them back to health after they'd been severely wounded in battle. We talked with them. Prayed with them. Learned from them. We were friends. So they honored our territory. They were not the barbarians the church and history would have everyone believe. Quite the contrary, in fact."

"Van Eyck came here?" Deal asked.

"He did," the abbess said. "He spent a few weeks, resting and painting. He was an inquisitive sort and the maidens at the time came to like him. That friendship proved invaluable a few years later when Joan of Arc was executed."

Claire heard a soft purr. The silence of the crypt amplified what would otherwise have been unnoticeable. The abbess reached into the pocket of her smock, removed a phone, and tapped the screen. The older woman listened for a moment, then ended the call.

"They are here."

CHAPTER 58

Fuentes stepped from the car, out into the midday sun. The reflective matte-black lenses of his sunglasses barely muted the harshness of the bright rays. A perfect bowl of blue sky stretched east-to-west. It had been a while since he'd last been in the mountains. He grew up on the Spanish side of the Pyrénées, close to Barcelona. He and his two brothers had hiked the hills repeatedly. One of them was now dead, while the other lived in Madrid and would surely be there the day he was crowned pope.

And that day was coming.

He had strong support within the College of Cardinals, more than enough to emerge as a serious contender. Many cardinals voted for themselves on the first ballot. Some just wanted to hear their name called out. A once-in-a-lifetime thing. Others did it to alert their brethren that they were interested in the job. But the serious contenders? The ones with a genuine shot to win? They voted for themselves simply to add one more to the tally they'd already established. And if that initial count came in hearty, then all challengers would know the race was on.

And he was ready.

But he was not unmindful of the idiom.

He who enters the conclave a pope, leaves a cardinal.

A warning about campaigning for the papacy, one many had not taken to heart. There'd not been a Spanish pope since Alexander VI at the turn of the sixteenth century. Not a man to emulate either. A Borgia. Ascended the ranks through nepotism. Kept multiple mistresses. Fathered several children. Bought his way to the papal throne with bribes. Regarded as one of the most corrupt popes in history.

He'd definitely do better.

He and Archbishop Vilamur had driven south from Toulouse in a diocese vehicle. They were now standing in a paved car park at the base of Mount Canigou, just outside the small town that sat below the Maidens of Saint-Michael's motherhouse. From the signage it appeared this was where visitors left their vehicles before making the trek up to the abbey. Only one other car was there, and a sign that normally displayed the hours the abbey was open for tours sported an over-sign that indicated the site was closed today.

Interesting.

Apparently, they were expected.

"Gerard," he said to Vilamur, "once we arrive up at the abbey, I will need your help to gain access. They will ignore my requests, but they would be hard-pressed to keep the doors locked to their archbishop."

He'd intentionally not said much on the trip. Nor had Vilamur said much hours ago on the nocturnal return to the rectory, after they'd dealt with de Foix. He decided that perhaps some explanation was now in order. "I told you yesterday that popes were fools. But these maidens? They are anything but fools. Which is why they have remained hidden for so long."

"How did you know they exist? To know to even look for them?"

He was waiting for the others to arrive, so he decided a bit more explanation was in order. Especially to a new ally.

"By the thirteenth century and the Albigensian Crusade, Marian worship was firmly entrenched within the Church. She had her backstory, feast days, and countless churches dedicated to her. She possessed a cult of worship and had become a vital part of our religion. But there's also *The Testimony of John*, which contradicted one of the basic tenets of the Blessed Virgin. She did not ascend body and soul into heaven. She died and was buried here on earth. Rome has long been aware of *les Vautours* and their connection to a possible tomb for Mary. How? I have no idea. That information has been lost. But during the Albigensian Crusade, Pope Innocent III instructed the Dominicans to find them. They tried, repeatedly, but were not successful. They did manage to locate a copy of *The Testimony of John*, which was hidden away in the Vatican." He paused. "Then, in 1933, a new document was found in the Vatican archives. An odd manuscript. But telling. Would you like to read it?"

Vilamur nodded.

He stepped back to the car, found the iPad in his briefcase, and opened to the file. He handed it to Vilamur. "This is a translation into English. It came to us in Flemish. We are not aware of its origins, but the best guess is it was written by Lambert, Jan van Eyck's brother, who completed Jan's unfinished works after Jan's death in 1441."

He watched as Vilamur read from the screen.

Praise and glory for the work,
Of paintings made by the one called Jan.

339

STEVE BERRY

Born in Maaseik, the Flemish Apelles.
Study diligently, understand, and you will see.
Through his eye for detail we see his patience.
And it is just as clear that he has a grand memory.

Come, you art lovers of all sorts,
And look at this precious treasure of paint.

You will deem Saint Peter's wealth as nothing
Because this is the true heavenly treasure.

Come, but with diligence and wisdom,
And pay attention to all things, as you will notice
That there is a line to abundancy
Because even a maid wants to make
A best impression and be praised.

Who wouldn't be rejoiced by those devotees,
Since all could learn some purity.
Notice how triumphant those judges ride
Toward kings, princes, counts and lords.

Notice the faces, along with the maid,
All things can be seen, toward and past her
And how well you will understand
Where she rests in peace.

Look how sound and honorable are the parts,
Of elders and clergy, standing and lying.
Here you see nothing but extraordinary,
Examples of all that is good.

But among the judges one sees the princely painters,
All the faces dissimilar, decorated with gracefulness
And without error, save for two.

His flower shot early off this world.
The one who came from Maaseik.
His life ended in Bruges.
But he will live for eternity
Among the holy.

"Jan van Eyck died in July 1441. He was buried in the grave-yard of the Cathedral of St. Donatian in Bruges," Fuentes said to Vilamur. "In 1442 his brother Lambert had the body exhumed and placed inside the cathedral. But when that tomb was opened in the mid-eighteenth century it was found to be empty."

"You think he's here? Among the maidens?"

"That is hard to say. But, if so, then this poem would be authentic. Before today, we had nowhere to look to verify."

"And that's why the *Just Judges* was so important?"

"Correct. This poem clearly references the altarpiece and that particular panel. It implies that the *Just Judges* can lead you to the Vultures. We were actively investigating that possibility in 1934, but the panel was stolen before we could examine it."

"Why was Rome so intent on it?"

"Pius XI was planning to declare the Assumption of Mary as dogma. But he wanted the matter of *les Vautours*, and what they may or may not possess, resolved. So the commission began an active investigation, involving both *The Testimony of John* and the poem."

"You must have been elated to learn the panel had been found," Vilamur said.

"To say the least. And I've been waiting patiently to view it.

But again, *les Vautours* struck first and destroyed it. This is a vexing issue. Pius XI died in 1939, declaring nothing relative to the Virgin. Eleven years later, in 1950, Pius XII invoked papal infallibility for the first time in almost a hundred years and defined the dogma of the Assumption of Mary. *Having completed the course of her earthly life, she was assumed body and soul into heavenly glory.* That was the last time full papal infallibility has been employed by a pope to this day. That dogma was preceded in 1946 by an encyclical, *Deiparae Virginis Mariae*, which requested all Catholic bishops to express their opinion on the Assumption. That was also a way to alert *les Vautours* to what might be coming. To see if they intended to keep their secret about the Virgin's grave. Hearing nothing, four years later, the pope moved ahead."

"And nothing has been revealed since. So why not just leave them alone? Obviously, they want whatever they have to remain secret."

"That's one course that could be pursued. But what if they change their minds? What if they abandon their mission? What if there is a traitor among them? That tomb could be found."

"How would anyone know it to be authentic?"

"There is a way. Not exact, but close enough to be sure. *The Testimony of John* speaks to it."

Another car wheeled into the lot and parked.

Friars Dwight and Rice exited, along with two other men, all dressed casually with jackets beneath which he spotted holstered weapons.

Good. He'd told them to come armed.

"Our troops have arrived," he said.

342

CHAPTER 59

Nick estimated he was about halfway up the zigzagging road, the path ascending the ridge like steps of a ladder. He'd finished his water and sandwiches, depositing the trash in one of the receptacles he'd passed along the way. He was fortified, ready for what lay ahead.

Whatever that might be.

He was probably a thousand to fifteen hundred feet up with a clear view through the trees. Flanks of green, narrow valleys lined with stands of beech, birch, and pine stretched for as far as he could see, more jagged mountains filling the horizon. It reminded him a lot of Colorado. The road he'd taken from town was also visible, traffic light today. The sun was high in the clear sky, warming the cool mountain air, the scent of pine strong in the breeze. How would he deal with the maidens? Surely, they were not going to appreciate his presence. After all, Sister Claire had driven off and left him in the Belgian countryside. Nothing unintentional about that. But he'd rebounded, and here he was ready to face what lay ahead. He'd dealt with a lot of tough situations across the globe. Delicate scenarios where he'd been required to think and act smart. He was an official UN representative and, as his training had made clear, his actions had consequences. Like stealing a body from a member nation's morgue? Reynaldo had told him that they'd be speaking more about that one when this was over, and he was not looking forward to that conversation. But he'd never encountered something like this. Definitely a first. Made more complicated by Kelsey's involvement.

He stopped for a short rest.

His gaze drifted back to the spectacular view, which also afforded a look down at the car park. Another vehicle had joined his there. Two men were standing outside the car. Visitors? Finding out the abbey was closed for the day? Maybe. One of them was reading from what appeared to be a tablet of some kind. Another car motored in and stopped. Four men emerged. He was too far away to make out faces, but the two from the front seat, one tall, the other short and stout, seemed familiar.

Dwight and Rice.

Dominicans.

With reinforcements?

All six men gathered for a moment, the pad was left inside one of the cars, then they started walking toward the inclined path.

Okay.

Game on.

$$\Omega$$

Kelsey felt the murmur of alarm that had skittered across the low-ceilinged chapel.

They are here.

Most of the maidens headed back up to ground level. The abbess directed four of the women to approach the altar and lift the wicker coffin with Sister Rachel inside.

"Take her to the cemetery," the abbess said.

"I'd like to go with them," Kelsey said to Sister Claire, and she caught the hesitancy in the woman's eyes. "I won't try to leave. You have my word. I have no desire to do that. I want to be here."

"May I ask why?"

"I want to know what this is all about. What Sister Rachel died for. What is it that compels all of you to do what you do?"

"Something wondrous," Claire said.

Kelsey was unpersuaded. "I hope so. Considering the price that was paid."

Claire turned toward the abbess and the older woman nodded. "Okay, go with them. But Sister Isabel will go too."

She nodded, understanding that trust came with limits.

The four maidens carried the wicker coffin up the stairs, then out of the building, into an open cloister dotted with topiaries, roses, wisteria, and lavender beds. Through the arches on the back side she caught a spectacular view of the mountains and the countryside for miles in the distance. The gorge just beyond felt like a sepulcher, the polished limestone a ghostly bone color, riddled with gaps and gashes that sprouted wildflowers. Not unlike the cliff face Jan van Eyck had painted on the *Just Judges*.

Sister Isabel took the lead and the procession continued out of the cloister to the front of the abbey, past the blooming cherry tree. The gate she'd seen earlier rose up ahead but the maidens did not carry the body that way. Instead, they veered right and headed toward the visitor center, passing the limestone building, and continuing into the trees, many of their pale trunks a silver blue gray. The trail they followed was well worn, a straight line through a wall of timber, like curtains on either side. Ferns and creepers littered the ground beneath the dense canopy. Box brush, green moss, and orange lichens grew in abundance among the shade.

The silent procession continued, with Sister Isabel in the lead. Kelsey followed behind the coffin. She felt out of place, here with another order and dressed in non-religious garb. A stranger in one way, but not in another. She sensed a connection to these women.

Strange that she would. But it was there.

Ahead she spotted a line of stacked gray stones that extended out to either side of the trail about waist-high. The low rock wall a barrier, but not an obstruction. A closed iron gate blocked the trail.

Beyond the gate she spotted graves.

Isabel pulled open the gate.

Above, in the stone arch was a chiseled inscription. In Latin. She silently translated:

> *O you who are in life,*
> *Enter and praise those*
> *who are not*

The coffin was carried through the gate and into the graveyard. The glade stretched for about fifty yards and gradually inclined upward. More loose soil here than rock, which was probably why it had been selected. Spring-green grass sprouted in patches. Violets added color. She surveyed the graves, which appeared to all have been there a long time, many of the markers worn to nothing. She felt the soft cushion of the grass beneath her shoes. Everything was neatly trimmed and carefully maintained. A freshly dug grave waited near a far corner close to the rock wall, the air pungent with the dank smell of turned earth. The maidens threaded a path through the crosses and markers, then gently laid the coffin on the grass.

She drifted off to the side, her head bowed in prayer.

Ω

Nick stood behind the trunk of a thick beech tree and watched the six men march ever upward.

Like an army.

Surely armed.

What did they plan to do? More important, what did the maidens plan to do? They had to know these men were coming. He should call in local law enforcement and let them handle it. He could even involve Inspector Zeekers back in Ghent. Everything happening here was directly related to what had already happened there. It might even smooth things over for Reynaldo, whom he hated placing in a difficult situation. But what could the locals do? Nothing had happened, and nothing would so long as they were involved. And was this a police matter?

Not really.

He had to handle this himself, which, he'd come to learn, was the wisest course. The good part was that the men headed his way were unaware he was there. The maidens? They knew. No question. Those women were smart enough to have either cameras or lookouts watching. Either way they knew about him and them. So he decided to allow the Dominicans to get ahead of him.

Then he noticed something else.

Behind the six men who were making another of the many turns, ascending and twisting their way ever closer, a fourth car had parked in the paved lot.

A man emerged.

Thin, dressed in dark clothes. Heading straight to the inclined road. But not making any effort to catch up with the others.

Instead, he stayed back.

As if following.

Who was this?

CHAPTER 60

Kelsey watched as the maidens fed ropes beneath the wicker coffin, then lifted and lowered it into the ground. None spoke, but all of them, including Isabel, cried.

She continued to pray.

But her gaze drifted to the nearby stone markers. Each was simple with no adornments. Just a name and a year. "Lana 1843." "Jamie 1786." "Viviana 1925." "Daniella 1828." So many women laid to rest here. There was a force about the place, which seemed almost animate, despite being only for the dead. No way that this was all the maidens. Given they'd been around for over a millennium, they would need a cemetery far bigger than this. Most likely, most maidens were returned to their families for burial and these were the ones without anywhere to go.

Like Sister Rachel.

She felt partially responsible for what had happened to her, though she knew it was not her fault. The decisions that led to Rachel's death were made by others. These women, living here in the mountains, dedicated to something that she as yet did not know, were determined. True, they'd destroyed a priceless work of art, but she was beginning to believe that there might have been a good reason for that, and she desperately wanted to know what that might be.

Isabel started and the other maidens began to sing the Ave Maria. She was not much of a singer but joined them.

Ω

Fuentes had not felt this satiated in a long while.

Of late his job had become more a depressant, one that had slowly drained him of talent and energy. But the news that the pope was dying had invigorated him. Now he could achieve so much more. Cardinals had, for centuries, taken advantage of situations that developed within the Vatican. Some had even managed to propel themselves to the papacy, and he wanted to follow their lead. Was it essential that this matter with the Virgin Mary be put to rest? Not really. The issue was only known within the most upper echelons of the Curia. But those dozen or so cardinals would be needed in the conclave, and this would be his way of showing them that he was the right man for the top job. The one who could get things done. Even those tasks that others had deemed impossible. The question of Mary's tomb had been hanging for an extremely long time.

Too long.

Over roughly seventeen hundred years Mary's exalted status had been good for the church. She'd brought comfort to millions of believers, softening the hard male edges that God and Christ could sometimes project. She was the perfect counter of female to male, and those early church fathers had been smart to invent her. And if this was five hundred, two hundred, or even fifty years ago it might not matter. But this was the age of instant, worldwide communication. Anyone and everyone had access to everyone else. So finding the tomb of the Virgin Mary and proving that Pius XII's dogma was far from infallible would have traction. True, the maidens had kept the secret and surely intended to keep doing so. But he wasn't going to rely on that.

Better to end this here and now.

Without further worry.

They came to the top of the road and an open gateway that led toward the motherhouse beyond. He heard singing. From off to the left. Away from the abbey.

He stopped their advance. "It's the Ave Maria."

Coming from the direction of the cemetery.

Earlier, he'd thoroughly scouted the local geography on Google Earth, noting that the maidens apparently buried some of their dead on-site. He'd planned on checking out the cemetery at some point.

Why not now?

He motioned and they all headed in that direction.

Ω

Nick had hidden in the trees, off the narrow roadway, and watched as the six men marched by and continued upward. Friars Dwight and Rice were definitely there. As to the other men? No clue. But one definitely seemed in charge, leading the way. A bull of a man, stoic, thick-set, with heavy cheekbones and a protruding jaw. It would take them a few minutes to make it to the top and he could easily catch up. In the meantime, he was more interested in the seventh man, still following the group at a discreet distance. He was not part of the Dominicans.

So who was he?

He kept to his hiding place, which afforded a clear view of the paved path. From around a bend the newcomer appeared. A slim, muscular youth with black curly hair and a flat face, dressed in jeans, boots, shirt, and jacket. Walking with a purpose. Almost marching. Eyes ahead. Arms at his side. So obviously looking like a tourist that he certainly was not one. Nick allowed him to pass, then stepped from behind the tree onto the road.

"Who are you?" he asked in English.

The younger man stopped and turned. Not a hint of surprise in the face.

"My name is Andre Labelle. Who are you?"

The English was excellent.

"Nick Lee. Are you following those guys up ahead?"

"I am. I need one of them."

"Might I ask who?"

"Archbishop Gerard Vilamur."

Interesting that so high a figure in the church was here, with the Dominicans. "Why?"

"That's none of your business."

Nick advanced a few steps closer. "There's trouble about to happen up there. Trouble I have to stop."

"Then stop it. I won't get in your way. I just want Vilamur."

"Maybe I can help you."

"I doubt it. Look, a friend of mine is missing. I was supposed to accompany him on a trip today, but he disappeared. I decided to stake out the archbishop and that led me here."

"Is the archbishop connected to your missing friend?"

"He is. And I'm sure he's also part of whatever may have happened to him."

"It seems the archbishop is also connected to my trouble. Does your friend have a name?"

"Bernat de Foix."

He instantly connected the dots. "I'm familiar with him. He was involved with the restoration of the Ghent Altarpiece."

"That's right. We were headed there today for a formal announcement on what was found. But he disappeared last night. He would not have missed that ceremony."

"Seems we're both on a mission."

"I'd like to get back to mine."

Fire burned in the dark ball-bearing-like eyes.

What had John Kennedy said? *Necessity has made us allies.*

And he might need the help.

"How about we head up together and let's see where this goes."

CHAPTER 61

Vilamur kept behind the four Dominicans as they followed a defined path grooved from the rocky soil by the soles of countless feet. The singing continued, the melody almost hypnotic, drawing them ever closer like a siren. They stopped at another iron gate that led into a cemetery. Across the closely trimmed grass and various stone cairns and markers six nuns stood around an open grave.

Singing.

Fuentes motioned and the four Dominicans withdrew weapons.

"Is that necessary?" Vilamur asked.

"I assure you it is. These women are quite formidable."

They advanced into the cemetery and headed directly to the maidens. Fuentes raised a hand and halted their advance, allowing the song to be completed. Five of the women wore gray smocks. One did not.

Who was she?

The maidens finished.

The Dominicans assumed positions to the left and right of the grave, their guns at their sides.

Fuentes stepped forward, removed his sunglasses, and pointed to the odd woman out. "Who are you?"

"I want to ask you the same thing. You have no business here."

"But I do. Again, who are you?"

"Sister Kelsey Deal."

"You're the one who found the *Just Judges*," Fuentes said.

"How would you know that?"

"It is part of my business here. I've been aware of your work for some time."

"Who are you?" Deal asked.

Fuentes raised a finger. "I'll ask the questions. My prerogative since I have the men with guns."

The other five just watched the conversation in silence.

"Keep them here," Fuentes said to Friar Dwight, then he motioned for Vilamur to join him as he walked off into the cemetery.

"Look for a headstone," Fuentes whispered. "It would be really old. Worn. Hopefully, it is here."

"How old?"

"Fifteenth century."

They fanned out separately, their eyes down on the markers. Many were crosses. Some simple slabs. Others just plain stone.

After a few minutes, Fuentes called out, "Here."

And he walked over, seeing a cracked and pitted stone marker projecting about half a meter from the ground. Not limestone. Marble. Which explained why it had lasted. Little was on its face. Just a few words and a number, eroded and nearly gone, but there.

ALS ICH KAN
1441

Fuentes bent down close. "Jan van Eyck was the only fifteenth-century Dutch painter to sign his canvases. He did that with a variant of the words"—the cardinal pointed—"*Als ich kan*. As I

Can. Or, As Best I Can. The year 1441 is when he died. No one really knows what he meant by the signature. It could be a type of modesty, where he prefaced his work with an apology for a lack of perfection. But that may be reading too much into things. It could be just a playful reference. No matter. Here it is."

He recalled what he read in the poem. *This flower shot early off this world. The one who came from Maaseik. Bruges keeps him. His life ended there. But he will live for eternity. Among the holy.*

Jan van Eyck was here.

Fuentes smiled.

"We are in the right place."

Ω

Kelsey had never before faced down a gun, much less four. The sight of them made her legs flutter with anxiety and her body shake. She worked hard to keep her nerves under control. The stoic calm of the five other maidens helped. Isabel had made eye contact and she drew strength from the woman's clear resolve. Not a hint of concern or emotion swept across that face.

The maidens stood dutifully, with their hands behind their backs, on one side of the open grave, facing the four men with guns on the other. What level of training had these women endured to prepare themselves for this? Obviously, quite a bit. They seemed ready.

But for what?

"Who are these men?" she asked Isabel.

"Dominicans."

"With guns?"

"They have a long history of violence. They led the crusade that slaughtered thousands of Cathars in this region. They also killed women and children."

355

Okay. Not the reassurance she was looking for. "What do they want?"

"That which we cannot give."

"Oh, but you can," the man she'd addressed a few minutes ago said, walking over. "And you will."

"I asked before," Kelsey said. "Who are you?"

"Hector Cardinal Fuentes," Isabel replied, the contempt clear in her voice. "The other man is our metropolitan archbishop. Gerard Vilamur."

"I've been a nun for a long time," Kelsey said. "Never have I seen prelates of the church act as all of you do."

"We do what is necessary," Fuentes said.

"A woman has died," she made clear to the cardinal. "This is her grave. What you do desecrates this sacred ground."

Her nerves had calmed. She was strong and defiant, defending what she swore to God to uphold.

"Sister Deal," Fuentes said. "None of this really concerns you. I did not involve you. The maidens made that choice."

"No," she said. "I made that choice."

"Fair enough. Gentlemen, bring all of these women along. It's time we visit the motherhouse."

$$\Omega$$

Claire lowered the binoculars from her eyes and set them down, unnerved by the quiet outside, like a prelude to a storm. She stood at the top of the abbey's conical tower, the highest point in the building, which came equipped with four dormer windows that opened in each direction. It was the building's crown, commanding a full view, through the trees, of the land the order had owned for generations. From her perch she could clearly see the main gate and watched as Fuentes, Vilamur, and the four Dominicans marched right through and headed for the cemetery. She'd managed to catch glimpses through the trees as Fuentes had found van Eyck's grave, which meant he was verifying the poem.

Of course he would.

The Vatican was predictable, she'd give them that.

The maidens had known about the poem in 1934, tipped off by friends in Rome. Its discovery, and Pius XI's intent to declare the Assumption dogma, had precipitated their ill-fated attempt to steal the *Just Judges* and prevent any close examination of its images. Though they'd failed to secure the panel, its ultimate disappearance had worked in their favor, enabling them to stay silent in the decades after, even when Pius XII sent clear signals that he was going to make Mary's Assumption dogma. They'd hoped that silence would keep the wolves at bay. But now they found themselves in the precise quandary they'd avoided for all those years.

She fidgeted, her hands groping for something to occupy them, as impatient as a caged animal. Below, she heard footfalls on the stone staircase as someone slowly climbed the spiral up toward her. Insects hovered just outside the window, beneath the eaves, buzzing in the still air. She brought the binoculars back to her eyes and studied the cemetery, the scene splintered by the branches and leaves in between.

They were all back around Sister Rachel's grave.

The abbess appeared at the top of the staircase. "The forward lookouts report two more persons."

"Where?"

"Near the main gate."

She refocused the binoculars in that direction and caught no movement. She continued to scan, looking for something, anything.

Then she saw them. Two men.

One she recognized.

Nick Lee.

Bleak thoughts chased one another through her mind at the unexpected possibilities. None of which were good.

She turned toward the abbess.

"We have a problem."

CHAPTER 62

Nick was wary of Andre Labelle. The young man seemed a volatile combination of nerves, alertness, and weariness, all swirling around a whole lot of anger. Ready for a fight. No. Looking for a fight.

Which was worse.

His parents had taught him many lessons from sport, especially world-class sport, where extreme feelings and uncontrolled emotions rarely led to success. Winning demanded good judgment, discipline, timing, and "a little bit of a lion, but a lot of a fox," as Dad always said.

And his father was rarely wrong.

They walked on, the path ascending and curving sharply, climbing ever higher. The entourage ahead of them had surely made it to the abbey by now.

"Are you sure Bernat de Foix has disappeared?" he asked. "Not just gone away somewhere."

"They took him. I'm sure."

He was puzzled. "The archbishop?"

Labelle nodded. "And others, probably."

"Why would they take him?"

"The archbishop and de Foix knew each other. From long ago. And it wasn't a good thing."

He wanted to know more but realized he probably would not get an answer. The young man's dry, callous, impertinent tone worried him. Clearly, something else was going on here. Something beyond the maidens. He tried to think, to connect the dots, his thoughts tracing back to the past couple of days, which seemed like a lifetime ago.

"There was another man. Shorter, stocky. Who is he?"

"I don't know, but he and the archbishop left the rectory at Toulouse a few hours ago and came straight here. I followed them."

Were the Dominicans involved with whatever happened to Bernat de Foix? Possibly. Warm beads of sweat trickled down his forehead and a chill of anticipation tickled his spine. He felt a familiar excitement as the net around him tightened, that element of chance combined with the possibility of error. Which always kept him sharp.

The road turned again and a tall stone gate came into view. No fence or barrier on either side, which surely once existed but no longer. This was for show and welcomed visitors into the shaded area beyond.

Then he saw movement.

Gray-smocked women appeared from the trees to the left followed by the four Dominicans with guns, all walking toward a rambling, multistory structure with wings, annexes, and a tower. The motherhouse. He grabbed Labelle and they sought cover in the foliage adjacent to the road.

He saw another man.

Walking behind the group.

"That's the archbishop," Labelle said.

And then he saw something that brought an ache to his gut.

Kelsey.

Being led at gunpoint by the last man.

360

Ω

Claire had caught a glimpse of Nick and a younger man, dark-haired, in jeans, as they appeared around the final bend in the main road, just as the entourage from the cemetery was making its way toward the abbey. Lee was clearly resourceful and had quickly made his way here. The abbess still stood beside her and they both watched the unfolding drama below as everyone was returning from the cemetery.

"We need to deal with Signore Lee," the abbess said, reacting to what Claire had just told the older woman.

"What do you want me to do?"

The abbess hesitated a moment, then told her.

"I'm not comfortable with that."

"Do it anyway."

Her vows were definitely being tested to the limits.

Reluctantly, she grabbed the bow and reached into a quiver of long varnished arrows with feathered tips. She slid one out and nocked it on the bow. She had to be careful, as a full draw on the fiberglass would be more than enough pressure to bring down a bear. So she drew the string toward her in a three-quarter pull. Anything more and the arrow would go right through. She lined up the peep sight, the feathered fletching just grazing her right cheek, sucked a long breath, and waited until the four Dominicans with guns drew closer. Sunlight sieved through the canopy spotting the ground in a patchwork of light and shadow, which affected her depth perception.

But she was a good shot.

She released the arrow and it snapped through the air with a faint, singing whistle, catching one of the four Dominicans in the thigh.

The man collapsed, howling in agony.

Never had she shot another living thing before.

"The purpose of that?" she asked the abbess.

"To create doubt."

Ω

Vilamur heard the wet thud of something slicing into flesh. An arrow had whined through the tall pines and one of the Dominicans went down with it protruding from his thigh. The man dropped his weapon and reached for the wound, writhing in pain, air squeezing from his lungs as he fought shock and struggled to breathe. Blood ran out of the wound in a long thick ribbon. Everyone stopped walking. Vultures might not kill, but they certainly maimed. He wanted to go and see if the man was all right, but his legs refused to move. Instead, his gaze shot upward to the top of the round tower that jutted up on the motherhouse's front façade. He saw a maiden with another arrow drawn back, ready to fire.

"I would not do that," Fuentes shouted.

He whirled around to see the cardinal with a gun nestled close to Sister Deal's right temple.

Ω

Kelsey's body was enveloped with fear, choking and electric, muscle spasms racing through her, terrified by the weapon to her head. Thankfully, she had the sense of mind to keep quiet and stand still. Two of the other Dominicans had gone to the aid of their fallen brother, which left one to keep Isabel and the other maidens at gunpoint.

"Lower the bow," Fuentes called out.

The maiden in the tower did not comply.

She heard the hammer on Fuentes's gun click into place.

A stale, poisonous taste invaded her mouth. Her throat went raw and hot from ragged breaths. Her eyes focused on the woman in the tower with the bow aimed straight at Fuentes.

Sister Claire.

Who lowered her weapon.

CHAPTER 63

Nick's body ached like a huge unhealed wound. Every part of his being wanted to spring from his hiding place and protect Kelsey. He could rush the guy with the gun to her head, but the trigger would be pulled long before he traversed the thirty to forty yards that separated them. Either he or she or both of them would get shot.

Not the smart play.

He knew how to handle a tough situation. He'd had his share of them. But he seemed ill informed on how to deal with this. Never had he had someone this close to him in dire jeopardy, everything depending on what he did next. His fear seemed a palpable ugly thing and the weight of indecision settled on his shoulders. Labelle appeared to be deep in a similar quandary. Not moving either. He could not see who'd planted that arrow into the man's thigh. The guy was in obvious pain but had gained a measure of control over his agony. Two Dominicans were dealing with him.

So he stayed quiet.

And waited.

Ω

Claire realized the abbess had gambled on Fuentes using Sister Deal as a shield. It seemed logical. But how would Nick Lee react? That was the unknown. He could go on the offensive, which would expose him and perhaps end all this right now. Or he could do nothing, realizing that they had things under control. The entire atmosphere was tense, theatrical, the scene below echoing a troubling combination of conflict and confidence.

"Make a decision," she muttered.

"We are coming inside," Fuentes called out, the gun still aimed.

"And if we refuse?" she called out.

"Must we go there? I came here for a reason, and nothing is going to stand in my way."

The abbess stood behind her, out of view. She kept her focus out the window. Lee had kept quiet and hidden.

"Let them in," her superior whispered.

"I'll open the doors," she called out.

Ω

Vilamur exhaled.

This was rapidly spinning out of all control. But what had he expected? These men were obsessed, and now he was right in the middle of their insanity thanks to his uncontrollable libido.

Was a red hat worth it?

Damn right it was.

But he was becoming concerned about Fuentes's promise to *silence* the maidens. What exactly did that mean? Shooting them? And these women were not without a punch of their own. One of them had just fired an arrow into a man's thigh. He understood Fuentes's need to establish an aura of dominance, but he resented the subordination that had been forced upon him. True, he'd broken his vows and violated the Tenth Commandment. But he never killed anybody, though he had allowed Fuentes to deal with Bernat de Foix. At the moment, though, he found himself on a massif, fifteen hundred meters up in the Pyrénées, with guns and arrows. Fuentes stood with eyes devoid of expression, casting an impersonal gaze like the glare of a predatory cat. None of which boded well. Sister Deal was clearly scared, but she was staying remarkably composed. He felt for her, but there was nothing he could do. This was all up to the maidens. Would they fight or concede?

He heard a sound and turned back to see the double oak doors part on their iron hinges and the abbess standing in the open doorway.

Thank God.

Ω

Nick was breathing fast, unsure as to what to do next. Maybe that gun he'd left in the helicopter would have been a good thing after all? He hadn't thought a weapon necessary. After all, he'd been headed to a convent. But he'd also never anticipated that Kelsey would be here. He'd believed the prioress on the phone last night when she said Kelsey was safe and he'd assumed that he could deal with things here. Bad mistake.

Labelle seemed anxious too.

"We'll let them get inside, then follow," he whispered.

"We can take them now," Labelle said.

"That woman, who had the gun to her head. She's special to me. I can't risk her life."

"I want Vilamur."

"And what are you going to do with him when you get him?"

"Make him tell me where Bernat de Foix is."

He knew that caution, rather than speed, was the best course. Let this play out and get into position to make a move when it made sense. The advantage was that none of the interlopers knew they were there.

The man with the gun at Kelsey's head told one of the other Dominicans to take the injured friar back down for medical attention. That left only Dwight and Rice, along with Vilamur and the other man, the one who seemed in charge. Kelsey and her captor started walking toward the other five maidens being held at gunpoint. One Dominican helped the injured man up and they started to leave back through the gate, the arrow still protruding at the thigh.

"Let them go," he whispered to Labelle. "The odds are getting better."

They remained in their hiding place, off the road, as the two slowly passed, the one with the arrow hobbling along with an arm draped around the other. The rest of the group advanced toward the abbey. Rice retrieved the gun that the injured man had lost. They all entered through the main doors, which were slammed shut after them.

"I recently was shown a truth," Labelle said. "One I've come to deeply believe in. Part of that truth is a pledge of no violence."

"Sounds like a good philosophy."

Labelle's eyes found his. "It is my life. Now. But I want Vilamur to tell me what happened to Bernat de Foix. I will do what's necessary to get that information."

Which really did not involve Nick or his mission. To this point the archbishop of Toulouse had not been a player. So he stared into the hard liquid eyes and said, "How about you help me out, and I'll help you?"

Labelle nodded.

And they both headed for the abbey.

Chapter 64

Fuentes was conscious that one error, one small omission, even a single piece of bad luck and the next step would be a desperate measure.

And those he could not afford.

Mistakes always bred more mistakes.

The arrow attack was not a mistake, but it was definitely a miscalculation, an underestimation of his opponent. And he would not repeat either of those fallacies.

He stood in a spacious entrance foyer, tall and lit from above with round arched windows. A hefty wrought-iron chandelier hung unlit. Wood-paneled walls exuded an oiled satiny glow. Framed art hung all around, mostly oil on canvas, pastoral scenes of the surrounding mountains, the varnish darkened with age and infested with fine spiderwebs of cracks. Four routes led out. One a stairway up, the other three blocked by closed doors, normal for a convent where access into the inner bowels stayed restricted.

All three doors opened and a maiden stood in each.

Friars Dwight and Rice kept their guns pointed at the five from the cemetery and Fuentes kept his trained on Sister Deal. His attention remained on the women in the doorways and the abbess, mindful that these people were just as determined as he.

"I have come on behalf of His Holiness to resolve a matter of long standing," he said.

"And what would that be?" the abbess calmly asked, a less-than-welcoming expression on her round face.

He told himself that les Vautours' success had always lay in deception, cleverness, diversions, and false trails. So don't go that way. "Where is the maiden who shot the friar?"

"That would be me."

And a woman descended the staircase, turned on the landing, and made her way to ground level.

"You are?" he asked.

"Sister Claire Haffner, Vestal of this order."

An officer. Second in command. Perfect.

He caught the attention of Friar Rice, who walked over and took charge of Sister Deal. He then stepped to the Vestal and, with no hesitation, swiped the butt of his gun across the woman's dark face, knocking her down. The other maidens gasped at the assault and reacted, but he fired a shot into the ceiling that kept them at bay. The bang bellowed in the high-ceilinged room, then echoed back. Chips of plaster rained down and dust twirled in the still air from the ceiling breach. Sister Deal rushed over to see about the Vestal. Sister Haffner was down on one knee, Deal beside her. A small gash bled on the woman's right cheek.

"There will be no more attacks," he said. "Is that clear?"

No one said a word.

"You will bow to the will of your archbishop, who is here, and His Holiness, of whom I am the duly appointed representative."

Haffner stood. "And the Dominicans with guns? Who have they come for?"

"They're here to ensure your compliance," he said.

"With what?" the abbess asked.

"Revealing the location of the Chapel of the Maiden."

Ω

Nick heard a shot.

He and Labelle were still outside, approaching the building, noticing that all of the windows were protected by filigreed iron grilles. No way to get through any of them. The sound of gunfire made it even more imperative that they find a way inside. The place seemed a mishmash of randomness. A wing here. A tower there. Annexes of differing styles. Lots of blue-gray limestone and a mantle of ivy beneath a slate roof defined by crenellated gables.

They rounded a corner and headed toward the rear.

The whole structure sat at the edge of a promontory, nothing but open air on the other side. They passed a small enclosure that held some wrought-iron tables and a few concrete chess pedestals flanked by wooden benches. Farther on they found a flight of stone stairs, built out from the wall and protected by a slender wrought-iron rail, that led up to a door.

Unlocked.

Finally.

A break.

A long barren corridor stretched ahead studded with more doors, not unlike the one from the convent in Ghent. Only difference, the ones here were all closed.

They hustled ahead.

Ω

Vilamur was becoming progressively more uncomfortable. Fuentes had brought him along to gain entry. That had been accomplished.

So why was he staying? These men were on a mission that certainly did not concern him any longer. And the guns? Then the battery on the maiden.

This was too much.

He was a metropolitan archbishop of the Roman Catholic Church. True, he had a problem. But that had been cured last night, no danger of any of it resurfacing as it would implicate not only him, but Fuentes and the Dominicans as well. Bernat de Foix was gone. All of the incriminating evidence was gone. True, his mistakes had compromised his reputation, credibility, achievements, even his probity, but not his title. He was *the* archbishop of this diocese, usually residing high above the world, free from worry, wrinkles, and harm. But he could not escape, or disguise, the leaden grooves which his thoughts had found and from which they could not free themselves. This was bad. And going to get worse. So he made a decision, then silently cleared his throat and drew saliva to the top of his mouth so that a cracked voice would not betray his anxiety when he spoke.

"I'm leaving," he said, his manner businesslike.

Fuentes turned to face him. "I did not dismiss you."

"Forgive me, Eminence, but I don't require your permission."

Ω

Fuentes assessed the situation.

Vilamur was challenging him in front of the maidens.

Not the best time.

Bishops could be that way. Within their diocese they were more powerful than a pope. They were the absolute rulers. Cardinals, not even those within the Curia, could not overrule them without consequences. This archbishop seemed different. He wanted to be a cardinal, and to do that he had to curry favor with those who could make that possible. But for some odd reason Vilamur was willing to throw that away.

Or was he?

He'd always judged people by gauging what they wanted in life. And this man definitely wanted more than he presently enjoyed. Of course, the blackmail on Vilamur cut both ways. God knows enough had happened that could be classified as out of the ordinary. No danger of the maidens lodging any complaints. But Vilamur? Possible. So why fight him? Not now anyway. That could always be done later.

"Of course, Archbishop, you don't require my permission," he said.

"You can handle whatever remains of this on your own. It does not need my presence." Vilamur faced the abbess. "Please know that I am bowing to the wishes of the Vatican here. This is a matter between you and Rome. It is a private affair that does not concern me."

"And yet you are here."

"Yes, abbess. I am. But now I leave this to you." Vilamur bowed to the older woman then turned and said, "Good day, Eminence."

And he left through the main doors.

Ω

Nick and Labelle headed down the corridor. They were toward the far end of the rambling building. The main entrance was more to the center, so he turned at a junction and headed that way, past a line of more closed doors. He assumed all hands were on deck dealing with the intruders, so no danger of encountering anyone. But, if so, they were all on the same team this time.

Right?

Voices.

He stopped. Labelle did too.

The sound was coming up through the open staircase ahead. Leading higher up were more narrow stairs, to probably where the archer had been stationed. He motioned and they retreated back, away from the stairs, stopping beside one of the outer windows.

Heavy doors opened and closed below.

They both stared out the window.

The archbishop was walking away from the building. He looked at Labelle, who pointed at his chest then down at Vilamur.

He understood.

Labelle turned, but he grabbed the younger man's arm and mouthed *good luck*. Labelle nodded, then hurried off the way they came.

Nick turned his attention back to the staircase.

CHAPTER 65

Kelsey had taken a chance rushing to Sister Claire's aid. But she'd never firsthand witnessed such heartless physical violence, and it was her duty to help those in trouble. The blow had been sudden and vicious and Claire seemed dazed.

"Are you okay?" she asked, crouching down beside her.

Claire nodded.

Kelsey stood. "You're a cardinal of the church. These are nuns."

"Get out of the way," Fuentes said to her, his voice lashing across the room with an iced menace.

Her resolve strengthened and she did not move.

"Now," Fuentes yelled, his face a mask of rage.

"Does it make you feel important to strike her?" she asked him. "To put a gun to my head?" She'd always been the one who'd plunged headfirst into things, no sense stopping now. So she checked the fear that threatened to swallow her and said, "What are you going to do? Shoot me? Shoot all of us?"

Fuentes raised the gun and motioned with it. "Not at the moment. But the situation is fluid, so who knows what I might do a few minutes from now."

"Are you truly here, Cardinal Fuentes," the abbess said, "on authority of the pope? Or is this a more...personal quest?"

"Does it matter? I'm here. You're here. And we have things to discuss. Where are the rest of the maidens?"

"In the chapter room. I assumed you would want to speak to us all."

"You assumed correctly. Please, lead the way."

Ω

Nick listened from the top of the stairs.

What the hell was Kelsey doing challenging that man, Cardinal Fuentes? Apparently, the Vatican was now involved with the Dominicans. Kelsey was headstrong as hell, but these men had come on a mission, and there was no reason to push the envelope. He heard everyone moving, heading off below to his left. Before him a corridor extended twenty feet or so to an open doorway in the same direction.

He edged that way.

The floor beneath him was polished pine planks atop stone. Solid. Not a sound betrayed his steps. At the open doorway he stopped and saw that he was on the upper level of the chapter room, small, not unlike the one in Ghent, only this one had a large barrel-vaulted ceiling and an upper gallery that wrapped on three sides, the fourth broken by windows with deep reveals high on the outer wall. He stood back, out of sight, and watched as the group from below joined the maidens already there. His thoughts were paralyzed with apprehension, so he dropped all speculation, tried to suppress his emotions and stop his mind from questioning.

But there was no denying.

Everything had changed with Kelsey here.

Ω

Claire reached up and gently caressed the gash to her cheek. It and her jaw hurt. Never had she taken a blow like that before. But she'd accepted the attack without rebuke. Retaliation would have accomplished nothing. Thankfully, the other maidens had practiced a similar restraint. She felt the power and threat that surrounded her, but was not afraid.

Not in the least.

She stepped into the chapter room and walked to its center. The other maidens were already seated on benches at the tables. The five from the cemetery, and the two Dominicans with guns, joined her among the others. Only their footfalls detonated across the deep silence. Her heart pounded with a heavy throbbing that seemed to beat through the center of her wounded face. Fuentes kept Sister Deal close. The room loomed like a mausoleum, illuminated only by shafts of weak sunlight filtered in through the high mullioned windows.

"I've come for the Chapel of the Maiden," Fuentes said. "Who among the legendary *Vautours* will tell me where it is?"

No one spoke.

The cardinal seemed pleased with himself. "I repeat my question. Who will tell me the location of the chapel?"

The knot of women continued to cling together in silence.

"All right," Fuentes said. "You give me no choice."

He motioned and Friar Dwight grabbed one of the maidens from the cemetery by the shoulder, forcing her to her knees, the barrel of his gun pushed into the soft flesh below the ear.

The hammer clicked into place.

"If I do not have an immediate answer to my question," Fuentes said, "he will shoot her."

Ω

Nick could hear and see what was happening below. He'd dropped down, lying prone on the wood floor, back from the iron railing that guarded the gallery's outer edge. He did not want to reveal his presence. But Fuentes's move on the maiden had changed his thinking. He'd assessed the situation, and was about to vault the rail, when he noticed Sister Ellen, the one he'd taken down in Ghent. She sat across the hall at one of the tables with an angle to spy up to the gallery. She seemed to be the only one not focused on the men in the room.

Their gazes locked.

And he immediately noticed the tiny shake in her head. He pointed to himself, then down. She shook her head again. He got the message. *Don't do it.* He decided to trust her judgment, though the situation with the gun below urged otherwise. Every fiber in his being told him to react and he debated ignoring her warning.

But he stayed still.

"Maidens," Fuentes said. "To your credit, you have managed to remain hidden for a long time. You've eluded Rome for centuries. But that all ends today."

The declaration was firm, direct, and without any equivocation.

"What will you do?" the abbess asked. "Kill her, then us all?"

Fuentes motioned and the gun was withdrawn from the woman's neck, the hammer replaced. The maiden scurried away from Friar Dwight, clearly shaken. "No, abbess, I will not harm anyone. But I will have this order dissolved and every woman here removed to another convent. Then I will dismantle this building, stone by stone, and search every millimeter of it and the land around it with the best scientific equipment, until I find what we both know is here."

No one said a word.

"That I will do," Fuentes said. "And with Rome's backing. Surely you realize that we are but the advance guard. More Dominicans are on the way."

Silence continued to reign.

No one moved.

"I'll tell you," one of the maidens finally said.

"No. Don't," another voiced.

"I'll tell you as well," another added.

More voices joined in urging them not to speak.

"Silence."

Sister Claire. Her voice loud and firm.

"None of you will say a word. Instead, I will lead them to the Chapel of the Maiden."

CHAPTER 66

Vilamur passed through the main gate and kept walking down the road between rows of trees, sunlight spearing the ground from openings in the leafy canopy. Certainly, it was much easier going down this switchback than coming up. So many thoughts tumbled around inside his head. Mainly, bad. And under all that troubling debris, he was concerned about what came next. He'd challenged Fuentes and there'd surely be repercussions. A man like that would not take a public rejection lightly, especially when he'd come to France bearing gifts. But he'd deal with all that later. The fact remained that Fuentes needed him. His was an easy vote for the conclave. Bought and paid for. One more in the yes column. And he was counting on Fuentes to place his needs above all else.

He kept moving.

Away.

Nothing good was happening. The smart play, the only play, was to get as far away as possible. He felt numbed, half awake, dream-like, confused and bewildered by all that had happened over the past couple of days. Usually, in life you got out of it in proportion to what you put in. And he'd definitely invested. But he was weary of the seemingly endless obstacles. Too late now, though, for remorse.

He heard quick footsteps behind him.

He turned back, expecting to see one of the Dominicans, or a maiden, and was met by a hard blow to the left side of his face that stunned and staggered him. The world around him blurred in and out of focus. He tried to stay standing but a wave of nausea and vertigo swept through him.

And he collapsed downward.

Ω

Claire stood her ground as the abbess stepped forward and confronted her.

"I order you to stay silent," her superior said.

"I'm done taking orders. This is ludicrous. We cannot subject these women to the dangers they now face. I voiced my opposition weeks ago but was overruled. And look what happened. Rachel died. That was my fault." She pointed. "Your fault. And all of the maidens who voted for that operation. And now, right here, in our motherhouse, Rome has come with guns, threatening to end us as an order. I won't bear the burden of this sisterhood being dissolved or of anyone else being hurt."

And several of the other women openly voiced their agreement.

"You're a traitor to us all," the abbess declared.

"Am I? Look around. Many of us opposed what was done. But you just kept going. We're something from the past that has no place in the present." Her gaze locked on the older woman. "I shot that man with an arrow, on your command. That was unnecessary."

"I ordered you to do what was needed to defend this house," the abbess spit out.

"And look what it got us. Not a damn thing," Claire said. "That

380

was my last act of blind obedience. This is going to end. Today. Right here. Right now. I'll give him what he wants, and he'll leave. No one will be hurt and our order will continue." She turned toward Fuentes. "Right?"

The cardinal nodded in assent, but added a smile that irritated her. "There will be no further repercussions."

"You'll be violating your sacred oath," the abbess noted. "Committing a mortal sin."

"I'll be violating common sense and my own conscience, if I don't," she declared. "And I'm not alone. Most here feel as I do." She surveyed the room. "Who agrees with me? A show of hands."

Slowly arms were raised. One at a time.

Eighteen of twenty-five.

A clear majority.

She faced the abbess.

"It's over."

$$\Omega$$

Nick could feel the tension. The maidens were clearly divided. The older woman, most likely the abbess, seemed caught off guard by Sister Claire's, and the other maidens', reversal. Concern filled the faces of Sisters Ellen and Isabel who, along with a few others, had not voted yes. An overwhelming majority of the maidens, though, seemed intent on giving Fuentes what he wanted.

"Abbess," one of the maidens said, "we tried to explain ourselves to you, to change your mind, but you would not listen. You went ahead with that reckless move in Ghent. I stand with the Vestal. This is no longer worth dying for and has to end."

"This is something we should discuss among ourselves," the abbess declared. "Outside the presence of strangers."

"That's not possible," Claire said, voice rising. "Do you think they're going away? They're just going to walk out of here while we debate the point? There's nothing more to discuss. They came for the chapel. I'm going to give it to them."

Many of the other women nodded in agreement.

There seemed a clear consensus.

On rebellion.

Ω

Kelsey felt the deep resentment that had seeped into the room like a creeping vine. She'd never before witnessed such opposition to a convent's central authority. Her own order was run like all of the others with power centered at the top. It was a democracy only to the point that the sisters freely chose their leader. But, once done, that leader's rule was absolute. Certainly, through the centuries, there'd been revolts and coups to priors and abbesses. But that had been long ago. In another time and place. Nothing of any recent vintage, nor would that ever be tolerated. The vow of obedience she'd taken to join the Congregation of Saint-Luke commanded her to imitate Christ and obey her lawful superiors.

Without question.

She looked at Sister Claire. "You're a disgrace."

"I'm complying with the lawful representative of the Holy Father. Our pope."

A few of the other maidens voiced their agreement.

"We're all servants of him," Claire said. "His word takes precedent over the abbess. And it is not for me to question that authority."

Kelsey faced Fuentes. "Are you here for the pope?"

The cardinal nodded. "I have a standing order to seek out *les Vautours*, as every head of the pontifical commission before me was given."

Not exactly an answer.

"Sister Deal," Claire made clear, "this does not concern you."

"Then why am I here?"

"Another example of me blindly obeying." Claire pointed at the abbess. "She wanted you here. Not me. As far as I'm concerned you should leave."

"She is right," Fuentes said. "This does not concern you. But you will not be leaving. Not just yet. Now, sister—what is your name?"

"Claire."

"Sister Claire, please take me to the chapel."

CHAPTER 67

Vilamur opened his eyes and immediately felt a throbbing in his head. He brushed away the cobwebs sticking to his brain and remembered. He'd taken a punch in the face. Out of nowhere. The blow had knocked him out. He'd been on the road, heading back down to ground level.

But now he was somewhere else.

An unrelenting breeze chafed his face and helped revive him. He was lying supine facing blue sky overhead. He brought a hand to his jaw and slowly worked the bone and muscle.

Nothing seemed broken.

He pushed himself up and saw he was lying about two meters away from the edge of a cliff. Beyond was open air with a commanding view of far-off peaks in sharp relief against the clear sky, a colorful valley of trees and meadows in between. The drop down was a hundred meters or more to rushing water. He shook off the dizziness in his head and managed to rise, turning to see a younger man standing a few meters away.

A face he recognized.

"You were at Montségur yesterday," he said in English.

"Where is Bernat de Foix?"

"I know nothing."

"You will tell me where he is, or I will shove you off that cliff."

The threat was concerning, considering the younger man had a clear advantage of age, muscle, and bulk. Maybe forty years separated them. And though the arthritis in his hands was not so bad, his knees were much worse. He doubted he could take him. And he was far too close to the cliff edge. But he could not tell his captor anything even remotely close to the truth. So he decided to divert the conversation. "You were there, yesterday, when I met with de Foix. Are you part of what he's doing to me?"

"If that means exposing your lies and deceit then, yes, I am part of that."

Not good. But he had to maintain the façade he'd so carefully crafted.

"God's holy word teaches us to reject all fleshly desire and all uncleanness," the young man said. "We are to do the will of God by rejecting the desires of the flesh and doing good, despite the unworthy servants that we are."

Now he understood. "You're Cathar too?"

"I am."

A clammy, tight band of anxiety nearly suffocated him. The danger here had just multiplied. So he summoned up his best pastoral voice and asked, "What is your name?"

"Andre Labelle."

He knew that name. From last night. The person who'd videoed him leaving Father Tallard's house.

Surely de Foix's accomplice.

Careful. Careful.

"Might I step away from this cliff?" he asked. "Then we can talk more."

Labelle pointed at him. "You'll stay right there."

He raised both hands in surrender. "Okay."

"Where is Bernat de Foix?"

"You speak as if something has happened to him. Why do you think that?"

"He disappeared during the night. Where is he?"

He started to step forward, away from the edge, but Labelle quickly blocked his way.

"I'll shove you right over the side, if you try to get around me," Labelle said.

And he believed every word.

So he stood still.

The wind kept whipping, drying his lips.

"I was one of those Father Tallard abused," Labelle said. "He touched me. Hugged me. Kissed me. He. Violated. Me."

"I am so sorry. Truly I am."

"No, you're not. You're only sorry that it was all revealed."

"Andre—"

"Don't call me that."

"Monsieur Labelle, Father Tallard was a bad man. He was in the process of being prosecuted when he died. A death that Bernat de Foix was definitely involved with."

"As was I."

"You and de Foix are both Cathar. Yet you killed?"

"We killed no one."

"But others did, who are not Cathar."

"*For many are our sins wherein we offend every day, night and day, in word, in deed, and by thought, voluntarily and involuntarily, and more by our will which evil spirits arouse in us, in the flesh in which we are clothed.*"

"Is that a prayer?"

"The *Apareilamentum*. A general confession that all Perfecti recite every month when we profess our sins. *Whereas the holy word of God teaches us we should put aside every desire of the flesh and every*

386

impurity and we should do the will of God by accomplishing perfect good. That man dying, going to your hell, was the perfect good."

"I could not agree more. He would have been convicted and spent the rest of his life in jail."

"Not good enough," Labelle yelled. "Not even close."

"Calm down. Nothing positive ever comes from anger." Something occurred to him. "How did you find me here?"

"I followed you from Toulouse."

This man had definitely connected the dots. He'd thought with de Foix's demise, and all of the electronic evidence erased, that his problem was over.

But he was wrong.

Andre Labelle knew way too much.

CHAPTER 68

Nick stayed hidden in his perch. The abbess, Kelsey, and the remaining seven maidens who hadn't gone over to the dark side, including Sisters Ellen and Isabel, were below in the chapter hall. Friar Dwight kept guard over them, armed. The rest of the maidens, along with Sister Claire, Fuentes, and Friar Rice, had left. Dwight had assumed a position at the exit out of the hall, which was below where he lay up in the gallery. Sister Ellen had positioned herself at one of the tables at the opposite end where she could still see him. He noticed she was careful with her glances so as not to attract Dwight's interest. But when Nick finally got her attention he motioned that he wanted to take the friar beneath him out.

She shook her head no.

He was puzzled. Why not? Too risky? Somebody might get hurt? That was definitely a concern. But he had to do something.

He heard Dwight call out in French. Unfortunately, he did not understand a word, but the man sounded angry. Below Sister Ellen had raised her hands and replied with some French of her own. She pointed above and spewed out more French.

Was this about him?

He rose to his knees.

Dwight came into view below as he emerged from beneath the gallery and began to angle his head upward, turning his body. Nick vaulted over the top of the rail and angled his descent so that he crashed down right atop the tall friar. There was a chance of an accidental discharge, so he made a point to sweep the hand with the gun downward. His body folded into Dwight's in a tangle of arms and legs. The friar broke his fall and together they slammed to the floor. He did not allow the man the luxury of any recovery. Instead, he wrapped an arm around the thick neck and clamped tight. He was banking on the fact that, for all his bravado, this bully had never been in a real fight. To make his point clear, he tightened his grip, which caused Dwight to gasp for breath. It wasn't quite a choke hold, but it was close enough.

The gun had fallen from Dwight's grasp.

Sister Ellen moved quickly to retrieve it and he released his grip. Dwight pushed away and began gasping for air with ragged breaths. Nick hopped to his feet and went straight to Kelsey.

"You all right?" he asked.

She nodded. "I'm fine." She looked into his eyes. "I'm glad you're here."

So was he.

Dwight was still trying to regain hold of himself. He'd choked the bastard pretty good.

"Looks like you have a full-scale revolution," he said to the abbess.

"It would appear so. You must be Nicholas Lee."

"I see my reputation has preceded me."

A couple of the maidens led Dwight over to one of the tables and sat him down. Sister Ellen kept the weapon pointed and ready.

"Who is he?" Kelsey asked.

"A Dominican named Robert Dwight," he told her.

"What in the world, Nick? What's going on here?"

He didn't have time to explain. "I'm going after Fuentes."

"Me too," Kelsey said.

"No, you're not," he said. "And please don't argue with me on this."

He caught the concern in her eyes, there clear as day despite the years of hurt and confusion between them. She did not want him to face things alone.

"He's right," the abbess said. "Sister Kelsey, you will stay here with me. We need to talk."

Kelsey did not seem to agree.

"Are you going to disobey me too?" the older woman asked.

Kelsey hesitated, then shook her head, capitulating to the command.

The abbess faced him. "Eighteen maidens left with Sister Claire, along with Fuentes and Rice. The cardinal and the friar are armed."

"Keep Dwight here, under control," he said.

The abbess nodded.

"You can't go out there unarmed," Kelsey said.

"I've been in tighter spots than this with no gun. I can handle myself."

"I understand your revulsion," Kelsey said. She knew all about Charlie Minter and Marvin Royster. "But don't be foolish."

"I got this." He winked, trying to put her at ease. "Besides, you need that weapon to keep Dwight from doing anything stupid. You stay here, with the abbess."

He turned to leave.

Kelsey grabbed his arm. "Be careful. Okay?"

He nodded.

Sister Isabel led him through the building to the main doors, which she opened. No one was in sight across the rocky, rolling grounds that spread out beneath the tall trees.

"Where are they?" he asked.

She pointed off ahead. "About three hundred yards that way. To the rock church."

He waited for more, but nothing else was forthcoming.

Okay. He stepped out into the afternoon.

The doors closed behind him.

$$\Omega$$

Fuentes entered the rock chapel, tucked away in the fold of the ancient mountain. Sunlight poured inside the towering rocky cleft, the limestone roof, walls, and floor all belonging to nature. Worn pine pews lined up in several rows, all facing three stone steps that led up to a raised platform, two more steps after that up to a marble altar. The whole place reminded him of the grotto at Lourdes. He felt that if he stopped and listened closely he might hear the beating of the mountain's heart.

"Centuries ago, people whispered that a secret portal to a feared other world was here," Sister Claire said. "Supposedly, a man who ventured through it in 1597 reappeared three days later insane and on death's door. His female companion was never seen again."

"I'm aware of this church's colorful history," Fuentes said. "But legends simply make a place like this more mystical, attracting people."

"Which it does. Mass is said here twice every month for the local population."

The maidens who'd accompanied them stood behind Sister Claire. He made a quick count. Eighteen. Of the twenty-five total still alive. That was a serious division. Hell, this order might self-destruct all on its own without any effort from him.

"Perhaps legends are not as fantastical, though, as they might seem," Claire said.

He was intrigued. "By all means, show me."

Ω

Kelsey sat at one of the oak tables, alone with the abbess. Most of the other maidens, including Sister Isabel, had headed off into the building. Two had stayed to keep watch over the friar, one of whom, Sister Ellen, was still holding the gun.

"Are you concerned about what's happening?" she asked the abbess. "I've never witnessed such a revolt before."

"I'm deeply concerned. The remaining maidens have gone to deal with it."

As had Nick. So she wanted to know, "Why did you bring me here?"

"Mr. Lee seems important to you."

Her question had been ignored. She'd been impertinent enough to superiors of late, so she decided to let it pass. "We almost married. I ended it, then joined the convent."

"A not-so-unusual story. I've heard it many times. You still care for him?"

"I still love him. And I always will. But I made my life choice, and I don't regret it."

Though she'd only met the abbess a few minutes ago, she felt a connection. This woman, with a tinge of an Italian accent to her English, oozed confidence and experience. Both of which seemed needed at the moment.

"This is a special place," the abbess said. "For nearly two thousand years we've had the honor of guarding the Chapel of the Maiden."

"What is it?"

"Your prioress did not tell you?"

She shook her head.

"It is the tomb of the Virgin Mary."

"That's not possible. She's in heaven."

"No. She's here and has been here for nearly two thousand-years."

How could that be?

"In 1431 the remains of a second maiden were added, the one who came to be known as Joan of Arc. We now call it the Chapel of the Maidens."

"You have Joan's ashes?"

The older woman nodded. "The church has no idea of that."

"Why is Rome concerned about the Virgin Mary?"

"Fear and arrogance fuel that quest."

A curious statement, said loud enough that the Dominican, Friar Dwight, could easily hear.

"It's a story that began long ago," the abbess said. "Christ came and died. Then men created a religion to worship him. They formed it. Molded it. Adapted it. So, understandably, they fashioned it in *their* thoughts and images. Eventually, they needed a woman, someone to counter the masculinity that they'd gone out of their way to infuse, so they invented Mary."

"She was real."

The older woman nodded. "Absolutely. The Bible tells us that she lived. But, beyond that, it says little more. It was up to the men of the church, in the second, third, and fourth centuries, to make her more. And they did. She was deemed born of an Immaculate Conception, free of original sin. The only human being ever afforded such status. Later, the Archangel Gabriel appeared and told her she would be the mother of God, though remaining a virgin for her entire life. And finally, she was assumed into heaven, body and soul." The abbess paused. "That story has survived sixteen hundred years, intact, never shrinking, only growing. Finally, in modern times, popes declared it all official dogma, worthy to be believed by every Catholic as absolutely true."

Which she herself fervently believed with all her heart.

"Imagine for a moment if the last part of that legend was false," the abbess said. "There was no assumption into heaven of the Virgin's body. She died like every other human being. Her flesh and bones remained here, on earth, like everyone else. If that was true, then the grievous error of the modern popes, who stamped her Assumption with papal infallibility, would be shown clearly."

That it would.

"The church has survived for two thousand years by being strong, defiant, and consistent," the abbess said. "It overcame the Reformation and so much other adversity. But the one thing it cannot endure, or survive, is the faithful believers questioning everything it says. Our religion, as every other, relies on unequivocal faith. Without that, there is no church."

Kelsey understood. "So they want to destroy Mary's tomb?"

"That is correct."

"So what the maidens just did, rebelling against your authority, that jeopardizes everything this order has worked for?"

The abbess nodded. "Without a doubt."

Kelsey now understood the gravity of the situation.

"Look at him," the abbess said.

And she turned her head to face Friar Dwight.

The man stared at them with a smug grin on his lips.

"The look of victory," the abbess muttered.

CHAPTER 69

Vilamur had to regain control of the situation.

Labelle stood three meters away, mumbling a prayer.

"Thou hast sworn unto Thy servants, for Thou alone art He who changest not. Thou alone art the Infinite and Boundless One. Thou only art ungendered, born of Thyself, Self-Father."

Had to be some sort of Cathar incantation.

"Thou only art immaterial and hast no stain, ineffable in Thy generation and inconceivable in Thy manifestation."

Definitely Cathar.

"Hear us, then, O Father Incorruptible, Father Immortal, God of Hidden Beings, sole Light and Life, Alone beyond Vision, only Unspeakable, only Unstainable, sole Primal Being, for before Thee was nothing."

"Why are you praying?" he asked.

Labelle pointed. "Why aren't you?"

"Do I need to pray?"

"We all need the God of Light. You particularly could benefit from him."

Keep the man talking. "Why is that?"

"For your sins against us all."

"Father Tallard is dead. Is that not enough?"

"Your sins are different from his. Where is Bernat de Foix?"

He decided to tell the truth. "Rome came for him."

That grabbed the young man's attention. "Who came?"

"Hector Cardinal Fuentes. The man who traveled with me from Toulouse today." He thought diverting this man's anger elsewhere a good idea. "He and some Dominican friars took de Foix last night."

"Where did they take him?"

"I do not know."

"You're a liar," Labelle yelled.

Stay calm. "I truly don't know."

Labelle began pacing back and forth in short steps, head down, muttering to himself.

"It was out of my hands," Vilamur said. "You need to be confronting them. Not me."

Labelle stopped pacing and pointed at him. "You're from the Church of Wolves, just as that cardinal is. A church that allows its priests to molest children. Its priests to sleep with married women. The last thing you wanted was for Tallard to be prosecuted or for de Foix to be heard. Both would only have brought attention to you. A disgusting adulterous bishop."

Apparently, his secrets were back on the table.

Good to know.

Ω

Nick hiked up the trail, past the cemetery. Wind moaned through the trees, the air cool with the scent of pine and earth. He noticed how the grounds were carefully tended, punctuated at regular intervals by clumps of flowers and trimmed shrubs. The gravel path wound higher, his soles crunching on the dry rocky soil, the terrain gaunt and bony. Off to the left was a magnificent view of the imperious cliffs that sliced down to the turquoise waters of a raging river. Ahead stood a huge plane tree, its trunk about six feet thick, the limbs spread out over a wide swath. Past there the trail turned right, then inclined farther up to what appeared to be a grotto.

And the rock church.

Ω

Fuentes watched as Sister Claire stepped past a marble altar, plain with no adornments, like the surrounding limestone walls that towered up twenty meters. He found it all a contradiction. Warmth without color. Character without definition. Statuary filled niches of varying shapes and sizes. Saints and Christ. Nothing of the Virgin Mary. Votive candles sat dusty and cold in wrought-iron racks.

"This can't be the Chapel of the Maiden," he said.

"It's not," she answered. "This was first a church in the eleventh century and has been in public use ever since. It serves as a diversion. What you want is there."

And she pointed toward a small devotional, carved into the rear rock wall, behind the altar, a three-dimensional projection with a pedimented top, a cross, and an image of Christ. Beneath the altar shelf a large *fleur-de-lys* filled the gray stone panel. Sister Claire knelt down and waved a small black rectangle she produced from her smock around the outer perimeter of the front panel, circum-navigating the flowery symbol. She then pushed on the panel, which swung inward, as if on hinges, revealing a hatchlike opening big enough to crawl through.

She motioned.

"Beyond is the Chapel of the Maiden."

Ω

Vilamur remained trapped near the cliff edge, Labelle still blocking the way. He was hesitant to press the man too far. He'd dealt with disturbed people countless times, both as a priest and as a bishop. They had to be handled with great care. One mistake could set them off.

"Have you been a Cathar your whole life?" he tried.

"I'm a Perfectus."

"As I understand it, that's important. Like a priest. Right?"

The eyes went hot. "Nothing like a priest. We are not chosen ones. We are not special. We are simply believers, finally ready to leave this evil world and never return."

"And evil it is," he said, playing to the man's convictions.

"De Foix is dead, isn't he?"

He debated how to answer that question. Lying would probably do little good. *I don't know*, even worse. So he opted for the truth. "I think he is."

He could see that realization had not settled well. This man had tracked him all the way from Toulouse. Definitely on a mission. But what that was? Hard to say. So he stood still, the steady wind battering the back of his neck, and tried to figure a way out.

"Everything I've been taught," Labelle said, "has proven true. The realm of the good God is filled with light. The realm of the bad god, this lousy material world, is nothing but a prison. The bad god fills this place with so much temptation. So much wrong. I fight those temptations every day. I am fighting them right now."

"I can help with that."

Labelle's faced screwed tight in puzzlement. "How could you possibly help? You. Are. The. Evil. You were de Foix's father. You defiled his mother, while a priest. You are every bit as much a sinner as Tallard was."

"I never touched a child."

"No. You just touched their mothers."

And he instantly regretted his words.

CHAPTER 70

Fuentes emerged through the narrow entrance portal and rose from his hands and knees. He and Sister Claire stood in a cave, the ceiling about three meters high, much tighter than the chapel on the other side of the rock wall. None of the other maidens had joined them. Instead they waited in the outer church, with Rice and his gun keeping a watchful eye on them. A total cloaking darkness, as if he'd been struck blind, enveloped him, the only light leaking in from the entrance. He heard a metallic grind then a loud click before lights dissolved the darkness.

"That's some entryway," he said. "How long has it existed?"

"There was once a larger opening, the original cave entrance, but it was sealed up centuries ago, when the rock church outside was first conceived. Eventually, the devotional was carved into the wall and the panel was opened and closed manually. Twenty years ago, when we electrified the church with lights, we went high-tech and added a magnetic lock."

They walked a few meters farther in until wrought-iron bars blocked the way, each one thick as a finger and fitted directly into the stone. In the center of the grate was a barred door fitted with hinges and a lock, the bars coated with a crusted layer of rust, the lock and hinges all of shiny brass. Sister Claire stepped forward and produced a key that opened the brass lock. With a sweep of her hand she gestured for him to step inside the lit chamber beyond. The light changed from a hard glare to a pearly glow, the stale air smelling of musk and incense.

He stared around.

In awe.

$$\Omega$$

Kelsey was trying to assimilate all that the abbess was saying. The older woman obviously wanted to explain things and for the Dominican to hear. But her mind remained on Nick and what was happening beyond the chapter hall.

"What's happening out there?" she asked.

"We are working to find out."

"Sister Claire's betrayal doesn't bother you?"

"Of course it does. All is in jeopardy now, thanks to men like that one."

The abbess pointed at Dwight.

"Do you really guard the bones of the Blessed Virgin?"

"We do."

"How is that possible?"

"Your tone suggests that it could not be."

"That's because I'm quite skeptical of the claim."

"No faith?"

"I have that in abundance. But you're asking me to ignore that faith and accept something else as real. For me, that *would* require proof."

"So you don't believe the Virgin Mary appeared to three shepherd children at Fatima? Or that the image on the Holy Shroud in Turin is of our Lord Jesus Christ? Or that the bones beneath St. Peter's Basilica are those of the first bishop of Rome?"

"Just like here, there are many questions surrounding all three of those."

The abbess smiled. "That there are. But we know, for a fact, that fifteen or so years after the death of Christ, the Blessed Virgin traveled by boat from Turkey, where she'd been living, and settled in the mountains not far from here. She stayed there until the day she died. The women who traveled with her, and others who already resided here, cleaned her body then entombed her. They cared for that tomb until each died, their daughters then assuming the duty. That continued for centuries. Eventually, the women who watched over the tomb organized themselves into a religious group, which became us."

"How is all that known?"

"We know our history. But everything else relative to Mary was recorded in a document known as *The Testimony of John*, the man Christ himself, from the cross, entrusted his mother's care to. We have that account, and so does the Vatican."

"Why was all this kept so secret?"

"At first, it was done simply out of respect. She was, after all, the Mother of God. The tomb was more maintained than guarded, and this region was quite isolated. But as time went on, and more people arrived, the level of persecution elevated. Christians were martyred. Churches destroyed. Relics defiled. Spies and informers loomed everywhere, and persecution found its way to the Pyrénées. That's when secrecy was imposed. Eventually, the greatest threat to Mary's peace came from the church itself. Those men who found her earthly remains threatening to their own fantasies. That's when women began to die protecting her tomb."

"Like Sister Rachel."

The abbess nodded. "So, to answer your original question as to why you are here? It is simple."

The older woman's face broke into a maze of kindly wrinkles. "We want you to join us."

Ω

Fuentes was amazed.

The room was not much larger than an oversized walk-in closet, the ceiling stained black from the smoke of countless candles. No choking miasma of ancient decay, though. Everything had been properly maintained, the layout exactly as described in *The Testimony of John*.

He recalled the words.

> We had tools with which to enlarge the tomb, for it was here that the Blessed Virgin's body was to rest. The cave was not as spacious as Our Lord's, barely high enough for a man to enter upright. The floor sank at the entrance, and then one saw the burial-place like a narrow altar with the rock-wall projecting over it. We did a good deal of work to prepare it, and also arranged a door to close the entrance. In the burial-place a hollow was chiseled in the shape of a wrapped-up body, slightly raised at the head. Beneath the resting place, into the rock we carved a symbol of how we regarded her. Ω. In the hollow we left another message that spoke to her life and death. τον εαυτό του.

The floor sank at the entrance about a quarter meter. And, yes, the burial niche in the rock wall appeared like an altar, the rock above projecting out over it. Inside, just as John had written, was a hollow, raised slightly at one end. Musty-looking bones, disarticulated and jumbled, lay scattered, and in the hollow's bottom were the Greek words.

τον εαυτό του.

Itself to itself.

He shut his eyes in a bid to clear his mind. He'd done what all of his predecessors had failed to accomplish.

He'd found Mary.

Ω

Nick spotted the entrance to the rock church and approached with care. He'd visited a couple of others around Europe, most notably the Ermitage Saint-Antoine and chapel at Gorges de Galamus, not all that far from here. This one was every bit as impressive, but definitely not as known. The maidens who'd fled the motherhouse sat in the pews. Rice was toward the far end, near the altar, toting a backpack and armed. Sister Claire and Fuentes were not in sight. Past the altar he spotted a devotional with its bottom front panel open, revealing a passage.

Fuentes and Sister Claire had to be beyond.

In the Chapel of the Maiden.

With only one way in and out.

He was unarmed, so it made no sense to escalate things.

No need.

He'd just wait for Rice and Fuentes to come to him.

CHAPTER 71

Vilamur kept trying to anticipate where this troubling encounter was going. He'd tried to sympathize, hedge, and divert, all to no avail. Andre Labelle had not budged, still blocking all escape and becoming more and more agitated. His plan had been to get far away before Fuentes and the Dominicans did whatever they were going to do. He did not want to know anything about it, and he surely did not want to be judged guilty by association. Bad enough he'd been involved to start with, but he doubted the maidens were going to lodge any official complaints. Far from that, in fact. Instead, his problem stood three meters away.

"Should we pray some more?" he asked Labelle.

"Your prayers and mine are not the same."

"Please, then. Use yours."

Labelle seemed unsure, then bowed his head. "*Holy Father, just God of the good spirits, you who are never mistaken, never lie, nor err, nor doubt, for fear of suffering death in the world of the alien god, for we are not of the world and the world is not of us. Give us to know what you know and to love what you love.*"

"That's a lovely prayer," he said.

"It is our tribute to the God of Light."

That dualism again. It's what originally brought the Cathars all their misery. Two gods. But he could not allow Labelle to detect even the slightest hint of ridicule or resentment.

"We have a tribute to God as well."

Labelle nodded. "The Lord's Prayer."

"Were you raised Catholic?"

"I was. It got me nothing but trouble. Our prayer, the Pater Noster, is primarily for Perfecti. Only a Perfectus can address God as *Our Father*."

Fascinating that a religion that professed to be without prejudices or classes, opportunity open to all, would restrict who could say a particular prayer to the almighty Creator. It made no sense. But elitism was inevitable with religion. Human beings just could not help themselves.

And he should know.

"*Our Father, which art in Heaven, hallowed be thy name. Thy kingdom come, Thy will be done on Earth as it is in Heaven. Give us this day our supersubstantial bread, and remit our debts as we forgive our debtors. And keep us from temptation and free us from evil. Thine is the kingdom, the power and glory for ever and ever.*" Labelle raised his head. "Ours is different."

"Yes, it is."

"But nothing in *our* belief system tells us to hide away a child molester and protect him from the law. Or sleep with married women and father children who are then denied and become bastards. Why would you do such awful things?"

He had no good answer, so he said nothing.

"Will I ever see Bernat de Foix again?" Labelle asked.

He shook his head. "No."

"He was a good, decent man, who cared about me."

He could see that was true. "I'm sorry for your loss."

Labelle's face tightened. "Really? The one person who could destroy your life and you're sorry he's gone?"

"He was my son."

"Which you cared nothing about."

He'd thought an acknowledgment might work, but it only seemed to make things worse. So he decided to be conciliatory. "You're right. I am a sinner."

"This world is nothing but sinners. Our task is to find a way out, to free our soul from this despicable place and find a way to the God of Light. That's our only purpose here."

Insanity, for sure. To live your entire life in misery and if you do not give yourself up and become some sort of Perfectus, then you're reborn into another miserable life, where you do it all again. Over and over and over. It made no sense. Surely the only reason the idea gained any popularity in the thirteenth century was that the Catholic Church had fallen into a state of total corruption. Even a largely illiterate population saw its hypocrisy. So anything had been deemed preferable. But today? In the modern world? The whole thing made no sense.

"You're evil," Labelle said to him. "Just like Tallard. Just like all those who came before you. Despicable clerics, abusing their positions. Nothing has changed in eight hundred years."

He did not know what to say.

"Christ, who was born in the earthly and visible Bethlehem and crucified in Jerusalem, was evil," Labelle said, voice rising. "Mary Magdalene was his concubine, taken in adultery. Just like you did with de Foix's mother. The good Christ, the real Christ, neither ate, nor drank, nor assumed the true flesh, nor was he ever in this evil world except spiritually. That's the difference between us and you. The difference in what we believe to be holy."

His vehemence stung and Vilamur saw the rage rising in the eyes like a cold mist. *Think.* How could this powder keg be defused?

"What of other believers?" he asked. "You, as a Perfectus, owe them a duty to look after them."

Labelle calmed a bit. "I do. And I have."

"Should you not be with them?"

Labelle stared at him. "Why do you care? We mean nothing to you."

"All who live within my diocese are my concern."

Labelle shook his head and stepped closer. "We don't need your concern. What we needed was for you to be true to your vows. For you to conduct yourself in a manner that is respectful and mindful of us all. Instead, you only looked after yourself. What would you have done with de Foix? How were you going to deal with the fact that you have a son? Tell the world? I doubt it. Of course, that's no longer a problem since de Foix is gone. Never to be seen again."

"That wasn't me."

"But you benefited from it." Labelle banged his chest with a closed fist, then pointed. "I'm here to finish what Bernat de Foix started."

What did that—

Labelle rushed forward in a quick, unexpected move, crossing the three meters that separated them, leaping into him with a flying tackle, wrapping his arms tight around Vilamur's chest. The momentum from the impact drove them both back toward the cliff edge. They slammed into the hard ground, which hurt. He tried to resist but the young man was strong.

"To hell with you," Labelle spit out in his ear. "And to the God of Light for me."

The younger man's feet dug into the rocky soil and, together, they slid forward, over the edge, out into open air.

He screamed in terror.

His eyes lost focus as he absorbed the weightless sensation of falling. Labelle kept his grip tight and their combined weight fell fast.

They slammed into a hard surface.

Labelle took the brunt. Surely, one of the many rocky outcroppings that dominated the cliff face.

Then more falling.

More shunting downward in repeated bounces. Eventually, Labelle let go and they dropped separately.

Then a final impact.

Hard. Solid. With no recoil.

And—

Nothingness.

Chapter 72

Fuentes surveyed the burial chamber. Everything appeared as described in *The Testimony of John*. Save for one addition. A ceramic urn in a wall niche with no markings on its exterior.

"The Maid of Orléans," Sister Claire said. "We gathered her ashes from the pyre after she burned."

He made the connection. "With the help of Jan van Eyck?"

She nodded. "He made that possible. Philip the Good betrayed Joan. Van Eyck disagreed with that but could do nothing to stop it. Instead, he aided us in recovering her ashes. He was close, on the inside. Without him we would not have been able to accomplish that."

"What was she to the maidens?"

"One of us. She'd been in training here when she first heard the heavenly voices. She left here to go north and wage war."

"Incredible that you have them. But van Eyck felt compelled to leave the world a reminder of his good deed, didn't he? In the altarpiece."

"Unfortunately, he did. Why? No one knows. He just did."

"He was unaware of the Virgin's remains?"

"Thankfully. No, he knew nothing of that."

"The Vatican was not aware of what van Eyck did with the altarpiece until 1934."

"We've known for centuries. But it only became an issue for us—in 1934."

He was curious. "This order stole the *Just Judges?*"

"We did. Then it was taken from us and the two maidens who stole it were murdered. We never found their bodies or the panel. The war then intervened and we thought it all gone for good, until a few weeks ago."

He pointed at the urn. "Those ashes have been here since 1431?"

She nodded. "Resting in eternal peace."

"She's a saint of the church and deserves so much more."

"She was murdered by the church."

"And then forgiven," he said.

"And that makes what was done right?"

He paused. "No, of course not." He turned back to the larger niche. "I suppose resting here, with the Blessed Virgin, is some consolation for our mistake."

He realized that he could not remove Joan of Arc's ashes. Their resurfacing would raise far too many questions. And he'd come to end all of the inquiries, not to create more. To the world, Jeanne d'Arc, the Maid of Orléans, died at the stake almost six hundred years ago, her ashes tossed into a river, gone, and there they would remain.

He examined the Ω chiseled into the limestone beneath the shelf. There, just as John described. "Clever. The final number in the Greek numeric system. But Revelation says that Christ was alpha and omega, the beginning and the end."

"Though Christ was first, she was, in many ways to the people who buried her, the last. Omega."

He recalled what John had written. *Beneath the resting place, into the rock we carved a symbol of how we regarded her.* Ω. "I suppose, to them, she was indeed the end." He examined more closely the Greek etched into the hollow. *τov εαυτό του.* Itself to itself. "An interesting choice in phrase."

"Not at all," she said. "She was a human being who lived and died, returning to the dust from which she came. Not a fiction that the church later created for its own selfish purposes."

More from *The Testimony of John* flashed through his brain. *In the hollow we left another message that spoke to her life and death.*

τov εαυτό του.

"All true, sister," he muttered. "But that fantasy served us far better than any truth ever could."

"Which explains why we have come to this point."

Yes, it did.

His plan had been to find the tomb and destroy it, thereby silencing the maidens. But now that he was here, standing inside something so ancient, so reverent, he was overcome. He'd been a priest a long time. He'd joined the church out of a love for God and a sense of duty to his chosen church. He'd risen in the ranks thanks to an unwavering devotion to that purpose, one that others had recognized and rewarded. Now he was one step away from the ultimate achievement. Becoming pope. Was God speaking to him? Here? In this holiest of places?

He knelt on the crusty floor.

And bowed his head in prayer.

Ω

Kelsey did not know what to say to the abbess.

We want you to join us.

So she asked the obvious. "Why?"

"You're the precise type of person we seek."

"I don't break into buildings, assault people, or set fire to priceless works of art."

The abbess smiled. "Not all of the maidens are sent into the field. In fact, only a small percentage take training for that. The rest work here, at the motherhouse. I would envision that for you."

She was both flattered and troubled. "Forgive me, abbess, but you have a civil war brewing here. There might not be an order to join."

"I will deal with that, once this situation with the cardinal is resolved. I have faith that we can work through our differences. Your expertise in art is something we could definitely benefit from. And don't sell yourself short. From all reports you've handled yourself exceptionally well. I saw how you stayed calm with a gun to your head. That coolness is something that cannot be taught."

She appreciated the compliments.

But at the moment her head was full of thoughts about Nick.

Hoping he was okay.

Ω

Fuentes tried to pray, but conflicting thoughts kept interfering. He could not help it. He was a planner. Always had been. Which explained his steady rise and why he, above all others, now found himself in this fortunate position.

Keeping this discovery to himself, sealing it away, and relying on the maidens to retain their secret had merits. They'd done that for nearly two millennia and would surely continue, only now with Rome's blessing. That course might even prove useful with a few of the more pragmatic cardinals, who would appreciate his discretion, though recognizing the problems that such a revelation could evoke. But that would place the maidens right in the middle of the equation, granting them a position of power and influence, one they could exploit in the future.

That was bad.

More cardinals, himself included, would want its destruction, which would silence the maidens and completely protect Mary's legacy. No chance then of any questions being raised. The church would remain inviolate, popes infallible, and the Maidens of Saint-Michael just another convent.

That made the most sense.

Especially considering he wanted to be pope, and he did not want to inherit a job weakened by scandal or threatened by extortion. He liked that when it came to dogma a pope's word was the last word, incapable, by definition, of being wrong.

He definitely wanted that to remain.

A difficult debate. Good arguments on both sides. But the decision was his. He crossed himself and stood. No sense delaying.

He stepped back to the iron gate.

And called out for Rice.

$$\Omega$$

Claire stood to one side, near the ashes of Joan of Arc, and watched as Friar Rice laid a backpack down on the dirt floor and removed a hammer. The Dominican then went to work obliterating the omega beneath the Virgin's resting place. The limestone easily chipped away and the symbol, carved so long ago, disappeared. He then chipped off the Greek epitaph. It hurt to watch such willful desecration. Maidens had labored for centuries to maintain what a fool with a hammer smashed in a matter of seconds.

"Was that necessary?" she asked.

Fuentes nodded. "Definitely."

She wanted to know, "Is it that important to be right?"

413

"It's not about being right," Fuentes said. "It's about preserving what exists. It's worked perfectly for a long, long time and I will not be responsible for its diminishment."

"The maidens and you have the same objective," she noted. "To keep this place secret."

"Maybe so. But the maidens have a distinct advantage in that partnership. Which could be used against Rome, if they so desired."

"That's not our way."

"I prefer not to take any chances."

Then the cardinal motioned and Rice replaced the tools and removed a canvas bag from the pack. The friar collected all of the bones from the Virgin's tomb, dropping each into the bag.

"They will be destroyed?" Claire asked.

Fuentes nodded.

"What of Joan's ashes?" she asked.

"They are not important."

No surprise. Rome had milked everything it could from the Maid of Orléans a long time ago.

Rice deposited the canvas bag with the bones into the backpack, then removed several bundles of a white, claylike material.

"Is that explosives?" she asked. "You plan to demolish this?"

"It has to be done. You said it yourself. Guarding this no longer makes any sense. So let it return to nature."

Rice laid two bundles in the empty hollow of the Virgin's grave, then inserted a metal igniter into each with wires running to a small black box, which he activated by flicking a switch. Fuentes lifted the urn with Joan of Arc's ashes and set it into the Virgin's niche, near the bundles. Rice stepped out of the chamber and laid three more bundles with igniters near the iron gate.

"I never intended for this to be destroyed," she said, both to Fuentes and to the Virgin.

"But it has to be. We both have issues that have to be addressed and, as unpleasant as this may be, destruction will resolve both of our problems."

$$\Omega$$

Nick was running on adrenaline.

He was exactly where he'd found himself so many times over the past few years. No backup. No partner. No team. No nothing, including no guarantees of the future.

Just the way he liked it.

At least all the cards from all the players were on the table. Everyone knew where everyone else stood.

He'd retreated off to the side of the opening that expanded inward to form the rock church. The maidens were still sitting in the pews. Rice had vanished behind the raised altar. Hard to see where.

But he told himself to be patient.

They'd have to come this way at some point.

$$\Omega$$

Claire climbed back out through the entrance and emerged from the hatch on the other side. Fuentes and Rice were already out, but she'd lingered a moment to switch off the lights, taking one last look around, and saying a prayer. May God and the Virgin forgive her. Nearly two thousand years ago a group of women had created a holy tomb from this cave in the mountains. They'd buried Mary, whom they believed to be the Mother of God. A woman who'd traveled to the region with John, the man Christ himself, from the cross, had entrusted his mother's care to. There she'd lived and died. Other women had protected her tomb, some, like Sister Rachel, even giving their lives. Now it would all be destroyed. Hers would be the last eyes that would see, intact, the Blessed Virgin's final resting place.

What had she done?

She stood.

"Please step back over here," Fuentes said.

She did.

Fuentes nodded and Rice pointed a controller at the devotional and pressed a button. The radio signal shot through the opening and activated the detonators. Explosions could be heard through the open hatch, rock crashing down as the ancient cave beyond collapsed onto itself. The ground and walls vibrated from the impacts. A cloud of limestone dust poured from the portal. She stepped to one side, reached down, and closed the panel with the *fleur-de-lys*. Debris continued to fall on the other side with muted thuds.

In an instant, the tomb of the Blessed Virgin was no more.

Ω

Nick heard the muffled boom. Then the rumbles. He spied inside the church, seeing Fuentes, Rice, and Sister Claire standing on the far side of the altar. The maidens in the pews had not moved.

Something had been destroyed.

The tomb? What else.

That meant Fuentes and Rice would be leaving.

He counted nineteen maidens, including Sister Claire, each of whom was worthy of respect.

21–1.

Not good odds.

CHAPTER 73

Kelsey stared across the chapter hall at Friar Dwight, who sat on one of the benches with Sister Ellen keeping guard.

"I never knew people like him existed within the church," she said to the abbess.

"Unfortunately, the Vatican has not survived over the centuries without men like him. The Dominicans and the church are two monolithic objects. One unstoppable, the other unmovable. Both have always done what was needed to be done. That friar is just the latest incarnation of a long line of sinners."

Dwight did not seem to appreciate the insult, but said nothing.

"The Blessed Virgin was always intended to magnify God within each of us," the abbess said. "On that point, the men who created her were clever. What they feared was that with her being just a human mother, that would make her unworthy of special veneration. But to the other extreme, where Mary became a heavenly idol so far removed from us, that was just as problematic. In her simplest form Mary was the full manifestation of a daughter of God, made in his image and likeness, as we all are. A woman who gave birth to Christ. Who lived and died and was buried. That should have been enough. But it wasn't."

She realized that the maidens who'd rebelled were likewise made in his image. As was she. All handmaids of the Lord.

"Am I being called?" she asked.

"I believe you are."

Sister Isabel reentered the hall and stepped over to where they sat. "The tomb has been destroyed. There were explosions."

The abbess crossed herself. "May God forgive them." Then the older woman stood and pointed at the friar. "Bring him."

Sister Ellen used the gun to escort Dwight from the room and they all headed for the main foyer. There, the oak doors were opened.

"Get out of this house," the abbess said to Dwight. "And never return."

The Dominican did not hesitate and fled out the open doorway.

"Wait," the abbess called out.

And Sister Ellen tossed the gun outside.

"Take that, too," the abbess said. "We have no need of it."

The friar retrieved the weapon and ran off.

"What are you doing?" Kelsey asked. "Nick is unarmed."

The abbess said nothing.

Sister Ellen closed and locked the oak doors.

Ω

Fuentes felt satisfied.

The tomb was gone. The bones collected. The maidens silenced. All was good except for Vilamur, who would have to be dealt with, but that should not be a problem. The archbishop wanted to be a cardinal, and he needed a few more of those, especially the kind with unquestioned loyalty. So an arrangement would have to be forged, but one that took into account the insubordination from earlier. Perhaps there would be no Curial appointment, or certainly not one of any standing.

No need to linger here any longer.

"Go and get Friar Dwight," he said to Rice. "I'll meet you both at the gateway."

Rice headed off with the backpack, down the aisle between the pews filled with maidens.

"Sister Claire," he said. "I'd like a word before I leave."

Ω

Kelsey did not appreciate the abbess' indifference. Nick was out there unarmed against three men with guns, one of whom the abbess had just rearmed. She knew how he felt about weapons, but surely in his line of work he had to use one from time to time. No matter. She wasn't going to allow him to fight alone. Sister Ellen and the abbess were already walking back toward the chapter room. She'd lingered in the foyer and now moved toward the oak doors, releasing the iron lock and swinging the heavy panel inward enough that she could leave.

The friar was a hundred yards ahead, moving away.

She ran after him.

"Sister Deal."

The abbess. Behind her. At the doorway.

She stopped and turned. "You're not my prioress. You're my captor. I owe you nothing."

And she headed off.

The door slammed shut behind her.

Ω

Nick heard what Fuentes had said to Rice.

He was positioned to the side of the entrance among a garden of boulders, out of sight. He fled his hiding place and moved from tree to tree, trying to get ahead of Rice, who emerged from the cleft and started back toward the cemetery and the motherhouse, a gun in one hand, the backpack in another. He waited until Rice drew close then stepped out onto the trail. It took a second or two for the friar to recognize him. Which he used to lunge forward and slug Rice in the face.

Something cracked. Probably Rice's nose.

He kicked the gun from the man's grasp.

Rice rebounded and they squared off, like boxers, trading blows. He could not allow this to go on too long. He needed to take this man out, but Rice was built like a fire hydrant and equally resilient. Blood poured from the nose. Rice dropped the knapsack and swung with his right fist. He ducked the blow and planted a kick to the man's chest, staggering him back.

But Rice kept coming.

Ω

Kelsey made her way down the trail, past the cemetery, following Friar Dwight, who'd disappeared around a bend ahead. She stepped up her pace and came to the turn.

Fifty yards away Nick and the other friar were fighting.

Thirty yards ahead Dwight had stopped walking, the gun in his right hand being raised.

And aimed at Nick.

CHAPTER 74

Claire was ready for Cardinal Fuentes to leave.

Enough damage had been done.

But the bastard seemed intent on gloating in his victory.

"I appreciate your cooperation," he said to her. "Along with the other maidens. What happens next for all of you?"

"That depends on you."

"As I said earlier, you will have no more interference from me. Or Rome. We'll leave the maidens to themselves."

"That was the point of this entire endeavor. I just hope Rome follows that course."

"We shall."

"You seem like an ambitious man."

"The church has grown soft of late, sister. Its voice devoid of thunder. We ask far more often than we demand. Hopefully, that will change in the future."

"By you?" she asked.

"By many."

"For me, this was not about you, or the church."

He threw her a wry smile. "No, I suppose not. May I ask what this *was* about?"

"Ending something that should have ended a long time ago. To do that, I defied the one woman on this planet I respect the most. I violated my oath to my order and my God. But at least no more maidens will be hurt or killed. That's what this was about." She paused and grabbed hold of herself. "Now take the bones and leave us to ourselves. There is much to deal with, thanks to you and me."

They stood toward the rear of the church, near the devotional with the secret panel. The altar was between them and the maidens were still seated in the pews.

Fuentes turned to leave.

"Cardinal," she said.

The man stopped and turned back to her.

"*If a man knows to do right and doeth it not, to him it is sin.*"

"Jesus to the Pharisees," he said. "Inspirational. But that does not apply to me."

"Then how about this? I hope you rot in hell."

Fuentes chuckled and shook his head at her impertinence.

A gunshot rang out.

Ω

Kelsey assessed the situation.

Friar Dwight was trying to lock an aim on Nick, swinging the gun back and forth, but the fight was making that hard. Nick and the other friar were tangled up and Dwight seemed unsure when and where to fire. His attention was totally on the brawl, so she used that moment of his confusion—the gun be damned—to rush forward and leap onto Dwight's back.

Taking them both down to the hard ground.

Ω

Nick caught movement to his right and pivoted away from Rice long enough to see Kelsey attacking Dwight, who held a gun.

Damn. He needed to get over there.

Fast.

So he swung off the ball of his left foot and slammed his right heel into Rice's chest. He followed with an elbow to the throat that sent the friar gasping for air and reeling back into the trunk of a tree. He then landed another kick, this time to the kidneys, which brought a yelp of pain. One more punch to the bloodied face and Rice went down.

Not moving. Done.

He whirled and felt as if caught in the midst of a kaleidoscope, everything around him changing shape by the second. He swiped away the sweat that stung his eyes, then a blast of energy exploded him into action and he rushed to where Kelsey and Dwight were wrestling on the ground. Dwight still held the gun, which he kicked from the man's grasp as the right hand swung upward. A round cracked off as it flew through the air, the bullet heading into the trees. He reached down and ended the struggle, grabbing Dwight by his jacket and yanking him up to his feet.

Kelsey twisted out of his clutch.

"Enough," he yelled at Dwight.

The tall friar wrenched himself free and was about to engage when his body jerked forward, as though hit from behind. Dwight's eyes went wide and his legs started to cave. The body went limp and folded to the ground. Behind him, Kelsey stood, holding a rock the size of a softball, which she'd used, two-handed, to take the man down.

"You could have killed him," he said to her.

She tossed the rock aside.

"God forgive me, but I wish I had."

Ω

Fuentes did not move, keeping the altar between him and the maidens beyond. Why had Rice fired a shot? What was wrong? He stared out into the rocky cleft, open sky, and trees beyond the pews.

A man appeared.

Medium height and build. Brown wavy hair. Clean-shaven. A gun in his right hand. The canvas bag Rice left with in the other.

The newcomer stopped where the pews began.

"And you are?" he called out.

"Nick Lee."

The man who'd intervened in Ghent. From the United Nations. He'd not made any calls to New York because he genuinely did not think it an issue. Clearly a miscalculation on his part.

"Where is Friar Rice?" he asked.

"Unconscious," Lee said. "Along with Dwight. It's just you and me now."

Ω

Nick stood at the rear of the church, fifty feet away from Fuentes who remained by the raised altar. Sister Claire stood off to Fuentes's right. The other maidens were seated in between, their attention varying between him and Fuentes.

"This does not concern the United Nations," Fuentes said. "You have no business here."

"I'd say I do. You put a gun to Sister Deal's head. That makes this my business."

"And what is she to you?"

"A woman I almost married."

Fuentes stayed behind the altar. "How gallant. But, again, this is not your concern."

Nick raised his arm and displayed the canvas bag. "I found these in Rice's backpack. They important to you?"

That grabbed the cardinal's attention. Which had been the whole idea of bringing them. Outside, Kelsey had given him the CliffsNotes version of what was going on. So it did not take a rocket scientist to figure out that the tomb had been destroyed and the bones removed. He'd also retrieved the weapons from Rice and Dwight. His "no guns" rule seemed a bit foolish at the moment.

So he kept one.

Which he raised and aimed at the altar.

"You're done."

Ω

Fuentes could not believe what he was hearing. After all that had gone right, now this.

He had to act.

So he dropped down behind the altar, drew his own weapon, and aimed it straight at Lee. He had cover. Lee did not.

One shot would end this.

"I am not in any mood to be played with," he said. "I'll shoot you dead, then get those bones back myself."

Ω

Kelsey had stayed to the shadows and slipped into the rock church at the far end of the cleft, away from the main route inside that bisected the pews. She toted the knapsack. Nick had told her to remain hidden and let him handle it with Fuentes. He'd said he was betting that Fuentes would not shoot anybody with so many witnesses.

But she wasn't quite so sure.

Ω

Nick was pushing his luck. No question. He was bare-ass-to-the-wind, out in the open. Armed, but Fuentes had the high ground and the altar between them. He debated sending a round that way, but a ricochet might endanger Sister Claire, who stood way too close and wasn't retreating at the sign of trouble.

"Maidens," Claire called out.

And all of the women rose from their pews, spilling out into the center aisle, forming a human barrier between where he stood and where Fuentes had taken cover.

Neither one of them could shoot the other now.

"Nick," Sister Claire said. "If you truly have the Virgin's bones, I ask you to hand them over to the cardinal. On one point he is correct. This does not concern you. The maidens and the church have fought a long-standing battle, which ends today."

"A choice you made," he said to her.

"Somebody had to. My friend Rachel died. A point you reminded me of several times. Sister Deal was placed in dire jeopardy. I cannot, and will not, allow any more harm to come to anyone. If the destruction of the tomb and the removal of the bones will end this, then I'm good with that. As are the other women standing in front of you."

Fuentes stood from behind the altar. "Maidens, know that this will all end today and your order will go on. Unaffected. You have my word."

He caught the self-righteous tone of a man realizing he was once again in control.

"We appreciate your efforts on our behalf," Claire said to Nick. "But I ask you to stop. We will not allow either one of you to harm the other. Please, just give him the bones and let him go. The damage is done and cannot be undone."

He debated all of the options.

None were good. So he decided to listen to her.

"Bring me the pack," he called out.

Ω

Kelsey had waited for Nick's instructions.

They'd both been unsure as to what to do with the bones they'd found. Nick had figured the bag would get Fuentes's attention, so they'd dumped the bones into the backpack and replaced them with stones. She'd been hesitant at such a desecration since Sister Claire, the maidens, the abbess, and Cardinal Fuentes all believed these were the mortal remains of the Mother of God. But this was an extraordinary situation, so the Blessed Virgin would just have to understand.

She stepped from her hiding spot and walked past the last pew toward where Nick stood, handing him the backpack.

Deception time was over.

"All right," Nick called out. "Here's what you want."

Ω

Fuentes decided to linger no further.

But there was a new matter he had to broach with Sister Claire. "This man and Sister Deal know a great deal."

He kept his voice low.

"I agree. But what does it matter? The tomb is destroyed. The bones will be gone. No one here is going to say a thing, nor are you. So they have nothing but a wild tale."

"Ordinarily, I would be hesitant. But there's little I can do, considering your show of defensive force. So I'll rely on you to deal with them."

"Not to worry. I'll handle it. The last thing we want is for this to continue past today."

He appraised her carefully, gauging for himself her credibility. "All right, sister. You deal with it."

He turned to leave.

"Cardinal," she said, her voice louder, "leave the gun."

He turned back and faced her. "I will not."

"Then you'll not be given those bones. And I have eighteen maidens to back that up. You may be able to shoot one, two, four, but not all of them."

A showdown? Interesting. But she was right.

He was outnumbered.

"I thought Vultures never killed," he said.

"We don't. But we can maim. Badly." He remembered the arrow to the thigh. "And I owe you for that blow to my face."

Good point.

Better to leave.

So he laid the weapon on the altar and walked away.

The maidens crowding the center aisle parted into the pews, clearing a way to Lee and Sister Deal. He approached and Lee handed him the backpack Rice had left with.

"Where are the friars?" he asked.

"Outside," Lee said. "But we have their weapons."

He accepted the pack from Sister Deal, unzipped it, and checked, seeing the bones. "How do I know you did not keep one?"

"You don't," Lee said.

He shrugged.

What would one fossil-like bone, with no provenance matter? "I certainly hope I'll never see, or hear from, either of you again."

And he left.

CHAPTER 75

Nick and Kelsey stood outside the church in the cool afternoon air. They'd watched as Fuentes roused both Dwight and Rice and the three had walked off down the path. Sister Claire and the maidens also left, heading back toward the motherhouse in silence. He'd tried to engage Claire, but she'd ignored him.

Finally, they too started walking, passing the cemetery.

"There are maidens lying here dating back centuries," she told him. "Sister Rachel is over there, in that open hole."

He stared across the markers at the fresh grave. "Do you believe that those bones were the Virgin Mary's?"

"I don't know. But it's clear that the maidens, and that cardinal, believe they are."

"And yet, all those women rebelled against that which they so fervently believed."

"We don't know the dynamics that have been happening within this order. There could have been trouble brewing for a long time. Trouble that finally came to a boil today." She paused. "The abbess wants me to join them."

That was a surprise. "What did you tell her?"

"Nothing. They turned Dwight loose before I could answer her and gave back his gun. That's when I came after him."

"Foolishness."

"You would have preferred I let him shoot you."

"Maybe a shouting match instead of an assault."

"So he could shoot us both?"

Good point.

They kept walking through the trees, the dense canopy shadowing everything more like twilight instead of midday. The grounds were quiet. Peaceful. No sign of Fuentes or his cohorts. Surely headed down the mountain with the bones, their mission accomplished. They came to the gate and he noticed, through the trees, that the front doors to the motherhouse hung wide open.

"That's really odd," he said, pointing.

"I agree. Those women are not the open-door types."

He wondered. An invitation? "Let's take a look."

They headed for the entrance and walked into the main foyer. No one was in sight, but all the doors leading out of it were open.

"Now, that's not normal at all," Kelsey said. "Especially with what just happened. In my convent all the doors leading into the building are kept closed and locked at all times. No exceptions. No excuses."

"I gained access to the inside through an unlocked back door."

"That would never happen in my convent."

Which made him wonder even more. Then he heard it. Soft. In the distance. Inside the building. Singing.

Kelsey heard it too. "The Ave Maria. They were singing it when I arrived. Down in the crypt."

"You know the way?"

She led him through one of the corridors to a stone staircase that wound downward into the earth. The singing had become more distinct, but still far off. Definitely coming from below. They descended into a crypt, the ceiling barely ten feet high, rows of heavy pillars supporting numerous vaults. Not much there other than a stone altar at the far end. Nothing on the walls. Incandescent lighting cast a yellow glow across the cream-colored stone.

"This is their chapel," Kelsey said.

He stepped forward, past a few of the pillars, and zeroed in on the sound. From his right. Past a section of stone hinged inward. They stared at each other, puzzlement slowly replaced by understanding. He decided to accept the invitation and entered the portal, admiring how it had been cleverly built, its axle a thick, greased metal bar embedded into the rock. When closed, the panel would have been indistinguishable from the surrounding rough wall.

A long flight of cupped, slick marble steps led down on the other side. They descended, the air becoming cold, but not dank. And he felt why. A draft signaled circulation. Down they went, ending in a spacious underground, barrel-roofed chapel with a small apse at the opposite end. Most of the walls were whitewashed, surely intended to emphasize the richness and color of the intermixed frescoed spaces. Enormous iron lanterns supported by chains hung from the vaults, their glow almost dreamlike. Not a speck of anything had peeled or chipped. Not a single sign of neglect. The maidens all knelt on the polished gray-green marble floor, singing in wonderful, lyrical tones. He studied the faces, some joyful, some relaxed. He glanced at Kelsey. A flash of joy seemed to pass through her, tears forming in her eyes. He too felt the elation.

The abbess knelt in front of the assemblage.

He stared around and noticed the frescoes.

The Virgin, wearing a mystic cylindrical headdress, hands raised in prayer, the swarthy face casting dignity and beauty. Figures of Christ, hands raised in blessing, the face a buff color with a wash of red-brown, a few splashes of black, and highlights added with streaks of white to the eyebrows, nose, and lips. More of the Virgin, each time depicted as a dark-skinned woman with clearly non-European features. Then he noticed the simple limestone ossuary, atop a marble plinth that stood before the far wall. Behind, in the apse, were two craggy recesses cut into the rock-hewn cavern. One contained a stone urn, the other what looked like a glass container.

He saw an inscription on the plinth. In Latin.

"What does it say?" he whispered to Kelsey.

"In the fifty-second year after the birth of our Lord, this tomb is in honor of Mary, the Mother of God."

The song ended. Silence reigned for a few seconds.

"Welcome," he heard the abbess say.

And the older woman stood and turned.

As did the others in gray smocks, who divided themselves to one side, allowing him and Kelsey to step forward, close to the plinth.

"This is the Chapel of the Maidens," the abbess said.

He was beginning to understand. "What just happened was all a dog-and-pony show. Theater. To convince Fuentes that he got what he came for."

"Proverbs is instructive," the abbess said. *"Like a dog that returns to its vomit, is a fool who reverts to his folly."*

He grinned. "And a fool he was."

"The quickest way to acquire a person's confidence," the abbess said, "is by seemingly trusting them with what they think is *your* secret."

Her expression seemed easy and calm, but she was intent on him, studying, judging. He stared around at the room. Everything had assumed a strange quality of unreality. "How old is this place?"

"It was completed in 1204, right before the Albigensian Crusade," the abbess said. "There was a real danger to us then. The pope sent an army to this region not only for the Cathars, but for us too. We were unsure what might happen, so the maidens of that time devised a clever plan. We kept the original tomb, as it was created in the first century, but replaced the bones with those of a maiden who'd died hundreds of years before. She'd rested in our cemetery. But, even in death, she was able to guard the Virgin. This room was forged out of an old cellar and the bones were brought and placed in that ossuary. Thankfully, the crusaders never came to this plateau. We escaped them entirely. But we were ready, just in case."

He stepped close and saw an inscription on the ossuary's exterior. Faint in the stone, but still there.

τον εαυτό του

"Greek for 'itself to itself,'" Claire said. "Those words were carved into the hollow of the original tomb. It was an epitaph, chosen at the time of Mary's death, that says it all. She lived and died and returned to dust, as all humans do. Of course, the women who left that were not interested in elevating Mary to any godlike status."

"None of which makes her any less holy," Kelsey added. "But it does make the men who made her into something more look foolish."

"That it does," the abbess said. "We are a place on a hill to which the world never comes. We would like to stay that way."

The abbess pointed at the ossuary.

Below the epitaph was a symbol cut into the limestone.

"Omega," the abbess said. "In the original tomb it was used as a way to covertly identify the occupant. For them, Mary was Omega. The end. The last vestige of Christ that remained on this earth. When this chapel was conceived, we created a plan, based on deception, playing off the wants and fears of those who might come here in search. It became our armor against failure. Twice before it was almost implemented. Today, it was finally used. We called it Omega."

"It was ingenious," he said. "And well played."

"Maidens," the abbess said. "Please excuse us. I need you to bring things to a close and secure the premises back to normal."

All of the other women, except for Sister Claire, left the chamber and headed back up to ground level.

He entered the shallow apse and admired the wall niche where the urn rested.

"That's the other maiden," Claire said. "Joan. Brought here in 1431. Unfortunately, she's proven a bit of a problem. She's the reason all of this happened."

"Jan van Eyck," the abbess said, "was the last person, not of this order, who knew some of our actions. He did not know a thing about the Blessed Virgin, but he helped us secure the ashes of the woman who came to be known as Joan of Arc. Then, for some inexplicable reason, he left a way for the world to find those ashes. We effectively hid that path for centuries, making moves on the Ghent Altarpiece, from time to time, through the centuries. But our luck ran out with the two of you. So we've decided to take you both into our confidence. Please do not make us regret it."

He knew the comment was directed straight at him. He was the official eyes and ears in the room, and they were surely wondering what he was going to do. But he'd already decided. "I won't say a word about any of this to anyone. It never happened."

He caught the relief in both the abbess' and Claire's eyes.

Kelsey's too, and she mouthed, *Thank you.*

He still had some issues with the Ghent police in the matter of stealing a body. Hopefully, Reynaldo would handle that. But he was going to take a hit, especially after he told his boss there'd been nothing to find.

"The tomb that was blown up. It was the original?" he asked.

Claire nodded. "Sacrificed for the greater good."

"A shame," he said. "Its historical and religious significance was immeasurable."

"I'm sure, in your line of work, you've witnessed many precious things destroyed," the abbess said.

"Sadly, I have." He paused. "The maidens rebelling was part of the show too?"

Claire nodded. "There was a division among us. A deep difference of opinion. Me on one side, the abbess on the other. Many of us thought our mission was no longer necessary. We decided to use that debate as part of Omega. But today proved us wrong. I was wrong. We're united once again. No debate. No dissension. Maidens, one and all. Our purpose reinvigorated."

"You made sure Friar Dwight heard you," Kelsey said to the abbess. "You wanted him to know that you guarded the Virgin."

"It only reinforced what he wanted to believe. It was a good addition to the plan."

"I assume I almost messed things up?" he asked.

"Your presence did add another dimension," Claire said. "We left all of the outer doors open, hoping you'd find one for entry. Sister Ellen was tasked with keeping an eye on you, and tried to dissuade you from interfering in the chapter hall, but I knew you would anyway."

He hated to be so predictable.

Claire smiled. "It seems your nature to jump right in. And, with Sister Deal involved, I realized you couldn't resist. So we made you part of what was happening. I think it all helped cement things in the cardinal's mind."

"Who speared the friar with the arrow?" he asked.

"That was me," Claire said. "The abbess was trying to send a message for you not to interfere."

"And I didn't. Not then, anyway. Again, you seem to know me real well."

"*Good guesses* is the way I look at it," Claire said. "One of the side benefits of being a nun. You learn a lot about people."

He told them about Andre Labelle and his connection to Bernat de Foix and Archbishop Vilamur.

"They're both dead," the abbess said. "When the main contingent headed for the chapel, I sent maidens out as lookouts. One of them watched as Labelle took Vilamur over a cliff."

He hated to hear that. But wasn't surprised.

"I suspect Bernat de Foix is dead too," he said. "There seemed a lot of issues going on with Labelle."

"How are you going to explain those deaths?" Kelsey asked.

"A hiking accident," Claire said. "They happen in these mountains all the time. We'll allow the bodies to be discovered by others. And they will. It won't involve us."

He stepped to the other niche and the rectangular glass container. Inside he saw loose pages, dry and brittle, edges curled, the surfaces all the color of brewed tea.

"That is *The Testimony of John*," the abbess said. "It is a first-hand account of the Blessed Virgin's life after the death of Christ, including her death and burial here in the Pyrénées. It's an original first-century manuscript."

"There aren't many of those in this world," he said. "How do you know it's authentic? How do you know the bones are authentic?"

"We actually don't," Claire said. "But we had a sample carbon-dated a decade ago, which verified the pages themselves are from the first century. We also know that a copy of it was taken during the Albigensian Crusade. A contingent of soldiers came south to the Roussillon, looking for us. They went to the village of Las Illas, not far from here, thinking we were there. Thankfully, their information was incorrect. We'd left that village hundreds of years before. But that didn't stop them from torturing and killing everyone there."

What a brutal time.

"A copy of this text was in the church at Las Illas," Claire said. "We were not aware of that until after it was taken. The crusaders delivered that copy to the pope, and it stayed in the Vatican archives, relatively unnoticed, until the twentieth century. We obtained photographs of those pages and compared them to this manuscript. They were identical, except for a reference that the one stolen was a copy."

Amazing.

"To answer your second question," Claire said, "we don't know if the bones are authentic. But we do know that they are the same bones interred in the first century in the cave that was destroyed today. The cave itself is exactly as described in *The Testimony of John*. And they are the same bones that have been guarded and protected continuously by this order ever since. They did not move from that cave, until we brought them here in the twelfth century. Fuentes knew of *The Testimony of John*. He quoted from it in the cave. Everything matched how the manuscript described the tomb. Which seems further verification of authenticity."

"And Jan van Eyck is in fact buried in our graveyard," the abbess said. "Which, to the Vatican, is further verification that this is the place they sought."

He wondered how, but did not ask.

"You let me go after Friar Dwight, who had a gun," Kelsey said to the abbess. "You closed the doors behind me. Why?"

"Was there any stopping you?" the older woman asked.

Kelsey said nothing.

"No, Sister Deal, you were intent on going after Dwight. I merely allowed you to do that. But Sister Claire was in the tower, with her bow, watching, just in case. Of course, you leaping onto the man's back did complicate things for her."

The abbess seemed fierce and dutiful, but also compassionate and understanding.

"What now?" Nick asked.

"We continue on with our duty," the abbess said. "The church is satisfied. In their minds, the issue is resolved. We'll never hear from them again. And the Blessed Virgin can rest here, in peace, forever."

"Why not tell the world the truth?" Kelsey asked.

"It would accomplish little and create more problems," the abbess said. "Better to allow the fiction to live on and for those men in Rome to think themselves so important."

"I still have those images from the *Just Judges,*" Nick said.

"Which are no longer a problem," Claire said. "Only us and the Vatican understand their significance as a road map to here and, thanks to Omega, Rome has no need to inquire into them. So let the world enjoy them."

He agreed.

Which might go a long way toward smoothing things over with the Belgians and Reynaldo. After all, he had retrieved them.

"I'll shortly retire," the abbess said. "To Ghent and our convent there. Sister Claire will almost certainly take my place. I have long thought she will need a competent Vestal. Someone with intellect and spirit. Someone we can trust. I was hoping, Sister Deal, you would join us and take up that task."

He stared at Kelsey.

A woman he'd once loved deeply, and still loved today, only in a different way. He was so glad she'd reached out to him. The past few days had been challenging, but also rewarding. He'd not only done his job but also made a new friend. And that's what she was. His dear, dear friend.

438

"I'd be honored," Kelsey said.

Time for him to go. He stepped over and gave her a hug. "Take care."

Tears welled in her eyes. "You too."

He gave the two other women a slight bow. "It's been a pleasure. And if you ever need anything."

He paused and pointed at Kelsey.

"She'll know where to find me."